The Twelfth Child

"Crosby's unique style of writing is timeless and her character building is inspirational."

—*Layered Pages*

"Crosby draws her characters with an emotional depth that compels the reader to care about their challenges, to root for their success, and to appreciate their bravery."

—Gayle Swift, author of *ABC, Adoption & Me*

"Crosby's talent lies in not only telling a good, compelling story, but telling it from a unique perspective . . . Characters stay with you because they are simply too endearing to go away."

—*Reader Views*

Baby Girl

"Crosby weaves this story together in a manner that feels like a huge patchwork quilt. All the pieces and tears come together to make something beautiful."

—Michele Randall, *Readers' Favorite*

"Crosby is a true storyteller, delving into the emotions, relationships, and human dynamics—the cracks which break us, and ultimately make us stronger."

—J. D. Collins, Top 1000 reviewer

Silver Threads

"*Silver Threads* is an amazing story of love, loss, family, and second chances that will simply stir your soul."

—*Jersey Girl Book Reviews*

"Crosby's books are filled with love of family and carry the theme of a sweetness for life . . . You are pulled in by the story line and the characters."

—*Silver's Reviews*

"In *Silver Threads*, Crosby flawlessly merges the element of fantasy without interrupting the beauty of a solid love story . . . Sure to stay with you beyond the last page."

—Lisa McCombs, *Readers' Favorite*

Cracks in the Sidewalk

"Crosby has penned a multidimensional scenario that should be read not only for entertainment but also to see how much love, gentleness, and humanity matter."

—Gisela Hausmann, *Readers' Favorite*

PRAISE FOR BETTE LEE CROSBY'S NOVELS

A Year of Extraordinary Moments

"One of those rare books that makes you believe in the power of love. Filled with memorable characters and important life lessons, a southern treat to the last page."

—Anita Hughes, author of *California Summer*

"Throughout this book, the author beautifully explores the theme of letting go of the past while preserving its best parts . . ."

—*Kirkus Reviews*

The Summer of New Beginnings

"This women's fiction novel is full of romance, the power of friendship, and the bond of sisters."

—*The Charlotte Observer*

"A heartwarming story about family, forgiveness, and the magic of new beginnings."

—Christine Nolfi, bestselling author of *Sweet Lake*

"A heartwarming, captivating, and intriguing story about the importance of family . . . The colorful cast of characters are flawed, quirky, mostly loyal, determined, and mostly likable."

—*Linda's Book Obsession*

"Crosby's southern voice comes through in all of her books and lends a believable element to everything she writes. *The Summer of New Beginnings* is no exception."

—*Book Chat*

Spare Change

"Skillfully written, *Spare Change* clearly demonstrates Crosby's ability to engage her readers' rapt attention from beginning to end. A thoroughly entertaining work of immense literary merit."

—*Midwest Book Review*

"Love, loss, and unexpected gifts . . . Told from multiple points of view, this tale seeped from the pages and wrapped itself around my heart."

—*Caffeinated Reviewer*

"More than anything, *Spare Change* is a heartwarming book, which is simultaneously intriguing and just plain fun."

—*Seattle Post-Intelligencer*

Passing Through Perfect

"Well-written and engaging."

—*Kirkus Reviews*

"This is southern fiction at its best: spiritually infused, warm, and family-oriented."

—*Midwest Book Reviews*

"Crosby's characters take on heartbreak and oppression with dignity, courage, and a shaken but still strong faith in a better tomorrow."

—*IndieReader*

EMILY, GONE

ALSO BY BETTE LEE CROSBY

MAGNOLIA GROVE SERIES

The Summer of New Beginnings

A Year of Extraordinary Moments

WYATTSVILLE SERIES

Spare Change

Jubilee's Journey

Passing Through Perfect

The Regrets of Cyrus Dodd

Beyond the Carousel

MEMORY HOUSE SERIES

Memory House

The Loft

What the Heart Remembers

Baby Girl

Silver Threads

SERENDIPITY SERIES

The Twelfth Child

Previously Loved Treasures

STAND-ALONE TITLES

Cracks in the Sidewalk

What Matters Most

Wishing for Wonderful

Blueberry Hill

Life in the Land of IS: The Amazing True Story of Lani Deauville

EMILY, GONE

BETTE LEE CROSBY

This is a work of fiction. Names, characters, organizations, places, events, and incidents are either products of the author's imagination or are used fictitiously. Any resemblance to actual persons, living or dead, or actual events is purely coincidental.

Published by Lake Union Publishing, Seattle

www.apub.com

ISBN-13: 9781542044929
ISBN-10: 1542044928

Cover design by Caroline Teagle Johnson

Printed in the United States of America

For Mom . . .
Who inspired my love of southern storytelling
and taught me that the most important
things in life are not really things.

"The heart of a mother is a deep abyss at the bottom of which you will always find forgiveness."

—Honore de Balzac

HESTERVILLE, GEORGIA

It's been forty-seven years since the music festival took place out at Harold Baker's farm, but everyone in Hesterville remembers that weekend. Not because of the music, which was so loud you could hear it clear over in Weston, and not even because of the nineteen people arrested—twelve for shoplifting, six for parading down Main Street naked, and one for breaking the front window of Brian's Pet Shop. No, the reason the people of Hesterville remember that weekend is because of what happened to the Dixon family.

None of the locals was in favor of the music festival being there; it was as if they sensed trouble before it even started. And just as suspected, trouble showed its face in the ugliest way possible. It began two days before the festival was to start and continued throughout that last miserable night.

You might think that on the final night, when the heat wave broke and a drenching rain turned the field into a giant mud hole, the partiers would have lost interest and left, but they didn't. They stayed. By then most of them were higher than a kite and didn't give a damn about anything but the thunderous sound of that music. A few people huddled under plastic tarps or cardboard boxes, but most didn't even bother. They just sat with their skimpy halters and T-shirts soaked through and beads of water cascading off their noses as they listened to the scream of electric guitars.

The festival was supposed to begin on Friday, but on Wednesday afternoon a van painted with peace signs and swirls of psychedelic colors turned onto Main Street. That was the start of it. George Dixon was standing out in front of his hardware store when the van slowed and a bare-chested man stuck his head out the window.

"This the way to Baker's Field?" he asked.

It was blistering hot that day, and a dozen or more people were packed into the van. With the windows rolled down, it was impossible not to catch the pungent smell of marijuana mixed with beer and sweat.

With a look of chagrin stretched across his face, George raised his arm, motioned toward the far end of Main Street, and said, "Yellowwood Road, twelve miles out."

The merchants along Main Street were already feeling uneasy about the festival, but George Dixon worried more than most. He had good reason; Yellowwood Road ran right by his house. If you were driving, the Baker turnoff was five miles past George's place. But traveling as the crow flies, the Dixon house was less than a mile from Baker's old cotton field.

As he stood there watching the van disappear, George flirted with the idea of having Rachel and the baby spend a few days at his mama's. It was a fleeting idea, quickly dismissed because the two women had no fondness for each other. Later he would recall having such a thought, but by then it was too late to do anything.

~

That van was the first, but it certainly wasn't the last. Throughout the day a steady stream of cars, trucks, and vans turned off the highway and rumbled down Main Street, their stereos and transistor radios blaring. Before the sky darkened and faded to shades of purple, thousands of partiers were camped out in that plowed-under cotton field.

The month of August was always sweltering in Georgia, but that particular year was worse than ever. On Thursday morning the sun came up looking like a fireball. Out there, where the land was flat and the shade trees few and far between, the heat was merciless. In a single afternoon it could scorch a person's scalp and cause their shoulders to blister.

After having caroused long into the night, the partiers woke with parched throats and empty stomachs. The concession trucks had not yet arrived and wouldn't until Friday evening. Left with no other option, most of them headed back to town in search of food and drink.

At first Mayor Walter Bruno claimed such an influx of customers would be good for the town's economy, and for a short time it looked as if he were right. As the day progressed though, bigger and bigger crowds made their way into town. By noon there wasn't a single seat available at a lunch counter or any of the three restaurants along Main Street.

Hesterville was small and ill prepared for such an invasion. With the restaurants jammed, the partiers swept through Piggly Wiggly, buying up what they could and pocketing any number of things they didn't bother to pay for. In what seemed the blink of an eye, the streets went from bustling to overcrowded. In a single day the population of Hesterville had more than doubled.

The wild-eyed and often shirtless crowd took over, and the locals, not anxious to get caught up in the melee, remained at home. Before nightfall the grocery shelves were nearly stripped bare; things like canned vegetables, boxes of laundry detergent, and wax paper were the few exceptions. Once the racks of Twinkies, chocolate bars, and beer were standing empty, a current of agitation took over. Cardboard signs got yanked down, a Coca-Cola display rack knocked on its side, and in the dark of night a rock shattered the liquor store window.

On Friday morning Herb Gallagher boarded up the broken window, tacked up a sign saying the liquor store was closed until Monday, and went home. Several other shopkeepers did the same, claiming there was nothing but trouble to be had.

~

Later on, when the investigation began, Big Sound, the organizers of the event, claimed they sold only five thousand tickets, but Sheriff Wilson estimated the crowd to be well in excess of fifteen thousand—more people than actually resided in Hesterville. Harold Baker swore the shops closing their doors on folks in need of food and water was to blame for what happened, but not one of the townspeople agreed with him. Least of all Rachel Dixon.

Of course, that was forty-seven years ago. To understand the truth of what happened, you would have had to be there.

A TROUBLED TOWN

Summer 1971

Big Sound kept the exact location of the music festival under wraps until four weeks before it was to take place; then the posters went up. Sadie Jenkins was just leaving the post office when she spotted one tacked to the telephone pole. She stood there for a full minute, studying the sign with her eyes narrowed and her shoulders squared back. Then she snatched the poster off the pole and stormed across the street to Sheriff Wilson's office.

"How dare you allow such a thing in Hesterville?" she screamed, then continued her tirade without giving him time for an answer.

The sheriff stood there unflinching, his chin jutted out and eyes steely as roller balls. He waited until Sadie stopped for a breath.

"Talk to the county commissioner," he finally said. "There's nothing I can do about it. The Baker farm is in an unincorporated area that's not part of the city. It's beyond my jurisdiction."

Not willing to accept what she called "a flimsy excuse," Sadie stood nose to nose with him and argued for a good half hour. Then she stomped out of the building, red-faced and looking as if she were ready to kill.

"Just you wait," she hollered back. "Come next election, I'll see you ousted or die trying."

As a founding member of the Hesterville Women's League and chairwoman of several committees, Sadie's threat wasn't without weight.

Before the week was out, she'd organized a protest march. The group, numbering almost two hundred, was mostly women armed with cardboard signs and banners made from painted bedsheets. They marched along Main Street, came to a stop in front of the sheriff's office, and stood chanting, "Stop the music! Send the hippies home!"

~

Sheriff Wilson's desk was directly across from the front window, so there was no way he could miss seeing the women. With his brows hooded and his mouth stretched into an angry-looking line, he pulled a stack of county bulletins from his inbox and started shuffling through them. As the noise of the shouts and catcalls got louder, reading became all but impossible.

"These damn women are trying my patience," he grumbled, but he kept his head ducked. He allowed the demonstration to go on for almost an hour. Then one of the women splattered a tomato against the front window.

"That's it," he snarled. Pulling the gun from his desk drawer, he slid it into his holster and stepped outside.

"Okay, ladies, I've been patient long enough," he announced. "It's time for you to stop this nonsense and go home."

Claire Madison, who stood two rows back, yelled, "We want that music festival canceled, and we're not leaving until you do something about it!"

The sheriff again tried to explain that Harold Baker's farm was outside the city limits and beyond his jurisdiction, but before he could finish several of the women began hooting, and someone too far back to identify yelled, "We're not buying that hogwash!"

Sheriff Wilson gave a flat-eyed grimace, making an obvious show of his irritation.

"Enough!" he shouted. "I want this crowd disbanded and out of here right now. Anyone still here in fifteen minutes will be spending the night in jail."

"You can't intimidate us!" Sadie Jenkins yelled, then pumped a defiant fist in the air and turned to the crowd. "Right, ladies?"

Standing in the center of the row, Claire gave an affirmative nod and echoed Sadie's cry. Not backing down, the sheriff folded his arms across his chest and fixed his eyes on Claire's face.

"You might want to rethink that, Mrs. Madison. That tomato attack is considered assaulting an officer of the law. With Edward being the principal at the high school, I doubt he'd want the school board to know his wife's been arrested."

His eyes scanned the crowd and came to rest on Bernice Turner.

"And, Mrs. Turner, what about Joe's job at the bank?" he said. "Do you think a banker wants to be seen visiting his wife in jail?"

As he called out the wives of businessmen and respected citizens one by one, a low murmur began to drift through the throng. Claire reached across and tapped Sadie on the shoulder.

"I've got to go," she whispered. "I'm sympathetic to the cause, but Ed would have a conniption if I got myself arrested."

Once the tide began to turn, Sheriff Wilson softened his tone.

"This is a onetime event," he said. "In three weeks, the music festival and the people who come here to attend it will be gone. Before the month is out we'll all go back to our daily routines, and the festival will be forgotten. Do you really want to risk going to jail over a cause that will ultimately turn out to be inconsequential?"

The three Barkley sisters standing in the far back shook their heads in unison, then turned and walked off. The Baptist minister's wife was right behind them. By the time Sheriff Wilson finished telling how he'd be on duty and keep a sharp eye out for any signs of trouble, only Sadie and a few friends remained.

Despite earlier enthusiasm, the protest march fizzled out, but it didn't end Sadie's efforts to stop the music festival. She and several of her friends carried petitions door to door asking people to sign them, and when they had more than a thousand signatures, Sadie tucked the papers into an oversize envelope and delivered it to Sheriff Wilson's office. While he stood firm on the Baker farm being beyond his jurisdiction, he placated her by promising to get the petition to county officials. In Primrose County, that was the same as doing nothing.

For the next two weeks, Sadie trotted out to the mailbox every morning in the hope of finding a response from the county, but one never came.

~

On the Thursday before the festival was scheduled to start, the town was already abuzz with tales of the shenanigans taking place out at Baker's Field. The whispers spread from ear to ear like a swarm of locusts. When Sadie ran into Elmer Bastrop that morning, she looked him square in the eye and asked if he'd heard what was going on out at the festival site.

"Heard?" he exclaimed. "Why, I seen it with my own eyes! When we were driving in we passed a bunch of them hippies on the road, most of 'em nearly naked, bobbing and weaving like they was drunk, radios turned up louder than the firehouse siren."

His wife, Barbara, nodded her agreement.

"I seen 'em too," she said. "And I'll bet my bottom dollar that tall fella was smoking marijuana."

"I knew this was going to happen," Sadie replied. She hurried off toward the Good Shepherd Church and told Reverend Caraway the women's Bible study group needed to hold an all-night prayer vigil.

"On Sunday evening, we could—"

Before he was halfway through the thought, Sadie started shaking her head. "It has to be tonight. We need the Almighty to nip this thing in the bud before it gets out of control!"

"But there are arrangements to be made, notifications to be sent—"

"I'll take care of that. You just make sure to have the church open and be ready with a good long sermon!"

Sadie turned on her heel and walked out, leaving Reverend Caraway standing there with a bewildered look stretched across his face.

Two hours later, most everyone in town knew about the prayer vigil.

~

That evening the Good Shepherd Church was crowded. Almost half the women of Hesterville came but only a sprinkling of husbands.

Rachel Dixon was one of the women. She carried six-month-old Emily in her arms and arrived after the reverend had begun to speak. With only a few seats still open, she edged her way along the side aisle and sat in the center of the second row.

Reverend Caraway raised his arms skyward and bellowed, "Rain, Heavenly Father, we beseech you, send us rain! Give us a storm powerful enough to drive this throng of unruly strangers from our land!"

The reverend slapped his hand against the Bible, and the congregation responded with a thundering chorus of "Amen." Once he knew the crowd was with him, he moved from asking for rain to calling for damnation of the devilish music. His voice got louder by the moment, and beads of perspiration rose up on his forehead. To emphasize the need for damnation, he slammed his fist down against the lectern so hard his Bible bounced and fell to the floor.

The noise startled Emily, and her eyes popped open. Rachel lifted the baby to her shoulder and began rocking her back and forth, but by then it was too late. Emily was already whimpering, and in a matter of minutes she'd be wailing.

Rachel stood and edged past the Carters and Mrs. Brimley, offering a brief apology. As she headed for the door, Sadie Jenkins rose from her seat and stepped into the aisle.

"Leaving so soon?"

Rachel gave a cautious smile. "It's way past Emmy's bedtime, and she's getting fussy."

"Bedtime? How can you expect the poor child to sleep with that outrageous noise practically in your backyard?"

While Sadie was prone to exaggeration, Rachel knew what she said carried an element of truth. On Wednesday night they'd heard the crackle of radios and shrill voices. Though it was annoying, it was bearable. But today she'd watched as a steady stream of vans and trucks drove down Yellowwood Road, headed for the Baker farm. This night would no doubt be worse, but she had no alternative. Emily's weary little eyelids were already fluttering shut.

Jostling the baby from one shoulder to the other, Rachel whispered, "Once Emmy's tired herself out, she's a pretty sound sleeper."

Sadie pinched her face into a dubious-looking frown and gave a huff. "Mark my words—none of you will get a wink of sleep tonight." Before she was halfway through her suggestion of spending the night there at the church, Rachel was gone.

As it turned out, Sadie's prediction was fairly accurate. Even though it was near dawn when the transistors stilled and the sound of laughter died down enough for Rachel to fall asleep, she still was not prepared for what was to come.

~

Before the Dixons finished their supper on Friday, the bright lights and loudspeakers came to life and thundered through the sky as no storm ever had. It was as if the hand of God had taken a sledgehammer to their roof. The thrum of bass guitars rattled the walls as the screech of amplified voices rolled across the rafters and filled every corner of the room.

Emily, still in her high chair, began howling almost immediately. Rachel jumped up from the table and lifted the baby into her arms.

"It's okay, sweetheart," she cooed and held Emily tight against her chest.

In the hours that followed, Rachel tried every way possible to quiet the baby: a pacifier covered with a sprinkling of sugar, a cool bath, back rubs, foot rubs, the colorful clown that laughed. It was all to no avail. Hour after hour, she paced back and forth across the living room floor, jiggling Emily from one shoulder to the other, humming softly, trying to ignore the vibration of the floorboards under her feet.

Twice George lifted the baby from her arms and suggested she get some rest, but for Rachel, rest was impossible. The sound of Emily's cries tore through her heart, and minutes later the baby was back in her arms. When he offered a third time, she shook her head and turned toward the kitchen, claiming the noise was a bit more tolerable in there.

Following along behind her, George shouted, "Do you think we ought to go stay with Mama for a few days?"

Rachel shook her head again, even though she hadn't actually heard the question and was too frazzled to think about anything but Emily.

"I'm okay," she said and waved him off.

It was near dawn when the music eased and became a distant rumble. By then Emily was so fitful that she still didn't sleep. The night had taken its toll, and not just on the baby; Rachel's eyes were narrowed to slits, and George, sprawled out in the club chair, had the look of a zombie.

~

On Saturday morning George opened the hardware store, even though he'd not had a wink of sleep. Thinking a good supply of caffeine would see him through, he downed a full pot of strong coffee before leaving the house, but it proved a poor substitute. Twice he nodded off and was jolted awake when his head plopped down on the counter. At eleven he gave up trying to work, hung a sign on the door saying CLOSED UNTIL MONDAY, and went home. He was standing in the living room wobbly as a windblown signpost when Rachel suggested he try getting a few hours of sleep before the music started up again.

George gave a feeble nod, then stuffed his ears with wads of cotton and climbed into bed. Before he could close his eyes, the music was again bouncing off the walls. The cotton did little more than dull the twang of guitars and screech of voices. After nearly two hours of tossing, turning, and pulling the pillow tight against his ears to cover the thrum of guitars, he realized there would be no sleep this day and got up.

Emily had dozed earlier in the afternoon, but she was now awake and crying. For a moment George stood watching Rachel pace the living room with the baby held to her shoulder. He saw the weariness with which she moved one foot in front of the other, one arm wrapped around the baby, the other dangling aimlessly from her shoulder. She was wearing the same clothes she'd had on yesterday, only now her shirt was pulled loose from the waistband of her slacks. Emily was no longer howling. She'd settled into breath-catching sobs with a hiccup or two in between, then another wail.

George crossed the room and lifted the baby from Rachel's arms.

"I'll take over for a while," he said, shouting to be heard.

For a moment Rachel just stood there, her eyes glazed over and that one arm crooked as if she were still holding the baby.

George leaned close and spoke directly into her ear. "You look really tired, honey. Try to get some sleep."

Holding Emily in his right arm, he put his left hand on Rachel's back and eased her toward the bedroom. She stumbled across the room and fell facedown onto the bed. Given the way she'd seemed on the verge of collapse, he thought she could have slept through anything, but like him, she couldn't close out the sound.

~

The music continued throughout the night and on into Sunday. There were brief pauses when the screams of guitars faded away for a few minutes, but each time they roared back louder than before.

It was late afternoon when Rachel heard a distant sound and cocked her head.

"Did you hear that?"

George pulled a cotton wad from his ear and asked if she'd said something.

She nodded. "Listen."

A long moment passed; then it happened again: a rumble of thunder, closer now.

"Praise God!" she said and smiled for the first time in days.

~

The wind came before the rain. It bent the tops of the tall pines and scattered remnants of dried brush as it swooshed across the open field. The sky west of Baker's farm blackened, and storm clouds rolled in. Still the thrum of guitars continued. As Rachel stood at the window watching, a slash of lightning creased the sky, and the downpour began. For a moment it was as if the music had disappeared, but all too soon it returned, now muffled by the sound of heavy droplets hammering the roof.

The pinging of rain against the metal roof was a familiar sound, something she'd grown used to. Rachel felt the pinched muscle in her neck start to loosen. Later that night she tucked Emily into her crib, then crawled into bed and snuggled up against George.

When Rachel closed her eyes and drifted off, she was dead to the world. Nothing short of a tornado was going to wake her—not the blaring sound of the last few sets by the Beastly Brothers, not the thunder that continued off and on throughout the night.

Not even the muffled creak of a door opening.

BAKER'S FIELD

Sunday Evening

On the final day of the concert, Vicki Robart sat cross-legged on the wet ground, her mouth pulled into a pout. The Beastly Brothers were onstage. The taller brother, who had red hair that stood like porcupine quills, was belting out a murderous rendition of the Carole King hit "I Feel the Earth Move," but Vicki wasn't feeling anything. Especially not good. Her clothes were soaked through, and the pain in her stomach was worse than yesterday. Smoking a few joints sometimes softened the ache and made the emptiness inside her seem less vast, but not tonight.

She looked up at Russ Murphy, his face bearded, his eyes glassed over, and his body swaying to the beat of the music. He'd been on his feet for the entire set, obviously not feeling the emptiness she felt. His ability to forget was something that boggled Vicki's mind. Murph, as she called him, had come home from Vietnam without part of his left arm, but he never spoke about it, never bemoaned the loss or cursed the enemy who caused it. Once, only once, did he say it happened during the Tet Offensive. After that, it was as good as forgotten.

She wasn't like him; she couldn't forget. Certainly not this soon. Maybe not ever.

She stood, took hold of his arm, and swayed against his shoulder. The sound system was amped up so high that the ground beneath them throbbed, and a person had to yell to be heard. She raised herself onto her tiptoes and put her mouth to his ear.

"I need another hit."

Murph glanced down and grimaced. He could see she was already at that halfway point where she swung back and forth, giggly one moment and tearful the next. "Really?"

She grinned. "Yeah, really."

"We're leaving after this set; you can't wait?"

"Now," she said, then narrowed her eyes, tilted her head, and smiled.

On the surface it seemed a sweet, almost innocent smile, but he'd seen times when she'd had too much and gone over the edge. Times like that, the anger came roaring back. Times like that she was capable of almost anything.

"Just wait twenty minutes," he pleaded. "We'll leave and find a place to get something to eat."

There was a momentary rise at the corners of her mouth, a too-wise look of irony perhaps; then she laughed.

"There's no place open. The food trucks left early this afternoon. I need something to tide me over."

Despite whatever misgivings he had, Murph handed her his knapsack, then turned back to the makeshift stage.

Once the knapsack was in hand, Vicki rummaged through the canvas bag, pulled out a rain poncho and the package of marijuana, then dropped to the ground again. With the poncho covering her like a tent, she rolled three joints and smoked two, one right after another.

As she sat there inhaling, she held the smoke long enough to feel the easy release, then let go with a slow breath. A year earlier she hadn't needed the comfort it brought; back then the promise of a new life was enough. Afterward, everything changed. In the early days, the ones following the loss of Lara, Murph was understanding, sympathetic almost, but before the week was out Lara became like his missing arm—something to be forgotten. For Vicki there was no forgetting; there was only numbness and the relief that came with a high.

After three more numbers, the performance ended with the wail of electric guitars, a naked woman climbing onto the stage, and fans still screaming for more. Huddled beneath the poncho and oblivious to the crowd, Vicki sat with her legs drawn up and face tucked between her knees. Murph reached down and took her hand in his.

"Let's see if we can get you something to eat."

He pulled her to her feet and circled the stub of his arm around her back. With his head and shoulders still bouncing to the beat of the music, he guided her across the field toward the road.

~

The rain slackened a bit as they walked to the car, and by the time they settled into the front seat of the old 1953 Pontiac, the heavy droplets had turned to a fine mist. Vicki reached for the plastic bag in her pocket and pulled out the third joint. As she lit up, a look of disappointment crossed Murphy's face.

There were times when he regretted being the one who'd introduced her to marijuana. At first getting blitzed meant laughter and fun, easy love, late-night food orgies. That was before Lara. Now a high meant Vicki could turn irrational and impossible to deal with.

He sat with his hand on the key in the ignition and gave a nod toward the joint she held.

"Save that for later," he said. "You've had enough; you don't need more."

She gave a cynical laugh. "Since when do you know what I need or don't need?"

"I know 'cause I've been there. Unless you're looking to end up brain-dead, you should set that aside and get some food into you."

"Food, yeah, that's what I need." She took a long drag, then handed him the joint.

He snuffed it out, dropped the roach into the ashtray, and started the car.

"It'll take about two hours to make it back to the highway. I think we can find a late-night diner or pizza place—"

Vicki gave a laborious sigh. "Two hours? I'm already starving!"

"Sorry, babe, there's nothing between here and there."

"Maybe in town—"

He shook his head. "There's nothing. That's why I said you should get something from the food truck earlier when—"

"You said, you said," Vicki echoed in a singsong voice. "Mister Big Deal, who always knows best. I wasn't hungry then, but I'm hungry now!"

Before they'd traveled a mile, the mist thickened into a heavy gray fog. As they bumped along the roughened dirt road, Murph leaned closer to the windshield, trying first the high beams then the low beams. Visibility was down to a few hundred yards at best.

"Shit, man," he grumbled. "It's gonna take forever to get outta here."

An agitated harrumph came from Vicki. "I'm starving! You said two hours!"

"Stop busting my chops. When I see something, we'll stop. Until then, I can't do a damn thing about you being hungry!"

The stump of Murphy's arm ached in the damp weather. Ached in a way that made him believe the missing arm was still there. For a moment he could feel himself making a fist, opening and closing the lost fingers, but then the feeling of having them back was gone and he was left with just the pain. Music, loud music, dulled the ache; the pulse of a guitar or thump of a drum pushed it aside. Now, in the still of night, with Vicki sulking beside him, his arm throbbed as it had in the beginning.

He steadied the wheel with the stump of his left arm, reached next to the ashtray with his right hand, and pushed in the lighter. After several seconds he put the joint he'd taken from Vicki in his mouth, lit it, then leaned forward, struggling to see the road.

Annoyed that he now had what she'd given up, Vicki turned her face and stared aimlessly out the side window. They inched along for a good twenty minutes; then she spied something in the distance.

"Stop here!" she shouted.

Murphy slowed the car and eased onto the grassy bank. "What now?"

She turned with a mischievous grin and pointed to a small house barely visible from the road. "I'm gonna knock on the door and ask if they can spare a bit of food."

Murph leaned toward the side window and saw the shadow of a sloped roof.

"Are you some kind of crazy? That place is pitch-black. Nobody's home, or else they're asleep."

Vicki giggled. "This is the boonies. Maybe they left the door unlocked like my mom used to do."

"So what? Even if it's standing wide open, you can't just walk in and take what you want. News flash, babe. That can get you tossed in the slammer."

"Not if I'm in and out before they know I'm there!"

Vicki slid out of the car before he could stop her. As she eased the door shut she heard him hiss, "If you're not back in five minutes, I'm leaving without you."

"Better not," she answered and disappeared into the darkness.

~

At first Vicki thought she would knock on the door, maybe lie a bit and say her husband was a wounded vet looking for work and they'd fallen on hard times. As she neared the house, the silence of it intimidated her. She bypassed the front porch and circled around the far side, passing a small window out of reach for her to see anything but the faint glow of a night-light.

Once she rounded the corner she found the rail of a back porch. Lifting her foot onto the first step, she exerted the tiniest bit of pressure and listened for a telltale squeak. There was nothing. Ever so slowly she ventured up the four steps and onto the porch.

Straight ahead was a door, and beside it a window. Vicki inched her way across the floorboards and peered inside. With the sky clouded over and no moonlight, the house was hidden in darkness, but when she pressed her face to the glass she could make out a large white cabinet.

This had to be the kitchen.

She moved over to the door, placed her hand on the knob, and turned. It gave way with no resistance—unlocked, just as her mom's always was. With a gentle push she eased it open and stood looking at the room. The refrigerator was on the far wall and beside it a stove. No, not a stove, a sink.

As her eyes grew accustomed to the dark she saw a clearer definition of the room. Feeling reasonably confident, she stepped across the threshold, made her way over, and opened the refrigerator door. She was hoping for some cold chicken, sliced ham or cheese, but when the light came on it lit the room. What she saw took hold of her heart and ripped it open again.

Baby bottles.

On the counter beside the fridge in a dish drainer, three baby bottles left to dry. Memories flooded her mind, and everything came rushing back: the dashed promise of a new life, a baby born with tiny fingers and toes but no heartbeat. Tears welled in Vicki's eyes, and the raging hunger she'd felt was gone. The piercing emptiness she'd lived with for the past seven months swelled inside her, and suddenly nothing else mattered.

She was already in the house. What harm would it do to take a quick peek inside the nursery? The light that had given her a glimpse into the room disappeared when the refrigerator door clicked shut. By then she'd already seen an opening to the hallway. She knew that's where it would be: the room where she'd seen the glow of a lamp in the window. Remembering the teddy bear night-light she'd bought for Lara, she traced her fingers along the counter and made her way toward the far end of the room. When the cabinets ended, she reached out for the wall and ran her hand along it until she found the doorframe, then stepped into the narrow hallway. The first thing she saw was a triangle of soft yellow light coming from the room on the left.

Lara.

It was a small room, and in two long strides she stood beside the crib looking down at the baby. The child, her hair the same honeyed blonde Vicki remembered, was lying on her tummy with tiny fists raised alongside her head.

Months later, after she'd returned home, after it was too late to change anything, Vicki would think back on this moment. She would tell herself the marijuana was to blame, that she was mindless at the time, possessed by a blurred reality and too stoned to think straight. But as she stood there looking down at the child who was exactly as she imagined Lara, she considered it destiny. God was giving her back what she had lost.

With a soft cooing that was little more than a murmur, she lifted the sleeping child into her arms. Emily stirred, shifted her weight slightly, then leaned against Vicki's chest.

Murph's words flashed through her head.

If you're not back in five minutes, I'm leaving without you.

No, she couldn't let that happen.

In the blink of an eye she snatched up the lightweight blanket lying at the foot of the crib and wrapped it around the child as she turned toward the kitchen. Retracing her steps with an uncanny certainty, she hurried out the back door and down the steps.

Covering the child with her poncho, she climbed into the car and said, "They might have heard me; let's get out of here quick."

Murph gunned the motor and drove off, believing Emily to be nothing more than a ham or roast chicken.

"Did you get what you wanted?" he asked.

"Yes," Vicki answered, then settled back, content to feel the beat of a tiny heart alongside hers.

THE DIXON HOUSE

The Next Morning

The rain continued on and off throughout the night, and when Rachel Dixon woke Monday morning it was to the sound of water dripping from the eaves. She cast a sleepy glance at the bedside clock, then nudged George.

"It's almost seven."

He rolled over and groaned. "Already? Is Emmy awake?"

Rachel shook her head and spoke in a whispery voice. "I haven't heard her yet. I guess she's catching up on all the sleep she missed, like us."

With the sky still gray and clouded over, the room was deep in shadow, the way it was in the predawn hours before the sun broke free of the horizon.

Rachel pushed back the thin blanket and sat up. "I'd better—"

"Not yet." George reached out, playfully pulled her back onto the pillow, and nuzzled his face in the curve of her neck. "It's been a tough few days; let's grab a few minutes more."

"Her diaper is probably soaked."

"If she were uncomfortable, she'd be fussing." George curled his arm around his wife's waist and pulled her closer.

"Five minutes," he said, then closed his eyes and nodded off.

Rachel couldn't go back to sleep, so she lay locked in his embrace with her ears pricked for the sound of Emily stirring. Later on she would blame George for selfishly taking minutes that could have changed the outcome, but for now she lay beside him, hearing only the tick of the clock as she waited for the baby's cry. When the five minutes were up she waited several more, then pushed his arm away, sat up, and swung her legs to the side of the bed.

"Time to get the day started," she said and jostled his shoulder.

George lay there rubbing sleep from his eyes as Rachel started down the hall toward Emmy's room. There was the sound of her bare feet padding across the wooden floor, the tick of the clock, rain splashing against the side of the house, then a scream that tore through George's heart like a jagged knife. He jumped from the bed and went flying down the hall.

Before he could ask what was wrong, he saw Rachel standing beside the empty crib. Her eyes were wide with horror, her face a ghastly white and her entire body shaking as she choked back the sound of a sob.

"Emmy—"

George's heart thudded in his chest. "Where is she?"

Rachel clenched her hands into fists and covered her eyes. The word *gone* was on her tongue, but she couldn't bring herself to say it. With her chest shuddering as if it were about to break open, she gasped. "I don't know!"

"Don't know?" George's voice quavered. "Did you put her in the crib last night?"

Unable to speak, she nodded.

For a fleeting instant George allowed himself to think Rachel was mistaken, physically exhausted and too tired to remember. It was possible Emmy was still sleeping on the living room sofa. He turned and started through the house, calling the baby's name and hoping to hear the sound of her happy babble.

His heart rose into his throat, and he felt the hammering of it as he went from room to room searching. He looked in corners and behind furniture, as if their daughter were a lost button that had somehow rolled away. Every room was the same, nothing disturbed or out of place. The house was exactly as it had been the night before; only Emily was missing.

When it became obvious that she was nowhere in the house, George called the sheriff's office.

Ted Braxton was on duty. "Good morning, Sheriff's—"

"This is George Dixon; get someone out here right away! Emily's missing!"

Hesterville was a sleepy little town where nothing much ever happened, and Braxton was a part-time deputy who did little more than answer the phone and hand out an occasional parking ticket, so it took a moment for the thought to register.

"Missing?" he repeated. "You sure she's not with her mama?"

"I'm certain. Rachel put her in the crib last night, and this morning she's gone!"

"But how—"

"Dear God, I don't know how!" George screamed. "Just get Sheriff Wilson out here right away! Hurry."

"Yes, sir." Braxton hung up, dialed Wilson's home number, and reported the situation.

"Call Dixon back and tell him not to touch anything in the baby's room," Wilson said. "Then get out to their place. I'm on my way."

Braxton made the call, then jumped into the patrol car and roared off with the siren wailing and lights flashing. When he arrived, Wilson was already questioning the Dixons. George was sitting beside Rachel on the sofa, her trying to stifle sobs, him with his arm around her back.

"The last time we saw Emmy was when Rachel tucked her in for the night," George said. "That was maybe nine or nine thirty."

Wilson glanced over at Rachel. "Was she asleep then?"

"Not sleeping but drowsy. She didn't fuss when I put her in the crib."

"Afterward, what did you do?"

"Nothing. I turned out the living room light and went into the bedroom."

"Where was George?"

"Already in bed. He was exhausted. We all were. We hadn't slept for two nights. The noise from that music festival—"

"So you could hear the music? Were the windows open?"

"They didn't have to be," George said. "You could hear it with the windows closed."

"When you went to bed, was the music still loud?"

"Not as much," Rachel said. "By then the rain had started, and with a metal roof . . ."

The sheriff gave a nod and continued. "During the night, did you hear anything? Footsteps, maybe, or a change in the sound of the music?"

The Dixons both shook their heads.

"When you got up, did you see any sign of a disturbance? Anything out of place? A window or door left open?"

"The window in Emmy's room was still locked," George said. "I checked."

"What about the doors?"

It seemed almost impossible, but Rachel's face turned whiter.

"I leave the back door unlocked during the day because I'm in and out, but we always lock it at night."

"Did you lock it last night?"

A blank look settled on her face. Try as she might, she couldn't remember. Locking the door was something she did by rote. She closed her eyes and tried to picture the evening moment by moment.

She recalled the sound of thunder in the distance, changing Emmy's diaper, and placing her in the crib. She could even see herself turning off the lights and climbing into bed, but she could not find an image of her hand twisting the lock on the back door.

Her sobs returned. "I can't be certain. I always do, but last night . . ."

Wilson turned to Braxton. "Check around outside. Dust for prints on the back door, the porch, and the baby's room."

Braxton disappeared out the door, and the sheriff went back to asking questions.

"Have you seen any strangers hanging around the place, stopping by to maybe use the phone or ask directions?"

George shook his head. "Because of the music festival there's been a ton of traffic up and down this road since last Wednesday but nobody coming to our door."

"What about phone calls? Any strange phone calls or hang-ups?"

Again George shook his head.

For the remainder of the afternoon the sheriff and Braxton went back and forth, asking questions, looking for some small piece of evidence they might have missed. They traveled up and down the road talking to neighbors as far away as a quarter mile, asking if they'd seen or heard anything unusual. Charlie Portman, plagued by insomnia, claimed he'd heard any number of cars rumbling by during the wee hours of the morning but had seen nothing.

As Wilson went from house to house, the story was much the same. People shook their heads and said they'd seen nothing but carloads of hippies headed out to the music festival. No one offered a license plate number or description.

In the late afternoon, Wilson drove out to the farm and questioned Harold Baker and some of the stragglers still camped out in the field. No one knew anything. Baker claimed Big Sound was responsible for ticket sales, and Big Sound claimed it was mostly cash sales, so there was no way of knowing who the buyers were.

At the end of the day, the sheriff had fingerprints and muddy shoe prints they'd found on the back porch, but there was little else.

"I'll have the FBI run the prints," he said, but his voice was already weighted with the sound of hopelessness.

~

It was after nine p.m. when Sheriff Wilson returned to his office, his shoulders stooped and his head hanging low. His body felt as heavy as a bag of wet sand as he dropped into the chair, but he sat there reading and rereading the notes he'd taken. Try as he might, he couldn't figure a motive.

Kidnapping was not usually a random crime. There was almost always a reason: anger, revenge, ransom. He couldn't see the Dixon family for any of these. George was the kind of guy everybody liked—no enemies, no baggage of any kind—and the same could be said of Rachel. They were churchgoers, the kind who came and went inauspiciously. George owned his daddy's hardware store, but it wasn't the kind of business that brought in a lot of money, so ransom seemed unlikely. Not impossible but unlikely.

After two hours of looking at one dead end after another, he began to hope the kidnapper would send a ransom note. Then he'd have a trail to follow, a paper match, a postal code, a handwriting style. Right now the only things he had were the fingerprints he'd sent off to the FBI. The rain had washed away any other tangible evidence.

The partial shoeprint from the back porch was of little use. No specific tread pattern or branding. It appeared to be a midsize women's sandal, but with more than fifteen thousand drugged-out hippies at the music festival, sandals were as commonplace as love beads.

It was almost midnight when Wilson snapped off the light and headed for home. By then he'd decided to start over again the next morning. There had to be someone who'd seen something they'd neglected to mention: the make or model of a car, an out-of-state license plate, a distinctive tattoo, some seemingly insignificant detail that would ultimately prove helpful.

ON THE ROAD

Russ Murphy was not looking for trouble. In fact, it was the one thing he wanted to avoid. When Vicki said there was a chance the people in the house might have seen or heard her, he pressed his foot down on the gas pedal and didn't ease off until they were zooming along the highway. By then Vicki had settled into the seat with an air of contentment surrounding her. Murph paid no attention to the way she hummed softly and caressed the bundle in her arms.

Given the motion of the car and the comfort of Vicki's arms, Emily snuggled up and slept until almost daybreak. Shortly after they crossed the Tennessee border, a faint blush of light began to show in the sky, and she whimpered. It was a soft mewl that had the sound of a kitten.

Murph glanced sideways. "What the hell was that?"

"The baby."

"Baby?"

He twisted his head, eyes bulging with disbelief, and saw Emily's tiny arms flailing and her eyes open. Suddenly she let out a wail. The sound of it unnerved him, and for a moment he lost sight of the road. The car swerved and thumped onto the grassy shoulder.

"Watch out!" Vicki screamed.

With his heart caught up in his throat, he yanked at the steering wheel and pulled back onto the blacktop. He didn't want to see what he'd seen, didn't want to know what he knew, but he couldn't hold back from asking the question. "Did you snatch the kid from that house?"

"I didn't *snatch* anything!" Her voice trembled with indignation. "This is Lara! I took what belongs to me!"

Murphy gave a mournful sigh. "Oh, babe, what in God's name have you done?"

For a long moment she sat silently, her lower lip puckered and a vacant look in her eyes. When she finally spoke, her voice was thick and weighted with emotion.

"Please don't be angry with me," she begged. "I saw Lara sleeping in the crib, and I knew I had to save her. It wasn't wrong. A baby belongs with her mama."

"Vicki, honey, you're not this baby's mama. This isn't—"

"Don't you think a mother knows her own child?" she cut in, blinking away the tears.

She eased the blanket back from the baby's face, and her blonde curls seemed to glow in the pale light of morning. The color of the child's hair was almost an exact match to Vicki's. She lifted the baby to her shoulder and placed the tiny pink cheek alongside her own.

Murphy was taken aback by the sight: mother and child, so alike it could go without question. It was like the phantom pain he felt from an arm that wasn't there, a false reality. For a long while he didn't answer. He stared straight ahead, focusing on the road, trying not to think, trying not to remember. But as the silence around them thickened, the thoughts he pushed back grew bigger and bigger.

He thought back on the first time Vicki had imagined another child to be hers. It happened at the Super Save less than a month after they'd lost Lara. She saw a blue-eyed baby in a grocery cart, and when the mother turned away for a second, she reached for the baby. That day he'd caught hold of her in time and hustled her out of the store with the shopping basket left sitting in the middle of the aisle.

Afterward he'd held Vicki pressed tight against his chest and waited until her sobs became a mournful whimper, then told her again how Lara had been born without a heartbeat.

In the days that followed, she grew more and more certain Lara was still alive, and nothing Murphy said seemed to sway her.

They'd been through this same scenario a number of times before, and he knew there would be no easy way of convincing Vicki this child wasn't her baby. Especially when she was still half-stoned.

A million thoughts raced through his mind, and every one of them was riddled with a sense of urgency. The festival had been too much for her, that was it. She was overtired and strung out. What she needed was food and rest. Once she was feeling like herself again, she'd realize this baby wasn't Lara and be willing to give the kid back. It was too dangerous to return to Georgia, but they could drop the baby off at a church or fire station with a note saying where she belonged. Once the family had their baby back, the police wouldn't waste time searching for the abductor.

Until then, he had to keep Vicki and the kid hidden.

It was a given that they couldn't go back to his apartment in Kentucky. Bardstown wasn't that big, and news traveled fast. The landlady knew their baby girl died the same night she was born. If they showed up with one now, it wouldn't take much to put two and two together and come to the conclusion that something was amiss.

He needed to get Vicki and the baby inside a motel room where no one knew them, then he'd have time to come up with a plan. *Not Tennessee,* he thought. *Too close to Georgia.* Arkansas was the next place that came to mind. That seemed less risky. It was two states away from where she took the kid and nowhere near Bardstown, Kentucky.

Instead of continuing north, he made a left onto Route 40 and headed for Arkansas.

Before they'd traveled another ten miles, the baby got fussy and started looking around as if she wanted to get free of Vicki. The soft mewling turned to a wail, and the closer Vicki held the baby the louder she screamed.

"Shhh," Vicki murmured, patting the baby's back and shifting her from one shoulder to the other. "Don't cry, sweetie, Mama's here . . ."

Trying to comfort the baby did nothing; she continued to howl, stiffening her body and screaming until she was red-faced and breathless. She cried for a good fifteen minutes, then slowed, gasping for air. Believing that was the end of it, Vicki cradled the baby in her arms and lovingly rocked her back and forth. Seconds later she started bawling again, this time louder than before.

With fear crowding his thoughts, Murphy's nerves were stretched paper thin. Concentration was almost impossible. How was he supposed to come up with a plan and figure out the next step when the baby wailing made it impossible?

When he missed the turnoff, he shouted, "Stop her screaming!"

"I would if I could!" Vicki snapped back. "She's probably frightened, and your yelling at her isn't helping one little bit!"

Murph took a deep breath and reeled in his anger. "Is it possible something's wrong with her?"

Vicki shook her head and lifted the baby onto her shoulder. "I don't think so. She's just hungry." Sliding her finger along the inner edge of the diaper, she added, "And wet."

"When you took her, did you take anything else? Food? Diapers?"

She wrinkled her nose in a look of disbelief. "I didn't exactly have time to look around. Stop somewhere and we'll buy stuff. Diapers, formula, some clothes, and—"

"Forget it," Murphy huffed. "This is no walk in the park! I'm trying to keep a low profile so everything doesn't blow up in our faces."

"And while you're keeping a low profile, Lara's supposed to go hungry?"

The name rolled off Vicki's tongue as if it had always been there, just waiting to be called upon. She touched the tip of her pinkie to Lara's lips, and the baby started sucking.

"This will keep her busy for a few minutes, but you're gonna have to stop and get some food for her."

Murphy drove for another fifteen minutes, then pulled off the highway and headed for Brownsville. The sun had cleared the horizon, and the stores would be open. In an all-night drugstore, a stranger buying a bunch of baby supplies was something a clerk might remember, but in a supermarket where people often shopped for these things, such a purchase would go unnoticed.

Once they left the highway he drove cautiously, slowing at amber stoplights rather than flooring it to beat the red and coming to a full stop at crosswalks. As he rounded the corner of Bowie Street, he spotted a Foodtown market and pulled into the sparsely populated parking lot. Reaching into his pocket, he pulled out a twenty and handed it to her.

"Try not to be too obvious," he said. "Grab what you need and get out as quickly as possible."

"Okay." She hefted the baby onto her other shoulder and reached for the door handle.

"You can't take her with you!"

"Why not?"

"For all we know, that kid's picture may be all over TV. If someone spots you with her, we'll end up in jail."

She looked at him with a blank stare. "That's crazy. Lara's my baby. Why would anyone even question—"

As she went on about how the baby looked exactly like her, Murphy sat there shaking his head. Obviously she was still blitzed and thought this kid really was Lara. *Too risky,* he decided and reached across to reclaim the twenty-dollar bill.

"Maybe it's better if you stay in the car," he said. "I'll get the stuff."

She listed the things she'd need: nursing bottles, cans of formula, diapers, wipes, jars of baby food. Although she'd never before cared for an infant, all the things she'd read in Doctor Spock's baby book were right there in her mind, tucked away and fully prepared for just such an occasion.

As he climbed from the car she called after him, "Try to get Gerber strained bananas."

Murphy rushed off without looking back.

It took less than fifteen minutes for him to be in and out of the store. He hurried across the parking lot, glancing back over his shoulder to make sure no one was following. As he climbed into the car he handed Vicki the nursing bottle and a can of formula, then tossed the rest of the bags in the back seat and pulled out of the lot. He headed north and a few blocks later turned west. When they neared the edge of town, he zigzagged in and out of several side streets until he was certain no one was trailing behind, then pulled onto a narrow two-lane road that meandered westward toward Arkansas.

Although he'd had little sleep for the past three days, Murphy was alert and on watch for any sign of trouble: a car following behind, a roadblock stationed around the next bend, a policeman eyeing them with a suspicious gaze. He zipped through towns that were barely a wide spot in the road, ignoring Vicki's suggestion they pull over and have a bite to eat.

"There're a few candy bars in the bag," he said. "Grab one of those."

"But I'm thirsty and want a Pepsi."

"You'll have to wait. When we find a place to stay the night, I'll get you a Pepsi and something to eat."

She stopping playing with the baby and turned with a puzzled expression. "We've already passed a dozen motels; what was wrong with them?"

"I'm looking for someplace special," he said and continued driving.

It was early afternoon when he saw the sign welcoming them to Arkansas. Shortly after they passed through Mound City, he spotted a sign saying HIDEAWAY CABINS—NEXT TURNOFF.

THE HIDEAWAY

The cabins were just as their name implied, hidden away behind an overgrown stand of oaks. Murph turned in and thumped along the dirt road until he came to the clearing. Three cars were parked alongside the cabin marked OFFICE, but other than that the place looked deserted. He parked on the far side of the clearing, climbed out, and headed for the office. The campground looked mostly empty as he crossed over.

Perfect, he thought.

~

"Eight dollars a night; checkout is noon," the clerk said and gave a toothy smile.

Murph registered as Mr. and Mrs. Russell with no mention of the baby.

"My wife's a light sleeper, so if the cabin in the back is available, we'd like that one," he said.

The clerk handed him the key marked 10. "No problem. How long you staying?"

"Two, maybe three days."

As the words left his mouth Murphy realized the thought of them hanging on to that baby for two or three days was crazy. Insane. He had to do something right away. Today if possible. Convincing Vicki to give up the baby wasn't going to be easy; he knew that. It would be like trying to pry a cub from the mama bear, but it had to be done.

Walking back to the car, he tried to pull his thoughts together, but the words he'd planned to use now seemed blurred and mismatched. They made little or no sense and were certainly not a convincing argument. *Too tired,* he told himself. *I'll grab a few hours' sleep and then . . .*

Once inside the cabin, he latched the door and fell onto the bed. Vicki gave the baby another bottle and changed her, then she too climbed into bed. They slept that way for nearly three hours: Murph on one side of the bed, Vicki on the other, and Emmy snug in the center.

The sky had grown dusky by the time he went in search of food. When he returned with a paper sack of hamburgers, french fries, and milkshakes, a newspaper was tucked under his arm.

~

Later on, when Vicki was gone from his life, Murph would remember that night and how, as he leafed through the *Gazette*, she'd spread the blanket on the floor and spent the evening playing with the baby. In his haste to get out of the store he'd forgotten a spoon, so she'd scooped bits of strained banana onto her fingertip and laughed as the baby hungrily sucked it down.

She'd looked up at him with a smile that would forever be printed on his heart and said, "See how wonderful it is to be a family?"

For that fractional moment of time, he'd agreed.

~

When Murph woke the next morning, Vicki was sitting in the chair with the baby in her lap.

"I made a list," she said and smiled.

"A list of what?"

"Things we'll need for Lara."

Murph winced as he rubbed the sleep from his eyes.

"We can't keep this baby," he said. "She's not Lara, and you know it. Lara died, remember?"

Her smile faded, and a row of ridges rose on her forehead.

"Liar!" she snapped. "That's what you'd like me to believe!"

He heard the denial rising in her voice, just as it had all those months ago. With a twitch of sadness pulling at the corners of his mouth, he shook his head slowly.

"We saw her, Vicki, don't you remember? We went to the cemetery; it was raining. Remember, we left roses for her?"

"No!" she shouted. "I don't know who that was, but it wasn't Lara!"

A crackle of tension bristled through the air, and the baby wailed.

"Now see what you've done!" She lifted the baby onto her shoulder and glared at him with her brows pinched tight. "Lara's upset because of the way you're acting!"

She snatched up the list she'd made and threw it at him. "If you won't go get the things Lara needs, then give me the car keys and we'll go!"

Murphy knew the "we" she was talking about included the baby. He couldn't let that happen.

"I'll go," he said wearily, then scooped the list from the floor and walked out the door.

~

After he left the motel, Murphy drove around for almost an hour just trying to clear the thoughts racing through his mind. There was no good solution, only a bunch of bad options, each worse than the other. During the month following Lara's death he'd feared he would lose Vicki too. She'd stopped eating, stopped laughing, and almost stopped living.

Drugs seemed the easiest answer. First it was painkillers, then after that . . .

He pictured himself rolling a joint, taking a puff, then handing it to her. After a second or third hit, the agony etched on her face softened, and they sat on the sofa sharing peanut butter and jelly sandwiches.

Back then the carefree easiness it brought seemed a good thing; now he wasn't so sure. It was one thing for him to get high; after Vietnam, he'd needed it. She didn't. Her thoughts were of making love, not war; that was, until the night of Lara's birth.

Early in the day she had started worrying that the baby wasn't moving. That night the pains began, and before daybreak the baby came—stillborn. The child she'd carried for seven months never took a breath.

For her, the loss of that baby was as devastating as the loss of his arm. Overnight they became two broken people living a patched life, finding moments of pleasure only in the oblivion of a high.

Over time the emptiness of Vicki's stomach grew into a cloak of sorrow that she wore night and day. There were ups and downs, but the ups came in soaring highs and fits of frenetic laughter. The downs were long days of sobbing into a tearstained pillow. In all those months, not once had Murphy seen her with the look of serenity she now had.

The endless sorrow, the need for drugs, it was because of the baby. Now she was unaware of the wrong she'd done; the only thing she felt was the baby in her arms.

Could he do it? Could he take this second child away from her, knowing that this time it would be an even greater tragedy?

Although he'd searched his mind a thousand times, he had no answer. He didn't know if her heart was strong enough to withstand the stress. Vicki was born with congenital heart disease and had nearly died giving birth. The doctor warned her not to try again.

If she couldn't live through another birth, could she live through another loss?

There were countless reasons for him to turn a blind eye and allow her to keep the baby, but an even greater number argued he should do the sane thing: leave the child in a place where she could be found and returned to her parents.

Sound as the logic was, he knew Vicki would never agree to that. She'd already convinced herself this child was her baby.

Murph was a million miles from finding an answer when he spotted a luncheonette by the side of the road and pulled in. The place was empty except for the gray-haired waitress behind the counter.

Before he was seated, she called out, "Coffee?"

He nodded and climbed onto the stool.

She set a cup in front of him and filled it with the steaming black liquid. "We got day-old Danish, fifty cents."

He shook his head. "No, thanks."

After a few more attempts at conversation, she moved off, and Murphy picked up the *Arkansas Gazette* lying at the end of the counter. The front page had pictures of a sinkhole that had opened up in a town called Milton but no mention of a kidnapping. He went through the newspaper front to back, but there was not one word about the music festival, Hesterville, or a missing baby.

If no one was out there searching for the baby, it might be safe to stay in the cabin.

For a short while.

Given a momentary sense of freedom, Murphy drove into town, parked on a side street, and went in search of a store where he could buy the things on Vicki's list. It was a stroke of luck that he spotted the thrift store on the corner.

Once inside he discovered there was only one clerk at the checkout counter. He ducked his head, gave a nod, and hurried past her. He was then free to roam the aisles, picking and choosing without having to explain.

He grabbed a carry basket and began the search. Tossing in a small silver spoon, a pair of rompers, a few nightgowns, and a teddy bear that was missing one eye, he reasoned buying these things did not mean they were keeping the baby; it simply meant she would be cared for and comfortable until he could come up with a plan. He'd seen the glow motherhood brought to Vicki's face, and yet he had to believe that after a few days she'd acknowledge the reality of the situation and agree to give the baby back.

It was like Christmas morning when Murphy returned to the cabin with the things he'd bought at the thrift shop. The smile on Vicki's face was happier than it would have been if he'd handed her a stack of gift-wrapped boxes from Saks Fifth Avenue. She reached into the brown paper bag and pulled the clothes out one at a time, oohing and aahing over everything, holding tiny shirts and dresses aloft to judge the size or admire the design.

When she came upon a white baby gown with lace edging, she squealed with delight. Even though the baby was napping peacefully, she lifted her up and pulled the nightgown over her head.

"Beautiful!" she exclaimed. "Absolutely beautiful!"

Dancing around with the baby in her arms, she turned to Murph. "Daddy, isn't our little Lara the prettiest girl in the world?"

He nodded and gave a tight-lipped smile.

With her blonde curls and huge blue eyes, the baby was beautiful, but she was not Lara. Murphy could feel the weight of this knowledge growing heavier with each passing moment. As he sat there watching Vicki twirl happily around the room, he knew this couldn't last. Today, tomorrow, next week, or possibly even next year, somebody, somewhere, would discover who the child was. Then what? Jail for him. For her jail or perhaps an asylum. Either way the baby would be gone, and quite probably Vicki's freedom for the remaining days of her life. She was too delicate; she'd never survive such an ordeal.

He couldn't let that happen.

For a long while he sat watching Vicki, her face aglow, a sense of guileless joy surrounding her as she played with the baby.

"Peekaboo," she'd tease as she hid her face, then merrily popped out from behind the pillow. After peekaboo there was patty-cake, and as Vicki clapped the chubby little hands against her own, the baby shrieked with laughter. Here and there Murphy found moments when he could push back the apprehension and feel that they were indeed a family, but before that contentment could take root in his heart the fear came roaring back.

AS THE NEWS SPREAD

George Dixon's hardware store did not open on Monday or Tuesday. Sometime late that afternoon a sign indicating the store would remain closed until further notice was taped to the inside of the glass door. No explanation was given, but by then most everyone in Hesterville knew about the kidnapping.

~

When Sadie Jenkins got word of what had happened, her first thought was of Helen Dixon, George's mama.

Helen lived alone in a big house, three blocks west of Main Street. She had a sharp tongue, an intolerant nature, smoked Chesterfield cigarettes by the carton, and purposely kept to herself. Although there were some who labeled her an unpleasant person and moved on, there were others who knew she wasn't always that way. At one time she'd been a good neighbor and considered a friend by half the women in town. But after she lost Henry, George's daddy, to a heart attack that didn't allow time for goodbyes, she'd grown resentful of life. Three years later, when George married Rachel and moved out, the bitterness inside her swelled to such a size it completely obliterated the loving nature she'd once had. With her now ready to snap the head off anyone who dared ring the doorbell, few people other than Sadie and the grocery store delivery boys came to the house. The windows that had been shuttered two years earlier remained so, and the wraparound porch sat devoid of furniture.

Early Tuesday morning Sadie filled a basket with her fresh-baked blueberry muffins, pulled on her walking shoes, and headed over to Pecan Street. She knew Helen was going to need a shoulder to cry on.

She rang the doorbell three times and, after standing there for almost ten minutes, began pounding on the door. Eventually she heard the shuffle of footsteps and Helen's angry voice.

"Hold your horses; I'm coming!"

When the door finally swung open, Helen was in a clumsily tied bathrobe with one side of her hair spiked up and the other side smashed flat against her head. Sadie held out the basket of muffins and strode in without waiting for an invitation.

"I rushed over the minute I got the news."

"News?" Helen echoed, her face as dark as a storm cloud. "It's not yet eight o'clock! Have you not heard of calling before you come pounding on a person's door?"

"I thought it was more important for me to hurry up and get here."

Sadie closed the door behind her and moved toward the kitchen. The two women had been friends since grade school, and Sadie knew Helen's kitchen almost as well as she knew her own. She filled the coffeepot, set it to brew, then dropped down in the chair across from Helen.

Pulling a pack of cigarettes from her pocket, Helen shook one out and lit it. "Now, what is so damn important that you need to be banging on my door at the crack of dawn?"

"Hasn't George called?"

A look of annoyance flickered in Helen's eyes. "Not that it's any of your business, but yes, he called yesterday evening. I was in the shower, and he left a message for me to call him at the house."

"Did you?"

"No. Not yet. I'm not overly anxious to talk with that wife of his. I figured it best to call him at the store later today."

For a brief while, Sadie sat there saying nothing. As the percolator bubbled to a stop, she searched her mind for an easy way to tell of the kidnapping, but there was none. She finally stood, poured two cups of coffee, and set them on the table.

"I know you've had your differences with Rachel, but right now she and George could use your support."

"I doubt that!" Helen took a long drag of the cigarette, then stubbed it out in the ashtray. "George doesn't need me. Not since he married *her*."

Sadie stretched her arm across the table and took Helen's hand in hers. "Actually he does need you, Helen. They both do. When Rachel woke up yesterday morning, Emmy's crib was empty. They think the baby was kidnapped sometime during the night on Sunday."

The angry set of Helen's face softened, and her lip began to quiver. "Kidnapped? Emmy? But how? Who would—"

Sadie gave her friend's hand a reassuring squeeze. "My understanding is that they don't know much yet. Sheriff Wilson is working on it, and he's got a team out there searching the woods."

Helen's eyes filled with water. "Lord God. They should never have been living way out there. I told George they ought to move in here with me, but Rachel wouldn't hear of it! She's the one to blame! A thing like this never would have—"

"Stop it!" Sadie snapped and withdrew her hand. "Rachel's already crazy with worry. The last thing she needs is for you to be blaming her."

"Well, it's true."

Sadie pushed back her chair and stood. "I don't want to hear it! If you were any kind of a mama you'd be out there comforting your family instead of sitting here on your righteous high horse!"

Leaving the full cup of coffee on the table, she turned toward the living room. Halfway to the door she stopped and looked back.

"I'm making a casserole for them, and I'll be bringing it out there later this afternoon. If you want to come along, you're welcome to do so."

As she reached for the doorknob, she heard a rather contrite voice say, "Pick me up on the way."

~

That afternoon Sadie not only baked a casserole, she also started a fund-raising campaign. She went through the directory and called every friend who lived within fifty miles of town. Once she'd given them a rundown of what happened, she said, "Right now there's not a speck of information on who the kidnapper might be, but if we were to offer a sizable reward for information . . ."

By late that afternoon, she had commitments for $7,850, and $500 of that came from Harold Baker. Although he'd told Sheriff Wilson he was absolutely certain the music festival had nothing to do with the disappearance of the Dixon baby, he had suspicions otherwise. The thought of that possibility needled him. He'd gotten a look at the people camped out in the field—most of them stoned out of their minds or rolling around in the mud half-naked—and although you couldn't tell one from the other, he wouldn't put it past any of them.

It was near five o'clock when Sadie pulled into the driveway of Helen's house and beeped the horn. Seconds later the front door opened, and Helen hurried down the walk lugging an overnight bag.

"I thought I'd best bring a few things in case they need me to stay," she said and climbed into the car.

When they arrived at the Dixon house George was standing on the front porch, his hands jammed into his pockets and his face tilted toward the sky. Startled by the sight of him, Helen felt her heart drop into her stomach. Never had she seen him looking so forlorn, not even five years earlier when his daddy died.

He looked at her and gave a barely perceptible nod. "Thanks for coming, Mama."

"Well, of course I'd come. I'm your mama."

He stepped down from the porch and came toward her. Although she had benevolence in her heart, Helen's sharp tongue got the best of her.

"Your message just said to call as soon as possible; you should have left word that it was an emergency and explained what happened! I'm Emmy's grandmother! I deserve to know when—"

She stopped midsentence when she caught sight of Sadie's pinched-up frown.

"No matter," she said and kissed his cheek.

Thinking this might be a good time for a mother-son talk, Sadie lifted the casserole from the back seat of the car and started toward the house. "Is Rachel inside?"

George nodded.

"I'll see if she wants this in the fridge or the oven." She hurried by and disappeared through the front door.

Sadie expected to find Rachel sitting on the living room sofa or trying to keep busy in the kitchen, but she was nowhere to be seen.

"Rachel?" she called out.

A small childlike voice came from the far end of the hall. "What?"

She set the casserole on the counter and followed the sound of the voice.

"It's me, Sadie Jenkins," she called out. "I've brought a casserole so you won't have to worry about cooking."

No answer.

Sadie slowly started down the hallway. The first doorway opened into the master bedroom where George and Rachel slept. The drapes were drawn and the bed unmade.

"Rachel?"

Again, no answer.

At the end of the hall she spied a room with the door pulled shut. She tapped lightly and said, "Rachel, are you in here?"

No answer, but Sadie heard the creak of a rocking chair swaying back and forth against the wooden floor. A feeling of apprehension gripped her as she eased the door open and looked into the room. She gasped.

"Dear God!"

Rachel was sitting in the chair with the rag doll she'd made for Emmy in her lap. She was wearing the same white nightgown and robe she'd had on Monday morning. Her face was whiter than the robe and drawn so tight you could see the skeletal structure of her bones.

Sadie crossed over and kneeled beside the chair. "Rachel, honey, what in the world are you doing?"

Rachel turned with a blank expression. "Doing?"

Sadie took the limp hand in hers. "You look like a dead woman. You're making yourself sick. I know how terrible this is, but you've got—"

Rachel blinked, and for a brief moment her eyes seemed to focus on Sadie's face. Then she turned away.

"No, you *don't* know how terrible this is," she said in a voice that was as flat and heavy as an iron skillet. "You can't possibly know, because you've never had your baby taken away."

"That's true. But just because someone else hasn't experienced the pain of what you and George are going through doesn't mean they can't understand it."

Rachel creaked back and forth in the chair, her eyes focused on the far wall and her lips pressed tightly together.

"When someone you love hurts, you hurt for them. That's how love is." Sadie reached in and wrapped her arms around Rachel. "Honey, there're a lot of people in this town who love you and George both, and as long as you're hurting, we're gonna be hurting with you."

Without saying a word Rachel leaned forward, lowered her face into the thick folds of Sadie's bosom, and sobbed as though her heart was broken—which it was.

~

Sadie and Helen stayed until late in the evening. They scurried about washing sheets, making the bed, and running a rag mop across floors that were already spotless. The sky was dark when Sadie heated the casserole and called everyone to the kitchen table.

George brought Rachel from the back room, keeping hold of her arm as he eased her into the chair. Like an obedient child she sat silently, her eyes as lifeless as an abandoned house. For several minutes, there was only the sound of a utensil scraping the bottom of the pan as Sadie spooned out the casserole.

Feeling this silence was more painful than that of her own house, Helen finally spoke. "I can help out in the store if you want," she said, looking to George. "Maybe wait on customers or tend the cash register?"

He looked into his mama's eyes for half a second, then shook his head and stuck a forkful of the chicken in his mouth.

Rachel just sat there, barely touching the little bit of food on her plate. Twice she moved a piece of carrot from one side of her plate to the other, then she left it there and set the fork aside.

At the end of the evening, Helen took George aside. "I know I haven't always acted real kindly toward Rachel," she said, "and I'm sorry about that."

"There's no need, Mama—"

"It's been a difficult time for me, but I want you to know I'm willing to help her out. I brought my overnight case, and I'm prepared to stay if you think she has need of me."

George shook his head. "Not tonight, Mama. Maybe when Rachel gets to feeling better."

Helen glanced across the room and eyed Rachel curled into a ball at the end of the sofa. A gut-wrenching feeling settled into her stomach as she came to fear Rachel was not going to get better, at least not anytime soon.

THE INVESTIGATION

The *Primrose Post* was a weekly newspaper distributed free of charge every Wednesday; that week they ran a headline declaring Infant Taken As Family Sleeps. The paper included a squint-eyed photo of Emily taken at the hospital just after she was born. Her eyes were almost closed and her hair still dark. Beneath the photo was a description saying the infant was wearing a pink nightgown; weighed approximately sixteen pounds; and had blue eyes, blonde hair, and a butterfly-shaped birthmark on her back.

Alongside Emily's photo was one taken of the music festival. That article estimated the crowd to be fifteen thousand and told of the featured bands. At the bottom of the column it said Continued on page 6.

~

When the newspaper arrived, Sheriff Wilson was in his office thumbing through the scraps of evidence he'd gathered over the past two days. Most of it amounted to nothing: fingerprints the FBI couldn't identify, a partial footprint of a girl's sandal, and statements from neighbors who had neither seen nor heard anything. Given the number of people at the music festival and the downpour that flooded the field, there was not a scrap of evidence to be salvaged.

The newspaper sat on his desk for almost two hours before he glanced over and spotted the picture. It wasn't the photo of Emily that piqued his interest; it was the one of the music festival. There were at least a dozen faces that might be identifiable. He studied the picture, then flipped over to page six. No names but more pictures. He checked the byline on the article: Joy Dancer.

As it turned out, Joy was a part-time reporter whose real name was Alice Montgomery. She worked special events and came into the office only on Fridays. With a bit of persuasion, Wilson got her address and phone number. That same afternoon he drove out to her house and met with her. Alice said she'd read the story of the missing baby and couldn't imagine what the Dixons were going through.

"It must be hell," she said sympathetically. "If there's anything I can do—"

"There just might be." Wilson went on to ask if she was there on Sunday and if she had any other shots of the crowd.

"I worked the festival all weekend. Did ten rolls of film, more than three hundred shots," she said. "If you think there's something . . ."

They spent the next two hours going over the proof sheets. Several shots were of the performers, and a large number were crowd shots taken from behind, but there were twenty-one shots with a clear view of the faces in the crowd. As the angle of the camera changed, so did the faces.

"Any of these people strike you as different? Maybe a bit out of the ordinary?"

She gave a wry smile. "They all like to think they are, but the truth is they look pretty much the same. Long hair, beards, and clothes that could use a washing."

Wilson nodded. It was the same story he'd gotten from everyone else.

He waited while she went into her darkroom and printed enlargements of all twenty-one photos. Once the photos were dry, she slid them into an envelope.

"Good luck," she said as she handed it to him.

He'd counted 103 individual faces; hopefully one of them would ignite a spark of recognition.

~

For nearly a week Sheriff Wilson went from place to place showing the pictures and asking if any of the faces looked familiar. He visited every house on Yellowwood Road and then went nearly five miles beyond the Baker farm showing the pictures and asking questions. Time after time he got the same answer from people. They'd heard the noise of the music festival but hadn't seen a thing.

"I'm not one to go looking for trouble," the widow Scoggins said. "I kept my blinds drawn and doors locked until those rowdies left town."

After he'd tried every house, he began canvassing the merchants in town. He went from one end of Main Street to the other asking if perhaps one of the faces looked familiar, possibly someone who'd shopped in the store using a credit card that could be traced. Abner Vanhouten, owner of Vanhouten's Drugstore, pointed out a lanky fella standing off to one side and said he looked vaguely familiar. The sheriff called Alice and asked if she knew anything about the man in question. She enlarged her copy of the photo, then said he was the lead guitarist with the Blue Bandits Band, so that also turned out to be a dead end.

~

When the reward fund grew to more than $10,000, Sadie turned it over to the sheriff, and he printed up posters with a grainy black-and-white picture of Emily in the center. At the top in bold red ink it read "$10,000 reward for information leading to the return of this child." Underneath was the same description that appeared in the newspaper—pink nightgown, blue eyes, blonde hair, and a butterfly-shaped birthmark. At the very bottom was a phone number for the sheriff's office.

A team of volunteers—mostly friends of Rachel and merchants who worked alongside George—went from town to town pinning posters on bulletin boards, placing them in store windows, and tacking them onto telephone poles. They went as far north as Ellijay and as far south as Needmore.

Before the day was out the sheriff began getting phone calls. A woman from Norcross claimed there was a five-year-old girl living two doors down who was the spitting image of the child in the photograph. A private investigator called and said he'd offer his services if the sheriff was willing to fork over a $500 advance.

That first week there were forty-two calls in all. Some seemed like crackpots from the get-go, but others appeared genuine enough until he paid them a visit. No matter how strange or how far away, Sheriff Wilson followed up every lead. At night he would come home bone-tired and too weary to eat supper, fall into his La-Z-Boy recliner, catch a few hours of sleep, then get up and start again. On mornings when his body screamed for more rest, he'd picture the haunted look in Rachel Dixon's eyes and force himself to push through the weariness.

A SEARCH FOR THE STORY

For a week Vicki and Murphy remained there in that one-room cabin—cozy, comfortable, hidden from the world. She and the baby never left, but he did. The second day he bought a small hot plate to heat food in the room, and each morning he shopped in a different store. One day it was ten miles west of the cabin, the next seven miles north of the place. He never returned to the same market, never allowed himself to become familiar or recognizable.

On every trip he came back carrying a copy of the *Arkansas Gazette*. Then for a good hour he'd sit and go through it page by page, front to back. In the early morning he listened to the news on the radio, and in the evening he sat with his eyes glued to the television, watching, waiting, wondering. He knew the police had to be searching for the child, but did they know Vicki was the one who had entered the house and taken the baby from her crib? Did someone perchance see his car or catch sight of the Kentucky license plate?

He had a million unanswered questions but could not find a single mention of the missing baby in the news. Not knowing was worse than knowing. At night he slept fitfully, always listening for the crunch of footsteps outside their door or the shriek of a siren turning off the highway.

On Saturday evening the baby grew fussy and screamed without apparent reason.

Murphy's heart rose into his throat. "Can't you keep her quiet?"

"Be patient," Vicki answered. "I think she's teething."

As if it were the most natural thing on earth, she lifted the baby into her arms, hummed softly, and walked back and forth until a sleepy little head dropped onto her shoulder.

~

The weekend passed without a speck of news, and Murphy could no longer stand it.

"I've got to find out what's happening," he said.

On Monday morning he left the cabin at eight o'clock and cautioned Vicki to keep the door locked and remain inside.

"Try to keep the baby quiet, and don't open the door for anyone. Not anyone. Do you understand?"

She nodded. "Of course I understand. I'm not an idiot. But it's so silly, all this hiding and—"

"Just do as I say, Vicki! I should be back by six or a little before."

She raised her face to his and kissed his cheek. "Drive carefully."

"I will." He held her close to his chest and hesitated, wondering if he should tell her what to do in the event he didn't come back.

There's nothing she can do. I'm the only protection she's got.

Without saying anything more, he broke away and disappeared out the door.

~

After a week of grocery shopping in first one town and then the other, he'd become familiar with the back roads. He drove north to Marion, dodging in and out of the streets until he was certain no one was following him. Once he was in the clear, he pulled onto Route 64 and headed west. In Crawfordville he picked up the southbound arm of Route 50 and followed that to Highway 40, which ran straight into Little Rock.

He hoped to be there before noon, and since it was lunchtime the place wouldn't be too crowded. The fewer people he came in contact with, the better.

On the outskirts of Little Rock he pulled into a small shopping plaza and went in search of a phone booth, figuring that a directory would be hanging alongside the booth. In the back of the drugstore he found what he needed and thumbed through the pages until he reached the section for the Little Rock listings. There were three pages of businesses named for the city, places like Little Rock Acting School, Little Rock Bookstore, and Little Rock Dry Cleaners. The public library listing was halfway down the second page. Three branches were listed; he opted for the main branch. He made note of the address, then tore the page from the book, folded it, and stuffed it into his pocket in case he couldn't find what he wanted and had to look elsewhere.

On his way out of the store, he spotted an elderly woman behind the counter.

"Excuse me," he said, "what's the best way to get to South Rock Street?"

"That's on the far side of the river." She waved a hand toward the highway that ran past the plaza. "Just keep heading west until you come to the junction of Route 30; that'll take you straight across the bridge. You looking for anyplace special?"

She caught him off guard, and without thinking he answered, "The library."

"Oh, it's just a little ways from the bridge, but you've got to make a few turns. Once you cross the bridge, make a right onto West Seventh Street, then a short bit later another right onto the street that goes down by the market. I forget the name, but—"

"Thanks," Murphy mumbled. Anxious to be on his way, he headed for the door.

"Come to think of it, the name of that street might be Louisiana," she called after him.

Murphy gave a wave in the air but didn't look back. Until he could find out what was happening he had to remain invisible, be a passerby nobody remembered. Stopping to chat was not part of the plan.

As she'd suggested, the library was easy enough to find. He drove past once, then circled around the block and came by a second time. Bypassing the empty parking spaces in front of the building, he took a left and parked on a side street three blocks south of the building. Before leaving the cabin he'd had coffee but nothing to eat. Now as he walked toward the desk, he could feel his stomach rumbling.

Nerves, not hunger.

At the front desk, with his face fixed in an expression that was neither smile nor frown, he said, "I'm looking for back issues of the Georgia newspapers."

"How far back?" the librarian asked.

Not wanting to raise a red flag regarding the date, he gave a nonchalant shrug. "Fairly recent, a month or so."

"The only one we carry is the *Atlanta Constitution*." She raised her arm and pointed toward a large alcove on the far side of the floor. "Try the reading room. The last five or six issues should be there. Anything older would be in the microfiche department."

Murphy gave a quick nod and hurried off.

Three long tables were set crossways in the reading room, and along the wall he saw a lineup of lounge chairs. On the side counter, stacks of newspapers were arranged by date with the most recent issues on top and those dating back on the bottom. After flipping past the *New York Times*, *Washington Post*, and *Chicago Tribune*, he came to the *Atlanta Constitution*. The bottom issue was from last Tuesday, and the headline told him this was what he'd been looking for. Right below the masthead a headline blared Search For Missing Baby Continues.

In all, there were five issues of the *Atlanta Constitution*: Tuesday through Sunday, with Saturday missing. He gathered them up, carried them to the back table, and sat. Starting with Tuesday, he scrutinized each edition, going page by page, making note of every comment, every mention of the kidnapping, the Dixon family, the music festival, and, most important, the fact that there seemed to be few if any clues as to the identity of the kidnapper. Tears filled his eyes as he studied the picture of the Dixons and read through the interview where Rachel pleaded with the kidnapper to leave Emmy in a safe spot where she could be returned to her family.

Her name is Emily Dixon. They call her Emmy.

Murphy's stomach churned, and the taste of bile rose in his throat. He was reminded of that day in Saigon when a grenade took part of his arm, and he'd fought to stay alive. Back then he'd thought dying was the worst thing that could happen to a person, but after reading Rachel Dixon's plea, he was no longer sure. Maybe there was a hell worse than Vietnam, and the Dixon family was living it right now.

For several minutes he sat there staring at the newspaper the same way he'd stared at his bloody arm—horrified at the truth but too frightened to move.

In Wednesday's issue, Sheriff Wilson was quoted as saying there was now a $10,000 reward for information leading to the child and/or the person responsible for the kidnapping.

"We believe the kidnapper may have attended the music festival," he said, "and we are currently going through photos in the hope of identifying potential suspects."

Although the story included two photos taken at the festival and another showing the Dixon house, it was no longer the lead article. It had been moved back to page five across from a quarter-page ad for Macy's housewares sale.

Murphy reread the article nine times, looking for some finger of suspicion pointing to him or Vicki, some piece of evidence or clue hidden among the lines. In the end, he could find nothing more than the broad statement saying they had pictures of the crowd. Staring down at the photo of the Dixon house, he could picture Vicki's slight frame as she darted across the lawn and disappeared into the darkness. Again, he reminded himself of the night: rain, heavy clouds, a thick blackness that swallowed up everything.

Seeing the car would have been impossible.

Moving his finger from face to face, he searched the crowd pictures. Neither he nor Vicki was in either of these shots.

Yes, but are there more pictures?

He moved on to Thursday's issue and found only one mention in the second section. No photos this time, just a brief half-column story with a headline that read Missing Baby Case Continues To Baffle Authorities.

There was nothing more on Friday or Sunday.

Before replacing the newspapers, he folded the first section of Tuesday's edition into a small square and stuffed it inside his shirt.

MURPHY'S PLAN

The drive back to the cabin was slower than it had been coming, with more cars on the road, more slowdowns, stops, and starts for no visible reason. Instead of being cause for agitation, it gave Murphy time to think. After he'd searched the Georgia paper, he'd looked through the *Knoxville News Sentinel* and the *Lexington Herald-Leader* and found nothing. Believing the search for the kidnapper had not bled into the surrounding states, he didn't bother circling through the back roads and looking in the rearview mirror at every turnoff.

Right now there was nothing tying them to the kidnapping. They could pin a note to the baby's shirt, drop her off at a church in Arkansas, then turn around and head home to Kentucky with nobody the wiser. The more he thought about this idea, the better he liked it.

It was the right solution, but the problem was going to be Vicki. He pictured the way she'd held the baby to her chest, happily humming, cooing, promising a lifetime of love. Her want of that baby was so intense that she'd lost sight of all else: the heartache she'd left behind, the lifetime of running and hiding that lay ahead.

As the traffic slowed and then came to a stop, he thought of waiting until Vicki was sound asleep, then lifting the baby from the bed and whisking her off to a church in some faraway town.

He stretched his neck and leaned toward the windshield, trying to figure out what was causing the holdup. For as far as his eye could see there was no roadblock, no accident, just a long line of red taillights, so he sat and thought.

A sadness he'd almost forgotten seeped into his heart as he recalled the days before Lara's birth. Vicki was so different then. She had an easy laugh that was almost magical. He smiled at the memory of how he used to laugh along with her, of how back then they'd thought that once the baby came, they'd settle down. Now it was as if their time together had a dividing line down the middle: before Lara was on one side, after Lara on the other.

It had been a difficult birth, and after long hours of labor Vicki was put to sleep so they could take the baby. Later on, with her body stitched together and her skin colorless as the sheets, she'd asked to hold her child. He could still feel the heaviness of her hand as he lifted it into his and told her the infant was gone. It was as if he had shot her through the heart. He couldn't do that again. It would be too much like losing Lara.

The line of cars began to inch forward, so he shifted into first gear and pressed his foot down on the gas pedal.

There had to be another answer, he reasoned, some way to convince Vicki to give the baby back willingly. He slid the gearshift into second and then third as the traffic sped up.

He thought back to earlier in the week, when the baby had snatched up the knife lying on the table.

"No, no, no," Vicki said, trying to pry the chubby fingers from the knife.

The baby didn't want to let go, so she tightened her grip and screamed.

Moving as though it was something she'd always known, Vicki grabbed her key ring and jangled it in front of the baby's face. The little one's eyes lit up, and she let go of the knife to reach for the keys.

Distraction. That's it. Something she wants as much or more than this baby.

Murphy's thoughts traveled back to the earliest days of their relationship, a time when they first began dating and Vicki was still living at home with her dad. As the weeks went by and they became fonder of each other, she began bringing things to his apartment and leaving them: a toothbrush, another pair of jeans, several sweaters, changes of underwear. Everyday things that seemed to be the building blocks of a relationship. Then came that fateful Tuesday when she showed up with a suitcase full of clothes and tears in her eyes.

"I can't live there anymore," she said and dropped onto the sofa.

"What happened?" he asked.

"Nothing. Yet."

There was more to the story, but it was the wee hours of morning before it finally came out. Her daddy had come home drunk and tried to climb on top of her. With tears streaming from her eyes, she told him this wasn't the first time she'd had to fight him off.

"I don't want to go back there," she said through her sobs. "If you'll let me stay here until I can find a place . . ."

That night Murphy held her in his arms and said she could stay for as long as she wanted. Four months later she was pregnant, and they started talking about a life together. Not necessarily marriage, but a life together.

Marriage meant responsibility, and responsibility wasn't something Murph was particularly fond of. He'd returned from Vietnam knowing that he'd never have the chance to be a licensed electrician. He'd worked as an apprentice for two long years. All the knowledge he needed was there, but the second arm necessary to hold a fixture in place or secure a junction box was missing.

It had taken the better part of a year for him to accept that the life he now lived—of social drugs, part-time jobs, and VA checks—was the new normal.

The car in front of him slowed, but Murphy was lost in thought and had to slam on the brakes at the last minute. The suddenness of a near accident jolted him from his reverie. As he sat there waiting for the line of cars to start moving again, his mind drifted back to Vicki and what he wanted her to do. He would be asking her to give up a baby that she'd already come to love, set aside her thoughts of motherhood, and come around to his way of thinking.

If she gives up those things, what am I willing to give up?

Murphy anxiously drummed his fingers against the steering wheel and tried to think. It wasn't enough to say, "Give up the baby and we'll go back to the way we were." That would be like stepping back in time; it would be like it was after Lara.

The traffic inched forward, then stopped again. Murphy moved with it.

He loved Vicki, loved her with all his heart, but he was not ready to go along with keeping this baby. At best, they'd have to live with the burden of guilt for the rest of their lives. At worst, they'd be arrested and thrown in jail. If that happened, he'd lose Vicki and whatever shambles of a life he now had. Keeping the baby was out of the question, but what would it take to convince Vicki to give her up?

He thought about the keys, jangling just beyond the baby's reach.

Marriage?

A horn blared. Murphy glanced up and saw the traffic starting to move. He shifted into gear and closed the gap.

He knew the answer but was slow to accept it. She wanted a child. Right now she had what she wanted. The only way to get her to let go of that baby would be to offer her one of her own. But how? The doctor had warned them not to try another pregnancy; her heart wasn't strong enough.

Adoption?

Maybe if they were married, and he had a steady job . . . Murphy remembered Richard Schaefer's offer for him to teach at the vocational school. Okay, so he couldn't be an electrician, but he had a degree and could *teach* electricians. The pay wasn't half-bad. With an income like that and his VA checks, they could probably buy a house. Something small to start with, and then . . .

Feeling a renewed sense of confidence, Murphy moved into the left lane and sped past a truckload of logs. He didn't bother to get off at an earlier exit and zigzag through the back streets but stayed on Route 40 and got off at the exit marked Mound Township. He glanced down at the clock. Almost ten p.m. Vicki would no doubt be worried, but when she heard what he had to offer . . . He smiled as he turned in to the Hideaway Cabins and followed the dirt road around to the far end.

A twitch of concern pinched his heart when the car came to a stop. Through the slatted blinds he could see the cabin was dark; even the flickering light of the television was missing. He unlocked the door and stepped inside.

"Vicki?"

AS TIME MOVED ON

After days of not eating, Rachel became so gaunt her bones stuck out like oversize knobs on a chifforobe.

"You have got to eat something," George said, his face stretched tight with worry.

Rachel looked at him, her eyes hooded and her mouth twisted into an expression of anger that was almost piercing. "How can you even think of eating when you know our baby is going hungry?"

"I don't know any such thing," he argued. "Whoever took Emily is no doubt caring for her the same as we did."

"Really?" she replied icily. "And just how do you think they're doing it, since she's still breastfeeding?"

Having no answer, George turned away and dropped two slices of bread into the toaster. He stood with his back to Rachel, listening as her ragged breath whooshed in and out like thin puffs of air from a faulty bellows. When the toast was ready, he buttered it and set the plate in front of her.

"Starving yourself is not going to help Emmy. You need to keep up your strength so when she does come home you'll be able to take care of her."

Rachel stared at the plate for a moment, then took a piece of the toast in her hand and lifted it to her mouth. After a single bite, she dropped it back onto the plate, stood, and walked away.

That first week the hardware store remained closed, and George stayed by Rachel's side. When she cried he tried to comfort her, and when she ranted he tried to calm her, but there was neither calm nor comfort to be had.

Sparks of bitterness bristled around Rachel like bees swarming a flower, and her mood changed from one moment to the next. She blamed herself, blamed George, found fault with everything, and was satiated by nothing.

The anger she allowed to fly loose, George held inside. "We've got to trust that God will bring Emmy back to us," he said, but his seemingly stoic behavior served only to infuriate Rachel further.

"Trust God!" she shrieked. "How can you trust a God who allowed our baby to be taken from us in the first place?" While her words were still hanging in the air, she doubled over and began sobbing.

By then, Mama Dixon was at the house every day, but she gave Rachel a wide berth and busied herself with chores such as cooking supper or dusting furniture that had no need of it. If Rachel was in the living room, Helen inevitably found something to do in the kitchen. Without intending to do so, she made it apparent that the abiding concern she had for her son was far greater than what was felt for his wife.

That Friday, Rachel became hysterical and charged that George was to blame for not pushing the sheriff to take action. Eager to stay clear of such a fray, Helen moved to the front porch and sat weaving a crochet needle back and forth through a shapeless square. With her ears perked, she listened as George tried to calm Rachel but offered nothing in his own defense.

"I know how much you're hurting," he said, "but laying blame will not bring Emmy back. Sheriff Wilson is doing everything he can—"

"He hasn't done anything!" Rachel screamed, the sound of her voice so thunderous it rattled the dishes in the cupboard and made Helen's ears ring. "He's asked a million questions but is no closer to finding Emmy than we are! How can he sit there in his office and do nothing when some monster has stolen my baby? Emmy is my flesh and blood! My baby, my only child!"

A late-summer breeze fluttered the filmy curtain at the front window, and Helen watched as George crossed the room to take Rachel in his arms. He held her against his chest, and in time her sobs grew softer and more muffled. When she was stilled with only the heaving of her chest against his, he spoke.

"I need you to stay strong," he said. "Emmy is not just your child; she's *our* child. I would give my life if it would bring her back, but it won't. Right now, all we can do is pray: pray that she's safe and well cared for and pray that she'll soon be returned to us."

His words didn't fill the emptiness of her arms and did little to comfort her. So Rachel continued to sob until the ache became so great that she could no longer bear it, then she swallowed one of the blue pills Dr. Elliott gave her and slipped into the oblivion of sleep.

Later on, when the sky was dark and the sound of crickets came from the field beyond the house, George sat beside his mama on the front porch. Helen creaked back and forth in the wooden rocker, the crocheted square now abandoned in her lap.

"Is Rachel sleeping?" she asked.

George nodded. "She's taken a sedative that should last through the night."

"I heard how she spoke to you, acting as if it were your fault."

"She's hurting, Mama. She didn't mean anything by it."

Helen lowered her eyes, took up the crochet needle, and twisted a loop of yarn around her finger. "All the same, it's not proper."

George leaned his head against the back of the chair and gazed up at the night sky. In a voice threaded with the sound of heartache, he said, "Mama, you've got to understand, Rachel's grieving. Her heart's crushed. She's struggling just to make it from one day to the next . . ."

His voice trailed off, and he sat there staring up at the sky, sorrow covering him like a shroud.

Peering over the top of her glasses, Helen said, "I didn't mean anything by it, only that—"

George lowered his face and turned to her. "I know you didn't, but right now we're both hanging on by a thread. Rachel needs forgiving, not somebody finding fault with her behavior. If hollering at me helps her to get rid of that anger, I can take it."

Without looking up, Helen caught the loop of yarn with her crochet hook and pulled it through. "Well, it doesn't seem—"

"She's my wife, and whatever she needs, I've got to be there for her," George cut in. "The one thing I couldn't take would be losing Rachel as well as our baby girl."

Nothing more was said, but they remained there for a long while, her creaking back and forth in the rocker, him looking out at the road that ran past their house. When he heard Rachel moaning in her sleep, he kissed Helen's cheek and claimed it was time for him to be going to bed.

"Tomorrow morning I'll be reopening the store," he said.

~

For a long while Helen sat there thinking of how George asked her to be sympathetic to Rachel, which under these circumstances shouldn't be hard to do. Yet . . .

She thought back to the first time she met Rachel and remembered how it had been easy to find fault: a clinging vine, she'd thought, frail-looking and not well suited for George, even though he seemed to hang on her every word. Six months later they were married, and George moved out of the house. Gone, just three years after his daddy died.

With George no longer there, she was alone in a house way too large for just one person. During those long, lonely nights she'd gone from room to room wondering, *What now?* Then Rachel called and invited her to dinner.

Helen remembered it all too well, the feeling that she had gone from being George's family to being a guest in his house. Cast out. Pushed aside. Replaced by Rachel.

Really?

She ran the images of those early visits through her mind one by one, searching for the singular word or action that had caused her to feel as she did. Although she could remember each visit—the chicken a bit underdone, a soggy piecrust, and George endlessly raving about what a wonderful homemaker his bride was—in all those memories she couldn't find the thing that caused her to dislike Rachel.

Jealousy?

The thought came at her like an angry wasp, landing and leaving a sting behind.

Impossible.

The rocker stopped, and she sat thinking of how she'd made an enemy of someone who should have been a friend. Instead of gaining a daughter, she'd lost a son. Over the past five years she'd grown bitter when there was nothing to be bitter about. She'd sharpened her tongue to a razor-like point and pushed her friends aside, angry at the world because Henry died before his time and Rachel took her son.

But the thing was, Rachel hadn't taken her son anywhere. They'd been there all along: inviting her to dinner, bringing Emmy for a visit, sitting alongside her in church. Now George was asking for her patience.

She was a mother, just as Rachel was. She'd turned her back on them once, and as the moon rose higher in the sky and the stars reflected pinpoints of hope, she vowed she would never do it again.

~

The very next day, Helen called the mechanic and asked him to come and service the 1957 Ford that had been sitting in the garage ever since Henry's death.

"Sand the rust from the fender and get it in tip-top shape," she said, "because I expect to be doing a lot of driving."

~

Nine days after the kidnapping, George reopened the hardware store, but he did so with a heavy heart. Although he went about his routines as always, first dusting the counter then stacking new merchandise on the shelves, his thoughts were with Rachel. That morning as he pulled out of the driveway, he'd glanced back to see her standing in the doorway, her shoulders stooped and tears rolling down her cheeks.

Hidden in the shadows behind her was Helen, standing at the ready like a watchdog. Just as she'd once been fierce in her disdain for Rachel, she was now fierce in her protection. She arrived in the morning and stayed until the supper dishes were washed and put away.

Helen was seldom more than an arm's length away, but Rachel seemed not to notice. She went for hours on end without so much as a word to her mother-in-law, and when Helen brought a soothing cup of chamomile tea Rachel left it to grow cold. In the past, Rachel's indifference would have been something to rankle Helen, but now she'd had a change of heart.

A FORCED MOVE

When he discovered Vicki missing, Murphy stood looking around the cabin. The baby blanket was still spread across the floor, Vicki's jeans hung on the back of the chair, but she and the baby were gone.

To where?

He lifted the pile of newspapers, moved the box of diapers aside, and just about turned the place upside down searching for a note, some explanation of where she was. Nothing. No note, no indication of anything wrong, and yet she was gone.

He stepped outside and eyed the wooded lot behind the cabins. It was thick with loblolly pines, downed branches, and overgrown brush. Not a place you'd take a baby—unless you were hiding.

A spiny burr of fear dug into his back. Had somebody seen them? Maybe recognized the baby? Reported their whereabouts to the police? His heart began to pound furiously, and beads of perspiration rose up on his forehead. A car door slammed, and he felt his knees buckling beneath him.

No, no, no!

As he fell into the chair, he heard the lighthearted sound of laughter.

"Thanks again. Maybe I'll see you tomorrow."

Vicki's voice.

The door swung open, and in she walked, the baby leaned against her shoulder, fast asleep.

"Where the hell were you?" Murphy screamed.

"Stop yelling! Are you deliberately trying to wake Lara?"

"I don't give a damn who I wake! Where were you?"

She gave him an angry glare, then scooped the blanket off the floor. With him right at her heels she crossed the room, tucked the baby into bed, then turned back.

"I got hungry and went out for a bite to eat, all right?"

He stood there dumbfounded for a half second, then screamed, "You went out? Where? With who?"

"If you'll stop yelling and give me a chance to answer—"

Murphy couldn't stop. All the anxiety, the fear, the anticipation of what could happen erupted inside his stomach and burst forth in a barrage of angry words.

"I told you not to leave here. Especially not with that baby!"

As his voice grew bigger and more aggressive, hers became smaller and more fragile.

"You also told me you'd be back by six. I was afraid—"

"Afraid of what? I was stuck in traffic and couldn't call. You had food here; why'd you have to—"

"I thought maybe you weren't ever coming back."

"Shit, Vicki, why would you—"

"Because you've made it obvious enough you don't want this baby."

"You're right. I don't want this baby. She's not ours to keep. If you'll listen to reason and let me drop her off someplace where they can see she gets back to her real mother, we can—"

"I *am* her real mother," Vicki said and turned away, sobbing.

They argued long into the night before she finally said the guy who owned the Hideaway had taken her to Beef 'n' Brew out on Route 50. As soon as he heard that, Murphy knew they had to leave.

Things were different now. Somebody knew they had a baby with them. He thought about the reward money and knew in many cases it would be enough to turn brother against brother. They were nothing more than two strangers renting a cabin. It was no longer safe.

In the middle of the night, with the sky pitch-black and heavy storm clouds obscuring the moon, he packed into the trunk of the car the meager belongings they'd accumulated. Before the first light of morning, he woke Vicki and told her they were leaving. She wrapped the baby in the thrift-store blanket, carried her to the car, and climbed into the passenger seat.

"Where are we going?" she asked.

Murphy gave a half-hearted shrug. "We'll have to find a place to stay until this gets resolved."

"Until what gets resolved?"

He glanced sideways with his brows arched in a way that suggested he was incredulous at the question. "What we're going to do about the baby."

"Stop calling her *the baby*! Her name is *Lara*, and I'm keeping her."

Murphy pulled onto Route 40 heading east and said nothing. He was confident this routine of pretending the baby was actually Lara would come to an end once he told Vicki of his plan. All he needed now was a place where they'd be safe until she had enough time to let the idea settle and grow on her.

~

Before the sun cleared the horizon, Murphy was nearing Memphis. He left Route 40 and started north on Route 55 with the intention of bypassing most of Tennessee. Kentucky was home. He felt more comfortable with the lay of the land there, and his car had Kentucky license plates, so it would be easier to blend in.

As he drove, he again thought through his plan and became even more certain of it. Once he'd convinced Vicki of his intention to get married and adopt a child of their own, she'd realize how foolish it was to try to hang on to this baby. It could jeopardize everything. They could end up spending the rest of their lives in jail. Caged. Apart from each other.

For now, they had to fly under the radar. Lie low. Remain hidden. Knowing he couldn't count on Vicki to be discreet and remain inside, they'd do the next best thing: hide in plain sight. Paducah maybe. It was more a city than town, busy enough and big enough for them to get lost in the crowd.

After having slept through most of the drive, Vicki finally opened her eyes and looked out the window. Gazing at the long stretches of land interrupted only by an occasional billboard, she asked, "Where are we going?"

As he turned onto I-24, he answered, "Paducah."

She gave a wide grin. "Good. I love Paducah. All those nice restaurants along the lake and cute garden apartments. I could meet other moms, and Lara would have kids to play with—"

"Being in a city doesn't mean you can start socializing. We've got to keep a low profile. At least for a while."

A look of annoyance settled on her face. "How long a while?"

Murphy was tempted to share his plan with her right then. He opened his mouth but then stopped himself.

Not now. Wait until the time is right.

He hesitated, shifting his eyes toward the side window as if searching for a sign or specific landmark. "Hard to say. Weeks, maybe. Months. It depends."

"Depends on what?"

"Let's get settled first, then we'll talk about it."

She turned away, her lower lip pushed out and her brows pinched together. "I'm not hiding away in some dingy little cabin like last time."

"I'm not asking you to, but you've got to be careful. Start making a bunch of friends and before long they'll be asking you questions about that baby. Questions you can't answer."

"I can answer anything," she said defiantly. "Go ahead—try me. Ask me something about Lara."

Murphy shook his head and said nothing. He wasn't about to get suckered into this no-win game. In the pit of his stomach he started to get a feeling of uneasiness about Paducah. I-24 circled around the edge of the city, and he considered staying on it, maybe looking at an area on the southeastern side of town, an area less busy, with fewer restaurants and no tourists.

As he neared Jackson Street, Vicki squealed, "Turn here!"

In a knee-jerk reaction, he did as she asked but regretted it almost immediately. Jackson Street curved around and became 21st Street. As they passed by the quaint coffee shops and ice-cream parlors, Vicki gave a lingering sigh.

"This is my favorite part of town."

The familiarity with which she said it intrigued Murphy. "Have you been here before?"

She nodded. "Several years ago, with my sister, Angela."

"You've got a sister? You never mentioned—"

She turned away from the window and focused her attention on the baby. "Yeah, well. We kinda drifted apart." She didn't offer another word of explanation.

It struck Murphy as rather strange that two sisters would simply *drift apart*. "What caused it? Was there some kind of problem?"

"I guess." Vicki continued playing with the baby, but it was as if a dark shadow had fallen across her face.

"Wanna talk about it?"

"Un-uh. I'd just as soon forget my sister, the same as she forgot me."

Turning back to the window, Vicki watched the streets whiz by and remembered that trip to Paducah. The two of them had been happy together, the kind of happiness she'd thought she'd hold on to forever, but it didn't work out that way. Once they were back in Madisonville, everything changed. Angela moved in with a girlfriend who said there wasn't room enough for anyone else, and Vicki was left at home with a daddy who was a mean-ass drunk.

She'd said she wanted to forget, but the truth was she couldn't. The memory of being left behind was still there, just beneath her skin, ready to pop open like a ripe pimple. It wasn't as if Angela didn't know how it was living in that house. She knew. It was her reason for leaving home.

"Family is family," Murphy said. "Maybe if you give her a call—"

Before he could finish the thought, Vicki started shaking her head. "Forget it."

At first he'd heard only the snap of anger in her answer, but when he glanced across and saw the downturn of her mouth, he realized that beneath her anger was an even deeper layer of sorrow.

"Maybe your sister didn't forget you," he said. "Isn't it possible that she's tried to get in touch but doesn't know where you're living?"

Vicki gave a cynical snort. "Madisonville's two hours from Bardstown; if Angela looked hard enough she would've found me."

Murphy was hard-pressed to come up with an answer for that. Vicki obviously had a lot of secrets buried too deep, or perhaps just too painful, to share. He wondered how it was that two people so in love knew so little about each other.

Give it time.

After they were married they could spend the rest of their lives getting to know each other. Once Vicki came to understand how much she was loved, she'd feel secure, then she'd open up. She'd reach out to him, knowing he'd always be there.

"I'm looking forward to us being a real family," he said; then with the stub of his arm steadying the wheel, he stretched his right hand out and affectionately traced a finger along the curve of her cheek.

"Me too," she replied, looking down at the baby as she spoke.

MARSHALL COUNTY, KENTUCKY

They stopped for lunch in a little out-of-the-way place close to the lakefront, and Murphy steered Vicki to a secluded table in the back. He'd cautioned her to be discreet, but as they made their way through the maze of tables she craned her neck, looking first one way and then the other. He'd also told her to keep the cap on the baby's head so the blonde curls wouldn't be quite so obvious. She didn't. Instead she sat the child on the edge of the table and made a big to-do over playing a game of patty-cake, almost as if she were looking for attention.

Murph sat on the opposite side of the table, his eyes narrowed and mouth stretched into a thin, stiff line. After a few minutes of impatiently drumming his fingers on the table and hoping she'd get the message, he glared across at her and said, "Do you have to do that?"

She looked up, wide-eyed. "Do what?"

He gave a nod toward the baby, shook his head, and said nothing. He knew a thing like this could lead to an argument, the kind that would most certainly cause people to turn and look.

As soon as the food was on the table, he wolfed down his burger. Vicki picked at hers and tried feeding the baby a french fry.

Still eyeing Vicki with a look of annoyance, Murphy said, "Cut it out, will you? Leave the kid alone and eat so we can get out of here."

"Are you in some kind of hurry? I was thinking of having a piece of cake."

"Think again," Murphy replied, then signaled the waitress for the check.

Once back in the car, Murphy pulled onto the winding road that circled the city.

"Let's look for a place on the northwest side of town," Vicki said. "Maybe Madison Street. I love that area."

Murphy gave a half-hearted nod and continued on, but once they got to I-24, he turned southeast rather than northwest.

"Hey!" she exclaimed. "You're supposed to be going the other way."

"Yeah, well, I figure it'd be better if we move on. I've got a bad feeling about Paducah."

She turned and longingly looked back at the city as it disappeared behind them.

"Too bad," she said with a sigh, "'cause I had a good feeling about Paducah."

He stretched his arm across the seat and put a hand on her shoulder. "We'll come back again real soon. Maybe someday buy one of those houses over on Madison Street. You'd like that, wouldn't you?"

She sat there saying nothing, the baby held tight in her arms and a look of disappointment plastered to her face.

A short while after they crossed over into Marshall County, Murphy saw a billboard advertising Lakeside Apartments. Now Available, the board said. Furnished or Unfurnished. He took a left and followed the signs for Wynne Bluffs.

~

Lakeside Apartments turned out to be nowhere near a lake, nor was it an apartment building. The slate-gray duplexes were lined up along the walkway with two doors in the front of each building, both doors painted a blue that in the late-afternoon shadows looked the same as the house.

Apartments Available, the sign read. Inquire Within.

Vicki watched as Murph walked up to the door, rang the bell, then stepped inside. Even though her knees were stiff and her back ached from the long hours of sitting in the car, she was hoping he'd come back with the corners of his mouth turned down and say nothing was available. The possibility of turning around and heading back to Paducah settled in her head, and she smiled. It would be too late to start house hunting tonight, but they could stay in one of those nice roadside motels with fresh sheets and fluffy towels.

She tickled the baby's chin and sighed. Wistfully looking at the drab doorway she said, "Your mama wants to go back to Paducah. Does Lara want to go back too?"

Happy for the attention, the baby wriggled and waved her arms in the air.

Vicki laughed. "You're just like your mama. We're city girls, aren't we?"

Lost in her reverie, she was startled at the sound of her name.

"Hey, Vicki," Murphy called a second time.

When she glanced up, he was waving his arm and motioning for her and the baby to come in.

"We're in luck," he said cheerfully. "They've got a furnished one-bedroom available right now."

With the baby in her arms, Vicki climbed from the car and started up the walkway. Standing alongside Murph was a woman with carrot-colored hair that poked out in a dozen different directions. She was twice as big around as he and a head shorter.

"Lou Palmeyer," she said and stuck out a beefy hand.

Vicki shifted the baby to one side, returned the handshake, then followed along as they went three buildings down. Lou unlocked the door, pushed it open, then stepped back.

"You young folks go on up and have a look-see," she said. "Climbing steps is hard on these old knees."

Vicki went first, and Murphy followed behind. The upstairs apartment opened into a living room with yellow walls, a comfy-looking sofa, and a scattering of other furniture.

Mrs. Palmeyer's voice called up from below. "This one goes weekly or monthly; electricity's included."

Vicki wandered through the rooms; the bedroom was painted the same yellow as the living room. The kitchen was small with a tiny table, two chairs, and a dish drainer atop the counter. She opened a cabinet and found it filled with an assortment of dishes, bowls, and glasses. Back at the Hideaway she'd had to make do with one small saucepan, paper plates, and cardboard cups. This wasn't Paducah, but it was far nicer than she'd expected.

She turned to Murphy and nodded. As he started down the stairs to tell Mrs. Palmeyer, Vicki called after him, "Ask if there're any stores or restaurants around here."

Mrs. Palmeyer, who at that point insisted they call her Lou, had bad knees, but her hearing was just fine. She called back up, answering Vicki.

"Eight blocks down on the right there's a shopping plaza with some little stores, and farther on there's a real nice Kaufman-Straus department store."

~

Later that evening, after Murphy unloaded the car, he went to the market and strolled through the aisles, picking up jars of baby food, spaghetti, bright-red tomatoes, and lettuce crispy to the touch. He took his time, selecting this brand over that brand and waiting while the butcher weighed a pound of fresh chop meat.

For the first time in more than a week, he wasn't looking over his shoulder or checking to see if someone was dogging his footsteps. Wynne Bluffs was a town where he felt unthreatened. It was big enough and small enough, off the beaten path, and slow moving. Chances were these people had not even heard of the kidnapping, never mind being on the lookout for the missing baby.

That evening after the baby was fed and placed in the center of the big bed with pillows safeguarding her on both sides, Vicki and Murphy sat at the kitchen table eating dinner from china plates and sharing a bottle of wine. For hours he'd been thinking about when and how to best approach the conversation, and this moment somehow seemed right. He stretched his arm across the table and took her hand in his.

"It's nice us being here like a family, isn't it?"

She smiled, and although her face was thin and colorless, he saw a flicker of happiness.

"It's nice here, but I would have liked to stay in Paducah. Those houses over on Madison—"

"We can still do that," he said, interrupting her. "We could get married, buy a house, adopt a child of our own . . ."

A smile settled on Vicki's face as she thought back to the summers of her own childhood and the happy days before their mother died, days of playing hopscotch and running through backyards with Angela.

"Having a sister is wonderful," she said softly. "Lara would like that."

Murphy loosened his grip on her hand, and his smile faded.

"Stop it, Vicki! None of this will happen if you keep that baby. As long as we've got her, the only thing we can do is keep running and hiding. We'll always be on the go, moving from place to place, looking over our shoulders, and wondering when somebody will recognize the kid. It's inevitable that sooner or later somebody will, and then—"

Before he was halfway through what he'd planned to say, the anger in Vicki's eyes flared, and her expression turned hateful.

"This isn't about us being a family, is it? It's about you wanting to take Lara away!"

"Wait a minute—"

"No!" she shouted, then stood so quickly the chair toppled backward and landed with a thud. "You think I don't notice how you keep calling her *the baby*, like she's a thing you can take or leave the way you would a worn-out pair of shoes? Well, Lara's not a *thing*; she's my child!

She's the only lucky break I've gotten in this crap-ass world, and nobody is taking her from me! Not you, not anybody!"

Before he had time to say a word, she turned away and stormed into the bedroom, sobbing.

That night she slept with the baby in her arms and her back turned to Murphy. Twice he reached across and touched her shoulder, but both times she shrugged him off, saying, "Don't touch me."

Long after Murphy was sound asleep and she could hear the steady wheeze of his snores, she lay there thinking of what to do if he tried to take Lara from her. In the back of her mind a plan began to take shape, but it was too early to do anything. Murphy loved her. She was certain of that. Okay, he could be unreasonable at times, but he'd never leave her, and he'd certainly never tell the police.

Or would he?

THE SEARCH CONTINUES

In the first week after the *incident*, as Sheriff Wilson had begun to call it, he stopped by the house every day, sometimes as often as three or four times. As the days wore on, his visits became fewer and fewer.

"It's because he can't face us," Rachel said accusingly.

"That's not true," George argued. "It's just that there's nothing new to report."

"It's been more than two weeks! Surely somebody has seen something! For God's sake, Emmy is a six-month-old baby, not a stolen piece of jewelry a thief can hide away in a dresser drawer!"

"Don't you think Sheriff Wilson is aware of that? He's driven clear across Primrose County to track down reports of some stranger with a baby. The man is doing everything he can possibly—"

"It's not enough!" she shrieked. "What if some madman has Emmy hidden away in his basement? What if she's wet or hungry? What if—"

"Stop it, Rachel!" George pulled her into his arms and held her tightly against his chest. He waited until her breathing slowed and she stopped flailing to get free. "You can't be thinking things like that. It won't help Emmy, and it certainly won't help you. You need to try to hold it together so when we do get Emmy back, you can be a mother to her."

"What if that time never comes, George? What then? You can't possibly understand how it is for me. You leave here every day. You get up in the morning and go open the store; you talk to customers, order supplies, do all the things you did before. But it's not that way for me."

"I understand. You may not realize it, but—"

"No, George, you think you understand, but you don't." Rachel's words had bits of bitterness stuck to them. "While you're off tending to business, I get down on my knees and pray. First I pray that Emmy will be returned to us, then I try to strike a bargain with God. I say if you won't give her back to us, then let the person who took Emmy be someone who loves her, who will be good to her and watch over her as I would."

Rachel lifted her face and looked up, her eyes reddened and tears rolling down her cheeks. "How terribly sorrowful is it that I should pray for another woman to love my child?"

George put his hand on the back of her head and held her close, so she wouldn't see the way his eyes had begun to water. He tried but couldn't quite hide the tremor in his voice. "It is sorrowful," he said, "but it's also the most loving thing I've ever heard."

~

Two days later, Sheriff Wilson stopped by early in the morning to say he'd be driving over to Billingsley, Alabama. "Caller claims to have heard a baby crying in some old man's trailer. The caller wouldn't identify herself and was kind of sketchy on details, but we'll see."

George stood with his arm wrapped around Rachel's shoulders and felt the tension as her back stiffened. "You think the baby could be Emmy?"

The sheriff rubbed his hand across the scruff on his chin and shrugged. "Maybe yes, maybe no. But it's worth looking into."

That day George didn't open the store until almost noon, and he closed an hour early.

Rachel had wanted him to stay with her, and he did as she asked for a while, but after two hours of pacing back and forth while she stood at the window watching for a man who wouldn't return until late evening, he gave up.

"It's a five-hour drive each way," he said. "The sheriff's not gonna make it back before six or seven."

"I realize that."

"Mama called and said she'd be here shortly, so I was thinking maybe I'd check things out at the store. Just to make sure everything's okay."

For a moment Rachel thought about telling him not to go, that there was no need. The store was closed and the door locked, so what was there to check on? She turned with those words on the tip of her tongue, then said, "Okay, go ahead."

The sad truth was that he wasn't like her. He was willing to do anything to bring Emily home, but the one thing he couldn't do was endure the endless agony of waiting.

That evening Mama Dixon fixed supper, but no one ate. Not even Helen herself. She picked at the pot roast half-heartedly, then left it to grow cold.

It was almost nine when Sheriff Wilson returned. He stood with his hat in his hand, making apologies for the time, then gave them the disappointing news.

As he spoke of how the baby turned out to be the man's great-grandson, Rachel could feel her heart sink.

That night George held her in his arms. "I'm as disappointed as you are," he said, "but let's not forget the sheriff has some other leads to follow up on, so there's still hope."

She nodded and said nothing.

It seemed that hope came and went like the ripples in a pond—there one moment, gone the next. It was never something Rachel could hold in her hand or carry with her from one day to another.

~

In time, the flow of neighbors stopping by to deliver a casserole or cake also slowed. George continued to open the store every day, and the townspeople resumed their lives. People at the lunch counter no longer spoke of the kidnapping. They'd grown weary of the tragedy and went back to more pleasant thoughts, such as the Labor Day parade and the way they'd laughed at Harvey Korman's antics on *The Carol Burnett Show*. On rare occasions there was a mention of how it was now necessary to lock your doors at night, but after a while even that disappeared.

In the third week of September, the mailman dropped an envelope in the Dixons' mailbox. It was midmorning; George was at work and Rachel was napping. Helen, who by then spent every day tending to her daughter-in-law, carried the mail in and laid it on the hall table.

The envelope was a light pink so pale it could easily be mistaken for white. The small, tight handwriting looked like that of a child attempting to learn cursive, the *Ls* crowded together and the small *H* no taller than the *A*.

The envelope remained on the table most of the day. Late in the afternoon Rachel spied it peeking from beneath the phone bill. She'd grown used to well-meaning friends sending sympathy cards with long-winded verses about love and loss, but this wasn't a card. It was a letter postmarked Culvert Creek, Kentucky.

She tore the envelope open, and as she stood there reading, her hands began to tremble.

"Mama Dixon," she called, "come quick!"

The letter was a single page that began with a scattering of thoughts referencing a golden-haired child with eyes as blue as the sky, guardian angels, and time without measurement. It went on to say a guardian angel watched over each child, and only that angel could take the child from her mother. In the last sentence, the handwriting became shakier and more difficult to read. Two of the words were blurred by what appeared to be tearstains. Rachel narrowed her eyes and followed the odd slant of the words.

When a child is taken, a mother must accept that it is for the best.

The letter was unsigned.

With her heart caught in her throat and her face growing ashen, Rachel heaved a ragged breath.

"Call George!"

Helen grabbed the phone, and her fingers flew around the dial. It had been two, maybe three years since she'd called the store, but the number was forever printed on her heart. In earlier years she'd called it a thousand or more times to ask what Henry would like for dinner or if he'd be working late. When George answered, his voice sounded so like Henry it startled her.

"Something's happened," she said and told of the letter. "This person spoke of *her* mother, so they're referring to a girl. It could be—"

Before she finished, George said, "I'm on my way!"

Moments later Helen called the sheriff's office and told Wilson the same thing she'd told George.

"I'll be right over," he answered.

The two men arrived at the house minutes apart.

~

There was no supper that evening, and Helen did not drive home as she had the other nights. Sheriff Wilson questioned both women about how the letter had arrived. Was it dropped at the door? Delivered by hand? Had they seen anyone near the mailbox? Did they know of any person who might have surreptitiously slid the letter between the phone bill and the Sears circular? Question after question came at them, but Helen and Rachel could do little more than answer with baffled shrugs.

For the first time in all the days Helen had spent at the house, Rachel sat beside her and held tight to her hand.

"I think this will lead us to Emmy," Rachel whispered.

"God willing."

Helen wanted to believe it, but she couldn't shake loose the memory of the night Henry died. It was the sheriff who'd called and said, *A mild heart attack. He'll be fine once he gets to the hospital.* Henry wasn't fine; he was gone before the hour was out.

Helen clung tightly to the slender hand she held in her own.

Emmy is just a baby. Please, God, watch over her and keep her safe.

~

That evening two of the sheriff's part-time deputies were called to Yellowwood Road. They dusted the Dixon mailbox for fingerprints, searched the yard for marks of a prowler, then went door to door asking about the mail carrier, unfamiliar faces, and cars pulled to the side of the road. After the sky darkened they continued, following flashlight beams as they moved about.

Sheriff Wilson remained inside with the family, asking the same questions over and over again, adding in a new thought or structuring the sentences differently in hopes of pulling loose some small fact that had been overlooked: an unusual sound, a car door slamming, a stranger in need of directions. The clock struck midnight, and when George insisted Rachel get some rest, the sheriff left.

~

In the morning Wilson was standing at the door before the Hesterville post office opened. For more than two hours he questioned the postmaster and Zack Cramer, the mail carrier assigned to Yellowwood Road. Like the Dixons, they had no answers. It was a plain, ordinary envelope, one of the hundreds that passed through their hands each day.

It was near noon when he finally left the post office. He stopped at the luncheonette, bought a can of Coca-Cola and a ham sandwich, then returned to his desk. As he ate, he pulled a road atlas from the drawer and reluctantly mapped out the nine-hour drive from Hesterville to Culvert Creek, Kentucky.

WYNNE BLUFFS

For two days after the big blowup he'd had with Vicki, Murphy didn't mention taking the baby back. They went from day to day avoiding each other's touch and barely speaking. In the evening they sat on opposite sides of the room, him stiff-necked in the club chair, her on the sofa with her legs folded beneath her and the baby in her lap.

On the third night, he again broached the subject, this time with a gentler voice and considerably more compassion.

"I understand you want a child of your own," he said. "I want the same thing. But it needs to be *our* child, an adopted child, maybe, but not one we've stolen from somebody else."

Vicki hiked the right side of her mouth and gave him a look of skepticism. "Nobody's gonna let people like us adopt a kid. I've got a lousy high school education, and you don't even have a job. Those adoption agencies aren't stupid; they check you out before they give you a kid. They come to your house, make sure the kid's got their own room and a place to play. All we've got is a rent-by-the-week one-bedroom apartment."

"I can change all that. Mrs. Palmeyer rents most of these places by the year. We'll sign a lease, settle in, and become part of the community."

"Yeah, and just how are you gonna explain it when Lara up and disappears?"

For three days he'd avoided telling her because he suspected she'd take it in a way different from what was intended, but now with the question flung at him, there was no way of skirting the issue.

"I already told Mrs. Palmeyer the baby isn't ours. I said we were taking care of your sister's kid for a week or two."

Speaking through clenched teeth, Vicki hissed, "You said she wasn't ours?"

Murphy scrubbed his hand across his forehead and grimaced. "She's not, and you know it, Vicki! You broke into that house and took this kid out of her crib. She's not yours. She never was."

"Really? Then why do you think that door was unlocked? Why do you think the baby bottles were left out for me to see? It's because I was supposed to take her, that's why! She's meant to be my baby!"

The compassion in his voice disappeared, and his words came at her as angry and stinging as the crack of a whip. "No, she's not! She belongs to the family who lives in that house; she's got a mother and father who are frantic because their daughter's been kidnapped."

"Stop it!" Vicki turned away and cupped her hands over her ears. "I'm not listening to another word."

He stood, crossed the room, pulled her hands from her ears, and held her shoulders in a firm grip.

"Whether you want to or not, you've got to listen. This is wrong in so many ways. Even if you don't care what that family is going through, at least care about what happens to us! If we get caught with this baby—"

She wrenched herself free of his grasp, then turned back. "God wants me to have Lara. He saw how I was hurting and led me to that house—"

"No, he didn't!" Murphy screamed. "It's what you want to believe, but it's not true! Thou shalt not steal! God would not tell you to steal that woman's child!"

For a moment she stood there looking like a chastised child, her lower lip quivering and her eyes filling with tears. When she did speak, her voice was thin and fragile. "In the Bible it says an eye for an eye, a tooth for a tooth; God took my baby, then gave me Lara to make up for it."

She brushed the tears from her cheeks, then dropped onto the sofa, her shoulders hunched and her arms wrapped around herself. Biting down on her lip, she sat there saying nothing.

He waited for a long while, hoping she would acknowledge the truth of his words. When he finally realized she was not going to, he sat beside her and took hold of her hand.

"Please understand, Vicki, I'm not trying to deprive you of anything. I love you and want you to be happy. I'm willing to work my fingers to the bone to give you whatever you want, but I can't stand by and let you do this. Keeping this baby will bring us more trouble than we ever dreamed possible."

Vicki's eyes narrowed and grew dark, no longer the blue of a clear sky but now the color of an angry ocean. "And if I refuse to let you take Lara away, then what?"

It was a long time before he answered, and when he did his words were heavy and almost tearful. "I'm hoping it doesn't come to that."

Vicki studied him, his neck bent, his face tilted toward the floor, his eyes now avoiding hers. She could tell his fear of what might happen was bigger than his love for her.

"Okay," she said. "You win."

He lifted his eyes and turned to her. "What do you mean, I win?"

She tipped her head in a solemn nod. "I'll let you take her if you prove to me that you're serious about us building a life of our own."

"How am I supposed to do that?"

"Start by getting a real job, not pushing bags of MJ or hanging out at bars. I'm talking about a job where you report in every day and get a paycheck at the end of the week. You do that, then I'll let you take Lara and leave her in a church, but until you actually do it I get to keep her."

He gave a troubled sigh. "I have no problem with getting a job, but I'm worried about keeping the baby here with us. It's dangerous. If somebody sees—"

"Don't worry. I'll stay inside, keep her hidden."

Murphy smiled and pulled her into his arms. "Thank you," he whispered. "I know how difficult this is, but it's something we have to do."

She gave an almost imperceptible nod, and he felt the moisture of her tears against his neck. A small crack opened up in his heart as he lifted her face to his.

"I'll make it up to you," he promised. "I swear I will. Tomorrow I'll drive back to Bardstown, get the rest of our stuff, pick up my VA check, and tell Mrs. Bachinski we're giving up the apartment. Monday I'll start looking for a job."

~

On Friday morning Murphy was up early and ready to leave the house before eight a.m. He kissed Vicki's cheek, said goodbye, and started for the stairs.

"What time will you be back?"

"Depends on traffic, but I won't be late. Probably before dinnertime," he said and disappeared down the stairs.

Vicki stood at the window and watched as he climbed into the car, then pulled away from the curb. Once the car turned onto the main thoroughfare, she hurried into the bedroom, pulled on a pair of jeans, and dressed the baby.

Speaking in a powdery-soft voice as she folded the diaper into place, she murmured, "We've got a big day today."

At 9:45 she walked over to Mrs. Palmeyer's building with the baby in her arms and rang the doorbell. When the door swung open, she gave an almost apologetic smile.

"I hate to bother you, but I was wondering if maybe you had a stroller I could borrow. Lara and I could both use a bit of fresh air, and I forgot to bring my sister's stroller."

Lou Palmeyer eyed her suspiciously. "Seems your sister would have remembered to give it to you."

Without a moment of hesitation, Vicki said, "She's expecting her second and is sick as a dog. Doctor has her on bed rest; that's why we volunteered to take Lara for a while. It's totally my fault for not remembering the stroller."

"Oh. Well then, I've got one in the basement, but it probably needs a good washing." She chuckled. "It's been down there for twenty-plus years. Since my youngest was a toddler."

"If you don't mind my using it, I'll clean it up spick-and-span."

"I can't say for sure what shape it's in." Lou Palmeyer pulled the door back and waved Vicki inside. "Come on in—we'll bring it up and have a look-see."

Trailing behind the short, stocky woman, Vicki followed her back through the kitchen toward the cellar door. Before they started down the stairs, Lou Palmeyer snapped a light switch, but nothing happened.

"Well, shoot, Elroy still hasn't replaced that blasted bulb." She turned to Vicki. "With my knees bad as they are and no overhead light, maybe we ought to wait till Elroy puts a new bulb in."

A flutter of panic passed through Vicki. "I've got real sharp vision. If you hold Lara, I'll go down and poke around till I find it."

A look of apprehension settled on Lou Palmeyer's face. "You sure?"

Vicki nodded. "Absolutely. Just tell me about where to look, and I can feel my way around."

"At the foot of the stairs, go left. There are a few itty-bitty windows over on that side, so you'll be able to see some. The stroller's behind a tricycle and a box of toys."

Vicki passed Lara to Mrs. Palmeyer and started feeling her way down the stairs. Before she got to the foot of the staircase, a spiderweb caught the side of her face. She squealed and swatted at it.

"You all right down there?"

Pulling pieces of the sticky substance from her hair, Vicki answered, "I'm fine. It was just a cobweb."

"That's Elroy's fault. He was supposed to clean the basement two years ago, and he still ain't done it."

"No problem," Vicki called back as she made her way across the room.

Butting up against the ceiling were three small windows just big enough to allow a sliver of light into the room. Vicki spotted the stroller right where Lou Palmeyer said it would be. She moved the tricycle, then slid the box of toys aside and reached for the stroller. The wheels refused to budge, so instead of rolling it across the floor, she had to drag it.

Lifting her foot and feeling for each step, Vicki climbed the stairs backward, bumping the stroller up one rise at a time. It was heavier than she'd expected and covered in years of dust. When she finally pulled it onto the top landing and out into the kitchen, Lou Palmeyer applauded.

"You've got spunk," she said with a laugh, "that's for sure."

Once Vicki unlocked the wheels and cleaned the stroller with Lysol, it turned out to be in fairly decent shape: a bit old-fashioned, perhaps, but serviceable. By ten thirty she had Lara in the seat and was headed toward the shopping area Lou Palmeyer had mentioned. Hopefully she'd find a pay phone.

FINDING ANGELA

A Mexican restaurant sat at the far end of the shopping plaza and to the side of it, a pay phone. No booth, just a small plastic shield on each side of the phone. Vicki pushed the stroller into the restaurant, handed the cashier a five-dollar bill, and asked for eight quarters and the rest in dimes.

With her pocket full of coins, she circled around to the side of the building, pulled the stroller close, and spread the scattering of dimes and quarters on the small counter just below the phone. She picked up a single dime, dropped it into the slot, and dialed 110.

"Long-distance operator," a crisp voice answered. "How may I help you?"

"I'd like to place a call to Madisonville, Kentucky." She quickly rattled off the number she had for Angela, hoping it hadn't changed.

There was a clink as her dime dropped into the coin return. The operator then told her to deposit $1.40 for the first three minutes.

She slid the coins into the slot one by one, and when the last dime dropped she heard the *click, click, click* of a dial spinning around. Moments later the phone began to ring.

A sleepy voice answered. "Why are you calling this early?"

"Um, sorry to disturb you. I'm looking for Angela."

"She's not here."

"Do you know when she'll be back?"

"She's not coming back. She got married and moved out."

Vicki felt her heart speed up. "Got married? When?"

"Who is this?" the girl asked in a prickly voice. "What business have you got with Angela?"

"I'm her sister, Vicki. I was hoping—"

"Where the hell have you been? Angela tried to get in touch with you, but your dad said—"

"Yeah, well, he and I didn't part on real good terms. You got a number for Angela?"

"Not anymore. Kenny got transferred, and they moved."

"Kenny who?"

"McAlister. Angela's husband. Before the wedding she was trying to get in touch with you so you could—"

"Where'd they move to?"

"Some small town west of Paducah. Fairfield, Fairwinds, something like that. I've got it here somewhere; you wanna hold on?"

"Yeah, okay. Try to make it fast; I'm calling from a pay phone."

Near Paducah, huh?

As she waited Vicki thought back to the trip they'd taken together. They'd been close, the way sisters were supposed to be. It was possible Angela had the same good memories. Vicki was remembering how they'd gone into the dress shop and tried on a dozen different outfits, knowing they didn't have enough money for even one, when the operator clicked on. "Please deposit forty cents if you wish to continue . . ."

She slid another four dimes into the slot and waited.

Finally, the girl came back. "Okay, here it is. Fairlawn. 288 Hillcrest Street. But there's no phone number."

"Crap," Vicki said with a groan. "What'd you say Kenny's last name was?"

"McAlister. M-C-A-L-I-S—"

"Okay, I got it," Vicki said and hung up. She scribbled the address on the top corner of a page in the phone book hanging alongside the phone, then tore off that portion of the page and stuck it in her pocket.

Dropping another dime into the slot, she redialed the long-distance operator. "I need to find a phone number in Fairlawn, Kentucky."

Her dime jingled back into the coin return, and she waited. After being shuttled over to the information operator, spelling out McAlister the way Angela's roommate had and hanging on for what seemed a longer time than was necessary, she had the number. Pulling the scrap of paper from her pocket, she wrote the phone number alongside the address, then dialed long-distance and placed the call.

The phone rang eight times before a man answered.

"Is this Kenny?"

"Yeah, who's this?"

"Vicki, Angela's sist—"

Before she could move on to what she had to say, he jumped in, telling how Angela was so disappointed about not having her as the maid of honor.

"She called everywhere trying to find you."

"Yeah, I got a few of her earlier messages and intended to call back, but things got kind of crazy. When I moved to Bardstown, I lost touch with almost everyone." Without mentioning how for months on end she'd remained bitter about Angela leaving her behind and tossed all those messages into the trash, she segued into asking if her sister was there.

"No, she works the early shift at the diner. She'll be home at three, maybe three thirty. How about I have her call you back?"

It was five after eleven. Three o'clock meant four hours of waiting. "Can I call her at work?"

"Afraid not. Give me your number, and I'll have her call as soon as she gets in."

Vicki hesitated a moment, then gave him the number of the pay phone. "Tell her I'm sorry about not calling sooner, but this is really important, so she should call the minute she gets in, okay?"

As she hung up the phone, Vicki felt a pounding in her temples. What if Angela was now angry with her? What if she decided to do as Vicki had done and not bother calling back? What if she had to work late, or Kenny forgot to give her the message? There were dozens of what-ifs, and each one of them was like a tiny mallet hammering the thought into her brain. This was risky, and she knew it. If Murph came home early and discovered her missing, there was no way of knowing what he'd do. Call the police? Tell them she had the baby?

She wheeled the stroller over to the bench in front of the restaurant and sat, hopeful that Angela would call earlier. From this distance she could easily enough hear the phone ring, and she could see the clock outside the bank a few doors down.

An hour passed so slowly that Vicki began to wonder if the clock was working properly. The sun rose higher in the sky, beads of perspiration settled on her forehead, and Lara became fussy. Taking the baby from the stroller, Vicki tried playing some of the games that usually entertained Lara. This time she would have none of it. After several minutes of cranky whining, she broke into a loud squall.

By then it was past lunchtime, and she figured the baby to be hungry. Lifting Lara to her shoulder, she cooed, "Mama didn't bring a bottle, sweetie; can you wait just a little while longer?"

The baby continued howling.

Finally, Vicki placed her back in the stroller and started for the food store at the end of the plaza. Her stride was long and her steps quick. She was in and out of the store within minutes, and without slowing she returned to her spot on the bench.

Opening the jar of bananas, she fed the baby as she had that first time, scooping tiny bits of food onto the tip of her finger and allowing Lara to suck them off. Once her little tummy was full, her eyelids grew heavy. Vicki cradled the baby in her arms and swayed back and forth in a rocking motion until Lara drifted off to sleep.

While she slept, there was little for Vicki to do except think. And worry. The minutes passed by in an impossibly slow manner until at last it was two o'clock. She still had another hour to wait. Hopefully not longer.

As she sat waiting, she prayed Angela would call. She also prayed Murphy would not make it back from Bardstown sooner than he'd thought.

~

At 2:45 Vicki slid the sleeping baby back into the stroller and walked across to stand beside the phone. From that vantage point she could no longer catch sight of the clock, and the minutes dragged by slower than ever. Twice she lifted the receiver and listened for a dial tone just to make certain the phone was working.

When the ring finally sounded, it was louder than she'd expected. She grabbed the receiver. "Angela?"

"My God, Vicki, where have you been? I just about went crazy trying to find—"

"Please don't be angry with me," Vicki said anxiously. "I meant to call, honestly I did, but with one thing and another . . ." She hesitated a moment, struggling with whether to tell the truth or not, then decided on a modified version of it. "When you wouldn't let me come and live with you, I moved in with this guy—"

"Wait a minute," Angela cut in. "I never said you couldn't live with me. I said it had to wait until I got a place where I had my own room. I stayed with Patty Summers for most of that first year; she had a studio apartment, and I slept on her sofa."

"Still, you never came back for me."

"I did so! I can't even count the number of times I called and left a message with Dad. I didn't come to the house because I just couldn't face him, not after what he did."

Although Vicki had intended to bypass the bitterness, there were splintery thorns on the edges of her answer. "Well then, you shouldn't be all that surprised to hear he tried it with me also."

Angela gasped. "That bastard! What did you do?"

"What could I do? I left home."

"I'm so sorry, honey—if you would have returned my calls or reached out to me, we could have—"

Vicki was nervous about the time and anxious to move on. "What's done is done," she said. "I'm hoping we can make up for it now."

"Of course we can," Angela replied warmly. "Would you like to come for a visit?"

"It might be more than a visit; I'm in kind of a fix and need a place to stay."

"What happened?"

"I've got a baby girl now, and this—"

"A baby girl!" Angela shrieked. "How wonderful!"

Without giving her a chance to go any further, Vicki cut in. "The thing is, this guy I've been living with has a terrible temper. Sometimes he flies into a rage, and I'm afraid he'll hurt—"

Angela gasped. "Oh no! Please tell me he hasn't hit you!"

The thought of Murphy with his laughing eyes and sweet smile flickered in front of her eyes, but she willed it away and continued. "There were a few times, but it's not me I'm afraid for—"

"You can't stay with him," Angela said, kicking into big-sister mode. "You know how it was with Daddy!"

"Yeah, I do. But other than you, there's nobody—"

"You don't need anybody else. You're more than welcome to come stay with us. Kenny and I have a two-bedroom with an upstairs where we can finish off a third if we want."

The offer was precisely what Vicki was counting on. "You sure Kenny won't mind?"

Angela assured her it would be fine. "Kenny's a great guy. He loves kids."

They spoke for another ten minutes, and Vicki explained her plan. As she left the shopping center to return to the apartment, the thought of what she was about to do pressed hard against Vicki's chest. She and Murphy had been good together. This wasn't what she wanted, but he'd given her no choice.

A CHILD REMEMBERED

Margaret Wilson had been married to the sheriff for more than thirty years and knew his thoughts as well as she knew her own. When he came home with his brows knitted together and the veins in his neck bulging, she knew something was wrong.

"Bad day?"

He nodded. Without saying a word he headed for the kitchen, where he plunked three ice cubes in a glass, poured an inch of bourbon over them, then dropped down into the straight-backed chair at the table. Since it was obvious he wasn't in the mood for dinner, Margaret lowered the flame on the green beans and sat across from him.

"Want to talk about it?"

He opened his mouth halfway as if to say something, then shook his head, lifted the glass, and took a swig.

"It doesn't help," he grumbled.

"What doesn't help?"

He didn't answer her question; instead he voiced his own thoughts. "How can an envelope just appear in a mailbox with nobody knowing anything about how it got there? Zack Cramer's been working the Yellowwood route for a good five years. How can he not know what he did or didn't put in the Dixons' mailbox?"

News traveled fast in a small town like Hesterville, and the minute he mentioned the Dixon name, Margaret knew what was wrong.

"So what now?" she asked. "Can you find the person who wrote the letter?"

"It's postmarked Culvert Creek, Kentucky. That's not around the corner."

Margaret knew there was more coming, so she waited.

"It's a nine- or ten-hour drive, and the blasted town is so small they don't have a law enforcement department. I had to call the Washington County sheriff to get any information."

"And was he helpful?"

"Hell no. Said he couldn't even look into it without having the envelope." Wilson downed the last of the bourbon, then sat there with his finger twirling the ice cubes around the empty glass. "Said my best bet was to ask around town, see if the locals knew anything."

"So is that what you'll do?"

He gave a disgruntled snort and shrugged. "It's a two-day trip. Ten hours there, another ten coming back, and there's no guarantee I'll find anything."

Margaret raised an eyebrow and eyed him with a look that was more doubt than agreement.

"Maybe not, but if you don't go, you'll never know." She stood, turned back to the stove, and started the beans bubbling again. "Dinner's in fifteen minutes."

~

That evening Wilson went to bed at ten o'clock, the same as always, but sleep was impossible to come by. He tossed and turned for hours, then plumped his pillow three different times. When nothing seemed to work he gave a sigh so thunderous it woke Margaret.

She snapped on the light and sat up. "What's wrong?"

"I can't sleep. This Dixon case has got me thinking about Becky."

"Becky?" She gasped. "Good grief, Carl, our Becky wasn't kidnapped! She died of diphtheria, and that was some twenty-seven years ago."

"I know, but losing a child is a thing you never forget."

"Well, of course you don't forget, but you move on. I spent more hours than I can count crying over Becky, but in time I made my peace with God. You've got to do the same, Carl."

"I have, Margaret. Still, I can't help thinking we at least had a chance to say goodbye to our baby; the Dixons haven't even gotten that."

"Emily is not dead! She's missing! And I sincerely doubt Rachel Dixon has given up hope that her daughter will be returned!"

"I suppose you're right . . ."

"I don't suppose; I know!" Margaret said, then she snapped off the light.

Wilson spent the remainder of the night thinking about whether or not he should go to Culvert Creek. He dreaded the long drive and tried to convince himself that this too would turn up nothing of value. The envelope was not remarkable in any way: no return address, an ordinary six-cent stamp, and no identifiable fingerprints. The notepaper was without a watermark, so it could have come from any stationery shop. As he lay there staring up at the ceiling, he could think of a dozen reasons for not going to Culvert Creek but only one reason for going.

Rachel Dixon.

He pictured the worn look on her face, the hollowed-out sadness of her eyes, the way her lip trembled as she pleaded for him to find her baby, and he knew that all the arguments for not going dwarfed in comparison. As long as there was a splinter of hope, he had to go.

~

In the morning when he woke, Margaret was gone from the bed, and the smell of bacon was coming from the kitchen. She heard the sound of him stirring and called out, "Hurry up, sleepyhead, breakfast is almost ready."

When he sat at the table, she sat across from him. "I've filled a thermos with coffee and made some sandwiches for the road."

He looked up, his eyes crinkling at the corners. "How'd you know—?"

She lifted the mug of coffee, took a sip, and smiled. "I've never known you to not do the right thing."

~

Early that afternoon Margaret drove out to the Dixon house with a freshly baked cake. Before she could rap on the door, it swung open.

Mama Dixon held her finger to her lips and made a soft shushing sound. "Rachel's napping," she said.

Margaret held out the cake and lowered her voice to little more than a whisper. "This is one of Carl's favorites, and I thought maybe . . ." Her words fell away when she saw Rachel standing behind Helen.

Rachel was thin as a shadow and her expression almost as dark. She was wearing a faded T-shirt and jeans that were at least two sizes too big. "Did he find Emily?" she asked. Although there was the tiniest bit of hope clinging to the question, her voice had the hollow sound of an echo.

"It's too soon to know," Margaret replied. "Carl's on his way to Culvert Creek, but he won't get there until later this afternoon." As she stood looking at Rachel's worn face, she recognized a long-ago version of herself.

Without waiting for an invitation, Margaret strode in and handed Helen the cake. "If you wouldn't mind, coffee would go nicely with that." She hooked her arm through Rachel's and steered her toward the sofa.

"It's n-nice of you to come," Rachel stammered, "but I'm afraid I'm not very good company these days."

"You're not expected to be," Margaret replied. "You're going through a hellish time, and you're entitled to feel as miserable as you want."

A look of surprise took hold of Rachel's face. "Why would you say—"

"Because I've been where you are, and I know how it feels." Margaret told of how they'd lost Becky and how she had suffered through a heartache much the same as Rachel. "Of course in your case, it's different," she said. "You've still got hope."

"I try to remember that and hold on to the belief that they'll find her . . ." Rachel hesitated for a long moment, the words stuck in her throat. She sucked in a laborious breath, then continued. "But it's been a month, and with every day she's gone, the probability of finding her lessens."

Margaret reached out and took Rachel's hand in hers. "That may be true in some cases but not all. Carl says the slimmest lead can sometimes turn out to be the break you need."

"Really?"

"Yes. And I can say for a fact, when he's working on a case like this, he's like a hungry dog with a steak. He just doesn't let it go."

The stiffness in Rachel's face eased ever so slightly. "So you think he'll find Emmy?"

"I think if it's humanly possible to find her, Carl will be the one to do it."

For a short while that afternoon, Rachel's spirits were lifted. Listening to Margaret tell of how the sheriff had overcome one obstacle after another, she could close her eyes and imagine him standing at the door with Emmy in his arms. She could again imagine the feel of Emmy's head against her shoulder and hear the sound of her musical laugh.

When Helen served coffee, the three women sat at the kitchen table. Rachel picked at the edges of the cake and ate a few pecans, which was more than she'd done on previous occasions.

~

That evening when George returned home from the store, Rachel told him about Margaret Wilson's visit. "The sheriff's gone to Culvert Creek to find the person who wrote that letter." She hesitated a moment, then, allowing some of Margaret's optimism to rub off on her, added, "I think this might be the lucky break we've been waiting for."

George eyed her with a raised eyebrow. "Is that what Margaret said?"

"Not exactly, but she was very positive about the sheriff finding Emmy. I wouldn't be one bit surprised if we get a call from him tonight."

George felt a prickly pinch of apprehension take hold at the back of his neck. He'd seen Rachel grow worse as each lead turned into yet another disappointment, and he was wary of it happening again. "I think it's too early to get your hopes up," he warned.

Her expression stiffened. "Do you have to be so negative?"

"I'm not being negative. I'm being honest. I'm hoping for Emily's return as much as you are, Rachel, but we've watched so many of these leads turn into disappointments. Every time a promising lead turns into a dead end, I see how it carves out another little piece of your heart. It's bad enough that we've lost Emmy; I don't want to lose you also."

Rachel's eyes became watery, and her words were garbled by the throaty sound of a stifled sob. "We haven't lost Emmy," she said. "Sheriff Wilson will find her."

"God knows I hope so." George moved toward her and held his arms open, but she turned and walked away.

~

When they sat down to dinner with Mama Dixon, Rachel was wearing her resolve like a suit of armor, her face a rigid mask of determination and her eyes deliberately avoiding George's. He ate, but she didn't even make a pretense of it. "That cake filled me up," she said and pushed the plate away.

Sensing the tension in the air, Mama Dixon left earlier than usual that night, and once she was gone Rachel stationed herself in the club chair closest to the telephone.

George sat across from her on the sofa. He read the newspaper, watched television for a while, then stood and crossed over to where Rachel was sitting.

"It's after eleven; let's go to bed." He offered his hand, hoping Rachel would take it.

Without looking up, she shook her head. "You go ahead; I'm waiting for a telephone call."

With a huff of frustration he turned and walked into the bedroom, leaving her alone in the living room.

As she watched him go, Rachel's heart seized. The crack that had opened up when she discovered Emmy gone suddenly grew wider and deeper. She wanted to turn back the hands of time, allow that moment to happen all over again. This time she would look up; this time she would take the hand that was offered. She no longer wanted to be alone in the chair, waiting for the telephone call that might never come. Her eyes filled with water, and despair snatched away the small fragments of hope she had mustered.

The thoughts that closed in on her were as dark and angry as storm clouds. How could it happen that in a single month, her life had turned to shambles? Emily gone. George angry with her. When the tears began, she lowered her head and covered her face with her hands.

She didn't see George return; she felt it when he knelt in front of her and pulled her hands away from her face. His eyes looked into hers, not angry or judgmental but filled with kindness and understanding.

"This isn't a war of who's right or wrong," he said. "We want the same thing, Rachel. We both want Emmy home. If it were within my power to make that happen, I would do it regardless of cost. I would trade my life for Emmy's in a heartbeat, if it would bring her home, but it won't. The only thing I can do now is pray for a miracle, pray that through the grace of God she is returned to us."

His voice suddenly became softer, and beneath the words Rachel caught a manifestation of her own sorrow.

"I know you think I don't understand, Rachel, but I do. I carry the same sorrow in my heart. But I keep it to myself, without words or tears, because I have you to care for. If you turn away from me, this burden that is already heavy enough to break a man will surely become too great for me to bear."

Rachel lifted her face and brought her lips to his. She kissed him softly, then whispered, "I'm sorry."

"There's no need for sorry." He circled his arms around her and lifted her from the chair. "Just come to bed and lie beside me."

She stood, and, leaning on one another, they turned toward the bedroom.

THE LONG DRIVE

The drive to Culvert Creek was mostly highway. Once Wilson turned onto Route 82, there were few distractions, and he was left with his own thoughts. Luckily he'd left early, and the traffic moved at a good pace, so he'd be there in time to check the satellite post office. Although the Washington County sheriff had offered little assistance, he had at least provided the address for what served as the local mail drop.

As he passed through Montgomery, Alabama, the traffic slowed, and Wilson pulled out the thermos of coffee and took a sip. It was just as he liked it, with plenty of sugar and cream.

His first stop would be the satellite post office, and afterward he'd try the local church to ask if the clergyman recalled seeing a new baby in town. According to the county sheriff, less than a thousand people lived in Culvert Creek. Even if the baby were kept hidden, any suspicious activity such as suddenly buying diapers or baby food was sure to be noticed.

Twice he pulled the letter from the envelope and eyed different passages, noting the significance of one word or another. He could tell the handwriting was that of a woman, and with the small, tight script he pictured her as being shy, an introvert possibly. A woman much like his aunt Marion. He thought back and remembered how she too wrote her *E*s narrow and close together just as these were. The stains apparently caused by droplets of water indicated the woman had been either crying or drinking when she penned the letter; in either case, a highly emotional state. Given the size of Culvert Creek, how many women would fit that description? Ten, maybe twelve. If necessary, he'd pay each and every one of them a visit.

By the time he crossed over into Mississippi, he was feeling a lot better about this mission.

~

At twenty minutes after five, Wilson pulled up in front of the Broadhurst Pharmacy, which, according to the lettering on the glass door, also offered postal services. Spotting an elderly man in the pharmacy area, he walked over.

"I'm looking for the postmaster."

"That'd be me." The old man reached across the counter. "Whitey Broadhurst."

As they shook hands, Wilson said he was looking for information on a letter that had been mailed from Culvert Creek.

"Official business has to wait until tomorrow," Whitey said. "The post office closes at five."

"But you said you're the postmaster."

"I am, but I'm only supposed to conduct official business from—"

"This isn't really official business; I just have a few questions." Wilson saw a flicker of hesitation, so he reached into his pocket and pulled out the envelope. "Recognize this handwriting or the notepaper?"

Whitey reluctantly took the envelope, looked at it, then turned it over in his hand.

"That's sure enough our postmark," he said. "But I can't say I'm familiar with this piece."

He squinted at the writing on the envelope a second time, then handed it back to Wilson. "You might check with Wilma Dobbs; she helps out part-time."

"Any idea where I can find Miss Dobbs?"

"It's Mrs. Dobbs. Wilma's married to the pastor. She and the pastor know most of the folks in town. Either of them might be able to help you."

~

Wilson's next stop was Christ the Redeemer Church, two blocks down. On the front of the small, steepled white building was a sign that read PASTOR'S OFFICE; an arrow pointed to the side walkway. He circled around the building and knocked at the back door. He waited a minute, then knocked a second time. When it became obvious no one was there, he returned to the pharmacy.

Whitey was stooped behind the counter, straightening the same shelf he'd been working on earlier.

"It seems no one is at the church," Wilson said. "Any idea where I can find Pastor Dobbs?"

Without looking up, Whitey shook his head. "Not this late in the evening, but he'll likely be there tomorrow."

As he stood there thinking of what to do next, Wilson sensed the optimistic feeling he'd had drifting away.

"Any place around here where I can get a room and a bite to eat?"

"Mabel's is the only restaurant in town. The food's good, but she closes at five thirty."

"What about a room?"

"Nothing here; Greenville's about the closest." Whitey stood and waved a hand toward the street. "Follow Creekside to the end, then take Route 1 south."

~

After a blue-plate special that left him with indigestion and a sleepless night on a lumpy mattress, Wilson was anxious to get back to pursuing what he'd come for. At seven a.m. he was parked in the back lot of Christ the Redeemer Church, waiting for the pastor's arrival. Thirty minutes into the wait, he got out of the car and began pacing back and forth across the parking lot. Culvert Creek seemed a town where time slowed to a crawl. Wilson was on the far side of the lot when an old Ford pulled in and parked alongside his truck.

"Excuse me," he called out. "Are you Pastor Dobbs?"

"That I am," the old man answered. "And you?"

"Carl Wilson." He offered his hand. "Sheriff, Hesterville, Georgia."

"Small world, isn't it? My granny came from Dawson, so I'm familiar with Hesterville. What brings you to this neck of the woods?"

"Official business, I'm afraid." Wilson pulled the letter from his pocket. "Have you seen any women with a new baby? Not an infant but maybe six months old or so."

The pastor scratched at the side of his face and tried to think through the congregation. He recalled a few teenagers and two preschoolers but no baby.

"Sorry," he said. "The Dumont twins are our youngest parishioners, and they're four—years not months."

"What about somebody who suddenly dropped out of sight? Maybe stopped coming to church?"

Dobbs shook his head. "There're plenty in this town who don't bother coming to church, but none of the regulars have stopped."

Wilson pulled the envelope from his pocket. "I'm looking for the woman who wrote this. You recognize the notepaper or handwriting maybe?"

Dobbs took the envelope, studied it, then handed it back. "Afraid I can't be of any help here either."

He turned, started toward the door, then stopped and looked back. "You might try Belinda's Beauty Shop; a lot of women who don't come to church are regulars down there."

Wilson smiled, gave a wave of thanks, and climbed into the truck.

~

Belinda was a big woman, as tall as Wilson and twice as wide. When he told her about the kidnapping and asked if there was a new baby in town, she laughed so hard her body quivered.

"Most all my ladies is well past the baby-wantin' stage," she said. "They's lookin' to take life easy."

"What about your customers? Has one of them maybe mentioned a neighbor or friend having a new baby?"

"I done told you—we ain't had no baby talk in here for twenty-some years."

Getting more discouraged by the moment, Wilson pulled the envelope from his pocket and handed it to her. "You recognize this notepaper or handwriting?"

She pursed her lips and squinted at the envelope. "It's somethin' like what Minnie Gray used to use, 'cept I think hers was pinker, more of that mauve color."

Wilson's face brightened. "What can you tell me about Minnie?"

Belinda chuckled. "Minnie sure ain't wantin' no baby. She's done passed seventy and ain't all together."

"All together?"

Belinda tapped a finger against her temple. "You know, her head. Minnie's mind comes and goes."

"When was the last time you saw her?"

"What with things the way they are, she's not a regular. But she come in for a nice 'do just 'fore Labor Day. Said they was going t' visit her sister in Ellijay."

"Ellijay, Georgia?"

Belinda nodded.

Wilson suddenly felt his optimism returning.

FUTURE PLANS

When Murphy returned from his trip to Bardstown, he found Vicki stretched out on the sofa, the baby asleep on her chest. The stroller had been folded and hidden under the bed.

She looked up and smiled. "How was the trip?"

"Good. I got the VA check, cashed it, and got our stuff from the apartment." He bent and kissed her forehead. "I told Mrs. Bachinski we were getting married, and she was happy for us; she even gave me the deposit money back."

With a smile curling the corners of his mouth, he added, "She said to give you a hug and consider it a wedding present."

Vicki lifted Lara into her arms and stood. "That's so like Mrs. Bachinski; she's such a kindhearted soul."

Murphy thought back on the wiry little woman who had been his landlady for the past three years, and his mouth broadened into an affectionate grin. "Yes, she is. I'm going to miss her, that's for sure."

"Maybe you can go back and—"

Murphy shook his head. "Once you cross a bridge, it's better not to look back. No matter how good or bad it was, yesterday's gone. Tomorrow's a new day, and whatever comes, we'll face it together."

Vicki had no answer for that, so she nervously shifted Lara onto her hip, then closed the space between them. With her free arm, she embraced Murph and pressed her cheek to his.

"Things may not always go the way we hope," she whispered, "but I love you more than you can possibly imagine, and I will for as long as . . ."

The remainder of what she had to say got caught in her throat.

He pushed back, took hold of her shoulders, and grinned into her teary-eyed face.

"Hey, this is no time for sadness! Things are gonna get better."

~

After Murphy carried in the bags of clothing he'd brought from the old apartment, he went out and came back with two roast beef sandwiches and a bottle of Chianti. They sat across from one another at the kitchen table, and he told her of all the things they would one day do: adopt a child, maybe two. Then they'd build a house with extra bedrooms and a wide front porch where on summer evenings they'd sit and look back on how it once was.

Vicki delighted in the earnestness of such a dream, and she allowed herself to believe in it as she listened to the tales of how in time their hair would turn white and they'd be surrounded by any number of grandchildren.

~

That night as they lay side by side in the bed, his breath warm against her ear, his fingers tenderly touching the places that gave rise to passion, their bodies became one in a union as loving as it had been in the early days of their courtship, before the marijuana and the tears that came without warning. Afterward they lay side by side, delighting in the simple pleasure of being together. They spoke of many things that night, but one thing was not mentioned: Lara. She was not part of the future Murphy had mapped out for them. In the big house with its wide porch and a spreading chestnut tree in the yard, there was no room for this baby.

In the wee hours of the morning when they were drifting on the edge of sleep, Vicki reached across and touched Murphy's chest.

"Can't you please let Lara be part of our plans?"

She waited a few moments, uncertain as to whether he'd heard the question. Then he turned on his side with his back to her. There was no answer, and she knew it would be useless to ask again.

~

Months later, she would remember that weekend as one of the best they'd ever had. She'd picture how his eyes crinkled at the corners when he smiled, and she'd ache for the feel of his hand pressed gently against her back. On nights when her heart felt as hollowed out as a jack-o'-lantern, she'd recall how he'd gone food shopping and surprised her with a bouquet of flowers: yellow roses with a fragrance so sweet it lingered like sugar on her tongue. When the memory of these things overwhelmed her, she'd turn her face to the pillow and let the tears come.

Once you cross a bridge . . .

~

On Monday morning, Murphy kissed Vicki goodbye and left the apartment a few minutes before nine. He was wearing the tweed jacket and gabardine pants he'd brought from the apartment with a tie knotted at his neck. After searching the "Help Wanted" section of the *Tribune Courier*, he'd come up with three good job possibilities plus an employment agency worth looking into.

"Good luck," Vicki said as she lifted her face to his and kissed his mouth.

The kiss was quick, there and then gone.

Once he was out the door, she stood at the window, watched him cross the parking lot, climb into the car, and drive away. When the car disappeared from view, she brushed the tears from her cheeks and turned toward the bedroom.

First she gathered the handful of things they'd bought for Lara and placed them in the bottom of a brown paper bag from the grocery store. Then she stuck in a few things of her own: a pair of jeans, a sweater, three T-shirts, and some underwear. By the time she added a stack of disposable diapers, two baby bottles, and three jars of Gerber baby food, the bag was full. She folded the top over and set it aside.

It was the time of year when the weather was changeable, chilly in the morning, sweltering in the afternoon sun. On this morning the sky was overcast with dark clouds and the menacing look of rain. Pulling the poncho she'd used at the music festival from the bottom of the closet, she folded it, placed it beside the bag, then opened the top drawer on Murphy's side of the dresser. The money, $600, was beneath a stack of boxer shorts. She took the folded bills, tucked them into the pocket of her jeans, then thought better of it. This was all the money Murph had. It would be almost two months before he'd get another check. He'd have rent to pay, need money for gas . . . She pulled the folded bills from her pocket and counted off five ten-dollar bills, then returned the remainder to its original hiding place. She'd be living rent-free with Angela and would soon be getting a job. Fifty bucks was enough to carry her for a while.

Keeping an eye on the clock, she fed Lara, dressed her in a warm sweater, then pulled the stroller from beneath the bed. At ten o'clock she sat Lara in the stroller, started for the door, then stopped and turned back. Using up five minutes of precious time, she rummaged through the kitchen drawer, found a piece of paper, and scrawled a note.

I love you now, and I'll love you always. I'm sorry it has to be this way. She signed it with the letter *V* and left the note lying on the kitchen counter. As she closed the door behind her, a swoosh of air crossed the room, and the note fluttered to the floor.

~

At ten thirty, the rain began. It started as a light drizzle and grew heavier as the minutes ticked by. Vicki draped the plastic poncho over the front of the stroller and moved back to stand under the overhang of the Los Burritos restaurant. She glanced at the clock: ten forty.

Angela should have been here by now.

A short while later the wind picked up, and the rain came at a slant, splattering the legs of her jeans and the side of the stroller. Vicki inched her way over and stood in the recess of the doorway with the stroller behind her. Although she was getting soaked, Lara was still dry. Pressing her nose to the window, she could see workers moving about, but the tables appeared empty. Could she possibly wait inside? Before making a move, she peered out at the parking lot again. Two delivery trucks and a half dozen cars but no white Ford Fairlane. She pulled open the restaurant door and ducked inside.

"That rain is really coming down," she told the girl at the register. "Okay if we wait in here?"

The woman behind the counter nodded. "Sure."

Vicki stood watching the rain for what seemed a very long time, and with each passing second she felt edgier. When two customers pushed through the door, she stepped aside and mumbled a feeble apology for blocking their way.

Lunchtime already? Where the hell is Angela?

Suddenly remembering the note she'd left lying on the counter, a sense of panic rose in Vicki's chest. She either had to get out of town or go back to the apartment. If Murph got home early and saw that note, there'd be no second chances. On the verge of tears, she turned to the woman at the register.

"I need to make a phone call; can you keep an eye on my baby for a minute?"

"The lunch crowd will be coming in soon, so make it quick."

"Yes, ma'am."

Despite the rain, Vicki darted out the door. She was halfway to the phone when a white Ford Fairlane pulled up alongside her and blasted the horn.

SISTERS

When Angela caught sight of Lara, she squealed with delight.

"She looks exactly like you!" she said and lifted the baby into her arms.

"Yeah, she does." Still feeling apprehensive, Vicki didn't waste time catching up. As she took Lara from her sister, she glanced around the parking lot, saw no sign of Murphy's car, and said, "Let's get going."

The poncho had kept Lara dry, but Vicki's shirt was soaked through. Angela noticed the way she'd begun to shiver.

"Want me to turn on the heat?"

Vicki nodded. "After we get on I-24, pull into a gas station so I can grab a dry shirt."

"I can stop now—"

"No, wait until we hit 24."

Vicki was chilled to the bone, but that wasn't what worried her. Murphy had gone in search of work, but he'd not said where. He could pop up anyplace within a fifty- or sixty-mile range. She'd come this far to keep from losing Lara and wasn't about to risk it for a dry shirt.

Turning it off as though it was no problem, she gave her voice a lighthearted tone and said, "So apparently a lot has happened since we last saw each other. Fill me in on everything."

Once Angela began talking, she bubbled over with chatter of Kenny and the new house.

"You're gonna love Kenny," she said with a grin. "He's a big teddy bear, the kind of guy who'll do anything for anybody."

She went on to say they'd met at a phone company party and fallen in love almost immediately. Vicki listened, nodding and smiling at one thing or another but saying little about her own life. There were only a handful of things she could say. So much of what happened during the past year had to remain hidden.

In the middle of telling how they'd moved to Fairlawn because Kenny was made group supervisor, Angela laughed.

"Listen to me prattling on about my life. What about yours? Now that you've got this precious little angel, you must have lots to tell."

Vicki gave a barely perceptible shrug. "Actually, I don't. The year after you moved in with Patty, Dad made living at home impossible. He got rip-roaring drunk every single night, so I had to sleep with my bedroom door locked. That June he took a crowbar and tore the door off the hinges. I called you the next morning, but as usual you weren't there, so I packed up my things and moved in with Russ."

"But you never called back to tell me what happened. Why?"

Vicki could feel the resentment she'd held on to for the past three years bubbling up in her throat. "If I'd told you about Dad, would it have made a difference?" she asked cynically.

"Of course it would. You know I'd do anything—"

"Well, you didn't," she cut in. "A dozen times I asked if I could move in with you, and you kept telling me you still hadn't found a place. After seven months of asking, I figured you just didn't want to be bothered with a kid sister, so I stopped calling."

"But if you had told me about what happened with Dad, I would have understood; I would have somehow found a way—"

Vicki turned and glared at her sister. "You already knew what Dad was like!"

"I knew what he was like with me, but he was never that way with you."

"Yeah, that was before you left. Once you were gone he came after me. Not the first five or six months, but afterward. He started with little things, putting his arm over my shoulders with his fingers drooping down on my boob, saying what a good daughter I was, talking about how a man without a wife gets lonely."

Angela gasped. "Shit! I'm sorry, Vicki, so sorry, but if you'd told me—"

Vicki's answer was quick and bristling with bits of anger. "I didn't want your pity! After our trip to Paducah I was hoping you'd want me to live with you because we had fun together, because I'm your sister!" She pulled in a deep breath, then added, "Because you loved me the same as I loved you."

"I did love you! I still love you! I called you for months afterward. Not once but dozens of times, and you never returned my calls."

"I was angry. I figured if you could live without me, I could live without you!"

"That's why you didn't return my phone calls?"

Vicki nodded. "It might sound kind of petty now, but back then it was a really big deal to me. I felt like I didn't have anybody but Murph." The moment his name popped out, she regretted it. She resolved to be more cautious. No last name. No ties to a daddy who wasn't really a daddy.

A look of sadness settled on Angela's face, and it was a long while before she spoke. "I'm truly sorry, Vicki," she said. "I'll make it up to you; I swear I will."

They rode in silence for several minutes, then, looking to find a subject less painful, Angela asked when Lara was born.

Without a moment's hesitation Vicki said, "February 5."

After that she started telling how she'd loved being pregnant and how having a baby made her feel fulfilled as a woman. All the emotional details were there: little facts that would wipe away any doubt of Lara being her child. And although she told of the baby's birth, she never once mentioned the exact time, place, or hospital where it happened. She also never mentioned that the first Lara came into this world with her eyes closed and her heart no longer beating.

Angela glanced across the seat at the baby. "She's small for seven months, isn't she?"

"A bit. It's because after that first month my milk dried up, and she's not too keen on formula."

Lies had begun to come easy for Vicki; first it was one thing, then another. Now she could pull a believable story from the air without a moment's hesitation.

Angela reached over and tickled the baby's tummy. "Well now, Auntie Angela will just have to fatten you up, won't I?"

Lara giggled happily.

~

With a stop so Vicki could change into a dry shirt and a second one for lunch, it was after four when they pulled into the driveway. The midsize Cape Cod with a wide porch and dormers overhead had a lamp aglow in the front window.

"Great, Kenny's home." Angela leaned on the horn, gave two short blasts, then jumped out of the car, motioning for Vicki to follow along. "He'll bring your things in."

As Vicki climbed out and stood looking at the house, a wave of nostalgia swept over her. If she allowed herself to think about it, she could imagine this to be the house Murph spoke of when he was sketching out a plan for their future.

Before they got to the end of the walkway, the door opened. A man with broad shoulders and a bright smile stepped out. He came toward them, gave Angela a quick kiss, then turned to Vicki.

"You must be the sister I've heard about!"

Bypassing the handshake Vicki offered, he wrapped his arm around her shoulders, gave her a warm hug, then reached for the baby.

"Allow me," he said as he took Lara from her.

There was something about the way he hoisted the baby into his arms, a gentleness that for a moment made Vicki want him as her husband. Countless times she had wished, even prayed, that Murphy would take the baby in his arms. She knew that if he had held Lara and felt the tiny hand wrapped around his finger, he would have fallen in love with her and given up any thought of ever letting her go.

~

That evening as they gathered around the dinner table, the conversation was light and lively, jumping from one thing to the next. The two sisters laughed at how on the last trip they'd taken together, they had walked up and down the streets of Paducah, looking at the houses and choosing which one they'd buy if or when they had the money.

"We had big dreams," Angela said with a grin, "but barely enough cash for bus fare home."

"Back then we thought we'd live next door to one another, have babies at the same time, and let the kids play together the way we used to do," Vicki said. "But look what happened. We totally lost track of each other, and if it wasn't for your roommate, I would have never found you."

"Now instead of next door, you'll live in the same house," Kenny said with a chuckle. With a twinkle in his eye, he added, "And before too long, Lara may have that playmate you were wishing for."

Vicki glanced at Angela's belly and gave a nod. "Are you . . . ?"

With a pale, almost regretful smile, Angela shook her head. "Not yet, but we're working on it."

~

Long after dinner was over, they sat in the kitchen and talked.

"Don't think I'm here just to freeload," Vicki said. "I plan to look for a job to pay for our board."

"There's no need," Kenny replied. "Angela's working part-time now, but once we've got a little one on the way she's going to stay home and be a full-time mama. She'll be looking for some company, and it'll be nice for you girls to spend time together."

~

Later that evening, when they were alone in the bedroom, Kenny noticed the pinched look on Angela's face.

"Is something wrong?" he asked.

She hesitated a moment, then gave a shrug. "I don't know. I'm sort of worried about Vicki. She seems so thin and . . . well, frail. At dinner tonight, she hardly ate anything. A few bites, but that was it."

Kenny tossed his T-shirt onto the back of the chair, then turned. "Maybe it's just anxiety. You know, the stress of going off on her own."

"Maybe," Angela repeated, "but Vicki can be pretty strange. Sometimes she acts playful and devilish, but inside there's a tornado raging. With her, you never know what's up until it's too late. For three years she didn't return my calls and never even told me she was angry with me."

"Well, yeah, that's a bit strange, seeing as how you're sisters."

"The thing is, when Vicki tells a story, what you get is *her version* of the truth. I have a feeling that's what she's doing with this guy who's supposed to be Lara's daddy."

"Why don't you come right out and ask her about him?"

"I did, but the only thing she'd say was that it didn't work out."

"Could be there wasn't much more to tell."

Angela raised a doubtful eyebrow. "Un-uh. I know my sister. The way she skirts around any mention of this guy is extremely odd."

"She's probably had a rough time and doesn't want to be reminded."

"Maybe. But if he's Lara's daddy, it seems she'd be going after him for child support."

"She probably will; give her time."

Angela shook her head. "She's not. On the drive home she said flat out that she wants nothing more to do with him. She's not going to tell him where she is or let him see Lara."

"Not wanting child support is strange, but she might have her reasons."

"She does," Angela said sadly. "He's supposedly roughed her up a few times."

"Did she tell you that?"

"Not the details, but she indicated that was why she wanted to get away . . ." Angela's words trailed off, almost as if she'd decided some things were better left unsaid.

Kenny climbed into bed, and she followed him, the look of concern still stuck on her face. Moments after he snapped off the lamp on his side, she sat up and clicked hers on.

"I'm not finished talking."

"Oh. Okay." He propped himself up on his elbows. "What else?"

"The clothes Vicki brought for her and the baby, that paper bag you carried in, is all there is."

The look of concern on her face spread to Kenny's. "She probably shipped some stuff—the crib, high chair, the rest of . . ." The remainder of his words trailed off when he saw the way Angela was shaking her head.

"There's no crib. The baby's been sleeping in bed with Vicki and her boyfriend."

"For seven months?"

"Yep, that's what she told me."

A stretch of furrows popped up on Kenny's forehead. "That's crazy. The kid needs a crib. She also needs to have a car seat, a high chair, and a decent stroller. That thing Vicki has is older than I am."

"I think money's a problem." Angela thought back to their earlier conversation and added, "Knowing my sister, she's not going to ask for help, no matter how bad things are. She thinks if somebody does something to help her out, it's because of pity."

"It's different with us; we're family."

"Doesn't matter. Vicki sees things the way she wants to see them."

"Maybe she's just embarrassed because the kid's daddy is a deadbeat."

Again Angela shrugged. "Possibly, but whatever the truth of the situation is, she's keeping it to herself."

Kenny hesitated a moment, shook his head, then said, "If your sister can't afford those things, then I guess we've got to help out."

"That's pretty much what I was thinking." The pinched look on her face gave way to a smile. "Do you think I should take Vicki shopping or just go buy the things Lara needs?"

"Take her shopping, but be careful you don't make it look like charity." Kenny lowered his head back onto the pillow. "After what you've said about your sister, I don't want her to think we're doing it out of pity. Say you're buying the things because before long we'll need them ourselves anyway."

"Hopefully we will," Angela said, then she grinned and snapped off the light.

Before the heat of the light bulb had cooled, her nightgown was lying on the floor, and she was kissing Kenny's face.

"You're gonna be the best daddy ever," she whispered.

FINDING MINNIE

Duck Tail Trail was a long and winding road with five small houses spaced a half mile apart. Minnie Gray's house was at the far end. From the outside it looked as if the place were deserted. The grass was six or seven inches high and the curbside mailbox stuffed full of mail and circulars.

When Wilson pushed the doorbell, there was no echo of chimes. He tried again, came to the conclusion the bell wasn't working, and rapped against the door. A dog barked. He knocked again, this time heavier, his knuckles cracking hard against the wood. Seconds later a male voice hollered, "Hold on, I'm coming!"

A thump. The sound of footsteps. When the door swung open, an old man with steel-gray hair peered out from behind the screen. Ignoring the sheriff's uniform Wilson wore, he gave a squinty-eyed look of suspicion.

"I ain't in a mood for listening to any sales pitch."

After two days of dead-end answers, Wilson was running thin on patience.

"Carl Wilson," he replied. "Hesterville sheriff. I'm looking for Minnie Gray."

"I'm Minnie's husband. What do you want with her?"

Wilson pulled the envelope from his pocket. "I'm hoping she can answer a few questions about this letter. Is she here?"

The old man shook his head and rubbed his hand across the whiskered growth on his chin.

"Lord God," he said with a groan. "That looks like one of Minnie's letters. What's she done now?" He clicked the screen door open and waved Wilson in. "Medgar Gray," he said and stuck out his hand. "I don't know what Minnie's done this time, but I'm hoping you can be a bit forgiving. She's not herself anymore and can't understand why she shouldn't be doing these things."

Wilson raised an eyebrow and asked, "What things?"

"Writing those crazy letters," he said sadly. "We lost our little girl forty years ago, and Minnie never got over it. She had a nervous breakdown and had to be sent away for three years. Ever since she came home, she's not been the same."

He turned and called out for Minnie, then took a picture from the mantel and handed it to Wilson. "This is us with Ellamae."

In the photo, the old man was young, clean-shaven with dark hair. The woman beside him wore a lace dress; her hair was in curls and her smile so bright it appeared almost dazzling. The child, a girl who seemed a miniature version of the woman, stood alongside them.

Wilson studied the photo for a moment, then asked, "What happened to Ellamae?"

"Influenza."

The word stood alone, isolated and without any additional explanation. It was weighted with the same kind of sorrow Wilson remembered, the same kind he'd experienced when they lost Becky.

"So young," he said sympathetically. "How very sad."

The old man nodded. "Minnie almost died giving birth, so she knew there wasn't going to be any more babies. When we lost Ellamae, she just couldn't find her way back from all that grief. The doctor said—"

He stopped short when Minnie came into the room.

Minnie Gray was almost childlike in size, and the cascade of curls she wore in the picture was gone. Her hair was tied back like a bundle of straw, poking out in a dozen different directions. Without acknowledging Wilson, she looked up at her husband and said, "Did you call me, dear?"

"Yes, Minnie. Do you see that we have company?" His words were soft and lenient, with a gentleness usually reserved for children. "This is Sheriff Wilson. He's had to come here all the way from Hesterville because of one of the letters you wrote."

She stood there looking like a deflated balloon, her shoulders slumped, her head bent, her gaze focused on the floor. "I'm sorry."

"Writing letters won't bring Ellamae back," Medgar said. "You know that, don't you, Minnie?"

She nodded.

"Sometimes the things you write frighten other people, and—"

She lifted her head and turned to Wilson. "I didn't mean anything bad."

He slid the letter from the envelope and handed it to her. "Did you write this, Minnie?"

She took the faded paper in her hand, studied it for a second, then gave an almost imperceptible nod.

"The letter says there's a child with golden hair and blue eyes. What child were you talking about?"

Her chin quivered as she sniffed back the threat of a sob. "Ellamae."

"Why did you say it's okay for a guardian angel to take a mother's child and she must accept it as best?" Wilson asked.

"Because that's what the angel told me the night they took Ellamae."

Medgar gave a disheartened sigh and shrugged.

"Believing it was a guardian angel who took Ellamae gives Minnie a lot of comfort," he said by way of apology. "Minnie and Ellamae both had a raging fever that night. Minnie was delirious and out of her head. It was five days before her fever broke, and by then we'd put Ellamae in the ground. That's when she started saying she'd seen the angels carry her baby off to heaven, and she's stuck to that story ever since."

Still looking down, Minnie peered at Wilson from beneath hooded brows. "Medgar's not a churchgoing man—that's why he can't see the angels."

"But you can?"

She narrowed her eyes, gave Medgar an apprehensive glance, then turned back to Wilson and nodded.

Wilson had come there holding on to optimism like a handful of marbles, but with each answer it seemed as if one of those marbles were taken away. Now he was left with only a single marble. He was counting on it when he asked the long-shot question.

"Did the angels tell you where they took the baby from Hesterville?"

There were a few moments of hesitation, when it seemed as though she might be thinking, then she shook her head. "They only told me about Ellamae."

He felt the hope he'd placed in that last marble leave his hand and fall away. "So why did you write that letter to the Dixon family?" he asked wearily.

Tears welled in the old woman's eyes. "Because I know how awful it feels to lose a child. I thought maybe if that mama knew about the angels, it would ease her burden a little bit."

With disappointment now weighing heavily on his soul, Wilson went through his questions one by one. He asked how it was she knew about the baby being kidnapped, how she got the Dixons' address, and if she'd written to other mothers. Each question had an answer that sounded logical but couldn't be proven one way or the other.

The facts were that Minnie Gray did have a sister living in Ellijay, a town fairly close to Hesterville, and there had been a front-page feature in the *Primrose Post* that told of the Dixon family and the baby's kidnapping. They'd run a picture of Emily beneath the headline that said Search For Missing Baby Continues.

After an hour of jumping from one possibility to another, Sheriff Wilson came to the conclusion that Minnie was simply a woman broken in spirit and addled of mind. While her letter might have been well intended, she'd wasted two days of his time on yet another wild-goose chase. He thanked the Grays for their courtesy, climbed back into his truck, and started for home.

It was after ten when Wilson pulled into the Dixons' drive. He climbed from the truck, the weariness of the trip dogging his footsteps. He was hoping Rachel had gone to bed. It would be easier telling George; his eyes had a look of sadness about them but not the soul-deep misery that Wilson saw in Rachel's face.

He stepped onto the porch and rang the doorbell.

George opened the door. Rachel was right behind him.

Wilson stepped inside, then stood there with his hat in his hand. "I'm afraid it's not good news—"

Rachel's eyes grew wide, and she gave a terrified gasp. Clasping her hand over her heart, she cried, "Oh my God, please don't say Emmy's—"

Wilson knew the thought before she spoke it. "No, no, it's not that," he said. "I didn't find Emily, but this turned out to be another dead end."

As he told how the death of Minnie's little girl had taken away her sense of reason, a sympathetic look settled on Rachel's face. "I can understand how such a thing could happen," she said remorsefully.

"So where do we go from here?" George asked.

"We keep looking and hope something turns up," Wilson replied. "We've got reward posters all over the state, and there've been several newspaper articles with Emmy's picture and some television coverage, so there's still a chance that one of those things will pay off."

Noticing the way Wilson was fingering the brim of his hat as he spoke, George asked, "How likely is it for that to happen?"

Wilson gave a reluctant shrug. "No telling. Could be tomorrow; could be never. The longer Emily's gone, the less our chances of finding her."

Rachel covered her face as a stifled whimper rose from her throat. "Don't stop looking," she begged. "Please don't stop looking."

UNEXPECTED BETRAYAL

Murphy didn't find the note Vicki left until almost midnight. That afternoon he'd come home with a bottle of wine thinking they'd celebrate his new job. Vicki wasn't in the apartment, but he didn't suspect anything more than her usual disregard for caution. Her clothes were still there: a pair of jeans tossed haphazardly across the back of the bedroom chair, her favorite sundresses hanging in the closet, and a pile of sandals still in the bag he'd brought from their old apartment at Mrs. Bachinski's.

"Dammit," he'd grumbled when he discovered her gone. It irked him that she'd defied his advice to stay inside.

He dropped down on the sofa and clicked on the TV. His upbeat mood from landing a job faded fast. Before the hour was out he was pacing the floor, his agitation made worse by worry, since she had the baby with her.

Until now, there'd been no indication that news of the kidnapping had reached western Kentucky, but there was always the possibility of a traveler from Georgia. Someone who'd seen the kid's picture, read about the reward, and was looking to collect some quick cash.

The thought of a passerby spotting them was a prickly reminder of Vicki's foolishness. He'd told her a dozen times that taking the baby out was stupid, just plain stupid. It was trouble they didn't need. Another day or two, then they'd drop the kid off at a church and be free to live their lives.

Why now? Why would she deliberately screw it up when we're so close to having this over and done with?

At six, Murph switched the TV station to CBS and watched the news. The local anchor told of a water main break and a need for more parental involvement in the school's PTA program, but there was no mention of finding a baby or apprehending a kidnapper. After the local news ended, Walter Cronkite came on. He told listeners Nikita Khrushchev had died at the age of seventy-seven, and a robbery had taken place at the Baker Street branch of the Lloyd's of London bank, but again, no mention of the kidnapped baby.

Vicki was capricious, that was a given, but with a baby and no money in her pocket she'd have limitations.

Money!

Murphy remembered the $600 he'd tucked away in the dresser drawer. He hurried into the bedroom, pushed aside the boxer shorts, and counted the money. Twice he fingered through the stack of bills and counted them: $550. She'd taken fifty dollars.

Maybe she needed something for the baby? Or herself? He doubted it was food, because there were jars of baby food in the cupboard and milk in the fridge.

So what else?

Murphy recalled Vicki's interest in the Kaufman-Straus department store Mrs. Palmeyer mentioned.

Yes.

He glanced at his watch: seven p.m. Some evenings the stores stayed open until nine. Maybe it was Mondays?

He clicked off the TV and scribbled a note telling Vicki that if she returned home before he did to stay inside the apartment.

I'll be back soon, he wrote. *I've gone in search of you!* He added the exclamation mark so she'd know he was pissed.

Murphy pulled away from the row of gray townhouses and turned onto Ledger Boulevard. He drove slowly, keeping one eye on the road and the other on the sidewalk, hoping to spot her on the way home. She didn't have a car, so she'd most likely be walking—unless there was a bus. So far he hadn't seen one on this road, but now it became another thing to look for.

He arrived at Kaufman-Straus just as the store was closing. As the last few stragglers hurried off, a uniformed guard stood there locking the door. By the time Murphy parked and ran over, the lights were dimmed and the guard gone. He knocked on the glass and waited, hoping someone had heard him. After a short while he knocked again, but when the neon sign in the store window clicked off, he knew it was useless. Even if someone answered his knock, it was obvious there were no last-minute shoppers left in the store. She wasn't here.

If not here, then where?

Murphy returned to the car and sat there, trying to think through a list of places she might have gone. At this point, he was stymied. She could be anywhere. Vicki was unpredictable; she did what you'd least expect and went where you'd never think of looking.

With no plan in mind, he began driving through town, up one street, down the next, stopping at small out-of-the-way restaurants and shops, peeking inside and moving on after not seeing her. When he returned to Lakeside Apartments it was after nine p.m. He'd found no trace of Vicki and was beginning to imagine the worst. He was out of ideas about where to look when he spotted the light in Mrs. Palmeyer's window and knocked on the door.

"I hate to bother you," he said, "but I'm looking for my wife, and she isn't at home. Have you seen her?"

"Not since she borrowed the stroller on Friday."

Stroller?

A sinking feeling settled in Murphy's stomach. Needing a stroller meant just one thing: she planned to keep the baby.

"Okay," Murphy said and forced a smile. "I guess she's gone to the movies or something. Thanks anyway." He turned and started down the walkway.

"I'm in no hurry to have that stroller back," Mrs. Palmeyer called after him.

"Okay, I'll let her know," he answered and, without turning around, gave a wave.

Once back in the apartment, Murphy opened the bottle of wine and poured a glass. He stood remembering how he'd expected it to be a celebration, then shook his head sorrowfully, took a long drink, and carried the glass into the living room. His heart felt heavy as lead when he lowered himself into the chair.

For a long while he sat there, thinking back on all that had happened. Time and again he pictured the night of their own baby's birth. He could close his eyes and see the wretched look on Vicki's face, hear the agonizing scream when she learned what happened. Yes, she'd suffered, but that didn't give her the right to take someone else's child, did it?

Where he'd been certain before, he now questioned everything, wondering if he'd done the right thing. Was there another way? A way he'd not seen?

When his glass was empty, he filled it a second time and then a third. As he drained the bottle, he noticed Vicki's note lying on the floor. He picked it up, and his hands trembled as he read.

I love you now, and I'll love you always. I'm sorry it has to be this way, it said.

Tears welled in his eyes, and he grabbed on to the counter to keep from falling. There was no longer any doubt.

She was gone.

~

In the days that followed, Murphy reasoned that since she'd taken just fifty dollars, the money would eventually run out, and she'd return. There was no way she could hang on to the baby and work. She'd return, and he'd welcome her back regardless of the circumstances. Somehow, someway, they'd work it out.

If keeping the baby was how he could hold on to her, he would do it. It was not his choice, but he would do it to be with her. And if in time they were caught, so be it. Spending the rest of his life in prison would be no worse than the life he was living now.

FAIRLAWN, KENTUCKY

Two weeks after Vicki arrived, Angela took the day off work, and the two sisters drove into Paducah for an afternoon of shopping. They had lunch at a waterfront café, then lingered over a second glass of iced coffee and shared a piece of lemon cake. They laughed remembering how as kids Vicki would come up with a plan to snitch a few dollars from their daddy's pocket or sneak in the side door of the Rialto.

With mock indignation Angela said, "You were always the one with the bright idea, but I was the one who usually got caught."

"Not true," Vicki replied. "What about the year you were in love with James Dean? We snuck in to see *Rebel Without a Cause* five times, and nobody was ever the wiser."

Sitting in the café and chatting as they were reminded Vicki of the afternoon she and Murphy had done almost the same thing, except then there was no dessert. He'd been irritable and anxious to leave. She'd wanted it to be leisurely, an afternoon such as this, but he'd spoiled it by looking over his shoulder as if he expected disaster to strike at any moment.

Before she could catch hold of herself, the memories began to come one after another, and a feeling of regret rose in her throat. The sorrow of it shadowed her face.

Maybe if I'd waited a little longer . . .

"Is something wrong?" Angela asked.

Pushing the thought back, Vicki forced a smile. "It's nothing. But we probably should get going if we want to find that crib for Lara."

They spent the entire afternoon in Paducah, strolling from shop to shop looking at baby clothes, cribs, and high chairs. While Murphy had tried to hide Lara, Angela did just the opposite.

"This is my adorable niece," she told the waiters and shopkeepers. "Looks exactly like her mama, doesn't she?"

Everyone seemed to agree. No one raised an eyebrow or questioned it.

While they were at the Baby Boutique, Angela took Lara from the stroller, sat her atop the counter, and played peekaboo as the sales clerk rang up an assortment of ruffled rompers and drawstring nighties.

"Just look at that smile," the clerk said. "She's going to be a heartbreaker for sure!"

It was easy to see why. With her golden curls and huge blue eyes, Lara was a beautiful child. Even when she was passed from person to person, she remained good-natured.

It would seem that given the situation, Vicki would shy away from such attention, but she didn't; in fact, she soaked it up. Gloried in it, you could say. In her mind, all those people seeing them as mother and daughter justified her decision.

~

Late that afternoon, with Lara sitting in her brand-new stroller and both sisters loaded down with shopping bags, Angela suggested they stop for a drink before heading home.

"There's a darling little place at the end of Clark Street," she said. "If we wait an hour before starting home, we'll miss most of the traffic, and it will be an easier drive."

Vicki grinned and gave a nod. "Sounds great. I think I know the place you're talking about; it has a garden terrace out front, with flowers and shade trees." She remembered it because when they'd passed through Paducah, she'd pointed it out to Murphy and asked to stop there. He'd given it no more than a fleeting glance, then declared it too crowded and driven right by.

In no particular hurry, they strolled down Marine Way, then made a left onto Clark. Halfway down the block Vicki glanced across the street and saw a familiar figure coming out of the Burgher House restaurant.

The woman was looking down, searching through her purse, then all of a sudden she lifted her head and started to smile.

Mrs. Palmeyer!

Vicki turned on her heel so quickly she almost knocked Angela over. "I've got to get out of here!" She whirled the stroller around and headed back down Marine.

Stunned and more than a bit confused, Angela hurried after her. "Wait a minute," she called. "What's wrong?"

Not certain whether or not Mrs. Palmeyer had caught sight of her, Vicki kept moving. "I feel really sick," she said, not slowing or turning back. "Like I could throw up any second."

Wrestling with the bulky shopping bags and almost out of breath, Angela finally caught up to Vicki and grabbed hold of her arm. "Wait a minute!"

Vicki kept up the rapid pace, and Angela stayed with her.

Tugging on her sister's arm, Angela said, "Rushing around like this is going to make you feel sicker. Slow down."

"I've got to get off this street!" Vicki glanced over her shoulder and saw Mrs. Palmeyer's carrot-colored head bobbing along Marine—a block and a half behind them. She turned into an alleyway that ran behind the buildings and came out on Fourth Street.

"Maybe if you stop and get something cold to drink, you'll feel better," Angela gasped.

Vicki shook her head and kept going. After they'd made the turn from Fourth Street onto Washington, Vicki glanced back again. There was no sign of Mrs. Palmeyer.

Vicki slowed her pace slightly but kept moving. "Sorry," she said. With no other explanation at hand, she claimed she was prone to panic attacks.

Angela looked at her with a puzzled expression. "Since when?"

After again glancing over her shoulder to make certain she'd lost Mrs. Palmeyer, Vicki breathed a sigh of relief and slowed her stride to a near normal pace. "It began just after Lara was born," she said. "And being in a crowd sometimes brings it on."

The quizzical look remained on Angela's face. "Marine Way wasn't crowded."

Vicki shrugged. "Maybe not, but it felt that way to me."

Still struggling to understand the cause, Angela asked, "Was it a difficult pregnancy? Was there some kind of trauma? What actually—"

"Oh, it was nothing like that." With the place where they'd parked the car now in sight and no further sign of Mrs. Palmeyer, Vicki was anxious to move away from the subject. "It doesn't happen all that often," she said. "I guess it was all the excitement of spending the day with you and Lara."

She gave an easy smile, then segued into talking about her pregnancy and how she suffered through two months of morning sickness, had a craving for cucumber sandwiches, and couldn't abide the smell of beer. She spoke of how in the sixth month she began to feel the baby moving and somehow knew it would be a girl.

"By the seventh month, I was big as a watermelon," she said, laughing, "but I didn't care. The only thing I wanted was a healthy baby."

Angela smiled. "Well, you certainly got your wish."

"Uh-huh." Vicki nodded. She stopped there and said nothing about the bright lights of the operating room and the heartbreaking news of a stillborn birth.

The stories she told were part truth and part lie, woven together so seamlessly there was no way of telling one from the other. She'd thought them through a thousand times until reality stepped aside and truth was reborn in the shape of what her heart wanted to believe.

The only thing she couldn't reimagine was Murphy. When Angela asked about the baby's father—why she needed to get away, what terrible abuse drove her to leave—Vicki said it was something she didn't want to talk about.

On the trip from Wynne Bluffs she'd tried to create a story of those horrors, but her thoughts of Murphy were always as she'd known him: concerned, loving, promising all he could give. When she tried to imagine him otherwise, the words felt bitter in her mouth, and they came out sounding broken. He was the one thing she couldn't re-create, so she said very little. On the rare occasion when there was cause to mention his name, she tried to refer to him only as Russ, no last name. But old habits died hard, and on three different occasions the name Murph was out of her mouth before she had time to stop it. Each time she'd chastised herself and made a mental note to avoid use of it in the future. She'd severed the connection, left no trail. For Lara's sake, it had to remain that way.

~

On afternoons when she and Angela were together, Vicki could convince herself she was happy. She had Lara, and that was enough. But at night, when the room was dark and the only sound was that of her heartbeat, loneliness overwhelmed her.

She couldn't rid herself of the thoughts of Murphy.

Hour after hour she'd lie there, remembering the times they'd slept curled together, his chest pressed to her back, his hand holding hers. When the memories became so real that she could feel the warmth of his skin against hers, there was no way to escape them. She tried to recall him giving her an ultimatum, but that picture wouldn't come.

Somehow the harshness of his words had been forgotten, and she could remember only the gentleness of his touch.

When the ache of missing him became more than she could bear, she lifted Lara from her crib and brought her into the bed. The warmth of having the baby sleep beside her as she had in the early days quieted the memories for a while, but they inevitably returned. On those nights when not even the tiny heartbeat alongside her own was enough, she buried her face in the pillow to muffle the sound of sobs.

She had come to the crossroad of life and chosen her path; now she could do nothing but live with it. The loss of the first baby, the finding of this one, and the heartache of staying away from the only man she'd ever loved were three ugly secrets she would carry to her grave.

A TIME TO MOURN

After Sheriff Wilson told Rachel that each passing day lessened the likelihood of finding Emily, she began to mark the days off. Every morning she'd look at the grocery store calendar hanging on the kitchen wall, stand there for several minutes, then scratch a big black *X* through the preceding day. Touching her finger to the current one, she'd say yet another prayer that this would be the day of Emily's return.

On the last day of September, she folded back the page, gave a mournful sigh, and turned to George. "It's been forty-two days."

He looked up from the newspaper he'd been reading. "I know."

"Do you really? I've never once seen you look at this calendar and count the days."

"I'm a man who keeps his own counsel, Rachel. I do it differently. I measure the time in my heart. You may not realize it, but I miss Emily just as you do."

"Miss her?" Rachel said cynically. "I don't just *miss* her. I fear for her, so much so that I can think of nothing else. Every waking minute I worry about if she is being fed and cared for! The fear I feel is like some strange monster swallowing up my insides. It grows bigger and fiercer every day. I go to bed frightened, wake up frightened. My breasts have turned dry and useless and my heart empty of everything but this fear."

With eyes narrowed and chest heaving, Rachel glared at him for a moment, then turned away and acidly asked, "Can you say the same, George?"

He set aside the newspaper, stood, and crossed over to her. Although she stood with her back to him, he placed his hands on her shoulders and leaned forward, his head touching hers.

"I worry about Emily as much as you do," he said, "but fear will not bring her home. Instead of giving in to it, I do what I can to find her. I keep pushing ahead and try to hold on to the belief that we will one day get her back."

Rachel broke free, then turned and looked at him curiously. "What exactly do you do?"

"I've been running ads in the *Atlanta Constitution* and working with Sheriff Wilson. Last week we ordered twenty thousand more posters. Soon Emily's picture will be all over Alabama, Tennessee, and Kentucky. Plus, the Main Street merchant's group has raised another five thousand for the reward fund and—"

"Why didn't you tell me all this before?"

George scrubbed his hand across his forehead. "I thought I was sparing you."

"Sparing me from what?"

"More disappointment. Another letdown."

As he spoke, Rachel could see something she'd missed before; it was the look of weariness that circled his eyes and gave his skin a ghostly pallor.

He hesitated a moment, as if he were considering the fallout of a thought before he gave it voice, then turned his head so his eyes were looking directly into hers and continued. "I have no way of knowing whether these things will work or not. That's why I've kept it to myself."

For the remainder of that week and into the next, Rachel's hopes were buoyed, but when October gave way to November, that hope faded.

~

The week before Thanksgiving, a cold front rolled down from Canada and brought with it a wind that howled through the night and well into the next day. Mama Dixon's car refused to start that morning, so she was stranded at home, and Rachel spent the day alone.

For most of the afternoon Rachel stood on the back porch watching the leaves of the red maple tear loose from the tree and blow away. As each leaf was carried off by the wind, she counted it as a loss, a thing to be mourned. In the tree she saw herself, a mother rooted to the spot, standing bare after the child she'd borne had been ripped away.

In time, the sky grew dark and the rain began. It came in spurts, starting as a drizzle, then in sheets so heavy she could barely see the shadowy pines across the yard.

George arrived home shortly after the rain started. With the house silent and no sign of life, he assumed Rachel was napping. He sat for a while, watched the evening news, then turned off the television and went to check on her. When he found she was not in the bedroom, he looked in the nursery. The room was as it had been ever since the night Emily was taken, and the rocking chair sat empty.

"Rachel," he called, then started through the house in search of her. From the kitchen window he saw the dreary figure standing on the back porch. With a thin gray sweater pulled tight around her shoulders, she at first seemed one with the rain, but when he opened the door and called her name, she turned.

"It's so sad," she said. "The leaves of the maple are gone."

Hurrying across, George wrapped his arm around her waist and eased her back toward the door. "It's too cold to be standing out here; your clothes are soaked."

She looked up at him, her face wet with a mix of rain and tears. "It's this place, George," she said. "They took Emmy because of this place. They took her on a night like this, when it was raining and dark. Standing out there I could almost see the way it happened. A man came from behind the pine trees; he crossed the yard and carried her off."

George took her icy-cold hand in his and said, "That's not what happened. The sheriff is certain it was a woman. A fairly small woman. He knows by the size of the shoe print and the depth of the impression it made in the mud. And he's reasonably sure she came from a car pulled over on the side of the road."

"But I saw—"

"No, Rachel, you imagined. Now let's get you out of these wet clothes and into something dry."

~

Later that evening, after they'd reheated part of a leftover casserole and he'd fixed her a mug of tea laced with brandy, they sat side by side on the sofa and talked.

"It's true this place is isolated and probably too far from town," he said. "Two years ago we thought it was perfect, but maybe it's time for us to make a change. We can sell this house, find a place closer to the store . . ."

Rachel set her mug on the coffee table and turned to him. "Part of me wants to leave here and get away from the memory of that terrible night, but a bigger part of me knows I need to stay, because here in this house I can hold on to the memory of Emily. I can still catch the smell of her, hear the bubble of her laughter, sit in the rocking chair and imagine her in my arms. I'll lose those things if we move away. This is our home, George, and when Emily returns, I believe this is the home she'll return to."

THE HARD TRUTH

For the first few weeks after Vicki left, Murphy believed she'd be back. Regardless of how thin the rationale was, he found reasons to cling to his belief. She'd left most of her clothes behind. She'd taken only fifty dollars. If she was never coming back, she would have taken it all, wouldn't she?

Assuming she was no longer drinking or doing drugs, he thought there was a possibility she'd come to her senses, had a change of heart maybe, and set off to return the baby. When that thought came to mind, deep furrows settled across his forehead and his heart beat faster. Sure, he'd been in favor of doing exactly that, but he doubted Vicki was clever enough to pull it off. Even on a good day she was filled with scatterbrained ideas; her taking the baby was proof enough.

He thought about that night, remembering how she'd simply walked into the house and walked out with the baby. If she was foolish enough to do that, she just might be gullible enough to believe she could return the kid the same way. Then she'd be arrested; he was certain of it.

During the day Murphy went to work, and the busyness of waiting on customers enabled him to push back those thoughts of her, but at night when he sat in front of the television and watched the flickering screen, his mind drifted. He pictured her in handcuffs, taken off to jail, unable to send word of where she was or what had happened.

News of the kidnapping hadn't made the newspapers there in Kentucky, so it was unlikely that news of the kidnapper being caught would either. If Vicki had been arrested, he'd have no way of knowing. After what seemed like endless nights of worrying, he decided to drive back to Georgia and sniff around. He wouldn't risk going back to Hesterville, but he could drive through Weston, the next town over, and grab a local paper. If there was any news at all, that's where he'd find it.

That Saturday, Murphy left Wynne Bluffs long before the sky turned light. He stopped only once to fill the gas tank and grab a container of coffee. Driving straight through, he'd be there in the early afternoon. That would give him time to get a newspaper, maybe have lunch, keep an ear open for local gossip, and be back on the road before sunset to head for home.

By the time Murphy arrived in Weston the plan was set in his mind, and everything was moving along just as he'd anticipated. Shortly after one he parked the car, found a copy of the *Primrose Post* at the drugstore, then crossed over to the luncheonette, sat at the counter, and ordered coffee and a grilled cheese sandwich.

He'd hoped the place would be a bit more crowded, but other than himself the only person at the counter was a big man with a stubble of whiskers. A group of middle-aged women chattered away in a side booth, but they were too far back for him to catch the conversation. He tried to listen for specific words—baby, kidnapper, arrested—but even that was impossible.

The man turned to him. "You new in town?"

Taken aback, Murphy sputtered, "Wh-who, me?"

"There's nobody else here." The man chuckled, then leaned toward Murph and offered his hand. "Carl Wilson."

"Russ . . ." Murphy caught himself. "Max Russell."

"So, Max, you new in town?"

Murphy shook his head. "Just passing through." He took a bite out of the sandwich and busied himself with chewing.

Wilson ordered a refill for his coffee, then turned again. "Where you headed?"

Long after he could have swallowed the food in his mouth, Murphy kept chewing. He needed to be somebody other than who he was and headed to a place other than Wynne Bluffs, where he'd be returning.

"Florida," he finally said, "to do some fishing."

"Good fishing down there. Margaret and I spent our honeymoon in a little town called Sea Breeze; that was some thirty years ago."

"Nice." Murphy nodded and bit off another mouthful.

"Yeah, it was nice," Wilson mused. "Every morning I'd go fishing and come back with a mess of snook or pompano."

Murphy gave a stiff smile, then grabbed the cup and started slurping his coffee. He'd turned away intentionally, hoping Wilson would take the hint, but obviously he hadn't.

"You planning to stay on the Gulf or someplace farther south?"

"No set plans," Murphy answered, then chomped down on the sandwich.

He hadn't counted on talking to anybody and sure as hell didn't want to be answering a bunch of questions. A rivulet of perspiration trickled down the side of his neck. He eyed the door. Walking out with most of the sandwich still on the plate would mean more questions. *Was there something wrong with the food? Can I get you something else?*

No, it would be better to just eat the damn thing and get out of there. He hurriedly took a second bite before he'd finished chewing, but when he tried to swallow, a piece of toast got stuck in his throat. He gagged, but the blasted toast wouldn't go up or down.

"You okay?" Wilson asked.

By then Murphy's mouth was hanging open and his face was starting to turn red.

Wilson jumped up and whacked Murphy on the back several times. The chunk of toast came flying out of his mouth and jettisoned across the counter. As Murphy stood there trying to regain his breath, Wilson signaled the waitress.

"Fran, get this guy a glass of water, will you?"

"Sure thing, Sheriff," she answered.

Murphy was still struggling to catch his breath when Fran set the glass of water in front of him. He grabbed it, tried taking a gulp, and started coughing again.

"Easy there, Max." Wilson took the glass from him and set it back on the counter. "You've got to learn to slow down, son. Take time to enjoy your meal; don't be in such a rush."

Murphy could feel his shirt growing damper by the second. He'd heard the waitress call Wilson "Sheriff," so he couldn't just bolt and run. His stomach rolled over, and the stink of fear was rising up from his armpits.

Wilson noticed but figured that kind of fear to be the aftermath of almost choking. "Relax, you're fine now." He gave Murphy's shoulder a friendly squeeze. "Just take your time and finish up lunch."

Murphy now had no choice but to be sociable; anything else would be way too suspicious a behavior. With a pencil-thin smile he stood, pulled two singles from his pocket, and laid them on the counter. "Thanks for helping me out," he said politely. "I think I'll wait awhile before trying to eat anything more. That episode kind of killed my appetite."

"Probably a good idea." Wilson gave a friendly nod, then added, "But when you do get around to it, slow down. Eating's like fishing; you've got to relax or you won't get the full enjoyment of it."

"You're right about that," Murphy said nervously, then he tucked the newspaper under his arm and scrambled out the door.

"Coming here was a damn fool idea," he mumbled as he climbed back into the car. "Stupid, that's what it was. Flat-out stupid."

Being face-to-face with the sheriff had unnerved Murphy, and he now wanted to get as far away from Georgia as possible. He headed for the highway and drove north until the needle on the gas gauge was fluttering past empty. By then he was across the Tennessee border.

At the gas station he filled the tank and bought a can of Coke. Then he pulled to the side of the lot and sat there reading through the *Primrose Post*. On page five he found a quarter-page ad with a picture of the baby and a notice saying the reward for information leading to the return of the child was now $15,000. Below Emily's picture was a line of bold type reading Emily Dixon, taken from her crib sometime during the night of August 19, 1971. Following that, a short paragraph describing Emily's blue eyes, blonde hair, and butterfly-shaped birthmark, said the Dixon family desperately wanted their daughter back. If left in a safe place and unharmed, no questions will be asked, the ad read. At the bottom were the phone numbers to call. Listed first was Sheriff Carl Wilson and, on the next line, a number for George Dixon. The thought that he'd been an arm's length from the sheriff sent a wave of nausea through Murphy's stomach, and the bitter taste of bile rose in his throat.

He sat there for a long while studying the ad, reading and rereading the statement by the Dixon family. It was now obvious that Vicki had not returned the baby, but the question was, where had she gone?

Before leaving the gas station, Murphy tore the ad out of the newspaper, folded it, and stuck it behind the back flap of his wallet. Then he tossed the paper in the trash can and headed back to the highway.

~

For several weeks he remained certain Vicki would be back, but in time that certainty gave way to probability. Once the trees became bare of leaves and the early-morning air carried a hint of frost, probability dwindled to a remote possibility.

On Thanksgiving Day, Murphy sat alone in the apartment eating a turkey sandwich he'd bought at the delicatessen and watching the Nebraska Cornhuskers play the Oklahoma Sooners. It was a tight game, and he was rooting for the Huskers to hang on to their number one spot, but even when Rich Glover made a tackle that caused the stands at Owen Field to erupt in cheers, his thoughts were preoccupied with Vicki.

He wanted to believe she loved him as much as he did her, but now it seemed almost impossible. She'd been gone nearly two months, and he hadn't heard from her. No letter, no note left in the mailbox, nothing. He reasoned that even if she were in jail, she could have written.

That's when he came to the realization that wherever she was, she wasn't in need of help. If she had been, she would have written. She'd have held her skinny little arm out and reached for his hand. He knew that's how Vicki was; she took what she needed and gave little in return. He'd been willing to risk everything to keep her safe, but she couldn't manage anything more than a scrap of paper saying she was sorry.

He stuffed the remainder of the turkey sandwich back into the bag and tossed it.

Sorry was no longer enough.

~

The next day Murphy carried a cardboard box home from the grocery store, packed the remainder of Vicki's clothes in it, and passed it off to Mrs. Palmeyer.

"I doubt she's coming back," he said, "but if she does you can give her this."

He then handed her a ten-dollar bill, said he was sorry about the stroller Vicki had taken, and hoped the money was enough to pay for it. Mrs. Palmeyer nodded and stuck the ten in her pocket.

That same afternoon, Murphy loaded the car with his things and headed back to I-24. He wasn't sure what he was going to do or where he was going. Vicki once mentioned a sister; maybe he'd try and look her up. Maybe not. When he got to the junction, he turned south. He'd never done much more than pass through Nashville, and that seemed like as good a place as any for a man looking to make a new start.

Murphy clicked the radio on, twisted the dial until he came to the group America singing "A Horse with No Name," then he hit the gas and joined in.

LARA'S FIRST BIRTHDAY

February 5, 1972

The fifty dollars Vicki took was gone before the month was out. Although she tried to stretch the cash, it went: a dollar here, a dollar there, until there was nothing but a handful of loose change in her pocket. In mid-October, after the leaves had changed color and the air had taken on a chill, they were sitting at the supper table when Vicki announced that she was going to get a job.

Angela was in the process of loading a mound of mashed potatoes onto Kenny's plate and stopped with the serving spoon in midair.

"You can't possibly!" she said. "What about Lara?"

"Don't worry—Martin Marietta has a night shift. If I get a job there, I could have her ready for bed and let you tuck her in."

A smile slid across Angela's face as she dropped the potatoes onto Kenny's plate.

"Well, I certainly don't mind taking care of her, but you working all night . . . ?" The thought trailed off with an implied question mark hanging at the end.

"I think it's a terrible idea," Kenny said.

Both women turned with a look of astonishment. Angela spoke first.

"Why?"

"Because Vicki isn't strong enough. Mothering a baby all day and working all night is enough to wear down a healthy person; what do you think it would do to someone as fragile as she is?"

"I'm thin," Vicki argued, "not fragile."

A look of disagreement had already settled on Angela's face. "I've seen you looking better. Kenny's right; the night-shift thing is not a good idea."

Without looking up, Vicki stuck her fork in a piece of chicken and aimlessly moved it from one side of her plate to the other. "I'm not comfortable with you guys paying for everything. I need to have some money of my own."

"We'll give you a weekly stipend," Kenny said, not backing down. "It's not much, but—"

Before his suggestion had time to settle, Vicki began shaking her head.

"Absolutely not. That's flat-out charity." With her eyebrows pinched together, she thrust out her nose, making it obvious there would be no changing her mind.

"Don't get insulted," he said. "It's not charity; it's family helping family!"

"Enough," Angela cut in, not giving the discussion time to become an argument. "There's no rush to judgment here. Let's take some time and think it over. With clearer heads I'm sure we'll find a way to work this out."

Later that evening, Angela took Vicki aside and asked if she'd be willing to work at the diner.

"Dimitri needs an extra server for the supper shift. It's part-time, from four o'clock until eight."

"Part-time? What's the pay?"

"With tips you'd probably make as much as you'd make working full-time at the factory, and you'd be able to spend most of the day with Lara."

Vicki gave a hesitant smile. "You wouldn't mind babysitting every afternoon?"

"Mind? Why, I'd be thrilled! You know how much I love that little munchkin."

And so Vicki became a part-time waitress, and Angela became a part-time mother. Every afternoon Angela rushed home at three, scooped Lara into her arms, and spent the remainder of the day with her. Before the first snowfall of December, Lara was calling both sisters "Mama." It would seem with all Vicki had done to make the child hers, she'd object to this, but she didn't.

"It's okay for now," she said jokingly, "but sooner or later she'll have to know who her *real* mother is."

Angela tried to laugh it off, but her smile was stiff and brittle.

~

That Christmas, Lara began crawling. Up until then you could sit her in the middle of the living room with a scattering of toys, and she'd stay put. That was before she saw the Christmas tree. With its colored lights and shiny ornaments, it was too much to resist. When the electric train whistled and began circling the tree, she stretched her tiny arm forward as far as it would go, then tipped over and took off. From that day forward, there was no keeping her still.

The Monday after Christmas, Kenny came home with a brand-new Kodak Super 8 movie camera and projector. By New Year's Eve he'd shot three cartridges of film and sent them off for processing. When Angela complained that $300 was a lot to spend on a spur-of-the-moment impulse, he laughed.

"Just wait," he said. "There will come a time when you'll be darn glad we've got these pictures."

Of course, time would prove him right, but back then no one could have possibly foreseen what the future would bring.

~

On February 5, they celebrated Lara's first birthday. The date marked the birth of the stillborn baby, but it was a full month before Emily Dixon would turn one year old. Months earlier Vicki had merged both babies into one, and this date would forever be their birthday.

She came home from work that day carrying a stuffed teddy bear nearly as big as Lara, a musical jack-in-the-box, and a set of stacking blocks that were soon scattered across the living room. Angela baked a cake, then frosted it with pink icing and placed a single candle in the center. When she tried to show Lara how to blow out the candle, the little one got so excited she smooshed her face into the creamy icing and came up laughing. Kenny filmed the party start to finish.

Once the film was processed, he set up the projector, and as they watched they all laughed as they had the first time. When the film flickered to an end, Angela threw her arms around Kenny's neck and kissed him.

"You were right," she said. "Capturing these special moments on film is the best present you could have ever given our family."

Perhaps it was the mention of family or the thought of celebrating such a milestone without him, but that night Vicki could not rid her mind of Murphy. Long after everyone else was asleep, she was remembering the touch of his hand and the feel of his body lying next to her. When she closed her eyes, she saw Murphy with the movie camera in his hand. She saw him laughing the way Kenny laughed, and she saw herself throwing her arms around his neck.

She tossed and turned for half the night. When the want of him became so powerful that she could no longer stand it, she climbed from the bed and tiptoed quietly into the kitchen. Sliding the drawer open, she removed an envelope and notepad, then carried them back to her room.

In the soft glow of the bedside lamp, she opened her heart and let her feelings bleed onto the paper:

> I hope you can forgive me. I know I was wrong in not trusting that you would keep my secret, but at the time I was frightened. Now I know how foolish that fear was. You are as much Lara's father as I am her mother, and you deserve to be part of her life.
>
> Perhaps it's not too late for us. Perhaps this love I still have for you is powerful enough to persuade you to pick up the pieces of the dream we once shared and start over. I pray for this every day.
>
> Lara and I are your family, Murph. We need you. I need you.
>
> I've never stopped needing you.

After she said all there was to say, she folded the letter, slid it into the envelope, and addressed it to Russell Murphy at the Wynne Bluffs address. Tucking the letter into the side pocket of the tote bag she carried back and forth to work, she climbed into bed and closed her eyes.

EMILY'S FIRST BIRTHDAY

March 10, 1972

Helen Dixon understood loss. She knew this day was coming, and she'd prepared for it. Sorrow was not a thing that could be forgotten or washed away, but it could be softened and made easier to live with.

As the first ribbon of dawn edged the horizon, she rapped softly on the front door of her son's house. They were seldom up this early, so Helen waited a few moments, then drew the key from her purse, unlocked the door, and made her way into the kitchen. After she'd set the coffee on to brew, she arranged the homemade raisin biscuits on a platter and took out the jar of blackberry jam Sadie Jenkins had sent.

She'd planned on making an omelet, but before she could crack the first egg, Rachel was standing in the kitchen doorway. Helen smiled, then turned back to the stove.

"I thought maybe we could get an early start today," she said. "I have several things to do and could use your help."

Rachel stood there, her hair hanging limp at the sides of her face and dark circles making her eyes appear hollow. She made a feeble attempt to tie the belt of the robe she'd pulled on over her nightgown, then left it hanging loose.

"What kind of things?" she finally asked.

"Mostly errands. Return some library books, pick up my prescription, stop by the fabric store. I need to make new curtains for the living room; the ones I have are just about falling—"

"Do you know what today is?" Rachel asked, her voice as pointy as an ice pick.

Helen pushed the skillet to the back of the stove, then crossed the room and took Rachel in her arms.

"Of course I do," she said softly. "My granddaughter's birthday is something I'll never forget."

The tears welling in Rachel's eyes overflowed, and she dropped her head onto her mother-in-law's soft shoulder.

"Oh, Mama Dixon," she said through tears. "I don't know how I can make it through this day."

Helen pulled Rachel closer, held her until the sobbing slowed, then spoke in a gentle voice.

"Grief is a terrible burden for anyone to bear, but it's sometimes easier to live with if you let others help you."

"How can anyone—"

"Emmy was George's baby too," Mama Dixon said. "And she was my granddaughter. Our hearts hurt the same as yours."

Rachel pushed back just enough to look into Mama Dixon's face. "But George seldom says anything . . ."

Mama Dixon gave a knowing nod. "Because he wants to stay strong for you. He loves you more than anything in the world, Rachel. That's why he keeps his sorrow to himself. It's his way of trying to lessen the load you're carrying."

Rachel lowered her eyes and looked away.

"I didn't realize . . . ," she said, but it seemed terribly inadequate in the face of such a revelation.

~

It was almost ten by the time Rachel was dressed and ready to leave. As she climbed into the car, she pushed aside the books scattered across the front seat. Helen glanced at her watch and said they'd have to hurry.

"Why?" Rachel asked. "The library is open all day."

"I know, but I promised Sadie I'd have these books back before eleven."

"Sadie? Is she working at the library now?"

"No, she's there for a meeting, but she asked that we stop and say hello."

Rachel gave a weary sigh. "I doubt that I'll be very good company today; maybe I should just wait in the car."

"And insult Sadie?" Helen gave a feigned gasp. "I think not. You need to come in and say hi." Noticing the frown on Rachel's face, she added, "We don't have to stay long. When you're ready to leave just give me a nod, and we'll get going."

Helen parked in an open spot near the front of the building, then hurried into the library, dropped the books on the front desk, and continued back to the meeting room with Rachel trailing behind. As soon as they stepped into the room, Rachel spotted a dozen familiar faces. She turned to Mama Dixon.

"You never mentioned this was a meeting of the Hesterville Women's League."

"I didn't?" Helen offered the pretense of forgetfulness, but a gentle smile tugged at the corners of her mouth.

These women were Rachel's friends. Friends she hadn't seen in months; women whose calls she hadn't returned. The desire to turn and run darted across her mind, but before she could move they surrounded her.

"Thank heaven you're here," Natalie Dennis said. "We're in desperate need of a chairperson for the library restoration committee."

"I'm willing to cochair," Kathy Foslein said, "but I can't handle it alone. I'm terrible with design concepts, and that's something you're good at."

"I don't really think—"

"At least say you'll consider it," Natalie pleaded.

The word *no* was in Rachel's mouth, but it didn't come out. As she stood there trying to find her voice, Sadie walked over, slid her arm around Rachel's back, and guided her over to the empty chair.

"We've ordered in lunch, so at least stay and have a bite to eat."

"It's not that I don't want to," Rachel said apologetically, "but I've promised Mama Dixon that I'd help—"

Already seated in a chair at the end of the table, Helen waved her off.

"We've got plenty of time," she said. "Those curtains can wait another week or two."

"Well, okay," Rachel said and gave a reluctant shrug.

When the ladies got back to their discussion of potential events to kick off the restoration campaign, Rachel at first seemed uninterested. She leaned back in the chair, picked at the loose button on her sweater, and fidgeted with her wedding ring, sliding it on and off. Although the conversation bounced back and forth like a tennis ball, she was lost in her own thoughts. When Kathy asked her opinion of the poster campaign, she came up short.

"Sorry," she said, shaking herself loose of the memories, "I missed part of that."

Kathy held up the poster a second time and explained how the plan was to put one in every shop window.

"It's less expensive than ads or mailings," she said. "What do you think?"

"It's good, very good," Rachel replied, but there was no fire in her words.

Lunch arrived a short time later, and the library restoration plans were pushed aside. After everyone was settled with a plate of food in front of them, bits of conversation began to circle the table. There was talk of new books to be read, recipes tried, and spring gardens that would soon be planted. Although a good portion of Rachel's thoughts were elsewhere, she gave a nod of agreement from time to time and twice mentioned the delicious raisin biscuits Mama Dixon had made.

The meeting ended at three, and by then Rachel had said she would consider their offer to cochair the library restoration committee but couldn't promise anything.

"I have good days and bad days," she said solemnly, "and on bad days I can barely force myself to get out of bed."

By the time they climbed back into the car and started for the pharmacy, Helen noticed the strained look on Rachel's face had softened.

~

Later that evening, after the supper dishes had been washed, dried, and put away, the two women took steaming mugs of coffee and sat on the front porch. The warmth of the afternoon sun had vanished. Rachel bundled herself in George's heavy cardigan and covered Mama Dixon's shoulders with a wool afghan. After they'd settled themselves with Rachel on the wicker settee and Mama Dixon in the rocker, Rachel looked over and smiled.

"Thank you for what you did today."

"Thanks aren't necessary. I was glad to have you along to help with my errands."

"Mama Dixon, you didn't need any help, and you know it. You dragged me to that meeting so I'd see my friends and not spend the day crying."

"That may have been a consideration, but I was telling the truth about needing those new curtains."

"We never did get to the fabric store."

Mama Dixon creaked back and forth in the rocker and smiled. "Well then, I guess we'll just have to try again tomorrow."

For several minutes Rachel sat there, her cold hands wrapped around the warm mug, her voice silent. Finally she set the cup aside.

"It's my fault," she said, the words sorrowful and heavy as a cast-iron skillet.

Mama Dixon's eyes widened. "Your fault for what?"

"Losing Emmy." Rachel swiped the back of her hand across her eyes and brushed the tears from her cheeks. "I forgot to lock the back door that night."

Mama Dixon pushed herself up from the rocker, came across to Rachel, took hold of her hands, and looked square into her face.

"You're not a perfect person, Rachel; no one is. You're human. You make mistakes just as any human does, but you can't go through life blaming yourself for what happens."

"This wasn't a little mistake. We lost Emmy because of it."

"You can't undo what's done. But you can forgive yourself and move on with life. I know right now that sounds impossible, but it's not. I did it, and you can do it too."

"You did what?"

"Forgave myself for what happened to Tommy."

Still holding Rachel's right hand, Mama Dixon lowered herself onto the settee. "I don't talk about this very often because even though I've forgiven myself and learned to live with it, the thought of what happened to Tommy still pains my heart."

"Who's Tommy?"

"He would have been George's older brother," Mama Dixon said, "but he died when he was two months old."

Rachel gasped. "From what?"

"The doctor couldn't give it a name. He said sometimes a baby just stops breathing, but I blamed myself for it." Mama Dixon gave a sad, drawn-out sigh. "Tommy was a colicky baby who'd cry and cry until he wore himself out, then he'd finally fall asleep. That night I had a terrible headache, and after I put Tommy in his crib, I closed the door because the crying made my head hurt worse. When I opened the door the next morning, Tommy was lying there dead."

"Oh, how terrible!"

"Yes, it was." Mama Dixon nodded. "For the longest time I kept thinking that if I hadn't closed the door that night I might have heard Tommy choking and been able to save him."

"Maybe, maybe not," Rachel said.

"Exactly my point," Mama Dixon replied. "And if the person who took Emmy was determined to get to her, they might have found a way whether or not the door was locked."

"I doubt—"

"But you don't *know*. Nobody does. And hanging on to that guilt will just cause you to stop living."

For several minutes they sat hand in hand, saying nothing. When the mantel clock chimed ten, Mama Dixon stood.

"It's getting late; I should go."

"Please don't," Rachel said and tugged her back down onto the settee. Returning to the conversation, she asked, "How were you able to move on?"

"A heart doesn't heal all that easily. It took a year, maybe more. I didn't just wake up one morning feeling better about myself; it happened slowly. George's daddy helped a lot. Henry was a lot like George: kindhearted and patient as the day is long. At first I used to snap at him for every little thing, but the truth was I was angry with myself and not him. Once I realized that, things started to get better."

She hesitated a moment, then gave a soft chuckle. "It's funny how thinking of somebody other than yourself can help your heart to heal."

"I've been pretty testy with George also," Rachel admitted. "And a lot of times it wasn't called for."

"I think George understands what you're going through."

Rachel thought back to the night she waited up believing the sheriff would bring good news. Even after she'd turned George away, he'd come back a second time and held out his hand for her. She smiled and gave a nod. "I think you're right, Mama Dixon. Absolutely right."

That evening the two women sat on the front porch and talked until almost midnight. When they went inside, Rachel took a nightgown from the drawer and handed it to Mama Dixon.

"Don't go home tonight," she said. "Stay here."

Mama Dixon smiled and gave a nod.

~

A short while later, when Rachel crawled into bed, she lay there for a long while thinking of the things Mama Dixon had said, remembering how more than once she'd jumped down George's throat saying he was at fault for keeping her in bed that morning, yet not once had he blamed her for the unlocked door. When she was angry, he was patient. When she cried, he comforted. They were different in a thousand ways, but perhaps that difference was as it should be. When she was weak enough to crumble, he was strong enough to hold her together. Although she'd heard the soft snores of sleep, she scooted her back up against George's chest and whispered, "I love you, sweetheart."

He curled his arm around her shoulder, sleepily mumbled, "Me too," then dozed off again.

RETURN TO SENDER

Spring 1972

Vicki carried the letter she'd written to Murphy in the side pocket of her tote bag for well over a month before she gathered enough courage to mail it. When she finally added a return address in the corner of the envelope, it wasn't the house on Hillcrest Street. It was in care of Dimitri's Diner at 1217 Clover Road, Fairlawn, Kentucky.

Although in the letter she'd sworn to trust him, the truth was she didn't. Not altogether. For now, it was better if he didn't know about Angela and she didn't know about him. Once he agreed to keep her secret, she'd gladly introduce them. She'd explain that Murphy wasn't truly abusive; they'd simply been at odds with one another. She'd laugh and say it was hardly more than a lovers' quarrel, then invite Murph to dinner at the house. Afterward Kenny could show the movies of Lara's first Christmas. As soon as Vicki dropped the letter in the mailbox, she began imagining the fun they'd have.

Her mind raced ahead, jumping from one image to the next. She pictured the surprise on his face when he saw how the baby had grown. With seven months having gone by, he could relax and stop worrying that someone would recognize Lara as the missing baby. In all that time, no one—not a shopkeeper, a neighbor, or even her own sister—had questioned the fact that Lara was her child. She was confident that when they were all three together again, they would have the perfect life he'd described.

Before the day ended, Vicki had begun to make plans. On the way home from work she lingered in front of the houses along Hillcrest Street, eagerly anticipating which one they might someday buy. Later that week, Lucky's, a department store two blocks down from the diner, had a winter clearance sale, and Vicki bought three bright-red sweaters: one for Murphy, one for her, and a matching one for Lara. That night as she lay in bed waiting for sleep to come, she imagined the three of them posed in front of the Christmas tree as Angela snapped the picture. It would be one she'd frame and keep forever, sitting atop a mantel or on the bedroom dressing table.

A week passed without an answer to her letter, and a bothersome tic began to settle in her mind. It started the day she saw a man crossing the street with his arm snugged around a woman's waist. From the back he could have been Murphy. For a fleeting second she'd thought about the possibility Murphy had moved on, forgotten about her, found someone new. The thought came and went in less than a heartbeat, and moments later she'd chastised herself for such a foolish notion.

Absence makes the heart grow fonder.

She'd heard it a million times and knew it to be true. After seven long months she loved Murphy more than ever, loved him so much that just the tiniest remembrance of his touch caused a burning sensation to wrap itself around her spine.

The next day the tic was there again. This time it came from the young family sitting in the back booth of the diner. When the toddler threw a tantrum, the daddy got up, paid the bill, and walked out, leaving the harried mama to deal with the problem. Vicki tried to picture Murphy's reaction given the same set of circumstances. She wanted to believe he'd lift Lara into his arms and soothe her anguish, but like the toddler's daddy, he was nowhere to be found.

When the weekend finally rolled around, Vicki's stomach was in knots, and even though she'd eaten next to nothing, nauseating waves of acid indigestion plagued her.

"Whatever is wrong with you?" Angela asked.

"Probably something I ate at the diner," she said, shrugging it off, but she knew it wasn't what she ate. It was the terrible uncertainty that was gnawing away at her.

~

Three weeks to the day when Vicki had mailed the letter, Dimitri gave a nod and said there was something in her cubby. The envelope was lying facedown, but even before she picked it up and turned it over, the familiarity caused a wave of nausea to rise in her throat. It was the same envelope she'd dropped in the mailbox. As she stood there looking at the rubber-stamped words MOVED, NO FORWARDING ADDRESS, her heart skipped several beats.

Murphy would never do that to her, she told herself. He most likely moved back to Bardstown and was again living in Mrs. Bachinski's furnished apartment. That would make sense. That's where they were happiest. Feeling somewhat satisfied with this explanation, she stuffed the letter back into her cubby and placed her tote on top of it. Then she began thinking of what she would say when she wrote the second letter. She changed into her Dimitri's Diner shirt, tied on an apron, and readied herself for work.

An hour into her shift, she was recalling how she'd predicted they might one day return to the tiny apartment and suddenly remembered Murphy's words.

Once you cross a bridge, you can't go back.

That thought was like a door slammed in her face. *Moved. No forwarding address!*

All those weeks she'd waited for his answer, and now she realized this was it. Without speaking a word, he'd said his final goodbye.

No matter how good or bad yesterday was, once it's gone, it's gone.

He'd never wanted Lara in his life, and now he didn't want Vicki either. This was his way of telling her. He'd moved on without leaving a trail of bread crumbs for anyone to follow.

Her hand trembled as she set the coffeepot back on the burner.

"Are you okay?" Dimitri asked. "You don't look so good."

She shook her head, moving it only fractionally from side to side. "I might be coming down with something."

He reached around, untied her apron, and said, "You look terrible. Go home. Get some rest."

Without stopping to change her shirt, Vicki grabbed the letter, stuffed it into the bottom of her tote, and hurried from the diner. As she thought of the past seven months, tears filled her eyes. She'd suffered in silence, always believing Murphy was missing her as much as she was missing him. She'd never set aside their love. She'd stayed true. He hadn't.

At the corner, instead of waiting for the bus, she walked on for another nine blocks, then crossed over and followed the walkway that ran through the park. When her thoughts became so heavy that she could no longer move one foot in front of the other, she dropped down on a bench and gave way to the shuddering sobs drawn up from the deepest part of her soul. A line of dark clouds rolled in from the east, but she took no notice of them, because her face was hidden in her hands.

"How can he move on and forget about me?" she asked herself through the sobs. "Doesn't he care that I'm still in love with him?"

A sharp pain ricocheted across her chest, but it was small in comparison to the heartache she felt. Moments later the rain began, a drizzle at first, then large drops that splashed against her skin and drenched her clothes. Lost in thought, she barely noticed. She was remembering all they'd gone through together, the good times, the bad times, the final weekend when he'd given her a glimpse of their future together. Gone. All of it, now gone.

The truth hit her with a sickening thud. She'd loved him with all her heart, but he hadn't loved her. Not in the way that counted. Sure, he'd been happy to enjoy the good times, but when she asked for the three of them to become a family, he'd turned his back and walked away. *Moved. No. Forwarding. Address.* "Screw you, Murphy!" she screamed. "If you can forget me, I can forget you!"

With her breath now coming in ragged little puffs, she stood and started back toward the walkway. She moved with long strides and her mind racing, her determination greater than ever before. She could do it. She could start over and build a life of her own. She still had Lara, and that was the only thing that mattered. Halfway to the park entrance, a bolt of lightning sizzled across the sky, and she took off running toward the bus stop.

Moments later, a pain more powerful than any she'd ever known slammed into her chest. It was as sharp and quick as the lightning bolt and knocked her to her knees. The pain spread like a river cresting. It flooded her arms and legs, making them impossible to move. She opened her mouth, sucked in a gasp of breath, and tasted the salt of her tears. Before she could cry out, a second pain hit, worse than the first. She toppled forward, her face crashing down against the cement walkway.

An angry belch of thunder rolled across the sky.

Moments before she lost consciousness, a single thought crossed Vicki's mind.

I'm sorry.

She never spoke the words, but even if she had, no one was there to hear them. Not Murphy and not Rachel Dixon.

ANGELA'S CHILD

When the doorbell chimed, it woke Angela. She glanced at the bedside clock, saw it was after two, then swung her legs to the floor and snapped on the lamp.

Kenny opened one eye. "What's going on?"

"Vicki must have forgotten her key."

He gave a groan and turned toward the wall.

Angela hurried down the hallway, but before she could reach the knob, the bell chimed a second time. Concerned the noise would wake Lara, she yanked the door open, ready to lay into Vicki because of the hour.

The moment Angela saw the uniformed officer standing beside Dimitri, she knew something was wrong. Dimitri's nose was redder than usual and his face crumpled into a horrified look of tragedy.

"Has something happened to Vicki?" she asked, her voice breathy and filled with fear.

Dimitri nodded, and her knees buckled. He caught her and held his arm to brace her back as he walked her to the living room, eased her onto the sofa, and sat beside her. The officer followed them in, explaining that a woman walking her dog had come across Vicki's body in the park.

"They took her to Saint Vincent's, but there was nothing they could do," he said sympathetically.

Angela gave an anguished wail.

The sound roused Kenny. He appeared in the doorway of the room, snapped on the overhead light, and asked, "What's wrong?"

"I'm so sorry," Dimitri said. "It's Vicki; they found her in the park—"

"She's dead," Angela sobbed.

"Dead?" Kenny stared at them in disbelief. "I thought she was working! What the hell happened?"

Dimitri pulled a handkerchief from his pocket and handed it to Angela. "She wasn't feeling well and left work early—"

"We don't have an official cause of death yet," the officer said. "The hospital thinks it was a heart attack, but they'll have to do an autopsy."

Angela listened as the officer revealed the minuscule bits of information they had. Vicki apparently had gone to the park alone. She was alone when she died. No one could say why she was at the park. Although there was money in her tote, she had no identification other than the Dimitri's Diner shirt she wore.

Alone. That was the word Angela couldn't move past. It was heartbreaking enough to lose Vicki, but knowing she died alone made it worse. No one should have to die alone. And Vicki wasn't just alone; she was lonely.

Angela had seen the loneliness on Vicki's face that very first day. It was a haunted look, the kind that comes from deep inside, from the place where a person hides their darkest secrets. Back then, she assumed it was a temporary thing, a sadness brought about by the breakup with the man who was Lara's daddy. But now she was beginning to wonder.

As the officer ran through the gruesome details, Angela thought back on how from time to time she'd seen the odd look of melancholy in Vicki's expression. It came and went sometimes in a matter of minutes. She'd be happily playing with Lara, then suddenly drift off, glassy-eyed and lost in thought.

Angela pictured the last time she'd seen that look. Was it yesterday? Or the day before? She'd asked what Vicki was thinking about, and as suddenly as the look came it went.

Vicki had glanced up with a forced grin and said, "Nothing special." But her eyes were the eyes of a lost soul, a person burdened by an unspeakable sorrow. Whatever secret she'd had, she would now carry it to her grave.

When Dimitri and the officer finally left, the sun was on the edge of the horizon, and Angela could hear Lara stirring in her crib. She stiffened her back, brushed the tears from her cheeks, and stood. She could do nothing more for Vicki, but she could be a mother to Lara, and that's precisely what she would do.

~

Two days later the autopsy came back saying there was a small hole in Vicki's heart that had interrupted the blood flow. Angela read the report through once, then folded it back into the envelope and slid it into a drawer.

GOOD DAYS, BAD DAYS

Summer 1972

Rachel eventually decided not to cochair the library restoration committee, but when the campaign kicked off in April she offered to help out with placement. Loading two cartons of printed posters in the trunk of the car, she and Mama Dixon went from store to store asking Primrose County shopkeepers for a spot in the front window. By the end of the week, both cartons had been emptied out.

That summer was just as Rachel had predicted. She had good days and bad days. But the good days were all too often punctuated with some incident that would again open up wounds that never quite healed.

In early July, she and Mama Dixon were in Weston having lunch at the Sweet Spot when a young woman walked in pushing a stroller. From where Rachel was sitting it was impossible to see the child's face, but she couldn't miss the wispy blonde curls; they were exactly the same as Emily's. The menu Rachel held fell from her hand, and she sat there, eyes wide and mouth hanging open.

Mama Dixon was in the middle of saying she thought she'd have an egg salad sandwich when she noticed the expression on Rachel's face. "What's wrong?"

Without taking her eyes off the child, Rachel gave a nod toward the woman.

Helen turned and saw the golden-blonde curls. "Oh dear . . ."

"That looks exactly like . . ."

"The child looks like Emily, but it's not her," Mama Dixon said knowingly. She set her menu aside, reached out, and touched her hand to Rachel's arm. "You can see that baby's still an infant; she's not much older than Emily was when she was taken."

"No, no, she's—"

"Look at how she's slumped over in the stroller. Emily would be sitting straight now, probably walking and talking."

Seeing but not hearing, Rachel kept her eyes fixed on the child.

"It's been almost a year," Helen said.

Suddenly the terrible ache of longing made it almost impossible to breathe. All these months Rachel had held on to Emily as she was, a cuddly soft infant, but now she'd be learning to talk, calling some other woman "Mama." For Rachel, time had stood still, like the glass-enclosed pendulum of a broken clock. She'd remained mired in her world of sorrow, but Emily had moved on, grown into a toddler.

She'd forever remember, but Emily was just a baby. Babies forgot so quickly. That year had seemed a lifetime to her, but . . . Rachel's eyes filled with water, and she bit down on her lip as she came to realize the truth: to Emily she would now be little more than a stranger.

"Dear God," she whispered tearfully and buried her face in her hands.

~

In August, when the anniversary date of Emmy's kidnapping was only a week off, Rachel took a turn for the worse. For three days in a row she was too weary to get out of bed, and that Sunday she skipped going to church.

On Monday morning Mama Dixon arrived at the house carrying a shopping bag filled with skeins of wool. Ignoring the fact that Rachel was not yet out of her bathrobe, she said, "I'm way behind on these afghan squares and need you to lend a hand."

Rachel had no heart for needlework, but she owed Mama Dixon, so she settled into the chair and began to crochet. Helen said she needed thirty squares, but that afternoon they passed thirty and moved on to forty. At first Rachel's squares were stiff and tight, half the size of Helen's, but as she began to take notice of what she was doing, her fingers found an easy rhythm. In time, you could not tell one woman's work from the other.

At the end of the day Helen suggested that if they were to keep working, they might be able to finish two afghans in time for the bazaar. And oddly enough, Rachel agreed.

~

The anniversary of Emmy's kidnapping was stretched over two days, because no one could say for sure whether she was taken late Sunday night or in the wee hours of Monday morning. On the first night Rachel was haunted by the memory of how the back door had been left unlocked. She blamed herself and there was nothing George could say or do to change that. Weary of such thoughts, she finally swallowed one of the little blue pills she'd taken during the first few weeks of Emmy being gone and climbed into bed. The moon was on the rise, and a narrow beam of light slipped through the summer-weight curtains. Before she had time to fall asleep, George climbed in beside her. He hesitated a moment, then moved closer, his shoulder warm against hers, his head resting on the edge of her pillow.

For a long while the only sound was the rise and fall of their breath, hers rapid and shallow, his long and labored. In time, she turned her face to his, and he saw the glisten of a teardrop on her cheek.

He touched his hand to her cheek and brushed back the tear. "Rachel, you might think I don't understand your heartache, but I do.

I swear I do. I don't say it all the time, but not a day goes by that I don't think of Emmy. The ache that's in your heart is just as heavy in mine."

"You hardly ever mention her name. I thought maybe you'd forgotten."

"Never," he said. "Every day I ask God to watch over her. I pray that she's loved and cared for . . ."

There was a moment of hesitation; then he added, "And I pray that He'll one day bring her back to us."

"Do you honestly think we'll ever see her again?"

His answer was slow in coming.

"Yes, I do," he said, the sound of hope in the undercurrent of his words. "I believe God has heard our prayers and will someday answer them."

"He hasn't answered them so far."

"I know. But I keep believing. When I feel doubt creeping up on me, I think back on what happened with Badger."

"Badger?"

George nodded. "The dog I had when I was a kid. I loved that mutt more than anything. Then one day he just disappeared. Daddy drove all over town looking for him, but he was nowhere to be found. I cried my eyes out over that dog. Two years later he came trotting up the front walkway as if he'd never been gone."

Rachel turned her face to his. "Did you find out where he'd been all that time?"

"No, but it didn't matter, because I had him back."

~

That first year was the most difficult. Everything seemed a reminder of what they'd lost. The days dragged on, long and heavy until they finally became weeks, and the weeks then struggled to become months.

Rachel was like the oak in Mama Dixon's front yard, which no longer had life in it yet somehow managed to remain standing. For a long while she was as dry and brittle as that oak. Then in the spring of 1973, the tree sprouted green buds, and she too began a return to life.

It didn't happen all at once but came in slow bits and pieces: an afternoon of shopping with Mama Dixon, a few meetings with the Hesterville Women's League, a night at the movies with George, and then the four-day trip to Atlanta for the Hardware Dealers Convention.

When George first mentioned it, Rachel claimed she wasn't up to socializing. "I'm not very good company these days."

"Maybe you'll feel better if you get away from the house for a while."

She shook her head. "I should be here in case . . ."

"It's going on two years, honey. If the sheriff comes up with something, he can call us at the hotel."

Although it took some convincing, Rachel finally agreed to go, and the trip, while not quite a turning point, became the start of one.

On the last night of the convention they dined at The Palm with a couple from Chicago, and for the first time in nearly two years Rachel found herself laughing. It was not simply a polite pretense of laughter but a musical sound that settled sweetly on George's ears.

After dinner, the orchestra played "Bridge Over Troubled Water," and they danced. As George held her close, his hand firm against her back, she lowered her head onto his chest.

"This is nice," she whispered.

For the first time since that fateful morning she allowed her body to feel what it had once felt. That night in a hotel room that held none of the painful memories, they found their way back to being lovers. His touch was slow and unhurried, her response filled with warmth and unbridled passion. Although they'd been married for almost four years, it was as if they were discovering each other for the first time.

Afterward as they lay curled together, her drifting on the edge of sleep, he whispered, "We're going to make it, Rachel. We've gone through the worst that can happen, but we will survive."

That year the good days outnumbered the bad ones, and Helen seemed to know when a bad day was on the horizon. Before Rachel could fall into a fit of depression, Mama Dixon was standing on the doorstep with yet another project that needed to be done. In December when the church held their Christmas bazaar, the two women donated five afghans. Prayers for Emmy were woven into every stitch.

THE JOY OF MOTHERHOOD

Fairlawn, 1972

Once Vicki was gone, the McAlister family's life changed. Angela never did go back to work at the diner. She couldn't. The thought of spending her days in a place so closely linked to her sister's death was daunting.

"You'll have to find a new counter girl to work the morning shift," she told Dimitri, and offered to return the uniform shirt hanging in her closet.

"Hold on to it," he said. "After a while you might feel differently. When you're ready to get back to work, we'll have a place for you here."

Although she doubted she'd be ready anytime in the foreseeable future, Angela kept the shirt. But before the week was out she realized that even the sight of it brought back the most terrible memories of Vicki's death. She pushed the black shirt to the back of the closet, behind a heavy wool coat she hadn't worn in years, and that's where it remained.

The truth was she blamed herself for Vicki's death.

"If I hadn't gotten her that job at the diner, she wouldn't have been working that day," Angela claimed, "and if she wasn't working she wouldn't have been wandering around the park alone and in the rain."

"Vicki's death had nothing to do with the job," Kenny argued. "It was her heart. The coroner's report said so."

"All the same, I'd feel better looking for a job elsewhere."

"You don't need a job. We can manage without a second income. Stay home and be a full-time mom to Lara."

At first such an idea appeared somehow foreign to Angela. She'd been working since she was sixteen years old and couldn't imagine getting up in the morning with no place to hurry off to. In an odd way, it seemed almost *lazy*.

Their discussion over the practicality of this idea went back and forth for a while, but after a few short weeks of being at home with Lara, Angela knew Kenny was right. By then she'd become Lara's mama, and the thought of whether or not they could afford a new car or summer vacation no longer mattered. She was focused on more important things, things such as good-night kisses, morning hugs, and afternoon walks to the park. An aunt's fondness had morphed into a mother's love, the kind of love that says you will never be left alone; you will always have a hand to hold.

When Lara learned to speak, Angela was "Mama" and Kenny "Daddy." They were a family. Angela held on to the hope that Lara would someday have a baby brother or sister, but it never happened. So she and Kenny poured all their love into Lara.

~

That first year, the McAlisters had a number of discussions about trying to locate the man who was Lara's daddy. Angela thought it was something they should look into; Kenny disagreed.

"He's her biological father," Angela said. "It's not important now, but in the future, Lara might want to know who he is."

"Why?" Kenny asked.

She gave a mystified shrug. "I'm not certain, but when I was at the telephone company I worked with a girl who was adopted, and she was always saying she'd give *anything* to know her real parents."

"Lara isn't adopted! She's your sister's child. Vicki was her birth mother, and you're a blood relative. Isn't that enough?"

"For now, yes. But with Vicki gone . . ."

"Listen, your sister wanted nothing to do with the guy, so there must have been a reason. He's probably trouble."

Angela was going to remind him that Vicki could be somewhat less than truthful and often saw things in an altered reality, but she held back. In the months before her death, Vicki had been different, softer perhaps, more accepting of life. It wasn't a specific behavior that Angela could point to and say this or that changed. It was more gradual, like a lazy sunset or the wind shifting direction.

Nothing was ever resolved. One year turned into two, and by the time Lara celebrated her second birthday, the thought was all but forgotten. Angela scheduled her days around afternoon naps, visits to the park, and library storytelling sessions.

The idea of finding Lara's daddy remained in Angela's head, but with the passing of time it became less and less important. On the rare occasions when she did think of it, his name was little more than a vague recollection. When she tried to remember, it came as a jumble of thoughts—Russ Morrissey? Morris Russell? Russ Murphy?

THE THING ABOUT LOVE

Spring 1973

In the early months of their marriage, George and Rachel had planned to have three, maybe four children. After losing Emmy, they never spoke of it again. Then one evening George found her standing beside the empty crib, looking down as if she were watching Emmy sleep.

Thinking this might mean a change of heart, he came up behind her, wrapped his arms around her waist, and kissed the back of her neck.

"Are you thinking about us having another baby?"

She shook her head, stood there for a few minutes, then began to sob.

"I can't," she said. "That would be the same as admitting we've given up on finding Emmy and ordered a replacement."

George took hold of Rachel's shoulders and turned her to face him.

"It's not like that at all," he said. "Having another child doesn't mean we'll ever stop hoping to find Emmy."

She lowered her eyes and looked away. "That's what you say now, but having a baby changes things."

"Yes, but it's always for the better."

"Not always. Most of the time, maybe. There's also a very real possibility that the baby will be a constant reminder of Emmy. What happens then?"

"Then we'll celebrate the fact that we have another child to help keep the memories of Emmy alive in our hearts." He pulled her close and traced his thumb across her cheek to brush back the tears.

"I know the thought of loving another child is a scary thing right now," he said, "but I trust the goodness you have in your heart, Rachel, and I believe you'll love our second child as much as you loved the first."

"Perhaps . . ."

Several moments of hesitation followed; then she turned away without ever speaking of the deeper fear hidden in her heart.

~

The next afternoon as she and Mama Dixon sat on the front porch crocheting granny squares, Rachel couldn't stop thinking of her conversation with George and of what he'd said about having another baby. At times the thought seemed a way of moving forward, then moments later it was simply too painful to bear.

The two women sat in silence for a long while before Rachel found courage enough to broach the subject. "Were you hesitant about having another baby after you lost Tommy?" she asked.

Mama Dixon lowered the square she'd been working on into her lap and gave a pensive nod. "Yes, I suppose I was."

Feeling her own fears justified, Rachel said, "Because you thought the second baby would be a reminder of Tommy, right?"

Mama Dixon picked up her crocheting and sat there with the needle not moving.

"Being reminded of somebody you've loved isn't a bad thing," she said. "But I was afraid I wasn't skilled enough. I worried that I'd do something wrong and lose the second baby like I lost Tommy."

She wrinkled her forehead like she was remembering something, then snagged a loop of yarn and pulled it through the slip stitch. "For a while I got so caught up in all that worrying, I almost forgot about how much joy having a little one can bring."

That thought intrigued Rachel. "So what changed?" she asked. "What made you decide to have another baby?"

"I didn't decide. I left it up to God. I told Him that I didn't know if I was deserving of another baby, but if He thought I was, I'd be mighty grateful for the chance."

"That's when you got pregnant?"

Mama Dixon gave a big round laugh.

"Not exactly," she said. "Henry and I tried for over a year, and I was almost to the point of believing that was God's answer; then it happened."

"You and Henry were pretty happy, I suppose?"

"Of course we were happy, but that wasn't the end of my worries about being a good-enough mama."

Rachel couldn't imagine Mama Dixon not being a good mama. She set aside her granny square and leaned forward. "George turned out just fine, so how'd you finally move past all that worry?"

Mama Dixon hesitated a moment, then smiled. "I never did, but before I had time enough to think about it, George was half-grown, out the door, and on his way to school."

She reached across and took Rachel's hand in hers.

"That's the thing about babies," she said. "They're not something you can hold on to forever. You get to enjoy them for a while, but in time they grow up and branch out to start having a life of their own."

"Good grief, that's so sad."

"No, it's not," Mama Dixon argued. "It's the way of life. The sooner a woman realizes it, the happier she'll be."

Thinking back on how Mama Dixon had made her disapproval of their marriage so blatantly obvious, Rachel said, "Well, you didn't seem to think that when George left home."

"I sure enough didn't." Mama Dixon snickered. "Most mamas aren't happy to see their kids leave home, but, ashamed as I am to admit it, I was the worst of the lot. I made everybody around me miserable, and it was a long time before I realized the only one I was really hurting was myself."

"How's that?"

"I was depriving myself of the thing I wanted most." Mama Dixon peered over her glasses and added, "A family."

Rachel smiled, gave her hand a squeeze, then went back to crocheting.

Mama Dixon set aside the granny square she'd been working on, then eyed Rachel's stack.

"You're way behind," she said. "You'd better get a move on."

~

In the weeks that followed, the two women had several more in-depth conversations. Rachel found it easy to confide in Mama Dixon, and as that spring turned into summer she began to talk about her fears.

They were sitting at Mama Dixon's kitchen table having a second cup of coffee when out of the blue she said, "George wants to have another baby, but I'm afraid that if we do, Emmy will be forgotten and we'll lose whatever hope we have of getting her back."

"That's one worry you don't need to have," Mama Dixon replied. "You won't ever forget Emmy. You're her mama, and once a mama has held her baby in her arms, that child is forever in her heart. There's no such thing as forgetting, even if you try."

"Why would any mother try to forget her own child?"

Mama Dixon pushed her cup to the side and leaned in. "It's obvious you haven't heard of the Lambert family. Now there was a mama who had plenty of cause for wanting to forget her boy, but even she couldn't do it."

"Why'd she—"

"Because he was a cold-blooded killer, that's why! Louie Lambert—you must've heard of him?"

When Rachel shook her head, Mama Dixon went on with the story.

"Louie was about five years older than George and spoiled rotten. Parents gave him the best of everything, but that boy grew up mean as a striped-ass snake. As soon as he got old enough to sass, him and his daddy would go toe to toe, and Alma, she was his mama, always took Louie's side. Then one day Louie just up and shot his daddy straight through the heart!"

Rachel gasped. "No . . ."

"Yes, indeed. Come to find out, the very same morning Louie had argued with his daddy about taking the car; then later that night he shot him. Claimed he mistook his daddy for a burglar, but everybody knew different, even Alma."

"What'd she do?"

"Throughout the trial she sat there sobbing, and most people figured it was because of Saul being killed, but when Louie was sentenced to twenty years in the state penitentiary, she up and moved to Reidsville so she'd be close enough to visit him once a week."

"I can't believe it!"

"Well, it's true. So you see what I mean, don't you?"

Looking more puzzled than not, Rachel shook her head.

"Alma had every reason to turn her back on that boy and forget about him, but she couldn't do it. That just goes to show a mama's baby is her baby forever, no matter what happens."

When Rachel didn't argue the point, Mama Dixon leaned back in her chair and downed the last of her coffee. With a bit of melancholy woven through the thought, she said, "I know a mama never forgets, because even after all these years I can close my eyes and picture Tommy's sweet little face."

"You sure that's not George's face you're seeing?"

"I'm positive. George has dark eyes like his daddy, but Tommy, he had my eyes: blue as the sky on the first day of spring."

Rachel could feel the truth of what Mama Dixon said. The image of Emily's precious smile would be with her forever. Even if she lived to be a very old woman, she would still be able to picture that innocent baby face and eyes as blue as her own. It was a thought that on cold nights would bring a measure of warmth.

~

In August, when the sun was blistering hot and they'd moved inside to sit in front of the fan, Rachel finally let go of the one worry she'd kept to herself. It happened an hour into the afternoon as they sat across from one another crocheting. Mama Dixon pushed aside the basket of yarn and swiped at the line of perspiration trickling down the valley of her bosom.

She stood and said, "It's too darn hot to be doing this. I'm going home and setting myself in a cool tub of water."

Rachel jumped up. "Don't go yet; I was just about to fix us a glass of sweet tea."

Mama Dixon raised a suspicious eyebrow. "Is there something special you want to talk about?"

"Why would you think that?"

"Because that crochet hook of yours hasn't moved in nearly an hour. So either you're feeling the heat as much as I am, or there's something on your mind."

"I guess it's a little of both," Rachel replied sheepishly.

The two women settled at the table with their tea, and Rachel told Mama Dixon something she'd carried around for almost two years without admitting it to herself.

"I didn't realize it at first, but I'm a lot like you were," she said. "Afraid of loving and losing another baby. Okay, I'll never leave the door unlocked again, but what if this time something else happens? Something I'm not prepared for?"

Mama Dixon wiped the condensation from beneath her glass and took her time in answering.

"Things will happen," she finally said. "That's life. You spend each day living, loving, and learning. The learning, that's the hard part. You might think you're ready to be a mama, but then something happens and you start doubting yourself."

"But I thought you got over being afraid."

Mama Dixon laughed. "You never truly get over being afraid. Fear settles in your heart the day you learn you're gonna be a mama, but somehow you stumble through doing the best you can, always hoping it's good enough."

That afternoon they talked for hours, Rachel giving voice to her fears and Mama Dixon telling of how she'd suffered through the very same misgivings. When she finally stood to leave, it was near suppertime, and the heat of the afternoon had begun to dissipate.

"Feels like it's getting cooler," Rachel said.

Mama Dixon nodded. "Yes, it does."

"George will be home soon, so why don't you stay for supper? Afterward we can sit on the porch and catch up on our crocheting."

A smile creased Mama Dixon's wrinkled face. "That sounds like a fine idea, a very fine idea."

That evening the three of them sat on the porch long after the lamp was lit and the moon high in the sky. As Rachel watched George reading his newspaper and Mama Dixon nodding off, she thought back on the day's conversation. After so many months of heartache and fear she'd thought she'd never have the courage to love again, but she was wrong. She loved George as much as ever, and now she'd also come to love Mama Dixon.

COMES THE FALL

Hesterville, 1973

In late September, when apples were at their peak of flavor and the smell of fall was in the air, Mama Dixon suggested she and Rachel pay a visit to the Penny Lane Orchard. It was said that Penny Lane had the sweetest apples in the state of Georgia, and during picking season people drove for miles to line up at the door and buy a bushel basket. The orchard was a two-hour drive away, but considering how fond George was of his mama's apple turnovers, Rachel agreed.

"It'll take us a while to get there," she said, "so maybe you should sleep over tonight so we can get an early start in the morning."

"I sleep better in my own bed," Mama Dixon replied. "And besides, I need to copy down my turnover recipe for you. When we get back, I'll teach you the secret to a crispy crust."

A short while later, she left. Before getting into her car and driving off, Mama Dixon said she'd pick Rachel up by nine so they'd be back in time to bake the turnovers.

~

For Mama Dixon, by nine meant closer to eight, but the next morning nine came and went without any sign of her. Figuring it to be nothing more than a slow-going start, Rachel poured a second cup of coffee and sat down to wait. Two days earlier, the mailman had delivered the new issue of *Good Housekeeping*, the one that boasted eighteen pages of recipes from their cookbook; she glanced at her watch, then began to leaf through the magazine.

Fifteen minutes later she closed the magazine and started considering whether or not to call. Twice she picked up the receiver, began to dial, then hung up. Mama Dixon's arthritis had been acting up, and there was no need to rush her if she'd had a bad night.

A half hour ticked by as Rachel sat there letting her coffee grow cold, and by ten she decided she'd waited long enough. Dumping the last bit of coffee down the drain, she dialed the number and listened as the phone rang a dozen or more times.

No answer—that's odd.

Thinking maybe she'd made a mistake, she redialed the number. Still no answer.

Rachel replaced the receiver and stood there thinking. It wasn't like Mama Dixon to make plans and not follow through. If she was sick or having car trouble, she would have called. Suddenly another thought hit: perhaps her car broke down somewhere along the road.

The notion of Mama Dixon alone and stranded was somewhat daunting. Rachel stepped out onto the front porch and leaned over the rail, hoping to see the old Ford chugging down the road. There was no sign of either Mama Dixon or the car.

She stood there for a few minutes on her tiptoes, craning her neck to see beyond the bend, but to no avail. The road was as quiet and lifeless as a church on Saturday night.

Returning to the house, she dialed the hardware store.

"George," she said, "I was expecting your mama this morning, and she should have been here by now. Have you heard from her?"

"No, but you know how Mama is. She may have stopped by the library or decided to run an errand on the way."

"I don't think so. We were planning to—"

"Honey, I've got to go," he cut in. "There are two customers in the store, and the guy from Black and Decker is waiting for me to approve an order."

Seconds later there was a click, and he was gone.

Rachel peered out the window. George had driven the good car this morning, so she was left with the troublesome Buick that sometimes turned over and sometimes didn't. She eyed the car sitting in the driveway. He knew how to jump-start it, but she didn't. All she could do was hope that today was one of its better days.

She grabbed her purse, hurried across the lawn, and climbed in. As she slid the key into the ignition, she muttered, "Start. Please start."

The Buick just sat there. When she turned the key, a click-click-click sounded, then nothing.

"Don't do this," she moaned, then turned the key again. Not even a click this time.

She pushed back from the steering wheel, trying to remember how it was that George got the car started. She closed her eyes and pictured him behind the wheel.

If you flood the engine, it won't start, he'd said. *You've got to be patient.*

He'd switched the key back and forth several times, turning it from "Off" to "Start," then with one foot on the brake and the other on the clutch, he'd shifted from "Park" to first gear, second gear, third gear, then neutral.

She slid the seat forward and tried again, this time doing everything just as she remembered. After shifting back into neutral, she pumped the accelerator and turned the key. The engine groaned, choked, and sputtered, then turned over, but before she could slide the gearshift into "Reverse," it died. Leaving her purse on the seat, she hurried back into the house and called George.

Before he'd finished his hello, she said, "I can't get the car started!"

"Rachel? Is that you?"

"Of course it's me," she snapped. "This god-awful Buick won't start."

"Did you floor the accelerator and hold it?"

"Floor it? I thought you said pump it."

"No, that'll flood the engine. When you tried to start the car, did you smell gasoline?"

"Yes, a little bit."

"Okay, wait five minutes, then try it with the accelerator floored. Why didn't you tell me you needed the car today? I could have taken the Buick."

"I wasn't planning on it. Your mama was supposed to pick me up, but she never showed. She hasn't called, and I'm concerned that she might have had car trouble on the way. I'm going to drive out and look for her."

"I'm sure she's okay," George said. "Mama keeps that Ford in pretty good shape. If you want, I can go look for her after I finish up with this guy from Black and Decker."

Rachel thought about it for a moment. "I'd just as soon do it myself. But if I still can't get the car started, I'll call you back."

The smell of gasoline was less pungent when she returned to the car. Sliding behind the wheel, she pressed the accelerator to the floor, held it for a good thirty seconds, then turned the key. The engine sputtered to life and kept chugging.

The trip to town was less than twenty minutes. As Rachel drove, she scanned both sides of the road searching for Mama Dixon or the broken-down car. There was no sign of either until she pulled into the driveway. The black Ford was parked back by the garage.

Her back stiffened, and the acid reminder of coffee rose in her throat.

Crossing the lawn rather than following the walkway, she hurried around, took the front steps two at a time, then stood on the porch ding-donging the bell. Standing where she was, she could hear the echo of the doorbell inside the house, but that was it. There was no shuffling of footsteps, no calling out, "Just a minute," nothing. She tried twisting the doorknob, but it didn't budge. Locked.

Suddenly Rachel felt the same sense of panic she'd felt the morning she looked down and saw an empty crib. She began banging on the door with both fists.

"Mama Dixon!" she yelled. "Are you in there?"

Nothing. Not even the smallest sound.

"Mama Dixon!" she screamed again and again.

A key. There has to be a spare key hidden somewhere.

Hauling over the wicker chair, she stood on the seat and ran her fingers along the top frame of the door. Nothing. No key atop the door or windows. She knocked over the flowerpots sitting along the rail; still nothing. As she searched she continued calling out for Mama Dixon, her heart now thudding against her chest harder than her fists had pounded on the door.

When Rachel ran out of places to search for a key, the thought of driving over to get George flashed through her head, but she dismissed it. It was a ten-minute drive to the store, and she had to do something right now.

Although she was small and not muscular, she hefted the wicker chair into her arms, then backed up and ran straight at the front window. The legs of the chair broke through, and the window shattered. She kept the seat in front of her face as chunks of glass exploded into the air. Most of the glass landed inside, but razor-sharp shards scattered across the porch. Stepping carefully, Rachel approached the window and leaned in.

"Mama Dixon," she yelled, "are you okay?"

No answer.

Using the legs of the chair, she knocked out the remaining pieces of glass, then climbed through the frame. Pushing aside the curtains, she moved toward the hall. That was when she saw Mama Dixon's body at the foot of the stairs.

Rachel heard herself scream. It was a shrill, ear-piercing sound that would linger in her head for months afterward. Although she did everything that was necessary, later on she would have almost no memory of it.

A PROMISE MADE

Glass from the window was everywhere, mostly in the living room but fanned out into the dining room and hallway as well. Instead of picking her way across the floor, Rachel rushed over and knelt beside the body. Brushing a piece of glass from the front of Mama Dixon's blouse, she ran a hand across her chest trying to feel the thump of a heartbeat.

Don't be dead. Please, please don't be dead.

Mama Dixon was on her back, her right arm twisted at an odd angle, her left hand wedged between her thigh and the bottom step. With panic swelling inside her chest and her hand trembling, Rachel pushed the thigh aside and freed the left hand. She took the limp wrist between her fingers and waited to feel a pulse. At first, there was nothing; then she felt the thrum. Weak and erratic but there.

She jumped up, grabbed the phone, and called for an ambulance. After that she dialed the number for the store and did not wait for George's hello.

"Your mama's had an accident," she shouted. "Get over here as quick as you can!"

"Rachel? Where are you?"

"At Mama's house. I think she fell down the stairs."

"Good Lord!" George exclaimed. "Is she okay?"

His question was so direct that for a moment her heart stopped beating. The realization that she couldn't answer was like a slap in the face. She began to sob, and the words felt sharp in her throat.

"I don't know."

When she hung up the phone, Rachel returned to Mama Dixon's side and knelt there, holding her hand and whispering a prayer for God to spare her life.

"Please don't take Mama away from us," she said through her tears. "You've already taken our baby. Isn't that enough?"

The words came in spurts, first angry, then prayerful, then fragile and broken with pieces of her heart stuck to every syllable.

The ambulance arrived first, and George came moments later. He rushed over and squatted beside Rachel.

"Any change?"

She looked up, her eyes red-rimmed and sorrowful. "None."

He reached in and pried her hand from his mama's. "Honey, you've got to move back so these men can get Mama onto the stretcher."

With his arm around her back and his hand lifting her elbow, he urged Rachel to her feet and stepped aside. The ambulance driver and attendant moved in. After they'd taken Mama Dixon's vital signs and slipped an oxygen mask over her nose, they eased her onto a stretcher and carried her to the ambulance. George looked at his mama as she lay there motionless, one arm swollen to twice the size of the other and her leg turned blue.

His voice cracked when he asked, "Is she going to be okay?"

The driver gave a helpless-looking shrug. "That's a question for the doc. But first we've got to get her to the hospital."

"Do you want to ride with Mama, and I'll follow in the car?" George asked.

Rachel nodded, then climbed into the back of the ambulance and sat alongside the gurney, holding Mama Dixon's hand. As the siren screamed through the quiet streets of Hesterville, she noticed the green blouse. The shoulder was ripped, and a button was missing, but it was the same one Mama Dixon had worn yesterday.

It happened last night, not this morning!

The ambulance took a sharp corner, and Rachel slid sideways, banging her arm against a metal rack as she braced herself. The radio squawked, the siren screamed, the attendant shouted numbers to the driver, but the only thing Rachel could think of was Mama Dixon lying there helpless and in pain throughout the night. She pictured her calling out over and over again when there was no one to answer.

If she or George had been there, it would have been different. They would have gotten help sooner or the accident would never have happened. Instead of lying on the floor with no one to answer her call for help, Mama Dixon would have been sitting across from her in the living room saying, "Rachel, would you be a dear and fetch my yarn basket from upstairs?"

Rachel would have done it in a heartbeat. She was young and could dash up the stairs and back down in less than a minute. But Mama Dixon, with her arthritic knee, was slower and less sure-footed, more likely to misjudge a step.

She was all but certain that if they'd been there, Mama Dixon would be sitting in a chair with a pile of crocheted squares in her lap instead of strapped to a stretcher with her eyes closed and her body broken.

She leaned over and whispered, "Please get well and come home to us, and I promise you'll never have to be alone again."

Although the ambulance attendant claimed such a thing was unlikely, Rachel swore that at precisely that moment the limp fingers squeezed her hand.

~

As it turned out, Mama Dixon had a broken hip, a fractured pelvis, and a hairline crack in the humerus of her right arm. That afternoon she was wheeled into surgery while Rachel and George sat and waited nervously. After nearly five hours of worrying, Dr. Wilcox came to the waiting room and told them the surgery had gone well, and Helen was now in recovery.

"Is she going to be all right?" George asked anxiously.

"I believe so," Dr. Wilcox said, "but because her bone was shattered it was a rather complex surgery. Until that new hip is secure, there's the risk of infection."

"Is there anything—"

Dr. Wilcox shook his head. "Not right now, but once she's released, she'll need someone to take care of her."

"That's not a problem," Rachel said. "We're family. We'll be there."

~

Mama Dixon remained in the hospital for two weeks, and Rachel came to visit twice a day. For the first few days while she was still groggy and in a fair bit of pain, Rachel sat silently by her bedside, sometimes crocheting, often just holding her hand and saying how fortunate they were that she'd gotten there when she did. Once she began feeling better, Rachel brought the yarn basket and stayed long after visiting hours were over.

She told of how she'd broken through the window and found Mama Dixon at the bottom of the staircase and spoke about the changes they would need to make moving forward.

"George is adamant about your not living alone," she said. "He's suggested we take the crib out of Emmy's room and fix it so that it's nice and comfortable for you."

Mama Dixon, as feisty as ever, shook her head and claimed she was just as adamant about staying in town.

"I've got a lifetime of good memories in that house, and I'm not about to leave it."

"Dr. Wilcox said no stairs for at least six months," Rachel warned.

"My hearing is just fine, and I know what he said." She gave a sly grin and added, "So I'm figuring I'd take the small sitting room downstairs for myself and let you and George have the rest of the house."

"Mama Dixon! You know we couldn't possibly—"

"Stuff and nonsense. When I pass on, the house will go to you and George anyway. All I'm suggesting is that the three of us could live together and enjoy it while I'm still alive."

For the next two days they went back and forth over it, Mama Dixon arguing that her house was big enough for nine people to live comfortably and close enough for George to walk to the hardware store. Rachel wasn't swayed and remained reluctant to leave their little house behind. She and George talked about it several times, twice over breakfast and every evening as they sat across from one another at the supper table.

"I'm okay with doing either one," he said. "The most important thing is that I want you to be happy. Whatever makes you happy will make me happy also."

Rachel kissed him and said she loved him all the more for having such an attitude, but it did nothing to solve the dilemma they were facing.

Then, five days before Mama Dixon was scheduled to be released from the hospital, Rachel returned home later than usual. As she pulled into the driveway, she noticed how the tall pines cast long, dark shadows across the lawn, and in an odd way it looked eerily foreboding. She sat in the car for several minutes, looking one way and then the other. No matter which way she turned, she could not see another house. Not even the smoke of another chimney. On Pecan Street where Mama Dixon lived, houses lined both sides of the street, and on the corner a streetlamp lit the walkways.

That evening Rachel stood in the doorway of Emmy's room and tried to imagine it without the crib, the changing table, and the rocking chair. She couldn't. Mama Dixon's house was filled with good memories, but this place would forever have the memory of the night Emmy was taken.

The next morning Rachel told Mama Dixon that she and George would be happy to live in her lovely house and would move in before she was home from the hospital.

In the few remaining days, Rachel went through the house packing the things she would take and pushing aside the things to be discarded. The nursery was last. Emily's rompers and frilly dresses held good memories and still had a faint scent of her clinging to them, so Rachel folded them carefully, layered them with tissue paper, and packed them into a box that would go to Pecan Street. It had been easy to decide they'd no longer need the flowered sofa and a kitchen table that was too small to begin with, but when it came to Emily's crib, the decision was impossible. There were both good and bad memories attached to it, and she couldn't decide which outweighed the other. She waited until George arrived home from the store that evening, then tearfully explained the dilemma.

She told him of how she'd saved the baby clothes but simply couldn't deal with the crib. "Every time I see it, it's a reminder of the night Emily was taken."

Looking at her, George could see the sorrow of such a decision draped across her shoulders like a leaden cloak. "I doubt the bad memories attached to that crib will ever go away," he said. "So maybe it's better we let go of it."

Rachel's jaw dropped, and she looked up with an expression of astonishment. "Just walk away and leave it sitting here?"

"No." George shook his head. "I was thinking I'd take it to Goodwill and let someone in need of a crib have it."

"But . . ." Rachel was going to ask if anyone would want a crib with such unhappy memories attached to it, but George addressed the thought before she gave it voice.

"There's nothing wrong with the crib itself; the bad memories that are part of it belong to us and us alone. They can't be passed along. To some needy family this will be nothing more than a nice sturdy crib for their new baby."

~

The next afternoon while Rachel was at the hospital visiting Mama Dixon, George closed the store and hung a sign on the door saying he'd be back in two hours. He drove home, cleared out the nursery, and brought the furniture to the Goodwill store in Chester.

The door to Emily's room was closed when Rachel arrived home that afternoon, and she sensed it was best left that way.

The following morning after the moving van carried off the things marked for Pecan Street, Rachel closed the front door and didn't look back. As she left the drive and started for town, a tear overflowed her eye and rolled down her cheek. She brushed it back and kept going. If she and George were ever going to find a future, she knew the sorrow had to be left behind in that house.

FINDING THE LETTER

Fairlawn, 1973

A year after Vicki's death, Angela received a telephone call from Dimitri.

"I've got something I think you might want to have," he said. "Would it be okay if I stop by this afternoon?"

"Of course," Angela replied. "It will be good to see you." She fully expected he'd be bringing some memento from the diner, along with a request that she think about coming back to work.

Two hours later the bell chimed, and when she opened the door Dimitri was holding a brown tote bag. "This belonged to Vicki, and I thought you might want to have it."

"Oh my God!" Angela reached for the bag as she swung the door back and motioned Dimitri inside. "I don't understand. How did you—"

"The same night Vicki died, there was a three-car pileup on the interstate and the emergency room at Saint Vincent's was crazy. With all those patients coming in, Vicki's tote was set aside and forgotten. When a nurse finally noticed it and couldn't find any ID in the bag, it was sent to lost and found. Two days ago, an aide was clearing out the older items and found a letter in the tote. It had Vicki's name and the diner's return address, so she called me."

Shaking her head in utter amazement, Angela said, "It's hard to believe that after all this time . . ."

"Yeah." Dimitri laughed. "It's been a while." After telling how they had five new waitresses come and go, he asked if she'd be interested in coming back to work.

"No way," Angela said and smiled. "I'm a mama now, and that occupies every minute of my day." Just as she started to say Vicki's baby had grown into a little girl and was talking a blue streak, Lara came running into the room.

"Mama, Mama, my book fell . . ." She spotted Dimitri, stopped, then edged her way over to stand beside Angela.

"Don't tell me this is Vicki's baby!" he said with a look of surprise.

"It certainly is." Angela's face was aglow with a look of pride. "Lara's going on three now. She already knows her alphabet and can count to ten."

"Wanna hear me sing the ABC song?" Lara volunteered.

Dimitri laughed. "Yeah, okay."

In a squeaky little-girl voice, Lara ran through the letters and did fine until she got to the *X*; then she looked up. "Mama, what comes next?"

"*Y* and *Z*."

Lara giggled, then finished off the song.

After saying what a wonderful job she'd done, Dimitri looked back at Angela, his expression a bit sorrowful. "I was hoping to convince you to come back to work, but I guess that's a waste of time, huh?"

Angela nodded. "Definitely a waste of time."

~

Later that afternoon, when Lara was settled in front of the television watching *The Mickey Mouse Club*, Angela went through the tote bag Dimitri had delivered.

Inside was a half-used tube of the peachy-red lipstick Vicki wore, a change purse with a few singles and some loose coins, a handful of tissues, several pictures of houses torn from magazines, and at the bottom of the tote an envelope with MOVED, NO FORWARDING ADDRESS stamped across the face of it.

The envelope was addressed to Russ Murphy in Wynne Bluffs, the town where Angela had picked Vicki up on the day she came to live with them.

Russ Murphy. Lara's daddy.

A sick feeling rose in Angela's stomach as she began to realize she now had a name. Not just a name but conceivably an address where she could start looking for the unknown stranger.

In the corner of the envelope were Vicki's name and a return address for Dimitri's Diner. *Why? Why would she list the diner as her return address?*

Angela slid the letter from the envelope and began reading. The letter made no sense at all. Vicki had said the guy mistreated her, but the first line of her letter read, "I hope you can forgive me." *Forgive her for what?* Angela's eyes moved to the next sentence: "I know I was wrong in not trusting that you would keep my secret." *What secret?* As she continued to read, more and more questions arose. *What was Vicki frightened of? Why did she question whether or not it was too late for them? What was the dream they shared?*

After she'd read the letter over five times, Angela had learned only two things—Vicki loved Russ Murphy, and she wanted him to be Lara's father—but there were also questions hanging on to those things. *If she wanted him to be Lara's father, then why did she say he'd abused her and she was afraid for the baby?*

~

Haunted by all the questions without answers, Angela waited two days before she told Kenny about the letter. And by the time she told him, she'd changed her mind three different times about trying to find Russ Murphy.

The moment she brought out the letter, Kenny's eyes narrowed, and his jaw stiffened. "Okay, you know Lara's father's name. But as far as I'm concerned, that changes nothing. It's pretty obvious that this Murphy guy is not looking for Vicki or the baby, so why stir up trouble by trying to find him?"

Angela was quick to buy into the thought. "You're probably right," she said. "Although the letter says she wants him to be part of Lara's life, I have my doubts. Vicki was always such a fickle-minded person—one day she wanted this and the next day it was that."

Kenny nodded. "I'm sure your sister meant well, but what she wanted and what's best for Lara may not be the same thing. Kids need stability. We're the only family Lara has ever known. Bringing some stranger in and saying he's her father could be devastating!"

He and Angela both found countless reasons for not trying to find Murphy, but neither of them voiced the real reason—they were petrified that Lara's birth father might try to take her away from them. Angela knew that losing the child she loved as her own would break her heart into a million little pieces.

Although thoroughly convinced they were doing the right thing, Angela couldn't dismiss the one niggling thought that remained in her mind. *What if someday Lara wants to know about her biological father?*

That night she tucked the letter in the far back of a dresser drawer with the intent that it would remain there.

A NEW BEGINNING

Hesterville, Winter 1973

Once the decision to move into the house on Pecan Street was made, Rachel came at it with fire in her soul. Whereas George had simply boarded up the broken window, she'd hired a glazier to replace the glass and ordered new curtains to take the place of the torn shreds left hanging. For two days she cleaned, vacuumed, scrubbed, and polished until every room was as sparkly as a new penny.

At Mama Dixon's insistence, she and George took the large upstairs bedroom with a window overlooking the backyard where she could plant a flower garden in the spring. A daybed was brought from the attic to the small sitting room downstairs for Mama Dixon. Then Rachel added a sunshine-yellow coverlet, curtains to match, and a potted chrysanthemum. Placing three colorful throw pillows in the center of the bed, she stepped back to study the results and smiled. It felt good to be doing something for someone else.

"Mama Dixon is going to love this," she said, then moved on to the kitchen, where she was organizing tins of tea and spices.

~

Two days later George brought his mama home from the hospital. She was pale, thinner than she'd been in years, and leaning heavily on a walker but glad to be home. She thumped from room to room, admiring first one thing and then another.

"The place looks better than it has in years," she said. Whereas she'd once found fault with every aspect of Rachel's housekeeping, she now couldn't say enough good things about it.

At the doorway of the small sitting room, she stopped and smiled.

"Why, I'd never thought of using yellow for this room," she said, "but it looks beautiful and brightens the place up."

She thumped over to the comfy-looking daybed, then plopped down. "All this excitement has worn me to a frazzle. If you don't mind, I think I'll take a nap."

"Go right ahead," George said and pulled the door closed behind him.

Minutes later she was sound asleep and remained so all afternoon. When she woke, dinner was ready.

"I hope you don't mind that we're eating in the dining room," Rachel said. "I used your good china because I wanted this to be a new-start celebration."

"Mind?" Her smile was stretched out as far as it could go. "I'm delighted."

When she finally pushed back from the table, Mama Dixon declared the dinner to be one of the most pleasurable she'd ever experienced, and, oddly enough, Rachel agreed.

~

The next day Sadie Jenkins came with a basket of freshly baked scones.

"I'm not going to stay," she said. "I just wanted to stop by and ask how Helen is feeling."

"She's doing much better," Rachel replied, then looped her arm through Sadie's and led her back to the kitchen before there was time to protest.

The three women settled at the kitchen table, and after a short while Rachel was laughing and talking as she hadn't in years. She listened eagerly as Sadie shared news of the town, told of the families who'd moved in and those who had left, and how the Women's League had raised money enough for new playground equipment. When Sadie suggested they were going to need a new chairwoman for the library restoration committee, Rachel smiled and said it was something she'd have to think about.

Later that evening when Rachel snapped off the light and climbed into bed beside George, she scooted a bit closer to him. "I'm thinking about helping out on the library restoration committee," she said.

He turned to face her and traced his hand along the curve of her cheek. "It would be good to see you getting involved in something like that again."

"Living here makes it easier. With people stopping by and my taking care of Mama and the house, it seems as if I'm busy all the time." She closed her eyes for a moment as though she were remembering something from the past, then said, "I still think about Emily a lot; I worry if she's being loved and cared for, but now it's not always my first thought in the morning and last thought at night."

"Isn't it better that way?"

She hesitated a moment. "Yes, I suppose it is, but I feel as if I have to learn how to breathe all over again. It would be impossible for me to ever forget Emmy; she's part of who I am. I don't expect that will ever change, but I'm finding a way to live with the ache in my heart."

The moon was high in the sky, and in the silvery light it cast across the room, Rachel saw a smile taking hold of George's face. "She'll forever be a part of me also," he said.

She raised herself up on her elbow, then leaned across and kissed his mouth. "Maybe your thought of us one day having another baby wasn't such a bad idea after all."

~

The week before Thanksgiving, Mama Dixon was getting around so well that she abandoned the walker and switched to a cane. By then, friends were stopping by most every day, and she claimed the walker was an eyesore, whereas the cane hung unobtrusively on the arm of the chair.

For almost a decade, the big house on Pecan Street had sat there with only a single lamp lit in the upstairs bedroom. That winter it came alive. Lamps were aglow in almost every room, cars came and went, and then two days before Christmas a tree appeared in the living room window.

It wasn't something they'd discussed or planned but a spur-of-the-moment impulse that turned out to be what George had been searching for. That Saturday after he'd closed the hardware store and was on his way home, he passed the empty lot where the Elks Club was selling Christmas trees. Bert Barker was working the lot that night, and as George passed by, Bert called out, "Got your tree yet?"

George hesitated for a moment, thinking he'd overheard a question meant for someone else, then realized he was alone on the street.

"You talking to me?" he asked.

Bert was a fellow merchant, a big man with a laugh twice his size. "'Course I am," he said and gave one of those huge belly laughs. "If you don't have a tree yet, I've got one for you."

"We don't have a tree, but—"

Before he could explain that after losing Emily, their family had made Christmas trees a thing of the past, Bert hooked a beefy arm around his shoulders and pulled him into the lot.

"This year's proceeds are going to the Crippled Children's Foundation, and we Main Street merchants aren't ones to turn our backs on a cause like that." He gave George's shoulder a squeeze. "Right?"

"I guess not."

"That's what I thought." Bert pulled a midsize tree from the bunch. "You want a five-footer or a six-footer?"

"Well, I'm not really sure . . ."

"Understandable," Bert said, then whipped out a tree that stood a foot taller than himself. "Here's one you can't walk away from." He turned the tree, showing first one side and then the other. "Look at this beauty. Not a bare spot to be seen! Measures a full seven and a half feet, but seeing as how we're both Main Street merchants, I'm only gonna charge you for a seven-footer."

George gave a half-hearted nod. "It's a beauty, all right, but I don't have my car with me, and much as I'd like to—"

Quick as a wink, Bert said, "It's yours! And delivery's free. I'm closing up in about fifteen minutes, so I'll swing by the house and drop it off."

George handed him the fifteen dollars and started for home. As he trudged up Hillmoor Street, he was lost in thoughts of how to explain the tree and didn't notice Bert's truck whiz by. When he turned up the walkway, Bert was standing on the front porch with the tree in his hands.

That evening, Bert, with his jovial laugh and bigger-than-life personality, stayed to help set up the tree. At first Rachel offered a weak protest, saying they weren't really ready and this was something that could wait until tomorrow, but Bert moved right past the thought and carted in a stand from the back of his truck. They slid the armchair aside, then stood the tree square in the center of the front window.

"Got any decorations?" he asked. "Lights maybe?"

"Upstairs, in the guest room under the bed," Mama Dixon said with a look of apprehension, "but it's been years, so they may not be . . ."

George was on his way up the stairs before his mama got to the part about the lights not working.

That evening the spirit of Christmas came to the Dixon house. It wasn't invited or even welcomed, but at some point it slipped through the brittle cracks of resistance and settled in. No one could say precisely when it happened or even how, but when George reached up to place a star atop the tree, Rachel noticed Mama Dixon was missing and her cane was left hanging on the arm of her chair. Fearing the worst, Rachel called out for her, and an answer came from the kitchen.

"Come on back; I'm setting out some hot chocolate and cookies."

As they gathered around the kitchen table with mugs of hot chocolate, Rachel noticed a sound she hadn't heard for a very long time; it was the lighthearted lilt of George's laughter. At first it seemed weak and far away, but when she turned to him and smiled, it grew stronger and settled softly on the inside of her ear.

Watching the plate of cookies being passed from hand to hand, she thought back on how she hadn't wanted a tree. She'd believed it would be a too-powerful reminder of the Christmas they'd once planned for Emmy, and George had agreed. Yet here he was, smiling and happy as he'd been the year they were married. Earlier she'd almost told Bert that Christmas trees had no place in the home of a family grieving the loss of a child, but she'd hesitated for a moment, and in that moment something changed.

She'd seen the look of longing on George's face. It wasn't simply a tree he wanted; he was trying to find a remnant of the life they'd once shared. He was reaching for things that once brought them happiness, hoping they could find it again.

Was it possible she could do the same?

BECOMING A FAMILY

Two days later, with the smell of pine still wafting through the house and the colored lights aglow, Rachel and George discovered that it was possible to set aside the past and enjoy the simple pleasure of being together. It began on a chilly winter evening when Mama Dixon had retired to her room early and they'd settled in front of the fireplace. She sat with her back resting against his chest, his arms encircling hers and the sweet smell of smoldering hickory wood tickling their noses. At first they talked only of the coming spring, the flower garden she hoped to plant and the new lawn mower he would need.

When the conversation stilled, she dropped her head back against his shoulder and leaned into the rise and fall of his chest with the tickle of his breath against her ear.

"I hadn't thought we'd have a tree this year," she said.

"Neither did I," George replied softly, then he lowered his face to hers and, with a featherlight brush of his lips, kissed the back of her neck. "Does the tree being here make you unhappy?" he asked.

"Not unhappy, but it brings back thoughts of all the things we'd planned for Emily." She paused a moment, then added, "I can't help but wonder if our moving ahead means we're leaving her behind."

"Never." George tenderly traced his fingers along her arm, then lifted his hand and pressed it to her cheek, turning her face to his. "Emily is not part of our lives now, but she'll always be a part of our hearts, yours and mine both. Given time, the memory of what happened is bound to grow less harsh, but the thought of who Emily was and what she meant to us will never be gone."

Rachel took the words and stored them in her heart. When memories of Emily came, as they inevitably did, she would be able to call upon this thought and remember it as a lifelong promise to their daughter.

Later, in the privacy of their bedroom, they moved beyond thoughts of Emily and George turned to her with his lips curled into a smile. His eyes were soft and warm, reassuring almost, as he bent and pressed his mouth to hers. That night they allowed their passion to flow as freely as it had in the early years. His touch was tender and she held nothing back as they came together. Afterward, they slept with their bodies so close that their arms and legs became entangled, and in the morning she woke to find herself pinned beneath his arm, her head nestled against his chest.

~

That spring, when the scarlet fuzz was just beginning to show on the red maples, Rachel missed her period. At first she attributed it to the long hours she'd spent digging in the garden, planting creeping phlox along the walkway and a bed of wax begonias in the backyard. But after three weeks had passed, she told George.

It was a balmy evening when nothing more than a light sweater was needed, and Mama Dixon had slipped off to her bedroom, leaving Rachel and George alone on the front porch. As they pushed back and forth in the glider, Rachel leaned her head on his shoulder.

"It's too early to know for certain," she said, "but I think I'm pregnant."

The glider came to an abrupt stop, and George turned to face her. "Really?"

She gave way to a grin and nodded. "It's only three weeks, so I can't be sure, but—"

Before she could say anything more, he pulled her into his arms and covered her mouth with his. It was what they had both begun to hope for. A new life. An opportunity to move beyond the heartache and become a family again.

"You should see Dr. Levine tomorrow," he said.

She laughed. "It's too soon. I'll wait another month or so until I'm certain."

"In the meantime, no more gardening. You've got to take it easy. If there's something to be done, just tell me, and I'll take care of it."

Although Rachel argued that a certain amount of activity was good for a pregnant woman, she agreed to let George finish up the garden they'd planned.

As spring turned into summer, a newfound joy crept into every corner of the house. Each morning George left for work whistling a happy tune, and Mama Dixon set aside her granny squares to begin crocheting tiny sweaters and caps. After she'd finished a white sweater with matching cap and booties, she went shopping and returned home with three bags of yarn. She'd bought yellow and mint green, the colors equally appropriate for either a boy or girl, and also skeins of pink and blue.

"A January baby will need plenty of warm sweaters," she reasoned, "and it's best to be prepared."

Although glowing with the prospect of again holding a baby in her arms, Rachel was plagued by morning sickness, not just in the morning but throughout the day. Her breasts became heavier than they'd ever been, and her ankles swelled to twice their normal size.

"My stomach is larger than a watermelon." She groaned. "And I'm gaining so much weight."

Mama Dixon pooh-poohed the thought, claiming a well-rounded stomach was assurance of a nice big healthy baby.

Dr. Levine saw it a bit differently. "Have you tried cutting back on salt?" he asked. "Maybe get a bit more exercise?"

"I've not had a grain of salt for weeks," Rachel replied. "And no cake, no pie, no cookies."

By then she was five months into the pregnancy, her skin stretched taut and her legs as stiff and heavy as tree trunks. With only the tiniest bit of exertion, she became so fatigued that she napped on the sofa, too weary to climb the stairs to the bedroom.

Leaning back on the examination table, she said, "I'm concerned because it wasn't this way with Emmy."

Dr. Levine scribbled something on her chart, then held his stethoscope to her stomach and listened. With his brow wrinkled and a look of intensity clinging to his face, he slid the stethoscope from one side of her stomach to the other, each time pausing to listen, then moving on.

With every second that ticked by Rachel grew increasingly nervous. The examination had never taken this long before, but when she asked what was wrong, Dr. Levine held up his hand, signaling her to wait, then moved the stethoscope a tiny bit higher.

"Just tell me the baby is okay," she pleaded. "Say something."

After almost ten minutes, he pulled the instrument from his ears and told Rachel she could sit up.

"I think you're going to like this," he said and smiled. "You're having twins. There are two distinct heartbeats."

For a moment Rachel stared at him in disbelief, unblinking and unable to breathe, then she gasped a mouthful of air and said, "Twins?"

He nodded, pulled a prescription pad from his pocket, and began writing.

"That's the reason for the weight gain and fatigue." He handed her the prescription. "This will reduce the swelling in your ankles, but I want you to start taking vitamins, get plenty of rest, and make sure you eat enough protein. Eggs, cheese, lean meats, and milk. Plenty of milk."

When Rachel left the doctor's office, she sat in the car for ten minutes before turning the key.

"Twins," she repeated over and over again, letting the thought of two babies bounce around in her head.

Although the news was ready to explode out of her mouth, she waited until she and George were alone on the front porch to say something. They were on opposite ends of the wicker sofa, her legs stretched out, her feet in his lap. He was telling how he planned to strip the yellowed wallpaper from the small room next to theirs and give the room a fresh coat of paint.

"Once that's done, we can start shopping for a new crib," he said.

She wiggled her toes playfully. "I think we're going to need two."

"Well, if the room needs two coats, then so be it. Have you got a color in mind?"

"Not the paint; I meant the crib."

He glanced across with a puzzled expression. "What about the crib?"

"One won't be enough. We're going to need two."

She smiled and waited as the realization of what she meant came to him. He looked at her stomach as if he were seeing it for the first time.

"There's two?" he said and laughed aloud.

She nodded. "Twins."

That evening they lingered on the porch, talking about the things they'd need and how to arrange two cribs in the small room. George suggested they might want to put both babies in the larger room at the end of the hall, but Rachel shook her head.

"I want to keep them close by," she said, "where I can hear every sound."

~

As welcome as thoughts of two babies were, the sight of two empty cribs sitting in the room next to theirs unnerved Rachel. Before the leaves on the oak turned color, the radiant glow she'd had during the early months began to fade. In late October, on a rainy evening when the sky was going from dusk to dark, George found her standing at the kitchen window.

He came up behind her and peered out the window. Outside there was a steady stream of raindrops falling from the eaves and shadows of the oaks covering the few remaining flowers in the garden, but nothing more. He touched his hand to her shoulder and leaned in, his cheek close to hers.

"Is there something out there?" he asked.

She gave a worrisome shrug, her shoulders hunched and her hands cradling her stomach as she would a baby.

"We probably won't know until it's too late." She turned to him, a tear rolling down her cheek. "What if it happens again? With two babies to protect—"

He gathered her into his arms, and with a gentle touch of his fingertip brushed the tear from her cheek.

"Nothing will happen," he promised. "I'll make certain of it."

~

A few weeks later, a crew of workmen came and installed a wrought iron fence that encircled the entire yard. Each spindle had a pointy spear at the top, and the gate at the front entrance opened and closed with a loud *clang*. The foreman suggested they could soften the sound by oiling the hinges, but George claimed it wasn't necessary. Once the workmen were gone, George called Mama Dixon and Rachel out to see the gate.

"Now there's no chance of an intruder," he said confidently.

His mama agreed, but Rachel eyed the gate with an expression of doubt stretched across her face.

"Where there's a will, there's a way," she said solemnly, then turned and went back inside the house.

Although George at first believed no intruder would be foolish enough to risk breaking into a house surrounded by an iron fence and lit by a streetlight, the thought of such a possibility settled in his head and refused to budge. That night and for several more following it, he tossed and turned, wondering if there was even a remote possibility that such a thing could happen. After two weeks of sleeplessness, he visited the ASPCA and came home with a German shepherd puppy who was nine months old and supposedly housebroken.

"This is Bruno," he said as the dog stood there wagging his tail. "He's a good watchdog and loves children."

Mama Dixon laughed. "And just how do you know all that?"

"The woman at the ASPCA told me he belonged to a family with two little girls. She said they wouldn't have given him up, but the dad was transferred to New York, and they'd be living in an apartment that didn't allow dogs."

Rachel bent over and offered her hand. "Here, Bruno."

The dog hesitated a moment, then ambled over. He sniffed her hand, then moved on to sniff her swollen belly. After a few moments, he came to rest with his snout nuzzled up against her stomach. She reached over, rubbed Bruno's ears, then looked up at George.

"Can he sense that I'm carrying babies?"

Even though George had no idea whether or not such a thing was true, he nodded.

"Obviously Bruno is getting ready to guard our twins."

Rachel eyed the dog with a look of skepticism. "We'll see."

Mama Dixon folded her arms across her chest, a look of disapproval wrinkling her brow. "With two babies on the way and a house to keep clean, having a dog is likely to be more work than we can—"

"We've got fourteen days to decide whether or not we want to keep Bruno," George cut in. "Let's give him a chance, and after that, if you want to return him I'm okay with it."

The dog looked up at Rachel and whined. She laughed.

"That's fine," she said and again rubbed his ears.

~

As it turned out, Bruno was not quite housebroken, and for the first two weeks Rachel went around mopping up puddles. On the fourteenth day, George said that since the dog wasn't as housebroken as he'd been told, they might want to consider returning him.

"Absolutely not," Rachel said. By then she could already envision Bruno lying beside the cribs and keeping a watchful eye throughout the night.

STARTING OVER

Hesterville, 1975

The twins were born the first week of January, the boy at five pounds, four ounces and the girl an even five pounds. They both came into the world healthy, their blue eyes wide open and a bit of light-colored peach fuzz covering their heads. The afternoon Rachel brought the babies home, Bruno was waiting at the door.

"He's been sitting there for the past five days," Mama Dixon said. "He missed you."

The dog followed Rachel over to the sofa and sat at her feet. For a few minutes he remained still, content to have his mistress back again. Then he turned his big head to the side, nosed the babies, and began sniffing them, the girl first and then the boy.

Rachel eyed George with a look of alarm. "Maybe you should put Bruno outside. I'm not sure it's safe to have him in here with the babies. What if he hits one of them with his paw or jumps up on them?"

"The woman at the ASPCA assured me that he's gentle as a lamb with children."

"Children maybe, but the twins are *babies*. Our babies!"

"Don't worry—I think he just wants to familiarize himself with their smell. Sort of get to know them. I'll stay here and keep a close eye on him if it makes you feel better."

A look of apprehension remained on Rachel's face, and she kept a tight grip on both babies. As she watched the dog sniffing the edge of the blanket, she hissed, "I'm warning you, Bruno; nothing had better happen to either of these babies!"

Bruno sat back on his haunches, looked up at her, blinked twice as if he'd understood the message, then went back to sniffing. With the fear of his lunging before she could whisk the infants away lodged in her chest, Rachel kept one eye on the dog and one eye on the babies as she sat and waited.

Bruno eventually caught Rachel's scent wrapped around the twins, then he sat with his snout at the feet of the girl. For the remainder of the day Bruno followed along, stopping wherever Rachel stopped, his head raised and eyes alert, his focus moving from one baby to the other and then back again. That evening as the infants were placed each in their own crib, he sat in the corner of the room, his eyes tracking the movement, almost as if he were trying to determine his place in the pack.

After both babies were asleep, Rachel turned off the overhead, clicked on the carousel night-light, and moved toward the master bedroom. She seemed to disappear into the hallway, but just beyond the doorway she stopped and turned back to keep an eye on Bruno. He stood when she left the room, raised his front paw as if he were ready to follow, but didn't. He lifted his nose, sniffed the air, then turned back to the cribs. He circled from one to the other, catching the scent, listening for an unfamiliar sound, and, when he seemed satisfied all was as it should be, he settled beneath the girl's crib with his ears perked and his eyes watchful.

Rachel gave a sigh of relief and turned toward the bedroom. That night she was up and down a dozen different times; with constantly peeking in to check on Bruno and the two predawn feedings, she barely closed her eyes.

Their routine was the same on the second night and again on the third, but by the end of the week Rachel had come to understand that Bruno was going to watch over her babies as closely as she herself would. On the fifth night, as she stood in the doorway and watched the dog settle into his spot beneath the girl's crib, the wall of fear she'd built around herself began to crumble.

After the twins were sound asleep, she sat on the floor alongside Bruno. With her arm draped across his back and her face level with his, she whispered, "I love these babies more than anything in the world, Bruno. I'm counting on you to help me keep them safe. Protect them from strangers and keep them from harm."

As she spoke, the dog sat with his head cocked and his eyes fixed on her face.

Rachel leaned in and scratched his ear. "You understand what I'm saying, don't you?"

The dog blinked, then returned to his spot beneath the girl's crib.

Although the sky was lit by only a handful of stars, Rachel was certain she could see the glow of a new beginning.

~

The following week, Sadie Jenkins stopped by to see the new babies. When she started across the room to take a peek at the girl in Rachel's arms, Bruno rose up on his haunches. He'd been lying beside the chair, but when Sadie ventured too close, he stood erect, his ears back and a menacing growl rumbling through his throat.

"It's okay, Bruno," Rachel said and patted his head.

~

A full two weeks passed before the babies were named. The boy's name came easily; he'd be called Henry, the same as George's daddy. Rachel originally wanted to call the girl Helen, after Mama Dixon, but Mama Dixon was staunchly opposed.

"Helen is such a boring name," she said. "I've never been overly fond of it."

She rattled off a number of other suggestions: Charlene after a twice-removed cousin they'd lost track of some thirty years ago, Barbara or Betty because of similarly named movie stars, and Jeannette, because Jeannette Rankin was the first woman to be elected to Congress and, as Mama Dixon reminded them, an inspiration to everyone.

"Jeannette's not bad," George said, but Rachel shook her head.

"They're twins; their names should start with the same letter."

"Henrietta, then?"

"Too much like Henry," Rachel said. "They may be twins, but we want them both to have a sense of individuality."

Any number of other suggestions followed, but each one had some sort of negative attached to it. Hester came too close to the town's name. Helga was far too stern. Hazel sounded like the nut. Each evening at the dinner table, Mama Dixon offered up several more possibilities, but most of them did not begin with the letter *H*.

Weary of having to call the babies "him" and "her," George said, "Well, they can't go through life nameless, so I hope you come up with something soon."

Rachel was on the far side of the kitchen stacking biscuits in a serving basket, but she caught the word *hope*, and it stuck in her head. It seemed so promising. It spoke of the future, of good things to come. Her thoughts flashed back to Emmy and the box stored beneath the bed.

When they had moved to the house on Pecan Street, George carted Emmy's crib to the Goodwill store; it was too painful a reminder to keep. But Rachel had packed Emmy's clothes into a box thinking someday there would be another child who would wear them. Now there was, but the word *hope* signified something born anew, not a child to be dressed in sorrowful memories.

She carried the biscuits to the table and sat across from Mama Dixon. As they joined hands and listened to George thank the Lord for all they had, her thoughts were elsewhere, bouncing back and forth between the word *hope* and the box stored beneath the bed.

That night sleep was impossible to come by. Rachel was still wide awake when she heard the first whimper of a baby ready for the two a.m. feeding. She climbed from the bed, slid her feet into her slippers, and hurried across to the small room. Bruno was again beneath the girl's crib. He lifted his head, saw Rachel, then went back to his original position with his snout resting on his front paws.

"Good boy," she whispered.

She crossed the room and lifted the boy from his crib. He was always the first to doze off and the first to wake. She changed his diaper, then sat in the rocking chair and held him to her breast. Later, as she lifted him to her shoulder, patting his back and hoping for a burp, the girl began to stir. Afterward, as she fed the girl, Rachel realized it happened this same way most every night. They had already developed patterns, their own individuality.

It was a long while before the girl fell asleep, and by the time Rachel returned to her own bed, she knew what she had to do.

~

The next morning when they sat at the breakfast table, Rachel said, "I've decided to call her Hope."

"I like it," George replied.

Mama Dixon smiled.

And so the babies were named Henry and Hope, both names culled from something good. Neither of them would ever replace Emmy, but they were individuals who would grow and prosper on their own.

~

Two weeks later when the babies went down for their nap, Rachel asked if Mama Dixon could take care of them for a few hours.

"There's something I need to do," she said, "but I'll be back in time for the next feeding."

Rachel closed the bedroom door and pulled the cardboard box from beneath the bed. Other than a few snapshots, these things were all she had left of Emily. Her hands trembled as she opened the box and lifted a tiny pink dress to her nose. Breathing in the familiar baby scent, she could once again see Emily wearing the dress, hear the soft round tones of a babyish chuckle, and feel the tiny hands clinging to her fingers. She pressed the dress to her chest and held it as tenderly as she'd once held her first child.

"Oh, Emmy," she cried. "My dear sweet baby . . ." The words fell away, and there was only the muffled sound of sobbing as she went through the box, lifting the tiny dresses and lace-trimmed shirts to her nose, her fingers touching each thing, seeing it not as a flat, lifeless garment but alive with Emily laughing, reaching up to be held, or dropping a sleepy head onto her shoulder. Each thing had a memory attached to it—coming home from the hospital, a Sunday at church, a stain left by the spill of sweet potatoes, the dozens of times George held her in his arms.

Pressing her face to the nightie Emmy had worn that last Saturday, Rachel allowed the tears to flow. She sat with her back hunched and her shoulders trembling as the enormity of her grief overwhelmed her. Letting go of Emmy's things felt like losing an arm or leg; they were part of a life that could never be replaced.

"I'll love you forever," she sobbed. "No one can ever replace you. Not now, not a thousand years from now. As long as I'm alive, you'll be alive inside me."

With tears streaming down her cheeks, she folded each garment and lowered it back into the box.

As she closed the flap, a sigh riddled with heartache and pain came from her throat.

"I hate to do this," she whispered tearfully, "but I have to. Your sister and brother deserve lives of their own, and the only way I can give it to them is by letting go of these painful memories."

She held her hand to the box and solemnly whispered a final goodbye. "I pray you have a good family, Emmy, a mama who dries your tears, fills your tummy, and loves you as I do. Hopes and prayers are the only things I can now give you, but I will forever hold in my heart the wish that you will one day know how much you were loved."

That afternoon, as the twins slept, Rachel carried the box to Goodwill and left it. As she came from the store, tears overflowed her eyes. Days afterward, she had to keep reminding herself that the things she had given away were only things. The part of Emmy she could hold on to forever was still with her, locked inside her heart.

SCHOOL DAYS

Fairlawn, 1976

Almost overnight Lara went from being a toddler to becoming a little girl with thoughts and opinions of her own. While Angela saw bits of Vicki in the child's blue eyes and blonde hair, her personality was nothing like that of her mother. Vicki had been a rambunctious child with little interest in books or studying; Lara was just the opposite.

By the time she was three she'd learned to read and was content to sit for hours leafing through the pages of a book. When a new word popped up, she'd come running into the kitchen with the book in hand.

"Mama, what's this?" she'd ask and point to a word like *hippopotamus* or *elephant.*

When things like that happened, Angela shook her head laughingly and wondered how in the world Lara came by such traits.

Eager as she was to learn new things, the child often followed her mama from room to room with an endless string of questions.

"Why does a zebra have stripes?" she'd ask. "Why is the sky blue? Where does the rainbow go when it disappears?"

Once those questions were answered, they'd be followed by a dozen more.

As Angela marveled at Lara's inquisitiveness, she inevitably thought of the letter hidden in the drawer. She couldn't help but speculate what Murphy might be like. *Studious? Smart?* Was it possible Lara was more like her father than mother? That thought came and went like a thief in the night. Curious though Angela might be, she was not willing to take a chance on Russ Murphy looking to reclaim his daughter.

For three years, Vicki's letter remained in the drawer. Out of sight, hidden away, but always there, always tempting Angela to peek inside the secret life of her sister.

~

Right from the start Angela had slid into the role of being a mom as easily as she would a comfy dress or a pair of slippers. For the first year or two she kept in touch with her girlfriends from the diner, but little by little the Saturday afternoons of shopping sprees and cocktail lunches gave way to backyard cookouts and planned playdates. Before long her closest friends were neighborhood women with children Lara's age.

Kimberly Melrose was just such a friend. She had three youngsters, twin boys going into the sixth grade and Brianna, a girl close to Lara's age. The summer after Lara turned three, Angela and Kimberly spent almost every afternoon at the lake. They'd pack a picnic lunch and set off early in the morning. After lunch, the two little girls napped in the shade of a beach umbrella while the older boys romped in the water. The two mamas sat in side-by-side folding chairs watching over the girls and chatting. The week before Labor Day, they were in the midst of talking through plans for a neighborhood barbecue when Angela looked over with a sad smile.

"It's been a great summer," she said. "I'm going to miss our time together when you go back to work."

"It's unavoidable," Kimberly replied. "Calvin loves coaching, but it doesn't pay all that much, and the boys are already talking about going to the University of Kentucky. Besides, the truth is that I enjoy working at the school. I can keep an eye on the boys without their knowing it."

"When Kenny first suggested I be a stay-at-home mom, I thought I'd miss working, but I don't. Lara is growing up so quickly that I'm afraid if I look away for even a moment, I'll miss an important part of her life, and I don't want to do that."

"I was that way with the twins. I didn't go back to work until they started kindergarten." She gave a soft chuckle. "By then I was more than ready for getting out of the house. Girls are a lot easier than boys, that's for certain."

"What about Brianna? Who takes care of her while you're working?"

"Calvin's mom. She loves doing it."

"Well, if you're ever in a bind and need another babysitter, I'm available."

"Thanks, I'll keep that in mind."

At the time the offer was little more than a passing conversation, but two years later Kimberly took her up on it. That year January roared through Kentucky with a vengeance. Halfway through the month an ice storm hit Fairlawn and made the walkways so slick they were treacherous. Three days later the ground was topped by several inches of snow, and the temperature never rose above twenty-two degrees. For two days the schools remained closed, but on the third day when they reopened, Kimberly had to work.

"No problem," Calvin's mama said. "It's only a few blocks; I'll bundle up and be there the same time as usual."

Kimberly offered to bring Brianna over, but Calvin's mama said it wasn't necessary. Instead she pulled on a wool scarf and rubber boots and started out. Halfway down the block, her foot slid out from under her, and she went down. Heloise Macintosh, who was standing alongside her front window, saw it happen and said the crack of poor Mrs. Melrose's head hitting the pavement was something she hoped to never hear again.

"Blood everywhere," was how she explained it to the police after the ambulance had carted Mrs. Melrose away.

Grace Melrose died that night, and when Kimberly returned to work a week later, Angela became Brianna's new babysitter. Five mornings a week Kimberly dropped Brianna off at Angela's house, and the two girls spent the day together.

~

A year later, Brianna and Lara were slated to enter kindergarten together, but it almost didn't happen. On registration day Angela showed up to enroll Lara. She was ready with the vaccination papers, but when the registrar asked for Lara's birth certificate, Angela was at a loss.

"I don't have one," she said. "Lara is my sister's child, and we adopted her after her mama's death."

The registrar gave a stiff smile. "Well then, we can use the adoption papers."

Angela feared something like this might happen, but she'd hoped to squeeze through with just the vaccination papers. She stood there stammering an apology about not having them when Kimberly happened by and caught wind of what was being said. She tapped the registrar on the shoulder. "You can take your break now, Sylvia," she said. "I'll sit in for you."

Kimberly finished Lara's registration. She checked the box allotted for birth certificate verification, scribbled her initials in the margin, then closed the file.

"How can I ever thank you?" Angela said gratefully.

Kimberly winked. "You already have."

~

Two days later Angela again thought of the letter hidden away in the drawer. A thousand times she'd wondered why she bothered to save it;

now she knew. She had to learn more about Lara's life—the life she had before Vicki brought her to live in Fairlawn.

To obtain a birth certificate Angela was going to need the answers to certain questions, and Russ Murphy was the one person who could provide those answers.

LIFE ON PECAN STREET

Hesterville, 1978

Early on Rachel had expected Hope to be a reminder of Emily, but it turned out to be Henry. His eyes remained as blue as they were the day he was born, and when she held him to her breast, she could see the peach fuzz turning lighter and starting to curl. At six months, if she had set those two babies side by side, she would have found it difficult to tell one from the other. They were almost identical, from the white-blond hair right down to the butterfly birthmark on their backs. The only difference was that Henry's birthmark was higher up, close to his shoulder, whereas Emily's had been just above her waist.

By the time they were nine months old, Hope's eyes had turned brown, and her hair had taken on a color somewhere between the gold of Rachel's and the brown of George's. Sun-streaked, Mama Dixon called it, the same as hers had been before it was peppered with silver.

In a few short years, the twins went from infants to toddlers. Their babble turned into an unending stream of questions, high chairs were carted off to the attic and forgotten, youth beds replaced cribs, and Rachel found time enough to help out at the library.

On the first Thursday of each month Mama Dixon kept watch over the twins while Rachel volunteered to teach the children's reading program.

That was the year Emily would have turned seven. On the day of her first class, a young girl darted by as Rachel was entering the library.

She'd caught little more than a fleeting glance, but seeing the child's golden hair flying loose had been enough to make her stop and turn for a better look. For one brief instant she'd allowed herself to think it was Emmy, then she saw the girl was older, eleven or perhaps twelve but small for her age.

For the remainder of that year, Rachel studied each girl's face as she looked at the class. She watched for a smile that resembled Henry's, blue eyes, blonde curls, but there was never a child she could point to and say, *This is my Emmy.* A piece was always missing. The blue-eyed girl had dark hair and the wrong nose; the blonde child had eyes the color of chocolate and a spread of freckles across her nose.

Emmy didn't have freckles back then, but did she now?

The passing of years made a tremendous difference in a child. Did Emmy still look like Henry? Had her hair darkened? She'd most certainly changed, but what were those changes? The thought of knowing nothing about her own daughter was an ache that never left Rachel's heart. As each grain of hope crumbled, it was replaced by a larger one of uncertainty and doubt; that was when she began to fear she might not recognize her own child.

"I'd like to believe I could look into Emmy's face and know right away that it's her," she told George, "but I can't be certain."

"Trust your heart," he replied. "You've got a mother's heart; that bond goes far deeper than just facial recognition. When you see Emmy you'll know it's her. I'm certain of it."

Rachel tried to hold on to the fact that he'd said *When* you see Emmy, not *If.*

But as her hope dwindled and the uncertainty grew heavy as a stone in her chest, she began to wonder about the wisdom of allowing the twins to share such a burden.

The knowledge of what happened the night Emily was kidnapped brought fear along with it. Rachel had lived with that fear since the day the babies were born, but it was hers to bear. She worried that it did not belong in the heart of a child.

~

One afternoon when she and Mama Dixon were sitting on the front porch and the twins were napping, Rachel asked, "Do you think we should tell Hope and Henry about Emily?"

Helen's crochet needle stopped moving, and she looked up. "I believe that's something you and George need to decide together."

"Oh, we will. But I thought, since you'd been through it, with telling George about Tommy, you'd have some advice on how best to handle it. I'm concerned that if the kids learn Emily was kidnapped, they'll become fearful the same thing could happen to them."

Helen gave an understanding nod. "I can see why you'd worry, but I doubt my advice will be of any help. George was going into his last year of high school when I finally told him about Tommy."

"Really?" Rachel leaned in and asked why Mama Dixon had waited so long.

Several moments ticked by before Helen answered. "At first I believed he was too young to understand, then as he got older, I saw little reason for bringing up such a sorrowful topic. I always figured I'd know when the time was right for talking about Tommy."

"And did you?"

As the memory of that year passed through Helen's thoughts she gave a wistful smile and nodded. "The summer before George's last year of high school, the Bracken family lost their three-year-old daughter. I'd known Phyllis for years, and George played ball with their oldest boy, so he and I went to the wake together. Seeing Phyllis so devastated made me remember how I'd felt the same after we lost Tommy."

She hesitated a moment, blinked back the tear welling in her eye, then continued. "On the walk home, I told George that I could understand exactly how Phyllis was feeling because his daddy and I had lost a young child. Then I told him about Tommy."

Rachel scooted forward until she was almost on the edge of her seat. "How did he take it when he found out?"

Mama Dixon gave a bittersweet smile. "George was just as you'd expect him to be, concerned and sympathetic. He asked a number of questions about what Tommy had been like and how he'd died; then we walked the rest of the way arm in arm, with me leaning on him. I remember at the time I'd thought how unusual it was for a lad his age to have such an understanding heart."

Rachel reached across and took Helen's hand in hers. "I think George gets his goodness from you."

Helen chuckled. "Much as I'd like to take credit for it, the truth is he gets it from his daddy. Henry was the kindhearted one, and George is exactly like him . . ." She continued on detailing the many similarities in father and son.

~

Later that night, when Rachel and George were alone in their bedroom, she said, "There's something we need to talk about."

George was bent over untying his shoes, but with the sound of her voice so serious, he stopped and looked up. "Is something wrong?"

Rachel shook her head. "Not wrong, but we need to decide when or if we are going to tell the twins about Emily."

George slid his foot from his shoe and stood. "Why is that a consideration right now?"

"They're three years old, and they understand more than you might think. I'm concerned that if we tell them about Emily, we'll have to admit that she was kidnapped, and they might become fearful the same thing could happen to them."

"But there's no reason for them to be afraid. Living here is a lot different than living on Yellowwood Road. There's a streetlight right outside the house. We've got a fence and a dog. The bedrooms are upstairs. Why, this house is as safe as—"

"What you say makes sense, and it's perfectly logical, but fear isn't logical. I'm a grown woman, and there are still times when I hear an unfamiliar sound or catch the moving shadow of a tree and feel fearful. I know that before an intruder stepped foot on the upstairs landing Bruno would have their throat torn open. Still, knowing that doesn't stop my heart from seizing when I hear the sound."

A look of concern crossed George's brow. "I'm sorry. I thought after we moved here . . ."

"It's better now. Much better. In the early years thinking of Emily meant feeling afraid, feeling angry, feeling sorry for myself. I prayed for her safety, but I couldn't stop crying over how much I'd lost. My tears should have been for Emily, just Emily, but I was crying for me also. I kept thinking, *Why me?* I almost lost sight of the fact that it didn't just happen to me, George; it happened to you as well."

"I can understand why you felt that way. It was a terrible time, and you had the worst of it. I was at the store most of the week, but you were there all day, every day."

"It's better that you weren't there, but thank God your mama was. I felt like she was the only one who could understand what I was going through. During those darkest days she told me she'd experienced the same kind of anger after losing Tommy."

"I never realized Mama went through—"

Rachel cut in. "That's because she didn't burden you with the knowledge when you were still a kid. You were sixteen years old before she told you about your brother."

For a while George stood there with his hand cradling his chin and a pensive look pinned to his face, then he said, "But if we wait too long, they might hear it from somebody else before we get around to telling them."

"I doubt that will happen. It's been almost seven years; whatever talk there once was has long since been forgotten. People seldom bother with remembering a tragedy that doesn't affect them. Everybody has their own problems."

After nearly an hour of considering how knowledge of the kidnapping could impact the way a child sees the world, they finally agreed to wait until the twins were older before telling them about Emily.

Later on, as they lay side by side in the moon-speckled darkness, George said, "I'd understand if you blamed me for what happened, Rachel; I also blamed myself. I thought having a house outside of town would give us room to grow; I never dreamed—"

She turned on her side and touched her hand to his lips, shushing him before he could finish. "Yes, I blamed you, but I blamed myself just as much."

"I never saw it as your fault. You were exhausted; why, either of us could have—"

She shushed him again. "That was a long time ago, and I've since stopped believing either of us is to blame." She hesitated a moment and moved closer. "All that anger was like a sickness inside me. I knew I had to either let go of it or walk away from our marriage, and I loved you too much to do that."

There was a long moment of silence, then he asked, "Have you ever regretted staying?"

She gave a soft chuckle. "Lord, no. If I'd have walked away, we wouldn't have this beautiful family we've got. We've gone through the worst life has to offer, but now we're at a place where we have a lot to be thankful for."

"Do you still think of Emily?"

"Well, of course I do! Don't you?"

"Yes. Sometimes on a slow day I'll walk down to Sheriff Wilson's office and ask if he's heard anything new, if anybody's called or inquired about the reward."

"And . . . ?"

"He says if he hears anything, we'll be the first to know." George hesitated a moment, as if weighing the worth of what he was about to say, then continued. "A year or so after her disappearance, I asked if he thought Emily was still alive, and he said yes. He told me when there's a kidnapping with no identifiable fingerprints and no obvious motive, the likelihood is that the kidnapper is someone desperate to have a baby and for whatever reason can't."

"I'm surprised you questioned whether or not she's still alive," Rachel said. "I've not for one minute doubted she is. I believe if anything happened to Emily, I'd know it. I think I'd feel it in my heart."

For a while there was only the sounds of the night, a soft wind rustling the oaks and the chirping song of katydids, then George asked, "Do you think of her often?"

"Not as much as I used to, but often enough. Mostly I try to imagine what she looks like now, what kind of a personality she has . . ." Rachel gave a lingering sigh. "Sometimes I look at Hope and Henry and imagine Emily being a cross between them—Henry's coloring and Hope's personality. I figure she's got to look a lot like Henry; at six months they looked exactly the same, even that butterfly birthmark. I mean, how uncanny is that?"

That night they talked into the wee hours of morning, and when they finally fell asleep, it was with her head on his shoulder and his arm flung across her chest.

SEARCHING FOR THE PAST

Fairlawn, 1978

For weeks on end Angela thought of how she could go about finding Russ Murphy. She had a name and an address where he once lived, but that was it. She had no idea what he looked like, what kind of job he'd have, or where he was from. The only thing she knew was that he'd lived in Wynne Bluffs. With nothing more to go on, she could only hope he had relatives in the area or was now living somewhere nearby.

She contacted the telephone company and requested a directory for Marshall County, which covered not only Wynne Bluffs but also nine surrounding towns. If necessary she'd call every Murphy in the county. Hopefully she'd find Russ Murphy or someone who knew him.

When she told Kenny of her plan, he looked at her with a raised eyebrow. "Are you really certain you want to pursue this?"

"I don't see that I have a choice," she said. "We were lucky that Kimberly was able to get Lara registered for school, but sooner or later she's going to need a birth certificate. Russ Murphy is the only one who can give us the information we need."

"So say you do find him; what will you do if he asks to have Lara back?" Kenny reminded her of how Vicki had taken off with the baby, not telling Murphy where they were or allowing him to see his daughter. "A father can get pretty vindictive over a thing like that," he warned.

It was something Angela herself had considered. "If I find him, I won't mention Lara," she replied. "Obviously, he doesn't know what happened to Vicki, so I'll just say I'm looking for my sister. Once I get him talking, he'll most likely tell me about the baby, then I'll casually ask where she was born."

A look of apprehension settled on Kenny's face as he stood there shaking his head; still, that didn't stop Angela. She had made up her mind and was confident she could pull it off without Murphy knowing they had Lara.

"What if he knows that when Vicki left, she came to stay with you?"

"He doesn't," Angela replied with an air of certainty. "She told me she didn't want him to know where she and the baby were."

"I don't know about this . . ." The look of doubt was still stretched across Kenny's face, only now his eyebrows were pinched together and his mouth jacked up on the right-hand side.

Three weeks passed before the Marshall County directory arrived on her doorstep, but the day it did Angela flipped open the book and started browsing through the Murphys. There were five pages but not one Russ or Russell. Undaunted, she plunged in and, thinking he may have used only a first initial, began with the *R*s. There were seventeen of them. On the five where an answering machine informed her that Richard, Roger, or Rosemary was not available, she left a message.

"This is a matter of the utmost importance," she said. "If you know or are related to the Russell Murphy who lived in Wynne Bluffs, please give me a call." Angela made no mention of Lara but left her telephone number, then moved on to the next name.

When she finished with the *R*s, she turned back to the first page and began with the *A*s. She skipped over the listings for Murphy's Beauty Salon and Murphy's Merry Maids but did call Murphy's Bar and Murphy's Garage, because they sounded a bit more promising.

For the next three weeks, Angela picked up the telephone and began dialing as soon as Lara was off to school. After the first week her index finger was blistered and her fingernail worn down to a nub, but she kept at it. Some days she could race through well over a hundred names; other days she encountered people like Henrietta Murphy, who wanted to chat.

"Russell," Henrietta mused. "Is he related to the Tennessee Murphys? Tall man, heavily bearded?"

When that happened, Angela would be forced to admit she knew nothing more than that Russell Murphy had lived in Wynne Bluffs some seven or eight years ago.

Three times the person she'd called asked why she was looking for Russ Murphy, and all three times she'd felt her heart drop into her stomach as she blundered her way through a feeble-sounding explanation of searching for her sister. When Michael Murphy told her he was a retired detective and felt certain this was a matter better handled by the police department, she hung up before he finished talking.

The one thing she didn't need was to get the police involved. Yes, it was more than likely they could do what she had been unable to do—find Russ Murphy—but what then? Lara was Murphy's daughter, that much Vicki had told them, so there would be no question. He was her father, and if he wanted to, he could take her away from them. The very thought of such a thing made Angela's heart stop beating. Lara was their child. Their *only* child.

After she'd hung up the telephone, Angela sat there with her stomach churning and her hands shaking. Enough was enough, she told herself. Kenny had been right. It was foolish to risk losing the daughter they loved in the pursuit of a birth certificate.

Yes, Lara would need one in time, but not right now. Not when she was only seven years old.

Angela closed the Marshall County telephone directory, then carried it out to the garage and placed it in the bottom of the trash bin. Even as the book left her hand, she knew that not having a birth certificate would someday present a problem, but hopefully it was in the far distant future.

Although she'd abandoned the project, the thought of learning more about Lara's birth never really left Angela's head. That winter she pulled Vicki's letter from the drawer time and time again. With each rereading she looked for a hidden clue, some small detail she'd overlooked earlier, but she never found one. The bold red stamp stating MOVED, NO FORWARDING ADDRESS made it seem as though the secrets of Vicki's life were buried along with her. With nothing more to go on, Angela shoved the letter to the very bottom of the drawer and left it there.

~

Two years later her hopes were suddenly reawakened. It began one spring morning when she answered the doorbell and found a stranger standing on her porch.

"Sorry to bother you, ma'am," he said, "but if I could trouble you for a few minutes of your time, I've got a couple of questions—"

"About what?" Angela cut in.

"Tyler Cushing, your next-door neighbor, is being considered for a position that requires security clearance, and I'm conducting a background check."

"I don't see how I could possibly—"

"It's just a few simple questions, ma'am." Without allowing time for any further objections, he continued on. "Have you known the Cushing family for long?"

"Only about five years—they moved in a year or so after we did."

"Mrs. Cushing ever say where they lived before this?"

"Actually, she did. Manhattan. Brenda hated the city, claimed it was way too crowded, and she thought the teachers at Josh's school were deplorable."

"What about now? Is she happy with the schools here?"

"Oh yes. Brenda's very involved in the PTA. Why, she practically ran the third-grade science fair . . ."

Each question led to another two or three, and before Angela knew it she'd spent twenty minutes talking to the stranger.

It wasn't until after she'd closed the door and returned to the kitchen that the thought hit her. Yes, Russ Murphy had moved away, but perhaps one of his old neighbors knew as much about his life as she did the Cushing family's. It was possible, maybe even probable, that a neighbor would remember where Lara was born. If so, they could easily enough get a copy of Lara's birth certificate without Murphy.

That same afternoon she called Kimberly's office and asked if tomorrow Lara could stay at school and participate in the afternoon activities program. "There's something I need to take care of, and I probably won't be back until about five."

"No problem," Kimberly replied, "and if you're longer, don't worry. She can come home with me."

~

The next morning Angela dropped Lara off at the school, then, armed with Murphy's onetime address, headed for Wynne Bluffs. Three hours later she pulled up in front of the townhouse apartment complex—twelve duplex buildings all painted the same slate gray. She got out of the car and started toward the building, where there was a sign indicating no vacancies. She rang the doorbell, waited, then rang the bell again.

After several minutes the door swung open and a squat woman who appeared to have been napping glared at her. "What?"

"I'm sorry if I've disturbed you," Angela said apologetically. "I'd like to inquire—"

With an obvious look of annoyance, the woman pointed to the sign in her front yard. "See that? No vacancies means no vacancies!"

"Oh, I'm not looking for an apartment. My sister used to live here, and I'm just trying to find out . . ." Noticing the look of irritation stuck to the woman's face, she quickly offered, "I'd be happy to pay for your time, if you wouldn't mind answering a couple of questions."

The pinched-up face softened. "I suppose I could spare a few minutes." She pushed the door back and gestured for Angela to come in. "Lou Palmeyer," she said. "Me and Elroy manage the apartments."

"Angela McAlister." She followed the woman into the living room and sat across from her. "My sister was Vicki Robart; I believe she lived here with her boyfriend, Russ Murphy . . ."

"Can't say as I remember the name. How long ago was it?"

"Let's see, Lara is nine now, so it would have been about eight years ago."

Lou Palmeyer's face brightened. "Yeah, yeah, I remember now. That baby was a pretty little thing, blonde curls, cute smile . . . We don't get many babies in here."

"Well, I'm Vicki's sister, and—"

"Oh, so you're the one with the baby? If I'm remembering right, you weren't doing so good then; how you feeling now?"

"Um, I'm fine, but did you know Vicki passed away?"

"Lord God, no!" Mrs. Palmeyer gave a gasp and collapsed back into the cushions of the sofa. "What's this world coming to? A young woman like her dying . . . She wasn't sick a day when they was living here."

"I know. It happened suddenly, before she had a chance to tell us anything about Russ Murphy. That's why—"

Cutting in, Lou Palmeyer asked, "What caused it?"

"Heart attack. Now, about Russ Murphy—"

"Heart attack, huh? You'd never expect it from somebody so young."

"Normally you wouldn't, but Vicki had a weak heart." Angela was anxious to move on. "So do you have any idea where Russ Murphy went when he left here?"

Lou Palmeyer shook her head. "People in short-term rentals like this, they come and go. They seldom say where they've been or where they're headed. To the best of my recollection he only stayed a few months after your sister left."

"Did they have any friends nearby? Women Vicki might have spent time with or guys he knew from work?"

Again she shook her head. "Not that I'm aware of. Your sister was only here a week or so, and her boyfriend was around for four, maybe five months."

Angela asked several more questions, and before long it became obvious that this woman knew very little about Vicki or Russ Murphy. With a feeling of disappointment pushing against her chest, Angela stood, thanked Lou for her time, then handed her a twenty and left.

She was halfway down the walkway when the door popped open again and Lou hollered, "Wait up—I've got something for you."

Angela turned and hurried back.

A few minutes later, a balding man came out carrying a cardboard box.

By way of introduction, Lou said, "This here's Elroy," then she moved on to saying Murphy had left the box for Vicki, should she come back. "It's been in my basement all this time, and I plumb forgot it till two seconds ago."

~

On the drive home, Angela couldn't stop thinking about the box in the trunk of her car. She was certain it held the answers she'd been searching for. Inside she'd probably find Lara's birth certificate, her baby bracelet, some pictures, possibly even one of the mysterious Russ Murphy, and who knew what else.

She waited until after Lara was in bed before telling Kenny about what she'd done that day. "The box is still in the trunk of my car," she said excitedly. "I wanted to wait so we could open it together."

Kenny carried the box in, wiped the dust off, then set it on the kitchen table. The top wasn't taped, just folded over with one flap tucked under the other. He pulled it open, and Angela reached in. On top was a red halter with some kind of stain on the front, and below that three sundresses. One by one Angela removed the layers of clothing, anxiously looking for something of greater significance—a birth certificate, a hospital photo, or something that would point to where Lara was born. Beneath the clothes she found a hairbrush, a ponytail clip, and a wristband from the Hesterville Music Festival in August 1971.

That was it. No pictures. No birth certificate. Nothing to bear witness to the early months of Lara's infancy, not even a tiny bonnet or receiving blanket.

Angela lifted her eyes and looked up at Kenny. "I don't understand it. Where're Lara's baby clothes and her birth certificate?"

He wrinkled his nose and eyed the contents of the box with a look of chagrin. "I hate to say this, Angela, but it appears your sister and Murphy were not very good parents. Maybe they ran into hard times, then after Vicki split he took off and left her stuff behind. Since there's nothing here for Lara, I'm thinking she might have been a surprise baby. One they'd not anticipated and didn't really want. It seems obvious they weren't prepared."

Gathering the pile of clothes on the table, Kenny stuffed them back into the box.

"But you saw how Vicki was with Lara. You could see how much she loved her."

"I guess there're a lot of things we don't know about your sister. I think we'd be better off leaving the past in the past. Vicki's gone, and I doubt that any good can come from us pursuing this Murphy character." Kenny picked up the box of clothes, carried it out to the curb, and left it for the garbageman.

Although Angela thought him wrong about Vicki loving Lara, they never again spoke of the box she'd brought back from Wynne Bluffs.

~

In the years that followed, the McAlister house was seldom without the sound of girlish laughter. Lara had more friends than Angela could count, and it was with good reason: she had a gentle manner and an easy-to-like personality. The pocketful of resentment Vicki had carried around with her was missing in Lara. There were times when Angela questioned that mother and daughter could be so different, but in the end she always attributed it to growing up in a more loving household.

MURPHY'S MUSIC

Murphy thought when he left Wynne Bluffs Vicki would be a thing of the past, but it turned out he was wrong. Small, seemingly innocent things were unwanted reminders—a woman with a child held to her shoulder, the carefree laughter of a girl in cutoff shorts, a song he could picture her singing. Things that would have once gone unnoticed now triggered painful memories.

He'd come to Nashville thinking it was a fresh start, but he'd brought his troubles along and realized this place was no better than Wynne Bluffs or Bardstown.

Having no real friends and even less ambition, he bounced around for almost three years, off and on clerking in a music store, bartending, working the register in a diner, tiring of one place, then moving on to another.

He was tending bar in the Long Neck Giraffe when a man with a gray beard and pulled-back ponytail came in and plopped down on a stool.

"I'm celebrating," he said. "Give me a double of the best bourbon you've got."

"Blanton's okay?" Murph asked.

He nodded. "Bring two glasses, and join me."

Not one to look a gift horse in the mouth, Murphy set the two glasses on the bar, dropped in a few ice cubes, and poured generously. "Whatcha celebrating?"

"Freedom. After today I never have to see Claudia's lying face again."

"Claudia's your wife?"

"Ex-wife," he corrected. "I should've never married her in the first place. You married?"

Murphy shook his head. "I was planning on it, but she up and left. No word of where she was going or if she was coming back."

"She might've done you a favor. If a woman ain't right for you, it's better to know it up front. Backtracking a road that you should never have traveled can be mighty painful."

"You sound like the voice of experience."

"I am. Claudia was my third mistake." He edged forward and stuck out his hand. "Buddy Copeland, three-time loser."

Murphy laughed and shook Buddy's hand. "Russell Murphy. Call me Murph."

Buddy Copeland remained at the bar for most of the evening; after four bourbons he switched to beer, and they continued talking. Once they'd exhausted the topic of ex-wives and runaway girlfriends, they moved on to talking about music. Buddy claimed he'd worked on Music Row since the early days. "I was with the Bradleys before they started recording in the Quonset Hut."

"Where are you at now?" Murph asked.

"Grand Ole Opry. They tapped me for the sound studio while they were still over at Ryman. When they finished building the new place, I came with them."

"Oh man, that's the job to have. That's like not even working."

"You want a tour? Come by tomorrow; I'll show you around, introduce you to some of the guys."

Murphy went, and two weeks later he was working as an assistant sound technician for the afternoon shows. Apparently his earlier experience as an electrician, along with Buddy Copeland's recommendation, was qualification enough for him to get the position.

For the first time since he returned from Vietnam, Murphy was doing something that made him deep-down happy. It wasn't the same kind of happiness he'd known with Vicki; this was more soul-satisfying and peaceful. He felt good about himself, about the job he was doing and the future he could now see. After a while he discovered that he no longer missed Vicki; he no longer saw the blue of her eyes in the sky or caught the fragrance of her skin in a passing breeze. She had over time become like the missing arm, a ghost pain that flickered across his mind and disappeared almost as quickly as it had come.

Two years after he started working at the Opry, he met Loretta. She had a soft smile and flyaway curls that were often dangling on her forehead or kissing her cheek. The first time he saw her she'd come to the sound booth to ask for an approval of the parts invoice they'd received in accounting, but after that day Murphy found a dozen different reasons to visit or stroll by the accounting office. After two weeks of conjuring up excuses for stopping by her office, he quit trying and asked if she might like to have dinner with him.

"It doesn't have to be t-tonight," he stammered. "I mean, it could be tonight, or it could be tomorrow, sometime next week, or . . ."

She looked up with a mischievous sparkle in her eyes and smiled. "I was wondering when you were going to ask."

That date led to several more, and two years later they were married.

Murphy had all but forgotten about Vicki until one night a few months after their first child came along. Loretta was down with the flu, so he warmed a bottle for the late-night feeding. After he'd fed and diapered the baby, he was standing alongside the crib watching her tiny eyelids flicker shut when the thought came to mind. It was like a quick stab to his heart.

He'd always seen the wrong of what Vicki had done, but he had never fully comprehended the heartache it would cause. Now, as he stood there looking down at his infant daughter, he understood.

He thought of the baby, the one she'd called Lara. The child would be about eight years old now; was it possible Vicki still had her? He sat there for several minutes remembering the first newspaper article he'd read and picturing the agonized look on the mother's face as she pleaded for the return of her child. He was trying to recall the name of the family when he remembered the reward ad he'd torn from the local newspaper and folded into a small square. That ad had telephone numbers where you could call in with an anonymous tip. He'd stuck it beneath the hidden flap of his wallet—not the wallet he carried now but the old one, the one he'd gotten rid of years ago.

He dropped down in the rocking chair across from the crib and sat there wondering if he'd actually put that wallet in the trash bin or tossed it into the catchall drawer of the nightstand. He couldn't say positively one way or the other, and even if he did have the wallet, what could he do? It wasn't as if he knew where Vicki was; he couldn't find her back then, so it was less likely he'd be able to find her now. And even if he did, then what?

He remembered how he'd come home that night and found her gone. No word of where she was headed, just a note saying she was sorry. What exactly was she sorry for, he wondered. Because she'd stolen another woman's baby? Because she'd walked out with not a word of goodbye? He could feel the old anger rising up in his chest.

It was not right for Vicki to get away with what she did. Not only did she kidnap that family's baby, but she'd used him as an accessory. He'd never wanted any part of what she'd done, but she pulled him in. Made him believe that as soon as he got a job she was going to give the baby back. She knew all along that she never intended to, but he was too blind to see. He hadn't done anything about it back then, but maybe it wasn't too late to do something now.

He couldn't find Vicki, but maybe the police could. He considered writing an anonymous letter but questioned how much good it would do. Vicki was no dummy; the likelihood was she'd changed her name or moved to a place where they'd never find her. If they didn't find her, they might trace the letter back to him, and then he'd be the one charged with the kidnapping. If it were only himself he had to think about, he'd chance it, but now he had Loretta and the baby. Was he willing to risk bringing that kind of heartache down on them?

When the first trace of a rose-colored dawn became visible on the horizon, Murphy was still sitting in the rocker. By then he'd decided to start looking for that damn wallet. The probability was he'd thrown it away, but if perchance he found it, then he'd figure out what to do.

CHANGING TIMES

Hesterville, 1980

The children's first day of school was a day Rachel had been dreading for years. It meant the twins would be on their own, without Mama Dixon's watchful eye or Bruno. Before her feet hit the floor that morning, a strange fluttering settled in her chest, but she was determined not to let it show. Hope was already apprehensive about school, and seeing her mama overly concerned would only make it worse.

Rachel had breakfast ready when the twins came down. Henry bolted into the kitchen with a grin on his face; he had been talking about school for a week and was anxious to get going. Hope followed along, her footsteps slow and her chin dropped down on her chest.

"Why can't Henry go and me stay here with Grandma?" she asked.

Rachel pulled her into a quick hug. "School is fun. Suzie will be there. You like playing with Suzie, don't you?"

Without looking up, Hope shook her head. "Un-uh. I like staying with Grandma."

"Well, Grandma's busy. She's got things to do, and you have to go to school."

"Why?"

Rachel placed a bowl of sugar-sprinkled oatmeal in front of each of the twins, then sat next to Hope. "Because the law says little girls have to go to school. But I'll make a deal with you. If you go every day this week and still don't like it, I'll reconsider letting you stay home with Grandma."

"Really?"

Rachel gave Hope an affectionate hug and nodded. "Really."

On their walk to school, Henry ran ahead, and Hope plodded along with Bruno at her side. The Hesterville Elementary School was a two-story redbrick building. Ms. Abernathy's kindergarten class was in room 1D, first floor center, according to the registrar. The courtyard hummed with activity, the older girls chattering with last year's classmates, boys playfully shoving one another, everyone hurrying toward the building.

As Rachel hooked the dog's leash to the bicycle rack, Hope looked up with tears in her eyes.

"Please, Mama," she begged, "don't leave me."

Rachel thought her heart would break as she squatted and looked into the tearful brown eyes. She brushed back a wisp of hair that had fallen forward and traced her finger along the trail of a teardrop.

"School's fun; there's nothing to be afraid of. Look how happy your brother and all these other kids are."

Hope kept her head ducked down and said nothing, but the tears continued.

Rachel slid her hand beneath the quivering chin and lifted Hope's face to hers. "Would it help if I come in with you and stay for a few minutes?"

Hope hesitated a moment, then asked if the dog could come. "Bruno's supposed to watch over me." She sniffled.

"Sweetheart, dogs aren't allowed in school."

The tears started up again. "But nobody will watch over me."

For a second Rachel's heart stopped beating; it was the same thought she'd lived with for the past week. She hesitated, knowing this was a moment of choice—she could pass along the fear she carried in her heart or give Hope the confidence she needed. She chose the latter. "That's not true, sweetheart." Folding Hope into her arms, she wiped away the tears. "I'll always be watching over you."

With Hope's hand held tightly in hers, she turned and started toward the building.

"Always and forever," she whispered into the small ear.

Once they were in the classroom, Rachel introduced Hope to her teacher. "You're going to have a wonderful time with Ms. Abernathy," she said. Then she bent and whispered, "School is nothing to be frightened of; being here with Ms. Abernathy is as safe as being at home with Grandma and Bruno."

There was no nod, just a wide-eyed look of fear.

"While you're in here having fun with the other kids, Bruno and I will be waiting just outside, and when school is over we'll all go for ice cream. Okay?"

Still no response, but the tears had stopped.

By the time Rachel slipped out the door, Hope was sitting in a chair next to her friend Suzie. For a long while Rachel stood outside the classroom door, peeking through the glass window, then pulling away before Hope caught sight of her, all the time counting the minutes until her children would be back in her arms. When at long last Hope began leafing through the pages of a picture book, Rachel left.

As she and Bruno walked back to the house, she again thought of Emily. It was a thought that had been in the back of her mind all morning. Retracing her steps along Mulberry Street, she wondered how Emily's first day of school had been. She and Henry were such look-alikes; had she also been eager and filled with excitement? Or was she like Hope, hesitant and afraid to let go of what was familiar?

The thought that Emily might have been frightened brought tears to Rachel's eyes, and she again wondered if someone had been there for her child. Did someone walk her to school and stand at the door of her classroom? Did they wipe away the tears, give her a reassuring hug, and promise to be waiting? Did they love Emmy the way she loved the twins?

Rachel's steps slowed, and as she turned onto Pecan Street she whispered a prayer that God had granted Emily someone to love her. "If it can't be me," she said tearfully, "then let it be a good mother with a loving heart."

~

Once the twins moved on to first grade, they left the house early in the morning and didn't return until after three o'clock. That same year Mama Dixon's crochet group began piecing together a friendship quilt, which they believed would take first prize at the county fair.

It was a project they'd planned some nine years earlier, but year after year something happened and one of the five ladies would suggest they set the quilt aside until the following year. Husbands died, nieces got married, grandbabies came along, and after Emmy disappeared, Helen almost dropped out of the group, claiming it was more important that she spend time with Rachel.

"We'll not hear of you quitting," Sadie said. "We'll simply postpone the project until next year."

Of course, one year turned into three, and then after the twins came along Rachel needed an extra pair of hands, and Mama Dixon didn't get back to the group until the summer after the babies had turned two. By then the ladies were content to simply crochet granny squares as they sat around the table sipping sweet tea and snacking on pimento cheese sandwiches.

Not until the early months of 1982 did they get back to working on the quilt, but once they did, they went at it wholeheartedly. The plan had always been to construct the quilt solely with fabrics that represented the most meaningful elements of their lives. Sadie warned against anyone showing up with store-bought fabric.

"We want this to be an authentic representation of who we are and the lives we've lived," she said.

That evening Mama Dixon told Rachel about the project and asked for some of the clothes the twins had outgrown. "We're doing a mix of fabrics, so it can be most anything," she said. "Playclothes, shirts, dresses, any of that. And if you wouldn't mind, I'd love to have a piece of that flowered apron you used to wear—oh, and a patch or two from one of George's work shirts." She gave a sly grin and added, "I want to make sure my whole family is represented."

"It won't be the whole family if you don't include something from George's daddy."

"I've already got that covered. I used the robe he—"

Rachel's eyes widened. "The green plaid robe? The one hanging on the inside of your bedroom door?"

Looking a bit embarrassed, Helen nodded. "I know I said I'd never in a million years part with it, but now I've thought better. Hanging on that hook, it was just a sad reminder of what a wonderful man he was, but by using his robe in our quilt, Henry can be part of something bigger, something that will last a long time and bring people enjoyment."

"Oh . . ." Rachel whooshed a long, drawn-out sigh. "That's such a beautiful thought."

"Yes, I only wish I would have kept something of Tommy's, but I didn't."

With a look of melancholy shadowing her eyes, Rachel said, "I'd also like Emmy to be part of your quilt."

It was Mama Dixon's turn to look surprised. "I thought you gave away everything."

"Not everything. I still have her pink dress. I'm not sure why I kept it, but . . ."

"You probably kept it for the same reason I kept Henry's robe: because it brought some small measure of comfort."

That evening after the twins had gone to bed and George had settled down to watch *Hill Street Blues*, Rachel pulled the tiny dress from the bottom drawer and held it to her face. It was unlikely that after so many years Emily's scent remained in the fabric, but for a brief moment she could imagine that it did.

The next morning, as soon as George was gone from the house, Rachel took her sewing basket into the bedroom and closed the door. It was almost eleven when she finally emerged and handed Mama Dixon a swatch of pink gingham. "Now the *whole* family will be part of the quilt," she said.

Helen looked down at the square of fabric, and there along the edge was Tommy's name, embroidered in delicate stitches of blue satin. She stood looking at it for a moment, then grew misty-eyed. "How can I ever thank you . . . ?"

Both women knew no thanks was needed.

~

At the next meeting, all five women brought shopping bags filled with remnants of things that were outgrown or outdated. Sadie offered lace appliqués that at one time were part of her divorced cousin's trousseau, and Josephine Jones brought the back of her late husband's bowling shirt along with scraps of a sundress she'd been photographed in some fifty years ago. Adele Scott had remnants of the naval trousers her brother wore in World War II.

"These have historic significance," Adele said as she laid the white squares on the table.

Helen waited until the other ladies had their swatches on the table, then she pulled out the stack she'd put together. One by one she went through them, describing how the colorful squares were taken from the twins' playclothes, the green plaid from Henry's bathrobe, the flowered print from Rachel's old apron, and the blue chambray from George's shirt. She saved the pink gingham square for last, and when she told how Rachel had given up her last keepsake of Emily and embroidered Tommy's name along the edge of the square, the ladies voted unanimously to have that piece be the center of the quilt.

That year the women renamed their group; they called it the Hesterville Crochet and Quilting Club. Sadie told the butcher's wife about what they were doing, and she told the pastor's wife. Before the month was out, the *Primrose Post* called, asking if they could do a story on the women and their quilting project.

When the story appeared on page nine of the *Post* along with a photo of all five women standing alongside a table covered with swatches of fabric, the project took on an even greater level of momentum. Whereas previously they'd had just one meeting a week, they now upped it to three or four.

Seeing Mama Dixon involved in such a wonderful project gave Rachel a feeling of happiness, but she now found herself with long hours of nothing to do. Before noon, she'd have the housework done and a dinner casserole ready to pop in the oven.

That November, on a morning when there was a chill in the air and a scattering of leaves across the lawns, Rachel wrapped a wool scarf around her neck and started out for a walk. She turned left at the corner of Pecan Street, then continued down Mulberry, making a right three blocks later and then a quick left. When she came to a stop she was standing in front of the library. It was a Tuesday not a Thursday, so there was no reading group scheduled, but still she went in.

Karen Molinari was behind the checkout desk going through a stack of books that had yet to be filed. She gave a quick wave and an apologetic smile.

"Sorry I can't stop to chat," she said. "I've got a million things to do today."

"Is there anything I can do to help?"

In the middle of marking index cards for the shipment of new releases, Karen looked up. "Help? You mean on Thursday?"

"No, now." Rachel started to say something about having no place to go and nothing to do, but it sounded lame so she switched to, "I'm free until three o'clock when the kids come home from school."

A smile brightened Karen's face. "Well if you really don't mind . . ." She pushed the stack of books across the desk. "These are fiction. They go alphabetically by author name. The A's start in the third stack across from the reading room."

~

For the remainder of that year and well into 1983, it was as if the bluebird of happiness had flown over the Dixon house and nested on the roof. It seemed as if one good thing followed another.

George's business flourished, the twins did well in school, Mama Dixon's group was moving ahead with their quilt, and Rachel was kept busy with her volunteer work at the library. She was there five days a week, but not on March 10. That was the day she set aside to spend with thoughts of Emily.

Over the years she'd imagined Emily learning to walk, losing her baby teeth, and growing from a toddler into a willowy little girl. That year Rachel saw her as a shy twelve-year-old, perhaps with braces and her hair pulled back in a ponytail. In time that image would change, but one thing never changed: the prayer Rachel said before the day ended.

"Please, God," she'd ask, "give her a family who loves her as much as George and I do."

~

After almost two years of working on the quilt they'd renamed Patches of Heritage, the Hesterville Crochet and Quilting Club entered it in the craft division of the Primrose County Fair, and it won the blue ribbon. The *Post* ran a second story on the ladies and their project, only this time it was featured on the front page of the Sunday edition. The photograph, taken at the fair, showed nine ladies clustered around the hanging quilt with Mama Dixon proudly holding up the blue ribbon.

~

That summer the hardware store's revenues exceeded George's predictions by a whopping 23 percent. Brad Grover became a full-time employee, and George got to take some long-awaited time off. He suggested a second honeymoon for just Rachel and him, and her eyebrows went up.

"And leave the kids alone?" she exclaimed.

"Not alone," George said. "With Mama and Bruno."

"But for five days?"

"They'll be fine. Mama loves those kids as much as we do, and Bruno never leaves Hope's side. There's nothing to worry about. What could possibly happen?"

Rachel didn't have an answer, but the look of apprehension was still stuck to her face. It took a fair bit of convincing and Mama Dixon's promise that she'd keep an eye on them every minute of every day, but eventually Rachel did agree, and George began planning the trip.

Two weeks after Labor Day, they drove to Savannah and checked in at a hotel overlooking the river. As soon as they were settled in the room, Rachel suggested they call home and check on the twins.

George glanced at his watch. "We've been gone less than five hours!"

"I know, but I'll feel more relaxed once I'm certain everything is okay."

After calling home, they went to dinner at the famed Pirates' House, then strolled the crooked streets along the water, walking hand in hand as they did in the days after they were first married. Afterward they stopped at an open-air café and sipped a sherry as the sky grew dark and the stars twinkled above them.

"It's strange, spending the night away from the kids," Rachel said. "As much as I'm enjoying this, I can't help but wish I could peek in on them to make sure they're okay."

George laughed. "I think you can relax, Rachel. With Mama and Bruno watching them, the twins are as safe as they'd be with us there."

"All the same, I'd feel better if we call once or twice a day, just to check."

"If we call twice a day, do you promise not to worry?"

Rachel gave a sheepish smile. "I'll promise to *try* not to worry; how's that?"

"I guess that's as good as I'm going to get." He playfully lifted her hand to his lips and planted a kiss on her palm.

In the days that followed they called twice a day, every day, but they also took carriage rides through the city, visited mansions with commemorative plaques that told how the building had stood since before the Civil War, and ate at taverns where Confederate soldiers had sat at the same tables. Although they were never without something to say to one another, the conversation was often peppered with thoughts of the twins or George's mama. Not necessarily worries but random thoughts of how Hope was going to love the musical jewelry box they bought for her, and Henry, likewise, the Dale Murphy T-shirt.

At night they made love passionately, without thought of yesterday or tomorrow. Although so many years had gone by, it was as if they were newlyweds, finding and taking pleasure from one another. When the last morning came, they remained in bed long after the sun was in the sky and then ordered breakfast brought to the room.

"This is so decadent," Rachel said, laughing. "I feel shameful being here and enjoying all this while the twins are at home with your mama."

"The only thing shameful is that we haven't done it more often."

George broke off a piece of his croissant, spread it with raspberry jam, and held it to her mouth. She playfully licked the jam, then bit off a piece of the buttery croissant. He laughed, then covered her mouth with a kiss and eased her back onto the bed. For the first time in more years than she could remember, they made love for a second time that morning.

On the drive home George reached across the seat, took Rachel's hand in his, and squeezed it lovingly.

"We'll do this again next year," he promised.

PECAN STREET TRAGEDY

Hesterville, 1985

In 1984 the weather remained balmy throughout most of December, but in January a cold front came down from Canada and dropped an icy chill over everything. People left their houses in the morning wearing lightweight sweaters and returned home shivering.

Before the month ended, every one of the women in Mama Dixon's quilt club had come down with some sort of cold or virus, and Helen herself was starting to sound nasal.

On Friday afternoon when Rachel returned from the library, Hope was at the kitchen table doing homework and Henry was watching television in the living room, but Mama Dixon was nowhere to be seen.

"Where's Grandma?" she asked.

Hope shrugged. "Taking a nap, I think."

Helen napping in the middle of the day was rather unusual, so Rachel went to check. She rapped on the door twice, and when there was no answer she opened it and walked in. Mama Dixon was buried under a pile of wool throws and comforters.

"Are you okay?" Rachel asked and touched her hand to Mama Dixon's forehead. "Good grief! You're burning up!"

"I'm okay," Mama Dixon mumbled and pushed herself to a sitting position. "I just needed a nap."

Rachel started peeling back the blankets. "You need more than a nap! I'm going to call Dr. Levine and get you over there right away."

"I don't need a doctor. It's just a touch of the bug Adele had. I'll be fine in a day or so . . ."

Her words trailed off because by then Rachel was headed for the kitchen to grab the thermometer and call Dr. Levine's office. Moments later she was back with the phone held to her ear as she popped the thermometer into Mama Dixon's mouth.

"You have reached the office of Dr. Levine," the recording said. "The office is currently closed. Our office hours are Monday through Friday, nine a.m. through five p.m. If this is an emergency, you may contact Dr. Levine's answering service, and they will locate him for you." The voice rattled off a phone number without allowing time to fetch a pencil. "If your situation is such that it requires immediate attention, we suggest you go directly to the hospital."

Rachel stood there for a moment, wondering if this was or wasn't a true emergency.

Almost as if she'd read Rachel's mind, Mama Dixon said, "Don't worry. I've got the same flu Adele had. I'll be over it in a week or so."

"Well, I *am* worried. I'm thinking maybe I'd best take you over to the emergency room and let a doctor check—"

"I'm not going to the hospital. I'll make an appointment with Dr. Levine and let him give me something."

"He won't be back in the office until Monday. I don't think you should wait that long."

With a flick of her fingers, Mama Dixon waved Rachel off.

"I'll be fine," she said, "if you just scoot out of here and let me get some rest."

~

That Saturday Mama Dixon didn't get out of bed. Rachel carried one glass of juice after another to the room for her, but they just sat on the nightstand with the pulp falling to the bottom of the glass.

"I'm not thirsty," Mama Dixon complained, "just tired."

When her temperature crept up to 103, Rachel carried a pan of ice-cold water to her bedside and wiped down her face, hands, and arms. After the cool bath her temperature dropped to 101, but Rachel feared it was a temporary measure.

"Please," she begged, "let me take you to the hospital."

Mama Dixon stubbornly refused, claiming she'd be fine waiting to see Dr. Levine.

~

On Sunday morning, Mama Dixon's temperature skyrocketed to 104, and she was too weak to continue her protest. Without offering an option, George called for an ambulance. When the paramedics loaded Mama Dixon into it, Rachel climbed in and sat beside her just as she had before.

"Once we get you to the hospital, you'll be all right," she whispered, but even as she spoke the words she was fearful of being wrong. After so many years of drawing strength from Mama Dixon, it was now time to give back some of what she'd taken.

It was Sunday, and the hospital was short-staffed on weekends. Once Mama Dixon was wheeled into an examination room, each small step forward was preceded and followed by long minutes of waiting.

Rachel stood beside the bed holding on to Mama Dixon's hand as she listened to the sound of labored breathing and violent spurts of coughing. After each coughing spell, Mama Dixon would fall back against the pillow, her breath coming in wispy thin gasps. The small room, a sickly green color, was icy cold and devoid of any decoration whatsoever. When the nurse came to draw blood, Rachel left Mama Dixon's side just long enough to hurry down the hall, find an orderly, and secure two heated blankets. She carried them back, covered the bed, and tucked Mama Dixon's bony hands beneath the warm covers.

George arrived two hours later, his face drawn and his brows pinched tight.

"How's Mama doing?" he asked.

Rachel gave a disheartened shrug. "Don't know yet. She was terribly dehydrated, so they've started an IV, but we're still waiting for results from the blood tests and X-rays."

They stood silent for a moment, then she turned and asked who was with the children.

"I called Sadie, and she came over. She said not to worry about time; she'll stay overnight if need be."

Rachel gave a nod, indicating the solution was okay with her. The twins were ten years old now; they understood right from wrong; they knew never to walk away with a stranger and to scream if they were in danger. Those were the things she'd taught them, and now when Mama Dixon needed her more than they did, she had to trust that they'd learned their lessons well.

She and George stood silently beside the bed, the same fearful look etched onto their faces. Over the years they had weathered many a storm together and seldom been at a loss for words, but now there seemed to be little either of them could say.

It was after seven when the doctor came in with a report.

"It looks like your mother is going to be with us for a while," he said. "She has a substantial amount of fluid in both lungs. We're treating her with some heavy-duty antibiotics, and we'll be starting her on oxygen. So far her temperature has remained steady at 104, but if it goes any higher we may have to put her on a ventilator."

After the doctor left, there were more hours of waiting. Each time a nurse or attendant stepped into the room to check a machine or change the IV bag, either George or Rachel asked how she was doing. The answers were generally "Stable" or "Holding her own."

After a while it became impossible to tell the nurses from the orderlies and the technicians. They came and went with little more than a nod or a stiff smile, leaving more unanswered questions and greater fear in their wake. At ten o'clock an orderly came and told them Mama Dixon was going to a room on the third floor.

"We'll be moving her shortly," he said.

Realizing that "shortly" could be a very long time in the emergency room, Rachel suggested George go home and get some sleep.

"I can stay here with Mama," she said, "at least until she's settled in a room."

George bent and kissed his mama's cheek. "Are you all right with that, Mama?"

She dipped her head ever so slightly and gave a frail smile.

"Would you rather I stay?" he asked.

She closed her eyes and wobbled her head side to side.

~

It was almost midnight when the orderly came and wheeled the gurney down the long hallway and into the elevator. Even after Mama Dixon was settled in her room and covered with three warm blankets, Rachel could see the way she was shivering.

"Are you still cold?" she asked.

Mama Dixon started to answer, but the moment she opened her mouth, a coughing fit took hold, and she struggled to catch her breath. When the coughing finally slowed, rivulets of perspiration dripped from her face, and the question went unanswered. In time, she was given a sedative that would allow her to get some rest.

Rachel stood by the bed and held her hand for a long while. Once Mama Dixon was sleeping somewhat peacefully, she whispered, "I'll be back in the morning," and left the room. In the lobby of the hospital, she called a taxi to come and take her home.

~

For the next nine days, Mama Dixon swayed back and forth. One day it would seem that she was improving, and the next she'd be worse than before. She slept when she could, but when she was awake the coughing fits came one right after another. They were so forceful they left her red-faced and wheezing for breath. From time to time she cried out because the pain in her chest was more than she could bear.

Rachel arrived at the hospital early in the morning, and she stayed until George closed the store and came to take her place. Mama Dixon spoke sometimes, but with the oxygen mask covering the lower portion of her face it came out muffled and hard to understand. Rachel sat by her side and watched as the machine counted heartbeats, rapid spikes one moment, then slowing to a near stop the next. She added blankets when Mama Dixon shivered and took them away when her face grew moist with perspiration.

On the tenth morning she found Mama Dixon's bed empty, the blanket folded back and the nightstand cleared of everything.

The memory of the empty crib flashed before her eyes, and suddenly it was that morning all over again, the fear as great as ever. It swelled in her chest and slammed against her brain as she turned and ran toward the nurses' station.

"Where's Mama Dixon?" she shouted.

"Dixon?" the nurse repeated. "Helen Dixon?"

"Yes, she was in room 305—"

"She's been moved to the ICU on the fifth floor."

Panic did not bode well in the ICU. Sorrow, yes, tears even, but panic gave the staff cause for alarm. When Rachel burst through the doors looking wild-eyed and frenzied, Cecile VanTyne left her station and hurried over.

"Is there a problem?"

Rachel bobbed her head from one side to the other, trying to see past Cecile.

"I need to find Helen Dixon."

"Ah, yes . . ." Cecile smiled. "You must be her daughter."

Rachel nodded. "Why is she—"

Cecile reached out and touched Rachel's arm. "Don't worry—your mom is stable for the time being. Last night she had difficulty breathing, but she's on a ventilator now and resting comfortably."

"A ventilator?"

"I know it sounds scary, but it's much easier on her. She doesn't have to work to breathe; the machine does it for her." Cecile turned and motioned for Rachel to follow. "I know she'll be glad to see you. You were the last person she spoke of before they placed the intubation tube in her throat."

When they reached the door of the room, Cecile stuck her head in and said, "Helen, dear, your daughter is here to see you." The cheerfulness in her voice seemed strangely out of place.

Rachel remained by Mama Dixon's side throughout the day. At first she spoke as though nothing were wrong, telling of the friends pitching in to keep an eye on the twins, of Hope studying for the school spelling bee and how Sadie had spent the night in the upstairs guest room.

As the sun dropped low in the sky, Rachel saw the weariness in Mama Dixon's face, and the terrible truth curled itself around her heart in a stranglehold. Tears welled in her eyes as she lifted the limp hand and held it to her heart.

"Oh, Mama Dixon," she said as she sobbed. "I hope you can feel how much I love you. I would have never made it through those terrible years without you. Please don't leave us now. I understand you're tired and hurting, but you've got to keep fighting. I need you, the kids need you, George needs you. You're the one who makes our family whole. Without you . . ."

Rachel couldn't finish the sentence, because the thought of being without Mama Dixon was too painful to even consider.

When George arrived, they both sat by his mama's bedside. George wrapped his arm around her back when a coughing fit seized her, and

Rachel held tight to her hand when she cried out in pain. It was long past suppertime when the pulmonary specialist came to talk.

"Dr. Kenneth Cornwell," he said and offered his hand first to Rachel, then George. He listened to Mama Dixon's chest, lifted her eyelids, and checked the intubation. After he'd made a few notations on her chart, he asked them to step outside the room for a chat.

With his eyes shifting back and forth between George's face and the floor, he said, "I imagine you've already sensed this, but I need to tell you that your mother's infection is not responding to the antibiotics. Her lungs are compromised, and she's not able to fight this off." He hesitated a moment, looking at George, then Rachel. "She was a smoker, wasn't she?"

George nodded. "But she stopped more than ten years ago, when the twins were born."

The doctor gave a regretful-sounding sigh. "The damage is sometimes irreversible. Right now, she's fighting so hard to breathe that her body doesn't have the strength to rebuild itself. I'd like to suggest that we put her in an induced coma. Chances are it won't change what's happening, but if she's able to rest easier there's a possibility she'll regain her strength."

"What's the downside of that?" George asked.

"She may not respond when we take her off the medication."

Rachel gasped. "Do you mean she might never come out of the coma?"

The muscles in Dr. Cornwell's face tightened. "I'm afraid so." He shifted his focus from Rachel to George, then back to her again. "I know it sounds harsh, but you need to know so when the time comes, you'll be able to make the decision that's best for you and your mother."

Tears overflowed Rachel's eyes and began rolling down her cheeks.

"There is no best decision," she said. "They're all horrible." Without saying anything more, she turned and went back inside the room to sit beside Mama Dixon.

When he finished talking with the doctor, George returned to the room and sat beside Rachel. It was a long while before he spoke. When he did, his voice was weighted with sorrow.

"I told him not to do anything yet; maybe Mama will come around. We'll see what happens in the next day or two."

George stayed until almost midnight, and when he left Rachel remained behind.

"I'm going to stay with Mama," she said, "because I know it's what she would do for me."

Sometime during the wee hours of morning, Mama Dixon slipped into a coma, naturally and of her own accord. Two days later, her heart gave out. She passed away with George and Rachel by her side.

ANOTHER SEARCH

Fairlawn, 1985

When Lara went from middle school into high school, no birth certificate was needed. Her school transcript was sufficient. No one thought to question a girl who was on the student council and got straight A's.

Each time Lara passed such a milestone, Angela breathed a sigh of relief. She knew eventually the birth certificate issue would become a problem—if not this year, then the next or the one after that. Shortly after Lara entered her freshman year of high school, Angela realized time was closing in on her and decided to do something.

That November the car was in the shop for repairs, and it rained almost every day, but neither of those things was enough to dissuade her. She pulled on her boots, covered her head with a plastic rain cap, and trudged over to the Fairlawn Public Library. Although she had only the vaguest idea of what she was looking for, Angela settled herself at the reading table in the research section and began poring over books loaded with words like *affidavit*, *whereas*, and *wherefore*. She found a wealth of information on establishing a property claim, filing for citizenship, or registering a business, but there seemed to be nothing on birth certificates.

She was on the verge of giving up when she came across a weighty tome published by the Health and Human Resources Department. Halfway through the book she discovered a section titled Delayed Certificate of Birth. It was a scant three pages long but clearly spelled out what a person could do to obtain a certificate of identity if a child's birth had previously gone unrecorded.

Previously unrecorded.

That thought stuck in Angela's head. Since no one had ever seen a birth certificate, she could easily enough slide into the assumption that Lara's birth had never been recorded. Which meant she could apply for one this way.

She read through the section five times; reading and then rereading each sentence to make certain she understood what had to be done. With each word, her pulse quickened. This was it, precisely what she'd been searching for all these years. A simple process for filing, a twenty-seven-dollar processing fee, and she'd never again have to worry about Lara not having a birth certificate. As she read through the pages one last time, Angela's eyes grew teary, and her heart swelled in her chest.

Pulling the pad and pencil from her bag, she began making notes.

- Full name of mother and father
- Date and county of birth
- Three pieces of documentary evidence
- Notarized affidavit signed by one parent or legal guardian

After she'd listed everything she was going to need, Angela copied down the address for the Vital Records Registration office.

It was near dark when she left the library; the wind had picked up, and the temperature had dropped another ten degrees. When she rounded the corner of Chester Street an icy gust took her rain cap, but she ducked her head down and kept going, all the while thinking of how she'd go about getting the documents she'd need. She arrived home drenched and shivering, but none of that mattered; she'd found what she'd been searching for.

~

That night Angela told Kenny of her plans. "It's not all that complicated," she said. "We have to submit proof of Vicki's death, a notarized statement saying we were Lara's guardians prior to the age of seven, and three forms of proof."

"That's it?" he replied. "We don't need a release from Murphy?"

She shook her head. "Nope. I've gone through the requirements word by word, and as far as I can tell, we'll be able to provide everything that's required."

"Which is . . . ?"

Angela ran through the list again; in a few short hours she'd memorized every last detail. "First off, there's Vicki's death certificate. Then we prepare a statement saying Lara has been with us since her mother's death and have it notarized. After that, we'll need three forms of proof that Lara is physically here and living under our care."

"What forms of proof are you—"

He wasn't asking anything Angela hadn't already asked herself, so she jumped in. "Her school records, her medical records, and a letter from the pastor."

After years of working with the telephone company, Kenny knew with a government organization, things were seldom as simple as they were said to be. "Once you submit those documents, what happens?" he asked.

"My understanding is that they verify your claim and send out the child's birth certificate."

"That's it?" he repeated, but there was no smile, and his jaw was rigid as a washboard.

Angela seemed not to notice the look of concern stretched across his face as she rambled on with a tale of how she'd found this obscure bit of information in a book the size of two encyclopedias bound together.

"When we finally get Lara's birth certificate, we should have a real family celebration," she said happily. "Maybe take her to Paducah on a shopping spree."

The ridges across Kenny's forehead deepened. "You haven't told Lara about any of this, have you?"

"Not about the birth certificate. She's always known Vicki is her birth mom, and we're her adoptive parents, but she doesn't know we don't have her birth certificate or adoption papers. Now, I was thinking that since we're this close—"

He was already shaking his head. "I know you're excited, but hold off mentioning anything until we actually have the document in hand. Right now she's not questioning any of this, so why give her something to worry about when there's no need?"

~

Before a week had gone by, Angela had all the documentation she needed. On Monday morning she wrote a letter explaining the situation and detailing her request, then packaged everything in a large manila envelope and mailed it off to the Vital Records Registration office.

She'd expected the birth certificate to arrive in a week or two, three at the most, but six weeks passed before the official-looking envelope appeared in their mailbox.

Angela anxiously slit the envelope open and trembled as she unfolded the single sheet of paper. Instead of Lara's birth certificate, it was a form letter.

It stated that in the absence of a parental signature and/or guardianship documentation, the Vital Records Registration office would require an announcement ad containing the name of the birth mother and/or the name of the child's father be placed in all applicable newspapers in the district where the birth occurred.

The second paragraph stated that once the announcement requirement had been satisfied, the court would set a date for the hearing.

The letter closed with a single sentence saying that the request for a Delayed Certificate of Birth would be held in abeyance until such time as proof of announcement was received.

With her knees about to give way and her heart feeling as though it would explode inside her chest, Angela lowered herself onto a chair. As she read through the letter a second time, her eyes filled with tears, and the words became blurred. A tear splashed on the paper, and when she brushed it away, the clerk's signature smudged.

"This is not fair," she sobbed. "It's not fair. We're Lara's parents. We're the only family she's ever known. What justice is there in some clerk who knows nothing of our daughter determining whether or not she should be granted a birth certificate? For God's sake, Lara's my sister's child! Why would a parent lie about something like that?"

For a long while Angela remained in the chair, feeling defeated, empty of hope, and fearful of what lay ahead. Yes, Lara would need a birth certificate for a number of things—a driver's license, college, marriage—but those were in the future. Right now she was only fourteen, and they had to weigh the risk of Murphy seeing the announcement and coming to claim his daughter against her need for a birth certificate.

Angela thought back to the day Vicki had come to live with them and remembered how she'd claimed Murphy was abusive.

Like Daddy.

Once that thought surfaced, Angela could not rid herself of it.

~

That evening, in the privacy of their bedroom, Angela told Kenny about the letter.

"We know nothing about Murphy," she said. "He or someone who knows him might still be living in the area, and if they see the announcement . . ." The remainder of her words trailed off because the thought was simply too overwhelming.

Kenny stood there and listened, his face tilted toward the floor, his right hand cradling his chin, one finger pressed to his lips. He waited until after she'd reminded him that Vicki claimed Murphy was an abuser.

"We don't honestly know if that's true," he said. "Your sister said a lot of things that leave room for doubt—"

Looking petrified, Angela gasped. "But are you willing to risk it?"

After a moment of hesitation Kenny shook his head. "No, I'm not. In four years Lara will be eighteen, and at that point she'll be able to determine her own fate."

He suggested they wait and revisit the issue after Lara's eighteenth birthday, and that's how they left it. Angela folded the letter back inside the envelope, tucked it away in the same drawer as Vicki's letter, and they never spoke of it again.

THE SMALL ROOM

The morning after Mama Dixon died, Rachel closed the door to her room. The room was full of memories, many of them good, but mingled in with the good ones were images of those terrible days before she'd gone to the hospital, and that was something Rachel was not ready to deal with.

In the days following the funeral, she had little time to grieve. She rose early in the morning to brew coffee and set out plates of food for the visitors who streamed in and out of the house. Friends who had known Helen as far back as grade school came to pay their respects. They brought casseroles and cakes or baskets of homemade cookies, then they sat and talked of how they would miss Helen. The twins stayed home from school, and George left the management of the store to Brad Grover.

Rachel busied herself from dawn to dark: greeting guests, hanging coats, serving cups of coffee or glasses of sherry, moving about the room listening to tales of Helen's youth and offering sympathy to those who pressed their hand to hers and shed a tear.

Sadie Jenkins came every day, but unlike the others she didn't sob or bemoan how much she would miss Helen. Instead, she went from room to room gathering the unwashed cups, refilling platters of cookies, and, on occasion, ushering out guests who overstayed their welcome. Late one evening, when the others were gone and the twins tucked in their beds, Sadie sat at the kitchen table with George and Rachel.

"If I can do anything to help . . . ," she said.

"There's nothing," George replied, his voice not quavering, his expression one of resilience and determination.

Rachel looked up, her eyes brimming with tears. "I'd like it if you could come by for coffee once in a while. Mama Dixon and I always had coffee together in the morning."

Sadie nodded.

Nothing more was said that night, but after everyone else had gone back to their regular routines of work and school, Sadie started stopping by. She'd come once a week, usually on a Tuesday or Wednesday, arriving after George left for the store and the twins climbed onto the school bus. She'd sit across from Rachel at the kitchen table, and they'd talk; sometimes it was just chitchat, but other times they'd reminisce about Mama Dixon, the good times they'd had and the sorrow of losing her.

It was on just such a morning that Sadie said, "Helen and I were best friends from before she married George's daddy. I was the maid of honor at her wedding, and she was the same at mine."

The picture of a young Mama Dixon dressed in a frothy bridesmaid dress came to mind, and Rachel smiled. "You must miss her terribly."

"Oh, I do. But when you get to be my age you've only got so many years left, and you can't afford to waste them on tears. When thoughts of Helen start crowding my head, I look up and tell her to save me a seat at the table 'cause I'll be there soon enough, then I switch over to thinking of all the fun we'll have when we're together again."

"I wish I could see it that way. For me, losing Mama Dixon is like losing Emily all over again."

Sadie pushed her coffee aside and leaned in. "Why, those things are not at all the same! Emmy was a baby, taken before you had your fair share of time with her. A mama has the right to expect to spend a lifetime with her baby, so I can understand your misery over Emmy. But Helen . . . Well now, that's a whole different story."

"How so?"

"You had a lot of years with Helen. She was a woman whose time had come."

"That seems rather harsh—"

"It's not harsh at all! It's the way of life. Kids can't expect their parents to outlive them. The good Lord calling Helen home when He did was the natural order of things."

Rachel gave an almost imperceptible shrug, indicating she didn't necessarily agree with Sadie. "I don't think—"

"Think what you want," Sadie said. "I'm just telling you what I know Helen herself would say: get on with your life and stop wasting the time you've got."

A few minutes later Sadie suggested Rachel had better hurry up and get dressed if she was to make it to the library on time.

~

Mama Dixon's room remained closed off all winter and through the sweltering months of July and August, but that September George said he'd like to set up an office at the house.

"It would enable me to do most of my paperwork after dinner or on Sunday instead of staying late at the store."

Rachel smiled at the thought of having him home earlier. "The upstairs bedroom at the end of the hall would be perfect."

"I'd rather have the small sitting room down here."

"That's Mama's room!"

"Was," George corrected. "It *was* Mama's room, but now it's a small room that no one's using."

"All the same. Why can't you take one of the upstairs rooms? They're bigger and—"

"Because they're upstairs. When I'm working, I don't want to hear the kids playing music or talking on the phone with their friends."

"I'll tell them to be quiet."

"That's ridiculous. Kids are kids. They shouldn't have to be quiet. All I need is enough space for a desk and file cabinet. That small sitting room is perfect."

Rachel's shoulders drooped. "I haven't cleaned it out yet."

"Take your time. It doesn't have to be tomorrow."

Rachel knew that even so, it was imminent. She would have to face up to what she'd been avoiding for the past seven months.

A week went by before she even peeked in the door, and when she finally did she regretted it immediately. Although the blinds were drawn, and there was nothing more than a sliver of sun lighting the room, she saw Mama Dixon sitting on the daybed, her face as pale and lifeless as it had been that last day. Rachel backed away, slammed the door shut, and stood there in the hallway, her forehead leaned against the wall and tears clouding her eyes.

She remained there for several minutes, remembering how for more than two years she'd kept Emily's room exactly as it was the night she was taken. She'd kept it as a shrine, a shrine dedicated to the misery of loss. Thousands upon thousands of hours she'd sat in the rocker looking across at the empty crib, and it had changed nothing. Mama Dixon, with sage advice and kind words, had helped her to move ahead, but even then Rachel had had to turn to George and ask him to carry off the crib. She couldn't find the courage to let go back then; could she find it now?

Rachel turned toward the door a second time, eased it open, and stood there. As the memories of Mama Dixon flooded her mind she felt her resolve waning.

"I don't know if I can do this alone . . ." Her words were whisper thin, her eyes again becoming watery.

Of course you can! a voice answered.

Rachel turned with a start. She expected to see Mama Dixon standing there but found herself alone.

"You're still here with me, aren't you?" she asked.

The voice remained silent, but by then Rachel was certain she knew the answer.

That morning Rachel emptied out the closet and the drawers. She lovingly folded Mama Dixon's dresses, slacks, and shirts into the shopping bags she would send off to Goodwill. After the clothes were packed, she filled a box with shoes and handbags and after that another carton with throw pillows, the yellow curtains, and the daybed coverlet.

When the room was cleared of everything else, she disassembled the dressing table and placed the pieces atop the mattress of the daybed. She then called for the Goodwill truck to come and take everything.

When George arrived home that evening, the small room was bare to the walls.

The only things Rachel kept were Mama Dixon's favorite apron and the small TV that she'd given to Hope so she and her friends could watch *American Bandstand* in her room. That evening when Rachel prepared supper, she was wearing the apron. What was once Mama Dixon's favorite had now become hers.

~

It didn't happen that same day, but little by little the painful memory of Mama Dixon as she was at the end began to fade. After a desk and file cabinet were moved in, Rachel started to see the room as George's space. One day without giving it thought, she told Hope to empty the wastebasket in her daddy's office. The words seemed to linger in the air for a few moments after she'd said them, and she smiled. Although it had been a painful process, she had taken another step forward and was still standing.

A NEW DIRECTION

Hesterville, 1987

Two years after George had converted Mama Dixon's room into his office, Rachel got a frantic phone call from Marilyn Byrd, one of the gals in the Hesterville Women's League.

"I hate to impose on you this way," she said, "but I'm desperate."

Given the sound of Marilyn's voice, Rachel envisioned the worst. "What's wrong?"

"With the kids off to college, I've been using the upstairs bedrooms as bed-and-breakfast rentals. My cousin Norma Jean showed up unexpectedly, and I've got a rental coming in tomorrow."

"I don't see how—"

"With those extra bedrooms you've got, I thought maybe this once you could help me out and take one of my rentals."

"Have a stranger stay here at the house?"

"She's not exactly a stranger. Cynde Louis has stayed with me once before. She's a businesswoman who came from the referral agency."

Several moments passed. The word *no* was perched on the tip of Rachel's tongue when Marilyn spoke again.

"Please . . . ," she begged. "I'm desperate. I can't toss Norma Jean out on the street, and my reputation with the referral agency will be ruined if I don't come up with something for Cynde."

Rachel gave a sigh of resignation. "Okay, I'll do it. But you're going to have to give me a rundown on what's expected."

Marilyn went over everything step by step, and to Rachel it seemed little more than having company. Of course, she would provide breakfast as she would for any guest, and having the room freshened up was no problem. It was something she'd been planning to do anyway.

Cynde Louis arrived shortly after four on Tuesday afternoon. She looked to be a few years older than Rachel herself but younger by far than Mama Dixon. Rachel took to her right away, and when George arrived home from the store he found the two women sitting on the front porch sipping lemonade.

After introductions were made, Rachel said, "Cynde's from Atlanta; I was telling her about the year we were there for the hardware convention. What was the name of that restaurant we liked so much?"

"The Palm," George said, and minutes later Cynde was telling of how she'd had the best steak she'd ever tasted at that very same restaurant. One word led to another, and before long Rachel asked Cynde if she'd like to join the family for dinner.

"I don't want to be a bother," she said. "Especially after you were nice enough to take me in on such short notice."

"You're no bother at all; in fact, we love having you."

Rachel gave a smile, and it was as genuine as any George had ever seen. In less than three hours, Cynde had gone from being a bed-and-breakfast responsibility to pleasurable company.

~

The next morning, long after the kids left for school and George hurried off to the store, Cynde lingered at the breakfast table chatting with Rachel. They talked of the new restaurants that had come to Atlanta, how Cynde had trained to be an insurance adjuster, and what it was like to be traveling five days a week.

"The money's good, but I don't love the travel," Cynde said. "That's why I stay at a bed-and-breakfast whenever I have the chance. It feels more like home."

Rachel confessed this was the very first time she'd actually hosted a bed-and-breakfast guest. "I might never have done it were it not for Marilyn asking me to help out."

"You should definitely continue," Cynde said. "You're a natural when it comes to making a guest feel at home."

When Cynde left two days later, Rachel stood on the front porch and waved goodbye. By then she was certain this was something she would do again and again.

~

That summer Rachel registered the Homestead Bed and Breakfast with the same agency Marilyn used, and in September she ordered a shingle to be hung beside the walkway that read WELCOME TO THE HOMESTEAD BED AND BREAKFAST. By then Bruno's muzzle had turned gray, and he was content to lie on the front porch and be petted by newcomers. His services as a guard dog were no longer necessary. He had done his job and done it well.

MOVING AHEAD

Fairlawn, January 1989

After twenty years of working for the telephone company, Kenny McAlister finally got the promotion he'd been waiting for. He would be based in Daytona and become the managing director for all of northeast Florida. The job paid half again what he was making, and the company was going to foot the bill for relocation expenses.

That evening when he broke the big news at the dinner table, he did not get the reaction he expected.

"Moving to Daytona!" Lara exclaimed. "When my graduation's only six months away?" She pushed back her plate and grew tearful. "Are you deliberately trying to ruin my life?"

Angela tried to calm her, saying things such as "Don't worry, we'll work this out," and "It's not nearly as bad as it seems," but Lara stomped off to call her cadre of best friends and tell them the devastating news.

Angela waited until she was gone and then voiced her opinion. "I'm not too crazy about the idea either," she said solemnly. "All our friends are here. Our home is here. Vicki is buried here. How can we just pack up and leave everything that's dear to us?"

Kenny reached across the table and touched his hand to hers. "Don't you think I've considered all that? Yes, it means a big upheaval right now, but it's only temporary. Once we're settled, our life will be even better than it is here."

"I'm not unhappy with what we've got—"

"I know you're not," he said and squeezed her hand. "But this promotion means a lot more money, which will come in pretty handy with Lara wanting to go to college. She's already applied to the University of Florida, and if we're living in Daytona, she'd qualify for in-state tuition."

"What if she doesn't get accepted? Or decides she'd rather go to Kentucky?"

"With Lara's grades, I think she'll be accepted most anywhere she applies, and as for her deciding to go elsewhere, we'll deal with that if we have to."

Angela sat there with a look of despondency tugging at her face. "I really don't want to leave here," she finally said, "and I'm certain Lara doesn't want to either. She wants to graduate with her friends. It's something she's been looking forward to . . ."

"I realize that, and I'm willing to compromise." Kenny suggested he would go ahead and make the move to Daytona, leaving Angela and Lara to stay in Fairlawn until after graduation.

She gave a half-hearted nod of acceptance, knowing it was the only workable solution.

~

Before the month was out, Lara received a letter of acceptance from the University of Florida, and as it turned out, her friends were thrilled with the thought of having someone to visit in the Sunshine State.

"Daytona is right on the beach," Kelly May said. "We can do a first-semester break at your folks' house."

Carrie Kendall agreed, adding that Daytona was a killer place for spring break. "I heard Brian Fitzpatrick is planning to go there with his friends from the football team."

"No way!" Kelly said. "How awesome would that be? We could have a party and invite them all!"

"I'd have to ask my parents," Lara said, "but my dad really wants me to be happy, so I'm pretty sure he'd be cool with it."

That same week, she and Kelly began planning a reunion for the first-semester break.

~

Kenny left for Daytona the twenty-ninth of January.

"I'm sorry I'll miss Lara's birthday," he said, "but my start date is February 1."

"She understands," Angela said. She handed him a thermos of coffee along with the sandwiches she'd prepared for his trip. With a look of sadness scrawled across her face, she gave a sigh and said, "I'm going to miss you terribly."

They kissed goodbye. It was long and sweet and filled with a desire they both knew would go unsatisfied for a long while. When the kiss ended he held her close for another moment, then broke free and climbed into the car. Tears clouded her eyes as Angela watched him back out of the driveway and disappear down the block.

"Take care of yourself," she whispered, but by then he was gone.

~

With Kenny gone, sleep was almost impossible for Angela. That first night she tossed and turned endlessly. For the past twenty years she had fallen asleep with her head on his shoulder and his arm curled around her. In all those years, they had not slept apart even once. Without him, the bed felt as big and empty as a snow-covered stadium.

For hours, she lay there remembering the warmth of his hand against her arm. She was always cold, but he seemed to radiate heat. She shivered, remembering how the brush of his thigh against hers or the touch of his hand was enough to warm her. Tonight she'd pulled on two extra blankets and a heavy comforter, but still she felt chilled.

She scuffed her feet together trying to warm them as she thought of other things: how over the next few months she'd be busy packing, deciding what to keep and what to give away. She pictured the long stretches of highway Kenny would drive and wondered if he had made it all the way to Daytona or settled in a motel along the way.

It would be only five months, Angela told herself. Next week she was hosting book club, and following that she'd take Lara shopping for some new clothes to wear on the class trip. Then there would be the prom, the graduation ceremony, and the parties that went along with it. Even though she could name dozens of things that would keep her too busy to miss Kenny, she couldn't move past the emptiness of that bed.

After several hours of sleeplessness, she got up and pulled on the sweater Kenny had bought the year they were married. It was stretched out of shape and had a hole in one elbow, but in it she could catch the scent of him, and, oddly enough, it kept her warmer than the stack of blankets piled one on top of the other.

A thin ribbon of daybreak was beginning to show on the horizon when Angela finally drifted off to sleep. By then she had come to the realization that it was going to be a very long five months.

A NIGHT OF MOVIES

Time is measured differently for everyone, and for Angela the days dragged by like an old man lugging a sack twice his weight. In April she began packing things away. Some would go into storage until they found a house, and others would be taken to the furnished apartment. Day after day she made trips to the Goodwill store with things they no longer had use for. First to go were the crib and high chair she and Vicki had bought in Paducah, then the baby clothes she'd stored thinking Lara might one day have a sister. Next were stacks of hardly worn wool sweaters and a pair of snow boots Lara had outgrown.

Each thing seemed to have memories stuck to it, some lighthearted and funny, others heavy as a sack of stones. The afternoon she folded her old Dimitri's Diner uniform and packed it into the Goodwill bag, her eyes clouded with tears. Vicki died wearing that same shirt, and although she could give the uniform away, she knew she could never rid herself of that memory.

When she moved on to clearing out the hall closet where they stored folding chairs and holiday tablecloths, Angela came across the movie projector Kenny had bought all those years ago. Behind it was a box filled with reels of film. For years he'd taken movies, documenting Lara's journey as she went from baby to toddler and in time to a gangly preteen. Afterward they'd continued sporadically until she moved on to junior high, then they stopped, but Angela couldn't remember why.

Even though the hallway was littered with piles of old sneakers, soccer uniforms, and guest towels, Angela carried the projector to the living room and plugged it in. At one time they'd had a screen, but she had no idea where it was now. She pointed the lens toward a blank wall, threaded a roll of film through the machine, and snapped on the power.

The light flickered, and then there she was: Lara at four years old at her birthday party, a Mrs. Beasley talking doll in her arms and a huge smile on her face. As Angela sat and watched the pictures jump from one spot to another, it was as if she were living it all over again. She smiled at the close-up of Lara with a smear of pink icing on her chin and laughed when she proudly held up four fingers to indicate how old she was. In the background Angela saw herself chatting with Mindy Snead, who'd moved away some five or six years ago. After a while the angle changed, and there was Kenny, younger, his face partly hidden by the beard he'd worn for a few years. The shadow of the tall pine was stretched across the yard and shading Lara's face as the film flickered to an end.

A door slammed. "Mom? Are you here?"

"In the living room," Angela answered as she flicked a switch to rewind the film.

Lara came through the door, tossed her backpack on the chair, then eyed the projector and grinned. "Are you watching the old movies?"

"Yes, this one was from your fourth birthday."

"Oh, I love that one! Play it again!"

Angela didn't need to be coaxed; there was nothing she enjoyed more. She snapped the projector back on and started the tape again.

"Oh my gosh. Look at Dad with that beard!"

"He had that for years. I think you were about six when he finally shaved it off."

Moments later the camera zoomed in on Lara hugging the doll, and she gave a squeal of delight. "That's my Mrs. Beasley talking doll!"

When the film came to an end she said, "Play the one from that first Christmas when I was a baby, the one with my birth mom in it."

Angela rummaged through the box, but none of the tapes was marked. "It might be this one." She pulled a spool of tape from the box and threaded the machine, but what came on-screen was the 1984 Girl Scout Jamboree.

"Oh, look, Mom, there's Amelia Baxter. She was my science buddy in eighth grade. We did that experiment where we almost blew up the classroom."

"Good thing Ralph Reed was your teacher. If it had been Mrs. Pennefort, she would have flunked you both."

There was a close-up of Lara waving the camera away from her, and after that a circle of girls gathered around a campfire laughing and toasting marshmallows. When that film ended, they continued to search for the first Christmas Lara had asked to see. Instead they found one of a group of eight-year-old girls crowded into Lara's room for a sleepover. The next reel was of the second grade school play where Lara had stumbled across the stage in a fairy costume and a flower garland that kept falling off.

She laughed. "Oh my gosh, I was so pathetic!"

"No, you weren't," Angela said. "You were only seven years old, and you had as much stage presence as any of the kids. Cathy Contino said you were wonderful."

Lara turned with a bright-eyed smile. "This is so much fun, Mom. Let's watch them all, then we can mark the cans with the name of the event and the date."

Angela pulled her daughter into an affectionate hug. "Pumpkin, that sounds like a perfect evening to me!"

"You haven't called me 'pumpkin' in ages," Lara said with a giggle. "Are you going nostalgic on me?"

"I guess so."

That evening Angela ordered a pizza, and they sat amid the piles of half-packed boxes watching the years roll by. Vicki was in only two reels: the first Christmas and that first birthday party.

Lara squealed. "Look at the size of that teddy bear. It's as big as I am!"

"Your mama was working at the diner then and had extra money. She went all out for your birthday, even got you a musical jack-in-the-box, but the thing petrified you."

"I don't remember that."

"Well, of course not—you were only a baby." Angela hesitated a moment, then asked, "Do you remember anything about your mama?"

Lara studied the image on the wall, then shook her head. "Not really. I know what she looked like because of the pictures, but I don't remember anything."

"It's a shame you never got to know your mom; you would have loved her."

"What was she like?"

Angela smiled as the memories flooded her mind. "She was funny and sweet with a 'let the devil take tomorrow' personality. She loved music, and sometimes she'd play the radio so loud it would feel like the floor was shaking. When we were kids, she was the wild and crazy one. She'd hatch a plan to sneak into the movies or steal a trinket from the dime store, and I'd go along with it." The thought hung in the air for a moment, then she laughed. "The funny thing is, I usually got caught and she didn't."

"What about when she got older? Did she still do crazy things?"

A look of sadness drifted across Angela's face. "I didn't see much of Vicki then, not until she brought you and came to live with us. After our mama died—"

"When did she die?"

"Mama?" Angela's thoughts drifted back to that year, to things she'd never spoken of, things she'd kept hidden in the back of her mind. "She died the year Vicki turned thirteen. With her gone, life was a nightmare for both of us. Our daddy was a terrible drunk. I took it for as long as I could, then I left, got a job as a waitress, and moved in with a girlfriend."

"Did you take my mama with you?"

Angela shook her head, then began rewinding the roll of film. She'd thought after so many years the memory would have dulled, but it hadn't. The regret was still there, as painful as shoes a size too small or an almost invisible paper cut. "I should have," she replied solemnly. "But I didn't. I was just a kid at the time. I promised Vicki once I got on my feet I'd bring her to live with me, but it never happened."

There was a moment of hesitation, a fleeting second when Angela could look back and see things as they actually were. She gave a wistful sigh, then said, "A year later your mama and I took a trip to Paducah together, but that was the last time we saw each other until she showed up here with you."

"Didn't you try to get in touch with her?"

"Of course I did, but Daddy said Vicki had left home, and he didn't know or care where she was."

"How awful."

"Yes, it was."

Lara allowed the thought to settle, then she asked, "What about my dad? Over the years you've told me a lot about Mama, but every time I ask about my dad, you say there's nothing much to tell. Did you ever meet him?"

Without looking up, Angela took another roll of film from the box and threaded it through the machine. "No, never."

As she slid the film between the rollers and tightened the reel, Angela felt a pang of guilt. She hadn't lied, but neither had she given Lara the truth. Perhaps she should have said that his name was Russell Murphy and that he and Vicki lived together in an apartment complex where the landlady knew her as a baby—but the avoidance of truth had begun a long time ago, and it was too late to turn back now. She remembered the forgiveness begged for in Vicki's letter and the contents of the box brought back from Wynne Bluffs; those were things Lara didn't need to know. Angela was a mother, and a mother's job was to shield her child from harm; that's exactly what she was doing. Like Pandora's box, the past was better off left untouched. Once opened up it could reveal truths no one wanted to know.

"I don't even know his name," she said, the lie slipping off her tongue. "Your mama was very secretive about him. She claimed he belonged to the past, and it would be better if the two of you never met."

"But jeez," Lara griped. "He's my dad. Mama should've let me decide that for myself."

"I'm certain she didn't expect to die so soon. Maybe she planned to talk to you about it once you were older . . ."

Angela allowed the rest of her words to trail off. She'd always believed there was more to the story, but she'd pursued it a number of times and each time came away knowing nothing more than what she'd known at the start. Lara had enjoyed a happy childhood, and that was what every mother hoped for. Perhaps Vicki felt the best gift she could give her daughter was the gift of not knowing.

Glancing down at the box of films, Angela said, "We've got five rolls left. Should we keep going or finish up tomorrow?"

Lara's look of sadness morphed into a smile. "Keep going."

~

The next five rolls jumped around; first there was her seventh birthday, then she was a toddler pushing a musical lawn mower across the living room floor, and after that a summer when she was nine and running merrily through the sprinkler.

The next roll explained why Kenny had stopped taking movies. Lara was sitting on the steps of the front porch painting her toenails, and when the camera approached she waved it off. She made a face and stuck out her tongue; although the sound was missing you could see her saying, "Get out of here with that thing."

"Oh my gosh," Lara said. "Why was I acting so horrible?"

Angela laughed. "I think it was because you didn't have any makeup on."

It was almost three a.m. when Angela threaded the last roll onto the machine. It was a smaller roll of tape and one she'd almost forgotten about. Vicki. Sitting in the rocking chair with Lara in her arms. She moved back and forth slowly, lovingly touching her finger to the tiny nose, then burying her face in the chubby rolls of Lara's neck.

Lara sighed. "Aw. It looks like she really loves me."

"She did love you, pumpkin, more than anything else in the world."

After Lara had gone to bed, Angela packed the labeled rolls of film back into the box and carried it to the bedroom. These were too precious to let out of her sight. When they left Fairlawn, she would carry these with her in the car.

~

The second week of June, Kenny flew home for Lara's graduation, and it was a weekend of nonstop craziness. First there was the ceremony, then a dinner with Lara's friends and their families. That was followed by round after round of picture taking and yearbook signing. It was not until Lara left for a party on Saturday night that Angela had a few moments alone with Kenny.

As they sat side by side on the sofa, she leaned her head against his shoulder and said, "It's hard to believe the time has finally come. In two weeks, we'll be leaving for Daytona."

"You've got the map where I highlighted the route, right?" Kenny said. "And you've scheduled the car for service?"

Both times she gave a nod without lifting her head from his shoulder.

"You'll be driving a thousand miles, so make certain you tell Harley to check everything over carefully."

"Uh-huh," she said and playfully trailed her finger along the inside edge of his thigh.

PECAN STREET REVELATION

Hesterville, Spring 1989

As the twins grew, so did the Homestead Bed and Breakfast business. Year after year there would be more bookings, and it was not unusual for both of the spare bedrooms to be filled. Only on a rare occasion did the guests have dinner with the family, but it was the breakfasts that Rachel enjoyed.

By then the twins were in the eighth grade, and like George, they were up early and out the door without sitting at the table for a full breakfast. George generally wrapped a fresh biscuit in a napkin and carried it out with him. Hope grabbed a container of yogurt, and Henry wolfed down a bowl of cereal so rapidly Rachel could at times almost believe it had never even been there.

The guests were the ones who lingered at the table. They told of where they were from and the families they would return to. They complimented Rachel on her scones or blueberry pancakes and often remained at the table to have a second and sometimes third cup of coffee. In an odd way, having strangers at the breakfast table eased the loneliness Rachel felt after Mama Dixon's passing.

Although she could sometimes go days or even weeks without missing Emmy, the memory was always there. Rachel never booked guests for March 10; it was Emmy's birthday and a day she kept for herself. On that day, after George and the twins were gone from the house, she took the locket with Emmy's picture from the drawer and allowed herself to cry. Each year she tried to imagine what Emmy would look like: at age two with pale-blonde curls and at five with two front teeth missing and a smile much like Henry's. As the years went on, creating an image of Emmy based on Henry became more difficult. As babies they'd looked almost identical, but as he grew he developed boyish features that would differ from Emmy's.

This year, a week before Emmy's birthday, Rachel had signed a permission slip for the twins to go on a field trip that would celebrate the end of the school year. Next year they would enter the freshman class, and the year after that they'd move to the big high school shared by three towns. Such a milestone caused her to start thinking about Emmy even before everyone else had left the house. She took the locket from the drawer and tucked it into her pocket; once she was alone she would visit with her lost child as she had for the past eighteen years.

The previous night she'd dreamed about Emmy and seen her laughing and dancing but from afar. She caught sight of the long blonde hair falling across her shoulders, but there were only glimpses of her face—there and not there and never long enough for Rachel to study it or commit it to memory.

Emmy would graduate high school this year, then she'd move on to having a life of her own. College perhaps? Or was she in love with some young man and anxious to start her own family?

Breakfast was a hurried affair, the twins anxious to get moving on their field day and George preoccupied with the expected delivery of a new line of faucets. Rachel stood on the front porch and watched as he pulled out of the driveway and the twins headed for the corner where they'd catch the bus. Once they were all gone from view, she went back to the kitchen, brewed a cup of chamomile tea, and stirred a spoonful of honey into it.

She carried her tea to the living room, sat on the sofa, and pulled the locket from her pocket. Snapping the catch open, she looked down at the sweet face of her lost child and whispered, "Happy birthday, Emmy."

For a long while Rachel sat holding the locket, telling Emmy all the things a mother tells a daughter standing on the brink of womanhood. She wished her happiness and hoped she would move on to college. Prayed she had known a loving family, a family who taught her right from wrong and hoped that one day she would have a husband, a good man who would give her children of her own.

The things she would one day wish for Hope and Henry were the same as she now wished for Emmy. The tears fell, and Rachel ached for want of the child she'd lost. In the end, she asked God to grant her the single thing she'd prayed for all these years.

"I ask nothing for myself," Rachel said. "I ask only that you keep Emmy safe, give her a life of being loved and knowing happiness."

The weight of remembering and prayers were such that they drained Rachel and left her feeling spent. With the locket still in her hands and her head dropped low, she closed her eyes.

A hand touched her shoulder.

"Mom, are you okay?"

Startled, Rachel rose quickly and looked at Hope. "What are you doing home?"

"I forgot my bathing suit, so I told Mrs. Crumbly you'd drop me off at the lake." She stooped and picked up the locket that had fallen to the floor. Seeing the baby picture, she asked, "Who's this?"

Years ago Rachel and George had agreed not to tell the twins about Emmy, so they wouldn't grow up fearful of the same thing happening to them. Now she was no longer certain that fear was valid. They were old enough to understand. Perhaps the time had come. She hesitated for a moment, then said, "I was remembering a child who was lost a long time ago."

Hope saw the tears in her mother's eyes. "Mom, you're crying! Who is this baby, and what does she mean to you?"

Rachel took the locket back and held it in her hands, looking down at the sweet face. She could so vividly remember the horror of finding the crib empty that morning. Over the years the rawness of her pain had healed, but the scar was still there and her memory of it as sharp as ever. She gave a long and deeply troubled sigh.

"Her name is Emily. We called her Emmy. She was our first child, born almost four years before you and Henry came along." Rachel's voice was sorrowful and the words slow in coming, almost as if each syllable were a heavy load that had to be hauled up from the depth of her soul. "Back then we lived in a small house on Yellowwood Road. When we bought the house, your daddy and I thought it would be a good place to raise children; we planned to put a swing set in the backyard, plant a garden, and . . ." Her words trailed off as she pictured the house as it was that rainy night—a lonely stretch of road where no one could bear witness to who came or went, tall pines shadowing the backyard.

With a look of alarm pinching her brows together, Hope asked, "Did Emily die?"

Rachel hesitated a moment, then shook her head. "No, she was taken from us."

"Taken? Like when the police take a kid away because you're abusing them?"

Rachel lifted Hope's slender hand into hers. "No, nothing like that. Your daddy and I adored Emily. We loved her as much as we do you and Henry. She was sweet and beautiful—"

"Then what happened?"

"She was kidnapped. Taken from her crib one night while we slept."

"Oh my God, Mom! That's so terrible!"

"Yes, it was terrible . . ." Rachel again hesitated, her breath ragged and shallow, her hand clutching Hope's a bit tighter. "Your daddy and I never got over losing her. In time we were able to move past the pain, but neither of us ever forgot."

"Oh, Mom, I feel so sorry for you and Dad. It must have been terrible. You don't deserve—"

"No parent deserves such heartache, but it happened all the same."

Hope scooted closer and lowered her head onto Rachel's shoulder. "What about the police? Couldn't they find the kidnapper?"

"They tried but never got very far. Sheriff Wilson chased down every lead that came in, Sadie Jenkins raised fifteen thousand dollars for a reward fund, and your daddy ran ads in the newspapers and printed posters that were distributed all over the place, but nothing ever came of it. It was as if Emmy had just disappeared from the face of the earth."

As they sat on the sofa, hands joined together, Rachel told of the music festival, how the town had been overrun with strangers, and how the house on Yellowwood Road was shrouded in darkness and so close to Baker's Field that they couldn't close out the thumping sound of the music.

"After three days of listening to it, we were so exhausted we slept like dead people. Neither of us heard a sound that night. Back then Hesterville was such a small town—nobody even thought twice about leaving their door unlocked."

With a look of surprise stretched across her face, Hope asked, "Did you and Daddy think that's why Emily got kidnapped?"

It was a thought Rachel had pushed aside years ago; now here it was back again. She hesitated a moment, then searched her soul to give what she believed the most truthful answer. "Yes, for a long while we did, and we both shouldered a share of the blame. But after a number of years we learned to be more forgiving. People make mistakes, and things happen—not because we want them to or don't care, but because life is a whole lot less than perfect. Your daddy and I realized we couldn't change the past but could do something about the future. Long before you were born, we made sure that you and Henry would be protected in every way possible."

"That's why we have Bruno and the big fence?"

When Rachel nodded, Hope jumped up and flung her arms around her mother's neck.

"You're the best mom ever!" she said. "But if you'd told us about Emily sooner, Henry and I would have understood and stopped trying to slip away from Grandma and Bruno."

"Parents make mistakes—no matter how hard we try, we still make mistakes. Your daddy and I didn't tell you when you were younger because we didn't want you to grow up afraid the same thing could happen to you."

Hope grinned and raised an eyebrow. "So instead, you were afraid for us?"

With a hint of a smile curling her lips, Rachel nodded.

Hope never did get to the lake. She spent the afternoon sitting alongside her mama, asking questions about the sister she'd never known.

"Do you think Emily looks like me?" she asked.

"She probably looks more like Henry. There's no way of knowing for sure, but when she was six months old she looked exactly like him: blonde hair, blue eyes, even that same butterfly birthmark." Seeing the disappointment on her daughter's face, Rachel added, "But I think she probably has your personality."

Hope's smile brightened. "I'd like her no matter who she looks like. It would be so cool to have a big sister."

For the first time in all the years she could recall, Rachel found happy thoughts of Emmy. They came from her baby sister.

"Today's her birthday," Rachel said. "That's why—"

"Mom, we should have a birthday cake!"

Rachel shook her head. "I hardly think—"

"Why not? Whether she's here or not, she's part of our family."

With Hope so excited about the thought of having a sister, Rachel couldn't say no. For the first time in almost eighteen years she would allow her heart to see Emily through happier eyes.

"Don't start broadcasting it yet. I'll tell your brother when he gets home from the field trip, and I'd like to talk to your daddy first, so he understands how this all came about."

~

That evening when George arrived home he spotted a bottle of burgundy and two wineglasses on the kitchen counter. Fully aware of the date, he eyed Rachel curiously and asked, "Are we celebrating something?"

"In a manner of speaking," Rachel said and told him what had transpired that afternoon.

The whole time she was telling the story George stood there shaking his head as if he were believing and not believing at the same time. Before she even got to the part about the birthday cake he asked, "So the kids weren't angry that we hadn't told them?"

"Not at all," Rachel said. "Henry was surprised to hear she had a birthmark just like his and suggested we could get *America's Most Wanted* to do a feature on Emmy's kidnapping. That way he could show them his birthmark and help find her. Hope was totally taken with the idea of having a big sister. In fact, she wants to celebrate Emmy's birthday tonight."

"Celebrate Emmy's birthday? Isn't that kind of weird?"

"It might seem so at first," Rachel said. "But actually, it's kind of sweet. I like the idea of believing that wherever Emily is, she's still part of our family."

That evening, dessert was a pink cake with eighteen candles. Since it had been Hope's idea, she had the honor of blowing out the candles and making a wish.

"Are you going to tell us what your wish was?" George asked.

"Un-uh," she said and shook her head, "because then it might not come true."

ROAD TRIP

On the first Thursday of July, Angela and Lara left Fairlawn. They'd planned to leave a week earlier but had stayed to enjoy the Fourth of July block party and to say one last goodbye to friends and neighbors.

With the car already packed and ready to go, Angela thought they'd be on the road by eight a.m., but it ended up being closer to eleven when they finally pulled onto the highway and headed west toward I-24.

Lara fiddled with the radio, twisting the dial until she hit upon the mellow sound of Phil Collins singing "Two Hearts," then settled back into her seat. Twenty minutes later she spotted the 69 West road sign.

"Why are we headed west?" she asked.

"Your father thinks we're better off sticking to the major highways. He wants us to get on I-24 and take it all the way down to 75."

Lara groaned. "Boring. Can't we at least have some fun on this trip?"

"We will. We'll stop for lunch and—"

"Mom! Stopping for lunch is not having fun. Let's explore. Find some out-of-the-way places, maybe go and see Nashville."

"Nashville?" Angela laughed. "I don't think—"

"Why not?"

After several moments of hesitation, she said, "We're supposed to be in Daytona tomorrow. Your dad is looking forward to spending the weekend with us."

"Can't you call and say we've decided to make some stops along the way? Dad's busy working; he won't care if we get there next week instead of tomorrow."

"I guess a day or two wouldn't make much difference."

"Mom, you'll have the rest of your life to be in Daytona, but this may be the only time we get to take a road trip together." When Lara looked at her mom's face and saw the thought settling in, she added, "In August I'll be going off to college, and we won't be able to do this."

The intensity on Angela's face softened, and she smiled. "All right. We'll take a few extra days and do some sightseeing along the way, as long as Daddy is okay with it."

"Yay!" Lara spotted the overhead sign saying PADUCAH 12 MILES as she lifted her arms and did a happy little jiggle. "Let's start here. I've never been to Paducah!"

"Yes, you have," Angela said with a chuckle. "You were just too young to remember."

They parked the car in the center of town, then spent the afternoon having lunch at a café along the waterfront and browsing the shops, with Angela reminiscing about the day she and Vicki came to buy the crib and high chair. As they stood looking in the window of the Baby Boutique shop, Angela told how Vicki had sat Lara on the counter and smiled when the clerks made a fuss over her.

"Your mama loved that; she was so proud of you."

Lara smiled. "I like that we're doing this, Mom. It makes me feel closer to Mama. Maybe I have the same wild and crazy streak she had."

"Lord God, I hope not!" Angela said and laughed.

~

It was near five when they left Paducah and got back on I-24. They drove for three hours, then left the highway and spent the night in

Clarksville. After having dinner in a roadhouse called Papa's Place, Angela called Kenny.

"If you have no objection, Lara and I would like to make this a real mother-daughter road trip. You know, take our time, do some sightseeing along the way, stop in Nashville for a day or two, maybe visit Chattanooga and Atlanta. The only thing is, we probably won't get to Daytona until sometime next week."

Kenny groaned. "I was hoping you'd be here tomorrow."

"I know, but try to understand. This may be the last opportunity I have to spend quality time with Lara. Once she's off to college . . . well . . ."

"I can appreciate your wanting to spend time together," Kenny said, "but it's a long time to be on the road just the two of you."

"Don't worry—we'll be fine."

He gave an apprehensive-sounding sigh. "Okay, but call me every night, and be careful."

"I will," she promised.

~

On Friday, Angela made it to Nashville. With no reservations and no specific plans, she drove through town looking for a place to stay.

"Let's find a fun place," Lara said. "Not one of the big hotels."

After an hour of scouring the side streets and finding nothing, Angela was about ready to spring for a night at The Hermitage when she spotted a bed-and-breakfast sign saying TURN LEFT FOR HANNAH'S HOUSE. She rounded the corner onto Bradford Avenue and saw it. A lovely turn-of-the-century stone house with a wide expanse of lawn and mounds of colorful impatiens. Alongside the walkway was a WELCOME sign.

Hannah's House was precisely the type of place she'd been looking for.

That evening they had dinner at Hattie B's, then strolled along Broadway. Later on, as she and Lara walked arm in arm, peeking in shop windows, eyeing the honky-tonk bars, and laughing as they hadn't in many months, Angela knew this time together was a good thing. Lara would soon be off to college and starting a new life, but both of them would forever remember the fun they'd had on this trip.

~

On Saturday they toured the Grand Ole Opry and the Country Music Hall of Fame, then had dinner at Puckett's. They were on their way back to Hannah's when Lara spotted a bustling coffeehouse and gave a devilish grin.

"The sign says it's open-mic night; let's stop and listen to some music."

After weeks of ups and downs—the excitement of graduation followed by the agony of leaving friends behind—Angela was glad to see Lara happy and smiling.

She glanced at her watch. "It's kind of late. Tomorrow we should get an early start if we're going to see the sights in Chattanooga."

"It's Saturday night, Mom, and nine thirty isn't that late! Let's skip Chattanooga and see the open-mic show instead."

Once they were seated at a small table in the back, they ordered lattes and sat listening to bluesy music until closing time. It was almost midnight when they started back to Hannah's House. Halfway down Belcourt Avenue, Lara leaned over and kissed her mama's cheek.

"This trip has been the best ever, Mom. Thank you!"

~

After such a late night the thought of an early start was forgotten, and it was ten a.m. when they finally climbed into the car. Angela slid the key into the ignition, but when she tried to shift into "Neutral," the gearshift refused to move.

"That's odd," she mumbled, then pulled the key out, waited a few seconds, and tried again. For a fleeting second, she regretted not taking the car in to Harley for servicing as Kenny had said. She'd intended to, but Harley had been booked solid, so she'd gone to the express lube place on the highway.

After three attempts, the gearshift popped into "Neutral," and the engine rumbled to life. She shifted into first and pulled away from the curb. Backtracking through the streets of Nashville, she circled the city and got onto I-40 East and headed back toward I-75 to continue the trek south.

"I'm thinking it'll take us four to five hours to make Atlanta," Angela said, "so we can find a place to stay, have dinner, and walk around the city for a bit."

Once they were underway, Lara found a country music station and began singing along with the Eagles.

"I hope Atlanta is as much fun as Nashville," she said, then went back to belting out "Take It Easy."

"Uh-huh," Angela answered, but her mind wasn't on Atlanta. It was on the strange feel of the car. She could almost swear she heard a strange noise that hadn't been there before. When they passed Chattanooga, she thought about getting off the highway and finding a service station to give the engine a quick check, but it was Sunday, and the odds of finding a mechanic working on Sunday were slim to none, so she sailed on by. If worse came to worst and the car did need some sort of repair she could have it done on Monday, and they'd spend a second night in Atlanta.

A few miles after they passed Dalton there was a clunking sound. The car shimmied, and it felt as though she'd downshifted into third. That was when she started to realize they weren't going to make it to Atlanta.

"Lara, honey," she said, "watch for an exit. This car has me worried. I think we'd better stop and have it checked out."

"I saw a sign saying there's an exit coming up in one mile, but I didn't catch where that road goes."

"It doesn't matter," Angela replied nervously. She eased off the highway onto what was a narrow two-lane road. With no signposts she had only two choices: go straight or turn right. She hesitated a few seconds, then turned onto Yellowwood Road.

They'd gone less than a mile when the car slowed to a crawl, and as Angela pulled onto the shoulder it stopped altogether. She sat for a few moments calming herself, then tried shifting into neutral to restart the engine. The stick shift wouldn't budge. Three times she tried, and each time the only result was an angry grinding sound.

The road was barren other than scattered patches of wildflowers growing by the wayside and, in the distance, what appeared to be a small farmhouse.

Angela pressed her back against the seat and groaned. "Damn. It won't go into gear."

"What now?" Lara asked.

"We'll have to call somebody and have it towed to a garage."

"Call how?"

Angela pointed to the farmhouse in the distance. "That looks like our best bet. You stay with the car. I'll go ask if I can use their phone and try to find out where we are."

"Un-uh, I'm not staying here alone. I'm coming with you."

"It's pretty hot out; are you sure you want to?" Angela asked.

By then Lara was already out of the car. "I'm sure."

Angela locked the car, and the two of them started out on foot. It was one thirty then, and the sun was directly overhead. Before ten minutes had passed they were both drenched in perspiration. Looking from a distance, the house had appeared to be a half mile away or less, but halfway there she realized it was well over a mile, possibly even two. By the time they turned up the long driveway, Angela was praying there'd be somebody at home.

When she stepped onto the porch, she saw the open window and heard the hum of a fan coming from inside.

"We're in luck," she whispered, then rapped on the door.

She waited for several minutes, and as she raised her hand to knock again, the door swung open. An old woman with silver-white hair and thick eyeglasses gave a cautious smile.

"I'm sorry to bother you," Angela said. "Our car broke down, and I was wondering if I could use your phone to call for a tow truck."

The woman peered around Angela and eyed Lara. "Is it just the two of you?"

"Yes. Lara's my daughter. We were on our way—"

The woman pushed the door back. "Well then, come on in. I'll get you the number for Ernie. The thing is, it's Sunday. I doubt he'll send the truck out on Sunday."

"Maybe if I paid extra?"

"I don't think so," the woman said. "He'll send the taxi and take you into Hesterville. Then come get your car tomorrow."

Angela breathed a sigh of relief. "That would be okay. Is Hesterville nearby?"

"Seven or eight miles." The woman fished through a basket sitting alongside the phone and pulled out a dingy-looking gray card. "Here it is," she said and handed Angela the card that read ERNIE'S TAXI & TOW. Below the address was a phone number.

Angela dialed the number.

"Ernie," he answered.

"Good afternoon," she said. "This is Angela McAlister, and it seems my car has broken down. I'm stranded out here on—" She turned back to the woman and asked, "Where exactly is this?"

"Yellowwood Road, out by Baker's Field. Ernie knows."

She repeated what the woman had said.

"Yeah, I know where that is. So are you calling for a mechanic or taxi?"

"Actually, I could use both," Angela replied. "I think the car might have to be towed, because the gearshift won't budge. When I try, it makes a terrible grinding noise."

"Sounds like it could be the transmission. I can send a taxi but can't get a tow truck out there till tomorrow."

Angela told him a taxi would be just fine and hung up the receiver. As she and Lara started toward the road, the woman stood in the doorway and waved goodbye. "Good luck with your car," she called, then disappeared back inside.

~

The walk back to the car was long and hot. Once they got there, Angela pulled out a suitcase of things they might need for a day or two. She knew for certain they'd be in Hesterville for one night, and it could end up being two or three. Hopefully there was a nice hotel where they could take a cool shower and have a leisurely dinner. After a day such as this one, they both needed it. She also had to call Kenny and give him the bad news.

~

As it turned out, there was no hotel in Hesterville. According to Ernie, there were two bed-and-breakfast places, a small inn that offered long-term rentals, and a Dozy Days Motel over in Weston. Hoping that she could have the car repaired and be on her way tomorrow, Angela asked which was closer to the garage.

"Probably the Homestead on Pecan Street," he said, "but if Rachel hasn't got a room available, Marilyn Byrd's place is just a few blocks farther."

When they arrived back at Ernie's garage, he called Rachel Dixon and asked if she had room for a guest.

"Someone you know?" Rachel asked.

"Uh-uh, a woman and her daughter from Kentucky. Their car broke down out on Yellowwood Road. I can't bring the car in until tomorrow, so they need a place to stay."

Rachel hesitated for a moment. She'd made it a policy to accept only guests who were referrals, people who had been checked out and worthy of trust, but something about a mother and daughter in need tugged at her heart.

What if it were Hope and me?

"Sure, I can take them," she said. "When will they be arriving?"

"They're here now. I'll drop them by your place."

Suddenly Rachel wished George hadn't taken the kids and gone off to a baseball game. She also wished she had asked Ernie if they at least appeared to be trustworthy people.

THE NEW GUESTS

When Ernie's taxi pulled up in front of the house, Rachel peered from behind the curtains to get a glimpse of the new guests. The mother was first up the walkway, her shoulders stooped and her expression weary. The daughter followed behind looking no less bedraggled. Rachel opened the door and moved out onto the porch to greet them.

"Welcome to the Dixon Homestead," she said and stepped down onto the walkway. "I'm Rachel."

Tired as she was, Angela forced a smile. "Thank you so much for accommodating us on such short notice." She introduced herself and then Lara.

"Here, let me help with that." Rachel reached out and took hold of the suitcase. "Ernie told me your car broke down, so I know you must be feeling exhausted. Would you rather freshen up or have a cool drink?"

Before her mom could answer, Lara said, "I want to take a shower. I've got to get out of these jeans before I roast to death!"

Angela gave a doleful nod. "I'm afraid the same is true for me. Walking such a distance in this Georgia sun was brutal."

"I'm sure." Rachel led them through the living room and up the stairs. "We have two guest rooms." She pushed open the first door, placed the suitcase inside, then continued along the hall. "Here's the bath. And this is the smaller room. We don't have any other guests right now, so you're welcome to use them both."

Before she'd finished explaining where everything was, Lara had kicked off her sandals and was shimmying out of her jeans.

"I'll see you downstairs whenever you're ready," Rachel said and ducked out the door. As she started down the stairs, she let go of a lingering sigh. For the first time in almost a decade she'd looked into the face of a girl and, for an instant, imagined her to be Emily. "How foolish is that . . . ," she muttered and shook her head.

When Angela came down, Rachel had a pitcher of sweet tea and a platter of pimento cheese sandwiches waiting.

"I thought maybe you'd enjoy a light snack. We can sit on the back patio where it's shady and there's a nice breeze."

"That sounds wonderful."

Angela followed her through the kitchen and out onto a patio edged with petunias in every shade of pink and purple. As they settled into the wicker chairs, she spoke of how lovely the house was and how delighted they were to be there.

"Lara will be down shortly," she said. "She's redoing her nails."

"Girls will be girls," Rachel replied. "I know, because I have one of my own. She's fourteen going on forty."

"Lara's eighteen. This fall she'll be going off to the University of Florida, and I'll miss her terribly."

Eighteen, Rachel thought, *the same as Emily.* She wanted to say, *I also have a daughter who is eighteen, and perhaps as beautiful as your Lara,* but of course she didn't. She'd learned long ago that to speak of a child who was missing only invited questions and, following the questions, a look of pity.

Instead she gave a lighthearted laugh. "I know exactly what you mean," she said. "There are times when they drive you crazy and you can't wait for them to be gone, and other times when the thought of it breaks your heart."

Angela nodded. "Isn't that the truth. Do you have just the one girl?"

Rachel hesitated a moment as the image of Emily flashed through her mind. For a brief second she thought of mentioning their other daughter, the one who was the same age as Lara, but she didn't. "Yes," she finally said. "Just one girl, but Hope has a twin brother, Henry. They're going into their freshman year of high school, so we have a few more years before we have to deal with the inevitability of losing them to college."

They spoke for a long while. Angela told of Kenny's relocation and how it saddened her to leave their friends behind.

"At first Lara was devastated by the thought of moving away, but since she'll be attending college in Florida anyway, she's come around a bit. You know how it is with kids; they're up one minute and down the next."

Both women laughed.

"The Richmond Braves farm team is playing an exhibition game today," Rachel explained, "and George took the kids to see it, but they should be home soon and for certain they'll be hungry. We'd love to have you and Lara join us for supper. It's just a buffet of cold chicken and potato salad, but there's plenty to go around."

"We don't want to impose; you've already been so gracious—"

"It's not an imposition; we'd love having you."

A short while later Henry came bursting onto the patio, followed by Hope.

"Guess what, Mom? I caught a fly ball!" He held out the signed baseball for Rachel to see. "It was awesome. Nick Middleton hits this pop-up, and I see it coming, so I jump up and *pow*, the ball lands smack in the middle of my mitt."

Hope grinned. "Then after the game Dad got Nick Middleton to sign the ball."

Rachel smiled. "It sounds very exciting, but before you two get carried away, don't you think you should take a moment to say hi to our guest?"

"Sorry," Henry said sheepishly.

Just then George came out, and introductions were made all around. Afterward Rachel told the twins to get cleaned up for dinner.

"Hope, when you're ready to come down, knock on the small guest-room door and ask Mrs. McAlister's daughter, Lara, if she'd like to join us."

"Okay, Mom," she said as she disappeared back into the house.

~

By the time they returned to the patio, it was obvious that Hope was enthralled with their new guest. She trailed after Lara, admiring the color of her toenails, the songs on her Walkman, and the thought of going off to college.

"That freedom must be awesome," she said.

"It is and it isn't," Lara replied. "I'm sad to be leaving my friends behind."

"But what an adventure! We've lived in Hesterville *forever*, and I'd be thrilled to be heading off to a college near the beach!"

"Actually, the university is in Gainesville. It's a city and nowhere near the beach."

"But still . . ."

When they gathered at the supper table the three young people sat together, Lara sandwiched in between Hope and Henry. It wasn't until Rachel had the food on the table and was sitting directly across from them that she noticed the uncanny resemblance between Henry and Lara.

Her breath caught in her throat. Looking at them individually, apart from one another, the resemblance hadn't seemed so striking, but side by side as they were, they had the look of family. She gave a nervous little laugh. "Good gracious, look at the two of you! If not for the difference in ages, you could be twins."

Hope grinned. "Lara and I look like twins?"

"No," Rachel said, her eyes still on Lara. "But she certainly does look like your brother."

They moved on to talking about Angela's experience out on Yellowwood Road and the unbelievable heat wave that Georgia was experiencing.

"It's been this way for a week," Rachel said, "and the weatherman claims there's no end in sight. This is the hottest summer I can remember; tomorrow it's supposed to hit a hundred."

"Oh dear." Angela gave a worrisome sigh. "I do hope the heat won't stop Mr. Maxwell from getting a tow truck out to Yellowwood Road."

"It won't," George assured her. "Ernie is slow as molasses, but he's dependable. If he said he'll have it towed tomorrow, he will. And he's a very good mechanic. If you'd like, tomorrow morning before I open the store I can stop by the garage and give him a nudge."

"If it's no trouble . . ." Angela told how Kenny had gone to Daytona in January, and she had stayed in Fairlawn so Lara could finish high school and graduate with her friends.

"Kenny and I both agreed it was the right thing to do, but having the family separated has been difficult, so we're anxious to get to Daytona."

"Mom's more anxious than I am," Lara said. "I'm hoping we'll have time to visit the university in Gainesville."

She leaned over, whispered something in Hope's ear, and they both giggled. Moments later Hope asked if they could be excused to go outside and play badminton.

As Rachel watched the two girls prance off together, she felt her heart skip a beat. The old sadness came and went like a cloud passing overhead, and in that brief moment she wondered if this was how it would be if Emily were still with them.

~

After the table was cleared George slipped away, saying he had paperwork that needed to be done. Angela then made her nightly call to Kenny. She told him that they'd had a spot of car trouble and stopped in Hesterville to have it checked out.

"Hesterville?" he replied. "Isn't that rather off the beaten path?"

"A bit," she said, "but we're staying at a lovely bed-and-breakfast, so it's worth driving a few extra miles."

She decided not to worry him with the extent of the car trouble, reasoning that for all she knew it could be something as simple as a blown fuse, and by tomorrow or the next day they'd be back on the road.

Later on, as the sun drifted toward the edge of the horizon, the two women returned to the patio. They watched the sky change from the crimson of sunset to the purple of twilight and in time to the black of night, lit only by the bright moon, a scattering of stars overhead, and the glow of lamplight coming from George's office.

On that hot summer night, when the breeze carried the easy conversation of two mothers and the laughter of young people singing along with a Sony Walkman, it seemed as if all was perfect with the world.

HOPE'S DISCOVERY

Monday morning dawned with the heat more oppressive than ever. Before the breakfast dishes were cleared away the temperature had climbed to eighty-five degrees, and the NBC weatherman was forecasting it would top one hundred.

"We've not seen a spell like this since 1923, but hang in there, folks, relief is on the way. There's a cold front coming down from Canada." He pointed to a large green mass on the map. "By next weekend we'll see rain, lots of it, and we'll be experiencing a cooldown."

When the projected high for the day flashed on the screen, Hope came running into the kitchen. "Mom, can we go swimming?"

"Yes, but ask Lara if she wants to go with you."

"Okay."

Hope darted from the room and was back minutes later. "Lara wants to go, and her mom said she could."

"Is Lara's mom going?"

"No. She said she needs to stay here to find out about the car."

At times Hope could stretch the truth a bit, so Rachel dried her hands and followed her back into the living room.

"Angela, do you mind if Lara goes swimming with the twins?"

"Not at all. It'll be a nice day for them."

"It's our local lake, but they've got two lifeguards on duty, and they keep a close eye on the kids, so there's nothing to worry about. I'll drop them off and pick them up later."

Hope's cheers were followed by a frenzied hour of lunch packing, swimsuit finding, sunscreen slathering, and a stern warning to listen to the lifeguards.

On the drive to the lake, Rachel listened to the kids chattering on about how they would swim to the raft, play water polo, and any number of other things. When she stopped at the pathway that led to the beach, everyone scampered out. As she watched them walk away there was a split second when the girls turned back and waved—that was when she saw it. Hope's eyes were darker, but they had the same nose, the same smile, the same curve of their cheek.

Rachel again felt her heart skip a beat. "Impossible," she murmured and bit down on her lip. These things were similarities, nothing more.

After they'd disappeared from view, she sat with her gaze fixed on the pathway where they'd been, still seeing the image she'd seen moments earlier. She didn't turn the key in her ignition until another car pulled up behind her and beeped the horn.

"Sorry," she called out, then pulled away and started for home.

When Rachel arrived back at the house it was after eleven, so she made a pitcher of lemonade and invited Angela to sit on the back patio.

"It's nice and shady, and we can hear the phone from there," she said.

For most of the afternoon they sat there sharing stories of life in Kentucky and living in Hesterville. Angela told of her reluctance to move.

"I guess change is inevitable," she said, "but it doesn't always come easy."

"No, it doesn't," Rachel agreed and told of how she'd been so resistant to letting George make an office out of the room that once belonged to Mama Dixon.

It was near four when Ernie finally called.

"I've got good news, bad news, and worse news," he said. "The good news is that we've towed your car, and it's now in the shop. The bad news is that your transmission is totally shot."

"Good grief," Angela said. "What can be worse than that?"

"It's gonna cost thirteen hundred to replace it, and since I've gotta send for parts, it'll take a good week to get the job done."

"Oh no." She gave a long, drawn-out groan. "Isn't there any way it can be done faster?"

"Nope," Ernie answered. "And a week is based on my not finding any other problems."

For a long while Angela just stood there saying nothing; finally Ernie asked, "So should I order the parts or not?"

"Yes," she answered. "Go ahead and order them."

When Angela returned to the patio, she had the look of a deflated balloon.

"That bad, huh?" Rachel said.

Angela nodded. "I hope you don't mind us being here for a while. Ernie said it's going to take a week to get the car fixed."

"Not at all," Rachel replied. "I'm enjoying the company. Some guests dash out right after breakfast, but having you stay and chat reminds me of how it was with Mama Dixon . . ."

She segued into the story of how one year they sat and crocheted together for so long that they donated seven throws to the church bazaar. Angela smiled but only half listened, because she was thinking about how she'd explain this to Kenny. At five o'clock when Rachel went to pick up the kids at the lake, Angela stayed behind.

"I'd like to go ahead and call Kenny," she said. "I know he's not going to be happy hearing the news, and I want to get it over with."

She was right; he wasn't happy. After she'd explained the cost and how long it would take to be repaired, she gave him the house phone number and told him they'd be staying until the car was ready.

"Look on the bright side," she said. "Nothing worse than this can possibly happen."

~

On the drive back from the lake, Rachel noticed that Hope was unusually quiet.

"Is anything wrong?" she asked.

"Un-uh." Hope shook her head without looking up.

"I imagine you're all exhausted after a long day in the sun," Rachel said. "You need to go to bed early tonight. I don't want you getting sick."

"I'm not tired," Hope replied, but she had a troubled expression stuck to her face.

As soon as they turned in to the drive, Rachel shooed everyone inside.

"Shower and get changed for dinner," she said as they headed up the stairs. She made her way into the kitchen and was in the midst of preparing a salad when Hope appeared in the doorway, still in her swimsuit.

"Mom, I need to ask you something." Her voice was uncharacteristically somber.

Rachel set the knife aside and took Hope in her arms. "What is it, honey? Did something happen?"

Hope gave a reluctant nod, then asked the question that had been troubling her all afternoon. "Didn't you tell me Emily had a butterfly birthmark just like Henry?"

Rachel hesitated and took a deep breath. After so many years of looking for similarities and finding none, she'd stopped imagining every blonde child was Emily. She'd stopped expecting the impossible to happen. At least she'd thought she had. "Yes, Emily did have a birthmark like Henry, but why would you—"

"Was it on her shoulder the same as his?"

Rachel's heart skipped a beat just as it had back at the lake, and a strange uneasiness crawled up her spine. "No, it wasn't; it was down lower, on her back."

"Like here?" Hope reached around and pointed to a spot just above her waist.

For a moment Rachel was dumbstruck, then she dropped down in a chair with her heart racing. "Yes. Why would you—"

The serious expression Hope wore was way beyond her years. With her voice lowered to a whisper, she said, "Lara has Henry's birthmark in that spot. I saw it when she changed into her bathing suit."

"Lots of people have birthmarks," Rachel replied apprehensively. "Are you sure it was the same as Henry's?"

"Mom, I'm positive. I was standing right beside her."

Rachel's heart swelled, and she could barely breathe. A million thoughts raced through her head. The possibility that Emily would one day simply walk back into their lives was too ridiculous to even consider, and yet here was Lara, the right age, looking just as Rachel believed Emily would look, and now with a butterfly birthmark in the same spot. Her stomach churned as her heart and mind battled—her heart crying out to believe and her mind arguing that such a thing was impossible.

She waited until she could catch her breath, then asked, "When you saw Lara's birthmark, did you mention it to her or Henry?"

"No, I wasn't sure if I should."

"Don't. At least not for now. Let me ask Lara's mom about it."

Trying to pretend this was not a matter for concern, Rachel gave her daughter's hand an affectionate squeeze. "It could be that you're a lot like me, Hope. When we want something to be true, we convince ourselves it is. I noticed how much Lara looks like your brother, and for a moment I let myself think she might be Emily. The problem is when you start believing things that are all but impossible, it's just wishful thinking."

"But, Mom—"

"No buts. I said I'd talk to Lara's mom about it. Now, scoot. Get ready for dinner, and don't mention a word of this to anyone else. Okay?"

"Okay," Hope echoed, apparently satisfied.

Rachel moved through the remainder of the dinner preparation like a robot. As she carried the dishes of food to the table her mind jumped from one thought to another. Yes, all the similarities were there—the birthmark, the age, the cerulean-blue eyes slanted upward at the outer edges, the curve of her cheek—all of it perfect and yet it made no sense. Not even an idiot would bring a kidnapped baby back to where the family could conceivably recognize their own daughter. Angela certainly wasn't an idiot. In fact, she seemed to be an intelligent woman and a good mother.

Seems to be . . . , Rachel's heart argued. *Not everything is as it seems to be . . .*

Despite the preposterousness of such a thing happening, Rachel knew there were too many red flags to let this go by without talking it through.

You've been disappointed a thousand times before, her heart warned, but Rachel pushed the thought aside. Even if she had to be disappointed a thousand times more, she'd never give up searching for Emily.

With a million different thoughts jumping around in her mind, Rachel hurried through dinner without speaking of what she'd heard to anyone. But before the table had even been cleared, she suggested George take the kids to the Dairy Queen for dessert.

"Angela and I will stay here and clean up," she said.

"We can wait awhile and then all go," George replied.

Angela was on the verge of saying that was a fine idea, but she caught the look Rachel gave George along with the shake of her head.

"Ice cream plays havoc with my stomach," she said. "I'd just as soon stay here and give Rachel a hand."

Something was wrong—she was certain of it. Hopefully it was not more bad news about the car.

THE QUESTION

Before George's car pulled out of the driveway, Rachel had the table cleared and the dishwasher loaded. As the water began swishing into the machine, she turned to Angela and said, "Let's sit in the living room and talk."

Rachel had not eaten a bite of her dinner, yet her stomach was churning. Her nerves were so raw that she could feel them pulsing against her skin. She knew how furious she would be if someone ever dared suggest the twins were not her babies, so she couldn't even imagine how Angela would react to such a question.

They sat opposite one another in the club chairs, and when Rachel looked across she saw a mother, not a kidnapper. Suddenly the whole idea seemed ludicrous. Other than Lara looking like Henry, the only thing she had to go on was Hope's word that she'd seen the birthmark. Hope was a fourteen-year-old girl with an extremely vivid imagination.

"Would you like a drink?" Rachel asked. "An after-dinner cordial, perhaps?"

She hoped Angela would say yes, because then she could pour one for herself also, and it might help calm her nerves.

Angela shook her head. "No, thanks. Dinner was delicious, but I'm absolutely stuffed."

Rachel smiled politely. She felt her heart fluttering, so she hesitated and took a few deep breaths. In and out . . . slow . . . slower. She glanced over, hoping to see Angela as she would have been eighteen years ago, a young hippie tiptoeing through a stranger's house to steal a baby, but the image wasn't there. She was too much like Rachel herself, a woman who cherished motherhood, a woman who'd likely as not cross a minefield to protect her child.

Rachel didn't think she could do it. After so many years of searching for Emily, it seemed strange that Hope, and Hope alone, had somehow unearthed her missing sister. Perhaps this actually was nothing more than wishful thinking. Hope had taken the idea of having an older sister to heart instantly. She'd even insisted they celebrate Emily's birthday. It was virtually impossible to believe she'd suddenly found that sister.

"You look as though there's something on your mind," Angela said. "Did you want to talk about it?"

Rachel answered with an edgy little twitter. "Yes, I think maybe I do . . ."

"Please don't tell me Ernie's called and there is something else wrong with the car."

"No, it's not the car," Rachel replied. "But since you've mentioned it, how was it you happened to be out on Yellowwood Road? There's not much traffic on that side of town. Have you been there before?"

Angela chuckled. "Good heavens, no. That was my first and last time, hopefully."

Rachel gave a stiff smile. It stood to reason that a person would give that answer if they were the one who had taken Emily.

As one thought pushed through to the next one, Rachel continued. "I hope you'll forgive me; I'm going to ask you a question that may come across as a bit insulting. I don't mean it to be that way, but . . ."

"Don't worry about it," Angela said. "I'm not that easily insulted, so ask away."

With her eyes lowered and her fingers nervously twisting the wedding band on her left hand, Rachel began.

"Yesterday, when you asked if Hope was my only daughter, I said yes, but we actually have two daughters. Emily, our firstborn, is eighteen years old now. I seldom speak of her, because when she was only six months old, we lost her."

"I'm so sorry," Angela said sympathetically. "But I'm not sure I understand—"

Rachel quickly clarified the situation. "Emily didn't die; she was kidnapped." Although she'd uttered those same words countless times before, they still stung as they rose from her throat. Pausing for a moment, she took another deep breath. "You're a mother, so I'm certain you understand that when anything bad happens to your child, it tears your heart to shreds."

"Of course I do. Why, I can't even begin to imagine the heartache."

"It happened back in 1971; that was the year they had the music festival out in Baker's Field. We lived on Yellowwood Road back then . . ."

As Rachel's voice droned on, telling of the loud music, the extreme exhaustion, the drenching rain, and waking in the morning to find Emily's crib empty, Angela began to think back on the cardboard box she'd carried home from Wynne Bluffs. Beneath Vicki's clothes she'd found an orange wristband. She'd held it in her hand and studied it, wondered if it might be a souvenir saved as a reminder of good times. It was from a music festival; Angela was almost certain of it. She closed her eyes and tried to bring the image to mind. There it was. *Hesterville Music Festival, August 1971.*

When Rachel finished telling the story and looked up, Angela's sympathetic smile was gone, and her face had paled.

"I hope you didn't think I was implying something tragic could happen to the kids now," Rachel said. "Hesterville is a very safe town. It was quite different back then. Thousands upon thousands of hippies descended on the town, and no one, not even Sheriff Wilson, could tell one from the other."

"Why are you telling me this?" Angela asked nervously.

"Because of something Hope said. She's a bit like me in that if she wants something badly enough, she almost wills it into happening. I realize she has a fanciful imagination, but after she told me what she'd seen, I knew I had to ask you about it; otherwise I'd never be able to live with myself."

There was no response. Angela now sat with her spine rigid and her arms flattened against her body.

Seeing this change boosted Rachel's courage. Maybe her question wasn't as crazy as she'd thought. The jitters she'd had earlier eased, and her voice grew stronger.

"When the twins were small, George and I decided to wait until they were old enough to understand before we told them about the kidnapping. Then a few months ago Hope saw Emily's baby picture, and when she questioned it I told her what happened. Well, as soon as she found out that she had an older sister, she became fascinated with the idea and wanted to know everything there was to know about her."

With her eyebrows pinched together, Angela said, "I really don't see how this—"

"It seems Hope now believes Lara is her long-lost sister."

Rachel slowed for a moment and forced a smile, but Angela's expression didn't change. There was no slightly bemused smile, no solicitous sigh, nothing. That struck Rachel as odd.

"You see, our Emily was a blue-eyed blonde like Henry, and like Lara. In fact, she and Lara are just about the same age." As she spoke, Rachel kept her eyes fixed on Angela and waited for a change of expression, but she remained as stone-faced as Mount Rushmore.

Whereas earlier Angela had leaned in to the conversation, she now sat with her back stiff. "I'm certain there are millions of young girls who match that description."

"At first, that's exactly what I thought," Rachel said. "I figured it to be more of Hope's wishful thinking, but then she told me about Lara's birthmark. Apparently she saw it when they changed into their swimsuits at the lake."

Suddenly there was a shift in Angela's voice. Her words became wobbly and more defensive. "It's true Lara has a birthmark, but it's not all that unusual. I've known other people with birthmarks. A woman I worked with had one shaped like a heart."

"Hearts and ovals, they're more commonplace, but the butterfly shape, not as much. Henry has a butterfly birthmark; his is on the back of his shoulder. Emily has one too, but I've never mentioned where it was. Then today when the kids came home from the lake, Hope told me Lara has a birthmark just like Henry's, only hers is low on her back. That's where Emmy's was." She hesitated, then asked, "Doesn't that strike you as rather odd? Two girls the same age, same coloring, and both with an unusual birthmark in precisely the same spot?"

Angela gave what was intended to be a casual shrug, but it came across as a hastily erected wall. "It's unusual, perhaps, but nothing more." She swiped her hand across her forehead and brushed back the perspiration beaded along her brow. "It's awfully warm in here. I could use a breath of air."

"If you want I could put the fan on, or we could sit outside."

Angela shook her head. "Don't bother. I'm really tired, so I'll be going up to bed soon."

With a sense of urgency now rising in her chest, Rachel reached across and touched her hand to Angela's knee. "Please don't go," she begged. "I'm not suggesting you had anything to do with Emily's kidnapping, but with so many coincidences you can surely see why I have to ask. You're a mother; if it were your child, wouldn't you ask the same questions?"

With her eyes avoiding Rachel's, Angela tilted her head ever so slightly. "Yes, I guess I would. But while I sympathize with your situation, I don't think I can be of any help."

Keeping her hand pressed to Angela's knee, Rachel pleaded, "Answer just one question, will you? A single question and perhaps we can put an end to this whole thing?"

Rachel's voice was high-pitched and edgy sounding.

It was as if Angela could sense what was coming. She cringed, and Rachel felt the twitch beneath her hand.

"I realize this is a deeply personal question, and I apologize for asking it, but are you really Lara's mother, and do you have a birth certificate to prove it?"

Rachel held her breath and waited. A second ticked by and then another and another. If the answer was yes and there was a birth certificate, there could be no argument, no further questions. This flicker of hope that had suddenly sprung to life would be snuffed out just as it had been so many times before.

Turning away, Angela gazed absently at something in the distance beyond the window. She'd known for years the birth certificate issue would one day be a problem—now here it was, uglier and more horrific than anything she could have ever imagined. The tears welling in her eyes answered before she did. "No, I don't have a birth certificate," she said solemnly. "Lara is my sister's child." She swiped the back of her hand across her eyes, then turned to Rachel. "Vicki was my younger sister; she died when Lara was only fourteen months old. At the time she and the baby were living with us, and her boyfriend, the baby's father, was nowhere to be found, so Kenny and I raised Lara as our own."

The thought that this child could be Emily ricocheted through the chambers of Rachel's heart, and she felt the thump of it against her breastbone. In a voice made more anxious by the years of waiting, she asked, "How old was Lara the first time you saw her?"

Rachel leaned forward, anticipating the answer.

Angela pushed farther back, her spine now pressed up against the rough fabric of the chair. "It's impossible for me to p-pinpoint . . . ," she stuttered. "Babies change overnight . . ."

"Was she an infant? A few weeks old? Months?"

"Months." Angela pictured Lara's blue eyes peering out from beneath the poncho Vicki had thrown over her. It was almost eighteen years ago, and yet the memory was as fresh as if it had happened just yesterday. Even now she could recall the haunted look on Vicki's face. Was this why? Was this the secret she was hiding? With her hands clasped in her lap, fingers locked together so fiercely they appeared bloodless, Angela prayed for it not to be true.

"Before your sister came to live with you, did she ever send you a picture of Lara as an infant?" Rachel asked. "One of those newborn pictures they take at the hospital?"

Angela shook her head without saying anything.

With her face taut, her eyes wide, and her voice more insistent than ever, Rachel asked, "What about a snapshot or a hospital bracelet? Clothing the baby had outgrown? Some souvenir of Lara's infancy, did she have any of those?"

Again, Angela shook her head.

Rachel's heart seized, and she had to hold herself back from crying out. Suddenly the impossible seemed possible. More than possible. Probable. She'd suspected it the first time she'd looked into Lara's face.

Angela lifted her eyes and looked across, her cheeks now wet with tears. "Vicki was different from most people. She was like a dandelion fluff that goes whichever way the wind blows. She didn't hold on to things or even people. One day she'd be there and the next she'd be gone. When she came to live with us, I hadn't seen or heard from her for three years. Then all of a sudden there she was, happy and smiling as if she'd never been gone."

"Did she have Lara with her then?"

"Yes. That baby was the one thing she did hold on to. She loved Lara more than I've ever known her to love anybody. I used to watch her holding Lara and think, at long last, Vicki's found something that makes her truly happy."

"Don't you think I felt the same about Emily?" Rachel asked. "When I discovered her crib empty . . ." The despair of all those years was threaded through her words, twisted tight around every syllable and clawing to be set free. She hesitated, then pulled in a deep breath and stiffened her resolve. The growing possibility of finding Emily pushed her past the memories of that horrible night.

In a voice filled with grit and determination, Rachel asked, "Was your sister at that music festival? Was she the girl who took our baby?"

The question hung there like the blade of a guillotine, and it was as if Angela had been stripped naked. Her face turned ashen, and her breath became so shallow it could no longer be heard.

For several moments the silence was so brittle it could have snapped, then the screech of a bird sounded from somewhere outside, and Rachel repeated her question. This time she spoke slower and with greater certainty.

"Did Vicki steal our baby from her crib?"

Angela covered her face and gave an anguished cry. "How could I possibly know that?" she said tearfully. "When Vicki came to me, I didn't ask where she'd been or what she'd done. I didn't ask . . . God forgive me, I didn't ask . . ."

"You didn't ask . . . ," Rachel repeated grimly. In the darkest part of her heart she wanted to rail and scream until the truth was ripped open and exposed for what it was, and yet from a place beyond what she felt there was a flicker of compassion. She saw in Angela a grief not unlike what she'd known.

For several minutes the two women sat there with a valley of silence separating them and the air so heavy it was difficult to breathe.

Angela finally looked up with a wretched look wrinkling her face. "I honestly don't know what Vicki did before she came to live with us, but I do know I've loved Lara as much as any mother ever loved a child. When she cried, I was the one who held her. When she was sick I sat beside her; I watched over her as any mother would. After my sister died I became Lara's mother, the same as if I'd given birth to her."

Rachel sat with her chin rigid and her lip quivering. "But you never wondered why the baby had no birth certificate? No pictures? No hospital bracelet?"

Angela had asked herself those same questions. Even now she could recall the edgy way Vicki's eyes had searched the landscape as they'd driven away from Wynne Bluffs, and how she'd always refused to talk about Lara's father, how she'd had none of the things a mother usually has—no diaper bag, no bibs, no extra nighties, not even a rattle or a favorite toy. She'd said that Russell Murphy was abusive, but in her letter she'd begged him to forgive her. What crime had he deemed unforgivable? Was it kidnapping?

The questions that had gone unanswered for so long now stood like giants, challenging the puny lies Angela had chosen to believe. She'd always suspected that Vicki had lied to her, but not until this moment did she realize that she too had lied—to herself.

When Angela finally spoke, her eyes were downcast, her breath ragged and uneven, her voice weighted with regret and the words little more than a throaty whisper. "Yes, there were times when I wondered about the truth of what Vicki said. I knew she could be irresponsible, that she'd done drugs and occasionally stolen things, but when she came to me with Lara I thought all of that was in the past. She got a job and was a good mother."

"A good mother?" Rachel's words were sharp and tinged with the sound of resentment. "How can you say that when there's a very real possibility your sister was a kidnapper? A crazy person who stole a sleeping baby from her crib?"

"You don't know for sure that she did," Angela said defensively.

"And you can't prove that she didn't," Rachel replied. "Can we get in touch with the guy who's supposedly Lara's birth father—"

Angela shook her head. "I've tried to find him but no luck." Each unanswered question led to yet another one, until Angela felt as though her heart would explode. "There's nothing more I can tell you," she finally said. "If I knew the details of Lara's birth I would—"

Without waiting for her to finish the sentence, Rachel asked, "Really?"

It was a single word, but it hit home like an ax striking the final blow to a tree that had stood for a lifetime.

"What would you have me do?" Angela asked.

"If you believe your daughter is not Emily, then prove Lara's existence before August of 1971."

"How? My sister's gone, and I don't have a way of—"

"We'll find a way. We'll find Lara's father, track down the places he's lived, call the surrounding hospitals."

As she sat listening, Angela felt her heart shriveling, becoming smaller and smaller until it was little more than a grain of sand that could so easily be trampled underfoot.

"You have two beautiful children," she said tearfully. "Lara is all we have. We're her family, her only family. A thing like this will destroy her, destroy all of us. Please don't—"

"Don't?" Rachel's expression was steely and unyielding. "After eighteen years of wondering what happened to my daughter, how can you possibly think I'd walk away now? I'm well aware of how painful this situation is, and I'm not trying to hurt anyone. That's why I'm not asking for a paternity test right now. If we find proof that Lara really is your sister's child, no one will ever know there was a question."

"Lara's not dumb; she'll know the minute we start—"

"We won't tell her what we're doing. Tomorrow, when the kids go to the lake, we'll start making phone calls and see what we can find out. Somebody has to know something about her birth, and if we can't find it, we'll hire an investigator who can."

Angela's face had all but collapsed in on itself. Deep ridges lined her forehead and cheeks, and a look of hopelessness had settled into her eyes. "What about Hope? You said she's seen Lara's birthmark."

"Yes, but I told her it was nothing. She's promised to keep it a secret. However, later tonight I am going to tell George. He deserves to know; he lived through the same agony I did."

Angela wearily pushed herself free of the chair and stood. "When the kids get back, tell Lara I had a headache and went to bed early." She turned and started toward the staircase, her shoulders stooped and her chin dropped down on her chest.

~

As she watched Lara's mother disappear up the staircase, Rachel saw a reflection of herself. Angela's brokenness was the same brokenness she had carried in her heart all those years, and yet, like herself, Angela had done nothing to be deserving of it.

Rachel remained there for a long while, trying to hold on to the certainty that Lara was in fact Emily. She placed her open palm on her stomach, remembering the feel of Emily's tiny heart beating inside her. She'd known, almost known, the minute she'd looked into Lara's face. George had predicted she would know and she had.

You have a mother's heart. When you see our daughter you'll know it's her no matter how many years have passed.

For the first time in almost eighteen years, Rachel could feel the hole in her heart starting to mend. There was work to do. Angela would try to prove Lara was Vicki's child, but Rachel had no doubt the child was Emily.

This time when the tears came, they were ones of happiness.

It was beginning to seem as if the miracle she'd prayed for had come to pass.

REMEMBERING VICKI

Once the bedroom door was closed, Angela gave way to the tears she'd tried to hold back. Were it possible, she would grab Lara, run away, and disappear into nothingness, but it was too late for that. Rachel knew their names, she knew they were headed for Daytona, and she'd seen Lara. Rachel was a mother on a mission and not someone who would give up. The only thing Angela could do now was search for some particle of truth hidden in the mess Vicki had left behind.

The questions Rachel raised were not without merit; Angela knew that. She'd asked herself the same questions a dozen times over. Each time she'd swept her doubts under the rug and moved on. She'd taken Vicki at her word, but was it because she believed it to be true? Or simply because it was what she wanted to believe?

For a long while she stood at the window looking out into the night, watching the sky fade from steel blue to black with nothing but a thin ribbon of pink to indicate the sun had been there. In time, even that narrow trace of pink vanished. The disappearing sun was like Vicki; it left nothing behind, no trace of light to prove it had once been there. Searching through the dark void of things unknown, Angela tried to recall a name, a place, a clue that would unlock the secret Vicki carried to her grave.

The memory of their talking about her pregnancy was there—Angela could readily call that to mind—but there was never a mention of a doctor or hospital. Nor was there any mention of the delivery, whether it had been easy or hard. And what about Murphy? Had he rushed her to the hospital, or did she go alone? All those pieces that were normally part and parcel of a birth were missing. Were they too painful to speak of? Or did Vicki have no memories of those things because they never happened to her?

Angela thought back to the day they'd met at the shopping center. Why the shopping center? Why not the apartment? Was she trying to disappear without a trace? And if so, why? She claimed to be running from an abusive boyfriend, but then why write and beg for his forgiveness? What unforgivable deed had she done?

Angela stood there for a long while, tears streaming down her face and her heart feeling as though it had been ripped loose of its mooring. She wanted to scream, to beat her fists against the wall and tear her hair out, but it would solve nothing. What she had to do was find the answers to Rachel's questions. The problem was that each answer only led to another question, and for so many years she'd turned a blind eye to them.

If Lara were Vicki's child, then where were the missing pieces of her early life—the first pair of booties that a mother saves forever? The hospital bracelet? Her birth certificate? The handful of things Vicki had brought were old and worn, too old to belong to a new baby, more like clothes that had been passed down from one child to the next and then the next after that. Even the stroller looked ancient. Thrift-shop ancient.

Thoughts began slamming into one another: Vicki in the car, her hair blowing loose, her hand on the radio knob, the music blasting. A cardboard box of clothes. A man who'd apparently waited for her to return. The cautious turn of her head as they drove through Wynne Bluffs. The orange wristband. *Hesterville Music Festival, August 1971.* She had been at the festival. She loved music and loved a good time. Yes, she was wild and unpredictable but never mean or malicious. She'd never once broken into a stranger's house, and she'd never steal another woman's baby. Why would she?

The why. That was the big question. It was possible, even likely, Vicki would steal a tube of lipstick or a few bucks from their daddy's wallet, but what reason would she have for stealing a baby?

"Why, Vicki?" she sobbed. "Why?"

She thought of Kenny. She needed him more than ever, but she couldn't call on him—not now, not after he'd warned her about having the car serviced and sticking to the major highways. She'd listened to Vicki, who'd lied, but she hadn't listened to Kenny, whose advice would have prevented this terrible disaster.

"Dear God," she moaned. "What have I done?"

Angela stood at the window until she saw the lights of George's car turning into the driveway, then changed into her nightgown and climbed into bed. She knew Lara would come into the room to say good night as she always did. Normally it was something she welcomed but not tonight. Not when her eyes were red and so obviously teary.

When the kids banged through the back door, she heard the sounds of their voices, shrill and lighthearted, then George's voice, deeper but sounding happy. A short while later there was a flurry of footsteps on the staircase and the sound of laughter. Then in the room next to hers, a door opened and closed. Lara was back.

She heard the soft shuffle of bare feet across the wooden floor, then the quiet closing of another door and the sound of water from the bathroom faucet. Lara, brushing her teeth. Angela knew the routine by heart; she'd lived with it for all these years.

A few minutes later there was a soft tapping at the door, and Lara eased it open.

"Mom," she whispered. "Are you asleep?"

Angela kept her eyes closed and did not move.

Lara waited for a few moments, then closed the door and returned to her own room.

When she was gone, Angela buried her face in the pillow and sobbed. It was a terrible thing not to answer your child's call, but the possibility that Lara was Rachel's stolen baby already had a stranglehold on her heart.

THE SEARCH FOR TRUTH

Rachel waited until they were in the privacy of their bedroom and then told George of all that had happened. As she spoke, he stood there with his mouth hanging open and a look of disbelief stretched across his face. She'd thought he'd be as deliriously happy as she was, but if so, he certainly didn't show it. The first thing he asked was whether or not she'd told the twins.

"I know you feel really certain she's Emily," he said. "But you've felt almost as sure on a number of other occasions."

"This is different! There's the birthmark, and Angela even admitted she'd never seen Lara as an infant."

"Remember, Hope is the only one who's seen that birthmark. You haven't. Also, Angela claims she and her sister were estranged for three years. A lot can happen in that time. Once she starts making phone calls, she just might come up with proof that Vicki actually is Lara's birth mother."

Rachel's smile faded. "Are you deliberately trying to discourage me? I'm happy; can't you be happy with me?"

Even though she'd turned away with her eyes narrowed and her mouth tightened into a pencil-thin line, George crossed the room and took her in his arms.

"I'm not trying to spoil your moment of happiness; I'm trying to protect you from the heartbreak of disappointment, just in case this doesn't turn out the way you want it to."

"But, George, you always said that when I saw Emily I'd know her, and I did. I felt it that first day. It's been at least ten years since I looked at a child and thought, *She could be Emily*, but that's exactly what I thought the minute I saw Lara."

"Yet you didn't say anything then—why was that?"

"Because I thought I was just being foolish. I figured our house is the last place in the world Emily's kidnapper . . ." Rachel's words fell away as she watched a look of concern settle on George's face.

"I want Lara to be Emily as much as you do," he said. "She's a beautiful young lady and everything we hoped our Emmy would be, but for the past eighteen years she's been Angela's daughter. Don't lose sight of that. Angela's the mother Lara has known all her life, and she loves her, the same way the twins love you."

When Rachel's eyes filled with tears, he eased her head onto his shoulder. "If you believe she's Emily, Rachel, keep right on believing. That way you'll want the best for her no matter what happens."

She pulled back and looked up at him. "What's that supposed to mean? Of course I'd want—"

"If we find out Lara actually is Emily, she probably won't be happy about it. She might even feel resentful. We see her as the daughter we've loved all these years, but to her we're nothing but strangers."

~

George's words stayed with Rachel, and as she lay in bed, unable to sleep, she began to have less and less certainty of her conviction. The hours ticked by, and as bits of doubt crept in, she began to wonder what she really wanted to happen. The thought of the child she'd given birth to seeing her as a stranger was heartbreaking, almost as heartbreaking as the thought of never knowing. When the first light of morning edged the horizon, she climbed from the bed, dressed, and went downstairs.

She'd expected to be alone, but Angela was already sitting at the kitchen table with a notepad in front of her.

She looked up at Rachel. "I couldn't sleep."

"Neither could I," Rachel replied.

Angela's face was blotchy and her nose rubbed raw. "I'm sorry I wasn't more understanding last night," she said. "I realize this is as difficult for you as it is for me. I was up most of the night, asking myself the same questions you'd asked."

Rachel set the coffeepot on to brew, then lowered herself into the chair on the opposite side of the table. "And did you come up with any answers?"

"No." Angela shook her head dolefully. "But I did come to the realization that we both deserve to know the truth, whatever it is." She slid the pad across the table. "I've made a list of places where Vicki lived before she came to stay with us. We need to find out where Lara was born, then we can see if her birth was registered."

Rachel began reading down the list. "What about the guy she lived with? Wouldn't he know where she gave birth to Lara?"

"His name is Russ Murphy," Angela said. "I looked for him years ago but came up empty." She went on to tell of finding Vicki's letter, going to Wynne Bluffs, and calling the long list of Murphys she'd found in the telephone directory. "My sister lied about a lot of things, so it's possible the guy's name isn't Murphy, but that's what he went by when they lived together. The one thing I am certain of is that they lived in the apartment complex. The manager remembered them having a baby."

"Was Lara born while they were living there?"

"No." Angela shook her head. "I asked that same question, but the manager said the baby was about six or seven months old when they moved in. Apparently Vicki was only there for about a week. Murphy stayed on for a few months, then he took off and left with no forwarding address."

"So where do we go from here?"

Angela scrubbed a hand across her wrinkled forehead, looked at the list and then back to Rachel. "I've racked my brain trying to remember places Vicki might have mentioned in passing, but I couldn't come up with anything. She bounced around a lot, but as far as I know she never lived anywhere outside of Kentucky."

"Kentucky?" Rachel groaned. "That's a pretty big area to search, when we're not even sure what we're looking for."

"Not as big as you might think. Vicki didn't have a car, so the likelihood is that when she had Lara, she was living somewhere in Wynne Bluffs or close by in the area where we grew up."

"We could call the county records department and ask—"

Angela again shook her head. "I tried that years ago. To order a copy from them, you've got to know the baby's date of birth *and* what hospital she was born in."

"Well, you know Lara's date of birth, don't you?"

"Yes, it's February 5. Vicki was still alive when Lara celebrated her first birthday, and I doubt that's something she lied about."

"Okay then, maybe we could try calling all the hospitals and . . ."

Angela hesitated, tracing her finger along the last name she'd written. This was the most difficult decision she'd ever had to make, but there was no longer a way to avoid it. After a moment she lifted her face and allowed her eyes to meet Rachel's. "Yes, that's what we have to do."

She'd toyed with the idea of telling Rachel about the orange wristband, but then pushed it aside. As a singular piece of evidence it was too condemning; she would wait and give the truth time to surface on its own. While she wanted the truth to be known, that didn't mean she wasn't praying it would turn out to be what she'd believed all these years.

Rachel stood, filled two mugs with coffee, carried them to the table, and again sat across from Angela. As she scooped a spoonful of sugar into her cup she heard the thump of footsteps overhead. "The kids are up," she said. "Let's put this aside until they're out of here."

Angela stuffed the notepad back into her tote and carried it off.

The next hour was filled with a frenzy of activity as the household came to life. With George running late, Rachel wrapped two biscuits in a checkered napkin and handed him a thermos of coffee. As he hurried off, she called upstairs for the kids to get dressed and grab their bathing suits. By the time they were seated at the breakfast table, a lunch basket was packed and ready to go.

Setting a platter of pancakes in the center of the table, Rachel said, "It's going to be another scorcher, so I thought you kids would like to spend the day at the lake."

The twins cheered, and Lara glanced over at Angela.

"You don't look good today, Mom; would you rather I stay here?"

"I'll be fine, sweetheart. Go enjoy yourself at the lake. It's just my allergies acting up."

"Well, if you're sure it's okay."

"Absolutely." Angela forced a smile. "It's a perfect day for the beach, and there's no need for you to hang around."

Minutes later Rachel had the kids in the car and was headed for the lake. As she drove she eyed the three of them in the rearview mirror and noticed that overnight the similarities in the children had become even more pronounced. Although Hope had George's coloring, all three appeared to be of the same family.

George was wrong. He had to be wrong. *She's Emily.*

~

When Rachel returned to the house, Angela was again sitting at the table with the notepad in front of her. She'd added another name to the list.

At the top of the list was "Wynne Bluffs—hospital unknown." Below that, "Madisonville and Bardstown." "Marsden County General" was written next to both towns.

Angela's first call was to the Wynne Bluffs police station.

"I'm thinking about moving to the area," she said, "and was wondering if you can tell me what hospitals are nearby?"

"Sisters of Mercy isn't far," the desk officer said, "ten miles west off I-24. If you're looking for a sophisticated medical center, you've got Lourdes Hospital in Paducah, but that's a good two-hour drive."

She thanked him, hung up, and dialed information for the Sisters of Mercy phone number. Minutes later she was talking to a woman in the records department.

After an explanation of Vicki's death and their relationship, she said, "My sister gave birth to a little girl on February 5, 1971, but I'm uncertain which hospital it was, and I need to get a copy of the birth certificate."

"What's the name again?"

"Vicki or Victoria Robart was the mother. The baby's name was Lara. But she might have used her boyfriend's last name for the baby."

"What's his name?"

After a moment of hesitation Angela said, "Murphy. Russell Murphy."

The clerk gave a huff of agitation. "Since you're uncertain about which name they used for the baby, I'm going to have to check patient records first. Hold on."

Fifteen minutes ticked by before the woman came back on the line.

"Sorry, hon," she said. "We've got no patient record for a Victoria or Vicki Robart, and nothing for that name under Murphy either, so I can't help you out."

"Thanks anyway," Angela replied and moved on to the second name.

She dialed the number for Marsden County General, gave the same explanation, and got the same answer: if she was unsure of the name on the baby's birth certificate, she'd first have to check with patient records. This time she was transferred to another line, and a man's voice answered.

"Patient records." His voice was quick and impatient-sounding.

Angela ran through the explanation again. "So that would be Vicki or Victoria Robart, or it could be under Murphy. She gave birth to a girl, first name Lara, on February 5, 1971."

"Please hold."

Angela listened to the sound of computer keys clicking. A few minutes later he was back, his voice still sharp, only now it was bristling with agitation.

"Ma'am, we don't issue birth certificates for infants who were stillborn."

"That can't be," she said. "It's a mistake. You've got the wrong record."

"I most certainly do not," he snapped. "Ms. Vicki Robart delivered a twenty-seven-week fetal-death female on February 5, 1971. A stillborn registration certificate was provided for cremation."

A fiery pain shot across Angela's chest, and several seconds ticked by before she was able to draw a breath. With her heart at a standstill and her voice quavering, she summoned her last ounce of courage and asked the final question. "Was the infant given a name?"

"Yes. Lara Robart Murphy."

The telephone tumbled to the floor as Angela fell forward sobbing.

Of all the reactions Rachel might have expected, this was not one of them. Something was terribly wrong. "What did they say?" she asked anxiously.

Angela continued to sob. She didn't even look up, just sat there with her face buried in her hands and her entire body trembling.

"Oh my God! What did they say?" Rachel bolted from the chair and grabbed the telephone off the floor. "What did you say?" she screamed, but by then there was nothing but the hollow sound of a dead line.

With a sense of desperation rising in her throat, Rachel squatted in front of Angela and pried her hands from her face. "Stop crying and tell me what they said," she commanded. "Please! Look at me!"

When Angela finally gathered herself together enough to speak, she did not lift her face or allow her eyes to meet Rachel's.

The words came between sobs, pieced together in rambling thoughts, intertwined with anguish, and barely understandable. "A thing like this never should have happened . . . I'm sorry, so sorry . . . I never—"

Rachel's eyes went wide. "Sorry about what?" she asked frantically. "What did they say? What happened?"

Angela pulled her hands back and again covered her face. "Vicki stole things; I knew it! But it was just junk, glittery trinkets from the five-and-dime. She never took anything big—"

Rachel's voice suddenly became high-pitched and panicky. "What are you talking about?" she cried. "What was it they told you?"

Oblivious to the question, Angela rambled on. "Especially not a baby. What reason would Vicki have for stealing a baby—that's what I kept asking myself. Why a baby? Why?"

With her eyes wild and her face growing more flushed by the second, Rachel stood, grabbed Angela by the shoulders, and shook her. "Talk to me! Tell me what they said!"

Angela made a sound so agonized it could have come only from the very depths of her soul. "Now I know why," she wailed.

She began to repeat what the clerk had told her, spilling out the thoughts in crumbled words and broken sentences. She told how Vicki had given birth to a little girl on February 5 and named the child Lara, but then she stopped, hesitating so long that it seemed the story had ended.

Rachel released her hold on Angela and stepped back with her arms hanging limply at her sides. In a voice weighted with eighteen years of sorrow, she said, "So Lara really is your sister's baby?"

Angela shook her head but kept her face buried. "No, Vicki's child was stillborn."

Rachel gave a horrified gasp. "Oh my God . . . She pretended Emily was her dead baby?" Rachel stood there for a moment looking too stunned to go on, then dropped down in the chair and repeated the thought as if she were struggling to understand it. "She took our Emily to replace her dead baby?"

Angela slumped back in the chair and continued to sob.

For a while they remained that way, not speaking but sharing a sorrow that belonged to both of them, two women, victims of the same crime, laying claim to the same child.

When the tears subsided and she could again find her breath, Angela spoke.

"I can't begin to imagine what drove my sister to do such a terrible thing. I can only guess Vicki was too sick at heart to understand the magnitude of what she'd done; she had to have been . . . There's no other reason why—"

"Sorrow does strange things to a woman," Rachel said, her tone not accusatory but touched with compassion.

As she spoke she could feel her heart slowing, returning to its normal rhythm. "No one understands what it feels like to lose a child until they live through it. I know how your sister felt losing her baby: I felt it too, only my heartache was a thousand times worse because I didn't know who had taken Emmy or what terrible thing they might do to her. Over the past eighteen years I've said a million prayers asking God to give my child to a mother who would love her—love her the way I loved her."

Angela lifted her head the tiniest bit and looked at Rachel from beneath hooded brows. "I can't even begin to imagine the heartache you went through . . . To say I'm sorry seems so very meaningless, but I am sorry, truly, truly sorry. If I had known . . ."

In the humility of Angela's words, Rachel sensed the same brokenness she'd once known. It was the kind of ache that splintered a woman's soul and robbed her heart of whatever happiness it had once held.

"What would you have done?" she said sadly. "You were Lara's mother. You loved her just as I loved Emmy. Would you have given up your child so that I could have mine?"

Even as the words came from her mouth, she knew there was no good answer. For Angela to say yes, she would have returned the child, would mean Lara was loved less than Emily. Rachel never wanted that. To say no would be pouring salt into the wound created by years of separation.

Without letting her eyes meet Rachel's, Angela said, "I wish I could tell you the answer is yes, that I would have sacrificed my happiness for yours, but the truth is I don't know."

Rachel gave a nod so slight it was like the blink of an cyc or the flicker of a shadow, then the two women sat there, close enough to hear the thunder of each other's heartbeat, but with a wall of silence separating them.

Angela thought back over the years, wondering where she'd gone wrong. What sign had she missed? How had she not known that in the same way she'd yearned for a child, Vicki had yearned for a family? She'd lost the mother she idolized; she'd been abused by her father, had no place to call home, no sister coming to her rescue, no husband to love her, and the final blow came when she lost the one thing she could have called her own—her baby. Although it didn't lessen the wrong of such an act, Angela now understood the *why*. Vicki had taken Rachel's baby because she was desperate to love and be loved. As the weight of that realization settled in her chest, tears overflowed her eyes.

It was several minutes before she gave voice to her thoughts. "I can never undo the harm that's been done, and I can never expect you to forgive Vicki for the heartache she caused your family. But I can tell you this: there was never a moment in Lara's life when she wasn't cared for and truly loved."

Angela turned and looked into Rachel's eyes, expecting to see anger, but there was none. In its place was a look of compassion, an understanding far beyond what was deserved.

"I realize that I have no right to ever expect forgiveness, but . . ." Angela continued on, telling of Vicki's life and how fate had taken far more than it had given back to her.

Rachel said nothing as she sat there replaying the last eighteen years in her mind. She pictured Mama Dixon sitting across from her, offering a ball of yarn and talking of how God makes things right in His own time. She remembered the birth of the twins and the years of them growing up with Bruno by their side. They weren't bad years; they were happy years. Year after year, she'd asked God to watch over Emily, to give her the same kind of happiness, a loving mother and a place to call home. Now, after all this time, she knew that her prayers had not fallen on deaf ears. He'd answered in His own way. At first she hadn't understood this strange new feeling pushing its way into her chest, but now she knew: it was gratitude.

Angela had taken a motherless child and loved her—was that really such an unforgivable sin? Rachel reached across and took Angela's hand in hers. "Perhaps forgiveness is the one thing that can make our families whole again."

CREATING A FAMILY

Later that afternoon, after Angela had spent hours talking with Rachel, discussing how they might move ahead and how they would tell Lara, she called Kenny with news of all that had transpired.

"You're kidding?" He gasped. "Lara's been with us for eighteen years! She's our daughter! They can't just expect—"

"Actually, they can," Angela replied. "They're struggling with this, the same as we are. They're good people who suffered a great deal because of what Vicki did, and given the circumstances, I think they're being extremely gracious. We're trying to make this as easy as possible for Lara."

"Have you told her yet?"

"No, I'll do it tomorrow. Rachel is going to take the twins to the lake, and I'll speak with Lara privately."

For several moments Kenny said nothing, and Angela felt the weight of his silence.

"I understand if you're angry," she said solemnly, "but it should be with me, not the Dixons. I'm to blame for believing Vicki's story." She sniffed back the tears that were threatening. "Then I made things a thousand times worse by not doing as you'd asked. If I had taken the car in for service and stuck to the route you mapped out, we'd be in Daytona, and this never would have happened." The sound of regret was wound around her every word.

There was another lengthy silence, but when Kenny finally spoke his voice was softer and more forgiving.

"You're not the only one who believed Vicki," he said. "I did also. At first I really thought she was on the up and up, but after I saw that box with nothing but a bunch of her clothes in it, I suspected there was something more to the story."

"You didn't say anything . . ."

"Yeah, I know. By then Lara was—what—ten or twelve years old? For God's sake, she was our daughter; what could I do?"

Although he acknowledged the wrong of what had been done, Kenny was slow to accept that the Dixons needed to get to know the child they had given birth to.

"We don't even know these people! How can we be certain Lara's safe there with a bunch of strangers?"

Angela gave a barely audible chuckle. "Remember how I used to say Lara's personality was nothing like her mama's?" she asked. And then without waiting for an answer, she said, "Well, I was wrong. She's exactly like her mama." She went on to say that Rachel was a generous and kindhearted woman who wanted only what was best for her child.

"But we are what's best," Kenny argued.

By the time Angela told how Lara had a brother and sister she needed to get to know, Kenny ran out of arguments and agreed to come to Hesterville for the weekend.

"If it will make things easier for Lara, then I'll do it," he said reluctantly.

"That's precisely why you should be doing it," she replied.

~

That evening as they gathered at the dinner table, there was no mention of the discovery that had taken place. The conversation, while not jovial, was pleasant enough. There was talk of the heat wave, Lara's upcoming visit to the University of Florida, and how the summer was rolling by at warp speed. Hope and Henry were both full of chatter about their day at the lake. Henry had spent much of the afternoon kicking around a soccer ball with Billy Olson, who was on the JV soccer team, and had begun to brag that he too would make the team. Hope held up her end of the conversation with stories of how Lara was teaching her to do both the backstroke and the butterfly.

"She knows how to do everything!" Hope said. "I wish she could stay all summer."

Lara laughed. "Wish all you want, but Mom said once the car is fixed, we've got to get back on the road."

Angela glanced over at Rachel with the warm glow of gratitude in her eyes. "We're not in that much of a hurry," she said.

~

Rachel waited until they were alone in their bedroom before telling George what they'd learned that afternoon.

"It's exactly as I thought," she said, a bittersweet smile tugging at the corners of her mouth. "Lara really is Emily."

He was in the middle of undressing, with his trousers hanging down around his knees, and almost toppled over. "Really?" He gasped. "Angela was the one who—"

"Not Angela. Her sister. She gave birth to a little girl named Lara, the February before Emily was taken, but the baby was stillborn."

George stood wide-eyed and listened as Rachel told of how Angela had called the hospitals and discovered the truth.

"Do you think Angela knew all along?"

"I'm positive she didn't," Rachel said sadly. "She was devastated by the news."

"Does Lara know?"

"Not yet. Angela will tell her tomorrow." Rachel heaved a heavily weighted sigh. "I certainly don't envy what she has to do."

George stepped free of his trousers, came across the room, and took Rachel in his arms. "I'm surprised that after all you went through, you can still feel compassion for her."

"You went through it the same as I did. What do you feel?" She looked up and noticed how his eyes had grown misty.

"It seems like a miracle that after so many years . . ." George's voice cracked, and he hesitated for several moments before continuing. "You always had faith, Rachel, long after I'd given up hope. Yesterday when you said there was a good possibility Lara was our Emily, even then, I was afraid to believe. I didn't want your hopes to be dashed again."

"You never said . . ." Her voice trailed off.

"How could I? As long as you held out hope that we'd one day find her, I couldn't say otherwise. You were the one, Rachel. Your faith is what finally enabled us to find Emily."

When he pressed her to his chest, she felt the hammering of his heart.

Long into the night they sat on the side of the bed and talked about the challenges yet to come. They spoke of how Lara might react to such news and the possibility she could turn away from them with anger in her eyes.

Although George knew such a thing could happen, he somehow believed the child was born with a heart like her mother's, a heart capable of great forgiveness.

~

The next morning Rachel and Angela were both up early, and the same edgy look was evident on both faces. Shortly after George left for the store, Rachel said she was taking the twins to the lake for the day.

"I've already packed lunch and a stack of towels, so get into your bathing suits."

Lara's face brightened. "Mom, can we go with them?"

Angela shook her head. "Not today. There's something we need to talk about."

"But—"

"Not today," Angela repeated.

Once they were alone, she poured two tall glasses of sweet tea and carried them to the back patio. She sat on the wicker settee and motioned for Lara to sit beside her. A worried expression tugged at Lara's face as she lowered herself onto the cushion.

Angela thought she was ready for this—she'd practiced what she would say until the wee hours of morning—but now the words were gone and her mouth so dry she could barely speak. She forced a cough, then reached for the glass of tea. Her hand trembled, and a splash fell on her skirt. Grabbing a napkin, she swiped at it with quick fidgety strokes.

"I'm so clumsy," she said nervously. "Terribly, terribly . . ."

Catching the jittery sound of her mother's voice, Lara asked, "Is something wrong, Mom? Daddy's not sick, is he?"

"No, no. Your daddy's fine. He's coming here to be with us this weekend."

Lara turned with a look of surprise. "Coming here? Why?"

Angela lifted her daughter's hand into hers and gave it an affectionate squeeze. "It's a long story that started before you were even born."

Her stomach churned, and the taste of bile rose in her throat as she struggled to find the right words. Suddenly it seemed there were none. Not one word that could carry comfort to her child and soothe the pain of what she was about to say. Even the tiniest word, the single letter *I* standing alone, seemed razor sharp and filled with anguish. She hesitated, pulling in a deep breath and then letting it go as she continued.

"You know how much your mama loved you, don't you?"

Lara nodded. "Mom, your hand feels clammy! Are you sure you're not coming down with something?"

"Don't worry, I'm fine." Angela swiped the palm of her hand across her skirt, then went back to what she'd been saying. "You know there's nothing in this world your mama wouldn't have done for you."

"I realize that, but I don't see how—"

"She once told me that she loved you long before you were born, that having you was the thing she wanted most in life." The fear in Angela's heart swelled and grew greater as she spoke. "But before you came into your mama's life, she gave birth to another baby. A baby who was stillborn and never took a single breath."

A look of compassion tugged at Lara's face, and she gave a faint sigh. "Oh, Mom, that's so sad."

"Worse than sad," Angela replied. "It was a life-changing tragedy that broke your mama's heart, and she never got over it. The thought of having a baby became an obsession, one she couldn't push aside or forget. I'm sure you've heard of people who want something so badly, they'll do whatever they have to do to get it; well, that's how your mama was about having a baby."

"But then she had me, right?"

With her heart pounding and her eyes searching Lara's face for a flicker of understanding, Angela shook her head ever so slightly. "No, sweetheart, that's not what happened. Your mama wasn't strong enough to go through another pregnancy, but she wanted a baby so badly that she did a terrible thing: she took another woman's child."

"Huh? I don't get it. What's that supposed to mean?"

"One night, when this family was asleep and there was no one around to stop her, your mama broke into their house and took their baby from her crib."

"Good God, Mom, that's kidnapping!"

"Yes, it is," Angela replied nervously. "I have to believe at the time she was so consumed with grief that she wasn't able to reason right from wrong. She only knew she wanted that baby, so she took it."

"But then she brought it back, right?" Despite the deep ridges that had settled across her forehead, Lara's words were hopeful.

"Unfortunately, she didn't. She kept the baby and told people it was hers. She gave the child her dead baby's name and birthday."

Lara jumped up and looked down at her mother with a horrified expression. "Oh my God, Mom, please don't tell me I'm that baby!" Her eyes began to fill with tears. "Mom . . ."

Angela stood and folded her daughter into her arms. She held her close for a moment, then, with her heart in her throat, she let go of the words she'd been holding back. "Yes . . . Lara . . . you are that baby."

Lara pulled back, her eyes wide and the color drained from her cheeks. She gave a gasp, then stood there staring at her mother. "But . . . you told me Vicki was my mom. You said I was with her when she came to live with you. Remember we saw those movies where I was a baby and she was holding me? She was my mom . . . You even said how much she loved me."

Angela's heart felt as though it would shatter into a million tiny fragments as she listened to the pleading sound of Lara's voice. Her child was asking her to take this ugly truth away, and it was the one thing she couldn't do. Struggling to hold back the tears, she said, "Vicki did love you, Lara; she loved you with all her heart. When I told you she was your mom, it was what I believed to be true."

"Then what changed? Why are you telling me she's not—"

"Because yesterday I learned the Dixons are your biological parents."

"The Dixons?" Lara's jaw fell, and she stood there looking dumbfounded. "Hope's mom and dad are my parents?"

"Yes. I had no idea until Rachel said—"

"Hope's mom and dad are my parents? The ones whose baby got kidnapped?"

Angela lowered her eyes and gave a nod. Seeing the despair on Lara's face was almost more than she could bear. She took a deep breath and tried to quell the anxiety rising in her chest. "It happened a few years before they moved to this house. You were only six months old at the time and . . ."

As Lara listened she tilted her head back and stood looking up at the sky, her eyes ready to spill over but fixed on a single cloud scudding across the blanket of blue.

Little by little the story unfolded. Angela related all the things Rachel had shared: the story of the music festival, the horror of waking that morning to find the crib empty, the years of searching, and how Hope had noticed the birthmark and told her mama.

"So because of this birthmark, they think I'm their kidnapped baby? Well, maybe they're wrong. Maybe my having this birthmark is just some weird coincidence. Maybe Mama was nowhere near this town when they had that music festival . . ." She dropped back down onto the settee, shaking her head sorrowfully.

Angela sat and wrapped her arm around her daughter's shoulders. "With all my heart I wish that were true, but I know for certain Vicki was here that weekend." She continued on, telling of how years later she'd found the letter and been given a cardboard box of the things left behind. "Vicki didn't hang on to many things, but she'd saved a souvenir from that weekend. It was a wristband with the name and date of the music festival."

Lara looked up. "Is that why we came here?" she asked solemnly, her words filled with doubt and uncertainty, as wobbly as a child learning to walk. "Has this whole trip been a search for my real parents?"

"Lord God, no! Kenny and I are your parents, and we're going to remain your parents. That's never going to change. Life as you've known it is not going to change. In the fall you'll go off to college just as we planned, and—"

Cutting in, Lara asked, "Well then, why are you telling me all of this? If nothing is going to change, what am I supposed to do now?"

Angela reached across, touched her hand to her daughter's cheek, and turned her face so that they were looking into one another's eyes. "Just give this family a chance to get to know you. If you're willing to do that, I think you'll see a lot of yourself in Rachel Dixon."

Lara gave a shrug of indifference and turned away. "We'll see," she said, then she stood and started back toward the house.

As Angela watched her walk away she knew that life would in fact change. The questions Lara had asked over the years would now be answered. In time, she would come to know her birth parents and have the siblings she and Kenny had been unable to give her.

She had to trust that this was a good thing, but when a tear slid from her eye and rolled down her cheek, Angela honestly could not say whether it was one of happiness or regret.

~

A short while later Rachel returned from the lake, and Hope bolted through the door with the sparkle of excitement lighting her eyes.

"Lara, Lara!" she screamed, then continued up the stairs, taking them two at a time. She knocked on the bedroom door with a quick rat-a-tat as if it were some kind of signal.

A voice from inside said, "Not now."

Hope ignored it and burst into the room. Her expression was one of pure joy.

"My wish came true!"

Lara was sitting on the bed, her back leaning against the headboard and her shoes on the bedspread, despite the rules. Without glancing up, she mumbled, "I said not now."

"Yeah, I heard, but I figured you didn't know it was me." Hope kicked off her flip-flops and leaped onto the bed beside Lara. "When I made that wish, I never in a million years thought it would come true, but it did, and now—"

"What wish?" Lara said. "What are you talking about?"

Ignoring the fact that Lara was unsmiling and stiff as a board, Hope continued. "Last March Mama told us about you, and that night we had a cake with candles to celebrate your birthday—"

"My birthday's not in March; it's in February."

Hope shook her head and grinned. "Un-uh, your real birthday's in March. March tenth. I know because it was the day of the field trip, but I forgot my bathing suit, and so I had to come home and—"

"Why are you telling me this?"

"Don't you get it? We're sisters! This is how it happened!" With barely a breath in between one sentence and the next, Hope went on to tell how she'd found her mama holding on to a locket and crying.

"Your baby picture was in the locket, only your name was Emily back then. That's when Mama told me about you and how every year on your birthday she took the locket out and said a whole bunch of prayers for you."

"She still has the locket?" Lara leaned in with a look of interest. "Where does she keep it?"

Hope shrugged. "Her jewelry drawer, maybe. I think she has a special locket box. I could get her to show it to you if you want."

Lara gave a nonchalant nod and scrunched her nose. "Yeah, maybe. I guess it would be fun to see when I was a baby. Mom has pictures from when I was a year old but nothing when I was real small."

"Oh, you were small in this picture. Really small," Hope said and snickered. "Mama told me she had you propped against a pillow so you wouldn't fall over."

"Aww . . ." Forgetting her anger for a split second, Lara smiled.

"But seeing the locket's not the most exciting part."

"Oh really? Then what's the most exciting part?"

"I said we should celebrate your birthday with a cake, so I got to blow out the candles. You get to make a wish when you blow out the candles."

“That’s not exactly news.”

“Maybe not, but this is! I wished you would get found and I could have you for a sister! Now here you are!”

No longer able to hold back, Lara laughed. “And you think I’m here because of that wish?”

“Not think.” Hope gave a wide grin. “Know!”

GETTING TO KNOW YOU

Lara spent most of that afternoon in her room. She thought through this new turn of events a dozen times and each time came away with a different observation or question. Since she had never known anything about her birth father, it wasn't difficult to see George filling the spot. He was a fatherly figure, with warm eyes and an easy laugh, all the good attributes she'd always imagined her daddy would have. But Rachel was a different story. To accept Rachel as her birth mom meant doing away with the image she already had in her heart. Over the years she'd taken the handed-down stories and a few minutes of home-movie clips and created comfortable memories. Vicki wasn't simply her birth mom; she was Angela's sister. She was the smiling face in home movies, the giver of huge teddy bears, and in an odd and rather unexplainable way, a piece of Lara herself. She'd held on to those memories for the whole of her life, and now letting go was difficult.

Lara thought back on the earlier suggestion that she'd see a reflection of herself in Rachel Dixon, but so far she hadn't, and she wasn't all that optimistic about doing so. While Hope's story of the locket was heartwarming, it was not enough to erase the memories of Vicki from her mind.

That evening at the dinner table, Lara was again sitting opposite Rachel. She'd planned to scoot over to the end of the table, where she could catch sideways glances without looking straight into Rachel's face, but Henry slid into the seat before she got there.

Throughout dinner Lara kept her head ducked and said little. From the corner of her eye she thought she saw Rachel smiling at her twice, but neither time did she look up to find out for sure.

Still excited by the thought of wishing her sister into being, Hope was not daunted by Lara's lack of conversation and happily rambled on about how they could write letters back and forth while she was away at college and spend winter breaks on the beach in Daytona. While she and Henry were equally pleased with having Lara as an addition to the family, Hope's enthusiasm was impossible to ignore.

When she finally wound down and took a breather, George looked over at Lara and smiled. "What are you planning to study?" he asked.

Surprisingly, Lara smiled back. "Journalism," she said.

"Well, I'll be darned." He laughed and shook his head. "I guess it runs in the family."

Lara eyed him with a puzzled expression. "What do you mean?"

Before George had time to answer, Hope did. "Mom was the editor of her high school newspaper, and I won the Mississippi River essay contest last year."

"Really?"

Hope nodded. "Yeah, I got a blue ribbon and—"

"No, I meant really your mom was an editor?"

"She wasn't just an editor, she was a darn good one!" George said. "She worked for the *Primrose Post* a year before we were married."

Again Lara smiled; this time it was more spontaneous and not quite so stiff. "I was the editor of our *Panther Paws* newsletter. Two years running."

Moments later Rachel came from the kitchen carrying a fresh pitcher of sweet tea. "Who's ready for a refill?" she asked.

Lara lifted her chin and peeked from beneath her brows. "I could use one."

When Rachel leaned forward to pour the tea, Lara looked up and caught another glimpse of her face. Although she was curious to know more, she wasn't ready to reach out.

Later that night as Lara lay in her bed thinking through the events of the day, she wondered why it was that she hadn't noticed the blue of Rachel Dixon's eyes before.

She was drifting on the edge of sleep when she remembered that copy of the *Panther Paws* she'd tossed into the back seat of the car. If they ever got the car back she could show it to the Dixons, maybe even ask Rachel's opinion. Lara fell asleep wondering if perhaps Rachel Dixon could give her a few professional tips to carry off to college.

~

In the days that followed, a strange curiosity picked at Lara. She'd wait until she saw Rachel occupied with something else, then look over and study her face, looking for a flicker of familiarity, something that would stir the memory of when she'd been this other mother's daughter.

From time to time she caught a glimpse of herself in Rachel—little things. The slant of her nose, the way laughter began low in her throat and then rose as an almost musical sound, the shape of her hands.

On Friday afternoon, she noticed her mom and Rachel sitting together on the back porch. Their conversation seemed friendly, almost intimate, and intriguing enough for her to want to be a part of it.

She strolled over and asked, "What's up?"

Angela laughed. "Actually, we were talking about you."

"Me?" Lara dropped down into a chair. "What about me?"

"I was asking about the future," Rachel said. "Wondering if perhaps you'd like to spend some time with us . . ."

Lara scrunched her nose, and a ridge of lines rose up on her forehead. "How much time?" she asked apprehensively.

"Only as much as you want, maybe come for a visit next summer when you're on break?"

"Do I have to decide right now?"

Rachel shook her head and smiled. "Take as much time as you need. We'd love for you to become a part of our family, but that decision will be yours to make."

For the first time Lara looked across and allowed her eyes to meet Rachel's. When she did, she found the spark of familiarity she'd been looking for. She could almost see herself twenty years from now looking exactly like this newly discovered mother.

~

Later that night, after Angela was in bed but not yet asleep, there was a soft rapping on the door. Lara eased it open and whispered, "Can I come in?"

"Of course." Angela sat up and snapped the light on.

Lara plopped down on the side of the bed, drew her legs up, and hugged them to her chest. "I've been thinking about it, Mom, and you're right. Mrs. Dixon and I are a lot alike. She puts ketchup and mustard on her hot dogs like I do, she has that same funny laugh, and her eyes are the exact same color—"

Angela laughed. "That's not the kind of thing I meant when I said you'd see a lot of yourself in Rachel."

"It's not?"

Angela shook her head and smiled. "You and Rachel have the same generosity and goodness of heart. Right now you're only seeing the surface similarities, but give it time, and I think you'll understand exactly what I mean."

It was a bittersweet moment but one Angela knew was inevitable. Lara's world was becoming bigger; she had siblings and parents she needed to get to know. Everything was as it should be. Although the sorrow of change was finding its way into her heart, she would forever be thankful for having had those precious years of Lara's childhood.

THE MISSING YEARS

Kenny arrived on Saturday afternoon. He'd spent a good part of the week thinking through the situation, and while he'd promised to be congenial with the Dixons, he had been Lara's father for the past eighteen years and wasn't going to let himself be pushed aside.

The minute he stepped out of the car Lara darted from the house and threw her arms around his neck.

"I've missed you, Daddy."

Her greeting was as enthusiastic as ever. Kenny wasn't certain what he'd expected. He kissed her cheek, then lifted her off the ground in a bear hug. "I've missed you too, pumpkin. From what I understand, you and Mom have gotten yourselves in quite a fix, haven't you?"

She smiled. "I don't think I'd call it a *fix*, but it was for sure a big surprise."

"Yes, it was," he replied sadly.

Moments later Lara wriggled free, and Angela slid into his arms. As he held her to his chest, he whispered, "How's it going?"

"Fine. I think you're going to enjoy getting to know Rachel and George. They're really good people, and, like us, they want what's best for Lara."

"We'll see," Kenny grumbled.

~

Rachel was in the kitchen readying things for a cold sandwich buffet, so George was the first to greet Kenny. He crossed the room with a broad smile and stuck out his hand.

"So you're Lara's dad," George said. "Glad you could make it. We've been looking forward to meeting you."

Kenny introduced himself, shook hands, then took his hankie and wiped his brow. "You should've come to Daytona; we've got a nice ocean breeze over there."

"Yeah, this weather's miserable, but it's supposed to cool down later tonight."

When Rachel came into the room, there was another round of introductions and hand shaking. Then George suggested he and Kenny have a cold beer and watch a few innings of the Braves game.

"You a baseball fan?" he asked.

"On occasion, but I prefer college basketball. The Kentucky Wildcats, that's my team. They've had a rough go of it the last few years, but they're coming back."

"Yeah, I hear you picked up the Knicks coach Rick Pitino. What's your take on him?"

"He looks good . . ."

Kenny wasn't prepared to like George Dixon, but oddly enough, he did. The man had an unassuming way and right off the bat acknowledged Kenny's role as Lara's dad, which broke down whatever barriers Kenny had anticipated.

As the two men headed toward the family room to settle in front of the television, Angela looked over at Rachel and gave a crooked smile. It seemed there would be none of the hostility she'd worried about.

~

That evening Rachel added a leaf to the dining room table and set seven places. George sat on one end, Kenny on the other, Lara between the twins on one side of the table, and opposite them were Angela and Rachel, sitting side by side like sisters.

The table was laden with dishes of roasted corn, creamy mashed potatoes, and salads so colorful they appeared to have been plucked fresh from the garden. By some odd coincidence it seemed as though every dish on the table was someone's favorite. When Rachel carried in the platter piled high with golden-brown pork chops and set it square in front of Kenny, he beamed.

"Oh boy, pork chops are my absolute favorite," he said, then speared two and lifted them onto his plate.

Rachel gave Angela a sly wink. "Really?" she replied.

As the dishes were passed from hand to hand, conversations crisscrossed the table, and bits of laughter slid in. There was talk of sports, family vacations, and the excitement surrounding Lara's first year at the University of Florida. When Daytona was mentioned, Kenny suggested everyone come for a visit.

"I'm in a studio apartment right now," he said, "but as soon as Angela gets there we're going to start house hunting."

"And it's going to be a house with a pool," Lara added; then she glanced down at Kenny and grinned. "Right, Dad?"

He nodded obligingly. "Yep, it will be a house with a pool."

Halfway through dinner, Rachel reached for the bowl of string beans and caught Lara staring at her.

"Penny for your thoughts," she said.

With the tiniest hint of a smile edging her lips, Lara replied, "I kinda think we look alike."

It was the moment Rachel had been hoping for, praying for actually. She smiled, and this time Lara didn't turn away. "I looked exactly like you when I was your age," she said. "Would you like to see some pictures?"

Lara gave a shy nod.

"Okay then, after dinner I'll pull out the old family album and bore everyone to death—how's that?"

Kenny laughed. "If you do, we'll be obliged to return the favor."

"I wish you would; I'd love to see pictures of Lara—"

Angela let go of a shriek that caused even the kids to turn. "Oh my gosh! How could I have forgotten this?" She looked over at Kenny with a wide grin. "The projector and films are in the trunk of my car!"

While Rachel and Angela cleared the table, George and Kenny drove over to Ernie's garage to pick up the projector and box of films. By the time they returned, the smell of popcorn was coming from the kitchen.

Although no one could point to the exact moment when it happened, that dinner marked the start of the two families coming together. It seemed as if they were distant cousins, somehow related but just now discovering one another.

~

That evening they all gathered in the living room and watched the home movies until almost midnight. With the reels now labeled, they started with Lara's first birthday and moved forward through the years. Kenny threaded the film through the machine, and moments after the light flickered on a tiny Lara waddled toward the camera with her arms outstretched.

Although Rachel knew it was coming, her heart seized at the sight of the happy smile. She grabbed George's knee and leaned forward as if she were trying to get closer, to step into the picture and be part of the moment.

"She was just learning to walk then," Angela said. As the reel continued she told how Lara pushed that musical lawn mower around the room, bumping into everything. After the lawn mower came scenes where Lara was hugging a rag doll, and then there she was, standing in her crib bouncing up and down.

"She's exactly as I'd imagined." Rachel's words had the sound of melancholy threaded through them. She thought back on all the years and how she'd pictured Emily at each stage of life. After the twins came along she'd prayed Emily would be as happy and loved as they were. Now she could see her wish had come true, even though she'd had no part in it. It was a bittersweet moment, tinged with both gratitude and heartache. She gave a wistful sigh and leaned back into the cushions.

Near the end of the reel there were a few shots of Vicki: first playing patty-cake with Lara on the floor, then with the baby at her shoulder as they turned and disappeared down the hallway. When the close-up of Vicki with her blonde curls and bright smile flashed onscreen no one said anything, but George's eyes narrowed, and his jaw stiffened.

Reel by reel they went through the years. Baths and bedtimes, little-girl tea parties, days at the park, swinging, running, the first day of school, a Halloween princess costume, and close-up after close-up of the childish face Rachel could for so long only imagine.

As she watched the years unfold Rachel thought back on all the things she'd missed. She'd not been there to teach her child how to brush her teeth, to say her prayers, or to tie her shoes. She'd never tucked her in, read a good-night story, or run beside her as she learned to ride a bike. All those moments were gone. Forever. They could never be recaptured. She would in time come to know her daughter, but she would never know her baby.

Rachel's eyes filled with tears, and she bit down on her lip in a useless effort to stem the flow.

Lara sat on the floor with the twins, adding her own dialogue to various scenes and laughing at others. When the image of her and Kenny at the father-daughter dance appeared, she turned to him intending to say something, but from the corner of her eye she saw the stream of tears rolling down Rachel's cheeks.

She hesitated a few seconds, then got up and came to sit beside Rachel on the sofa. When Rachel turned with a tearful smile, Lara scooted closer, hooked her arm through Rachel's, and leaned in to her shoulder. In that single moment Rachel felt a tiny piece of the heartache she'd carried for all those years break off and fall away.

As Kenny rewound the final reel, Lara put her mouth to Rachel's ear and whispered, "I'm kind of hoping it'll take that garage another week or two to get the car fixed."

Rachel brushed back a tear and kissed Lara's cheek. "I think that's something that can easily be arranged," she whispered.

A secretive grin passed from one to the other, and in the silence of her own heart, Rachel whispered, *Thank you, God.* No one else heard her, only The One who'd obviously been listening to her prayers all those years.

~

In the wee hours of morning, when the others were asleep and the only sound was the soft rise and fall of George's breath, Rachel heard the rumble of thunder in the distance. It echoed through the night again and again, each time drawing closer, until at long last the sky broke open, and the rain began. For a few moments, the sound was soft like the swish of a silk skirt, but it quickly changed to the slam of a book and then the crash of an oak being felled.

She climbed from the bed and stood at the window watching the rain and listening for the remembered sound of music. It was in her ears for a split second, then gone.

It's a memory, she told herself, *only a memory.*

She turned, slipped out of the bedroom, and started along the hall. With her bare feet stepping lightly on the wooden floor, she made no sound as she opened the first door and tiptoed across the floor.

Henry had his back to her, but she could hear the steady cadence of his breath. She took the summer blanket, covered his shoulder, then left, closing the door behind her.

Hope's room was next. She eased the door open but had no need to go any farther. Lying at the girl's feet was Bruno. He lifted his head, ears perked and eyes reflecting the glow of a night-light.

"Good boy," Rachel whispered. Then she closed the door and moved to the door at the end of the hall.

That's when she heard it again: the sound of music, not imagined but real. She tapped ever so lightly on the door and listened. Suddenly the music became softer, and in a whispery voice, Lara called, "Come on in."

When she eased the door open, she saw Lara with the Sony Walkman on the nightstand and the faint sound of "Downtown Train" coming from beneath her earphones.

Lara looked over, wide-eyed. "Sorry, I didn't think anyone could hear this." She reached over and snapped off the Walkman. "Did I wake you?"

Rachel smiled. "No, I wasn't able to sleep, and then with this storm—"

"I couldn't sleep either," Lara said. "Wanna come in and talk?"

~

A year from now, even ten thousand years from now, Rachel would still remember that moment. She would remember the way her heart swelled and the ocean of tears began to ebb. She would never have the yesterdays of Lara's life, but she now knew she would have a lifetime of tomorrows.

While the wind howled and the rain slammed against the house, she sat on the side of Lara's bed and told of how the weather had been much the same that last night of the music festival.

"Scary!" Lara said. "No wonder you're checking on everyone."

Rachel said only that it had been a terrible storm. She remembered every agonizing moment of that weekend and the dreadful days that followed. But those memories were ones she would keep to herself.

In time, the storm blew through, and the rain became little more than droplets falling from the eaves, but still they sat and talked.

Ribbons of pink were feathering the sky when Lara grinned and said, "I've sort of been wondering what I should call you."

"I guess that's kind of up to you. What feels comfortable?"

Lara hesitated a moment, then said, "Well, you are my mom, but since calling two people Mom might be confusing, how about I call you Mama Dixon?"

Rachel pictured Helen sitting across from her, a ball of yarn in her lap and a stack of crocheted squares lying on the floor. She heard the joyous sound of the laughter they'd shared and remembered how Mama Dixon had stood beside her on the darkest days. She'd taught Rachel how to hold on to the good memories, to push the painful ones aside, and to make room in her heart for forgiveness. They'd been closer even than mother and daughter.

Rachel smiled. "There's nothing in this world I'd like better."

Although this was not the time to talk of it, Rachel could already imagine the day when her hair would be threaded with silver and she would sit across from Lara with a ball of yarn in her lap just as Mama Dixon had once done.

When she finally returned to her room, George was already awake. "Where were you?" he asked.

Rachel told him of how she and Lara had spent much of the night talking. With a smile curling the corners of her lips she said, "She's decided to call me Mama Dixon."

"Mama Dixon?" George laughed. "How's that feel?"

"Pretty good." Tears of happiness welled in Rachel's eyes, and her smile grew even broader. "I'd like to believe that one day I'll be as wise and forgiving as your mama. I'm not there yet, but maybe having Mama Dixon's name will help me along the road."

EPILOGUE

The storm that roared across Georgia that Saturday night broke the heat wave and left a refreshing coolness in its wake.

That July, Rachel's long-suffered sorrow seemed to fade along with the oppressive heat. When Ernie said he'd need an extra two weeks to replace the transmission, Angela told him to take his time. They were in no hurry.

By then, Rachel and Angela were already planning a Thanksgiving in Hesterville and a Christmas on the beach in Daytona.

In August, Lara went off to the University of Florida just as she'd planned. She kept the name she'd used for the past eighteen years but began celebrating two birthdays. The one in February was generally spent with the McAlisters, but the second one in March was always spent in Hesterville with Daddy Dixon, Mama Dixon, Hope, and Henry.

Years later, Lara married a young lawyer with a promising career in the State Department, and they settled in Tallahassee. By no coincidence, it was a four-hour drive from either Hesterville or Daytona. Soon after Lara married, Rachel got her long-awaited Emily: a granddaughter with the same blonde curls and blue eyes as her mama.

Although Rachel never got to enjoy the growing-up years with Lara, she got to relive the experience with Emily. She watched her granddaughter grow from a toddler into a young woman who was as beautiful as her mother had been. And when Emily was married, the Dixon family were all there—Hope, whose last name was now Williamson, and her five teenagers. Henry; his wife, Charlotte; and their son. George, who now carried a canc. And Rachel, whose hair was indeed threaded with silver.

ACKNOWLEDGMENTS

When a reader holds a finished book in hand, they see only the face of the author, but in truth, many people contribute to the successful making of a novel. I consider myself blessed to have had the wonderful team at Lake Union working with me on the development of this book.

I am extremely fortunate to have been paired with Alicia Clancy, my editor. She goes above and beyond what might be expected and comes to know my characters as well as I do. Her advice is both wise and insightful. I am delighted and honored to have her as my partner on this exciting journey.

I owe a huge debt of gratitude to Tiffany Yates Martin, my developmental editor, for forcing me to dig deeper and find the treasure trove of emotions hidden beneath the surface.

My utmost thanks also goes to Nicole Pomeroy, my production manager, along with Stacy Abrams, and Sarah Vostok, my copy editors, for their attention to detail and thoughtful handling of this story. And a note of appreciation goes to the Lake Union author relations team for carefully following up on each and every detail, answering my endless questions, and seeing this project through to completion.

I remain truly grateful to my agent, Pamela Harty, for introducing me to Lake Union and continuing to provide day-to-day support with such unending grace and wisdom.

A special thank-you to Lynn Ontiveros, Trudy Leasure Southe, and Joanne Bliven, the friends and story partners who listen to my earliest thoughts, poke holes in my plots, and continually challenge me to broaden my vision. I also thank beta reader Suzie Welker for her guidance on the roads and hospitals of Kentucky during the time period of this story.

A sincere note of thanks to Ekta Garg, fellow author, beta editor, adviser, and friend.

I would be lost without Coral Russell, the do-everything person who keeps my blog on target, organizes fan events, and steps in to help when I need a third hand. Thank you for all these things and the thousands of others you do.

And to the ladies in my BFF (Best Fans & Followers) Clubhouse, I am eternally grateful. They read my books, share them with friends, review them on Goodreads, and eagerly await each new release. Loyalty such as this is something to be treasured.

For things too numerous to count, I thank my husband, Dick. He is, and will always be, my partner, my best friend, and life's greatest blessing.

ABOUT THE AUTHOR

Photo © 2018 Bryan Adams Photography

Bette Lee Crosby is the *USA Today* bestselling author of twenty novels, including *The Twelfth Child* and the Wyattsville series. She has been the recipient of the Reader's Favorite Gold Medal, Reviewer's Choice Award, FPA President's Book Award, and International Book Award, among many others. Her 2016 novel, *Baby Girl*, was named Best Chick Lit of the Year by the *Huffington Post.* She laughingly admits to being a night owl and a workaholic, claiming that her guilty pleasure is late-night chats with fans and friends on Facebook and Goodreads. Her 2018 novel, *The Summer of New Beginnings*, published by Lake Union, took First Place in the Royal Palm Literary Award for Women's Fiction and was a runner-up for book of the year. The sequel, *A Year of Extraordinary Moments*, is now available.